BLUE MAGIC
ON
MUSHROOM ISLAND

A NOVEL BY

DAVID C. EDMONDS

A PEACE CORPS WRITERS BOOK
2024
OAKLAND, CALIFORNIA

A PEACE CORPS WRITERS BOOK

BLUE MAGIC ON MUSHROOM ISLAND

A Peace Corps Writers Book – an imprint of Peace Corps Worldwide

Printed in the United States of America

By Peace Corps Writers of Oakland, California.

For more information, contact peacecorpsworldwide@gmail.com.

Peace Corps Writers and the Peace Corps Writers colophon are trademarks of PeaceCorpsWorldwide.org.

Cover art by Awan Designer

David C. Edmonds website: www.dedmonds.com

ISBN-13: 978-1-950444-78-6

Library of Congress Control Number: 2024906739

First Peace Corps Writers Edition, May 2024

DEDICATION

To the memory of my beautiful sister,

BARBARA EDMONDS BOYKIN

and

To all who loved her

"Falling in love is like eating mushrooms. You never know if it's the real thing until it's too late."

--Bill Ballance

CHAPTER 1

Managua, Nicaragua, October 1994

There should have been a warning about the gringo—a State Department Advisory, a message on the bulletin board—anything to keep me from falling for his magic like an abandoned housewife, drinking too much wine, leaving an embassy reception on his arm, doing things I'd never done before on a first date (if you could even call it a date) and agreeing to see him again tonight. Which was why I scooped up the phone the second it rang.

"Change of plans," he said. "Are you ready?"

"Change to what? Where are you?"

"Same place as last night. Don't say it on the phone."

An image of the luxurious Hotel Intercontinental popped into my head. Was he crazy? Had I been that easy?

"What's this about, Matt? I'm not going to your room."

"Not my room. I'm in the hotel restaurant. You won't believe who just walked in?"

"Who?"

"Can't say on the phone, but this is big. He's in disguise—dark glasses and a wig. Something's going on. Can you get over here right away? It'll make one hell of a story."

"Wait, Matt, this is going too fast. What do you want me to do?"

"Interview him for your show. Ask what's going on. Who he's meeting? Why is he taking a dangerous risk? There's an extra chair at his table. Near the exit. All you do is walk over and sit down next to him. He wouldn't dare make a scene."

"Is he alone?"

"Two other men are with him, muscle types."

"But what about my cameraman? What about—"

"Kodak's already on the way. Can you hurry? Please. I sent a taxi. It should be there any second. And one more thing…"

"What?"

"Can't stop thinking about you."

He hung up, leaving me breathless. How did he know Kodak was my cameraman? And who was the mystery man in the dining room? Howard Hughes? No, he'd long since moved out of the country. Oliver North? No, that bastard wouldn't dare show his face in Nicaragua.

I checked myself once more in the mirror. Black leather jacket. Designer jeans. White blouse. Heels. Should I change? No, not enough time. I glanced out the window into the parking lot. No taxi yet, only darkness, broken streetlights, and a security guard walking around with a flashlight and assault weapon. Dear God, what to do? Should I call my station manager?

No, bad idea. How could I explain the gringo? Best to call Ignacio at the hotel restaurant. He was my go-to for everything. I picked up the phone again and waited for a dial tone—which wasn't easy in Nicaragua—and soon had the maître d' on the other end. The background stir of music and conversation was the same as when I'd spoken to Matt. "Ignacio," I said, "what's going on in the restaurant? Anything unusual?"

"Same as when you were here last night. A lady with a noisy baby. I also see your…um, amigo from last night. He's sitting at the bar, dressed in a white guayabera."

My face grew warm. How did Ignacio know about last night? Matt and I had gone straight to the elevators clandestinely—or so I'd thought. God, this was bad. He probably asked the maids about the bedsheets. Suppose my station chief found out? Suppose it got into the tabloids?

Channel Four TV Woman in Hotel with US Embassy Spy.

"He's just a friend," I said, knowing he knew better.

"Of course, Adriana. Anything for you. No problem. I can get you and your friend a nice corner table. It's private."

"No, Ignacio, that's not why I called. I need you to check out the table near the exit. Three men. One with dark glasses. Can you see them?"

"Hold on…Oh, yes, I see them. They haven't ordered yet."

"Anything unusual about them."

"Well, they keep glancing around like escaped convicts."

"Locals or gringos?"

"They're speaking Spanish."

"What about the one in dark glasses? Do you know him?"

"Hold on. I'll take a closer look."

A car horn blared. I glanced out the window and saw my taxi. "No, that's okay. I'll be there in a few minutes. Can you please escort me to their table?"

CHAPTER 2

The drive to the hotel took eight minutes and would have been five, except for potholes, broken traffic lights, flower vendors at every intersection, and a broken-down army tank. Worse, the driver never shut up. Nicaragua is going to hell. Too much violence and kidnappings. New construction looks like crappy strip malls from the States, and on and on.

I tuned him out and tried to concentrate on the gringo. Was he using me? Had his words and charm last night been genuine? And who was he anyway? He'd said he was an economist at the embassy. But what kind of economist snoops on hotel guests?

"Here we are, señorita."

I glanced up. We had stopped in the circular drive directly in front of the hotel entrance. "No, no, no," I said. "Over there, that side street."

He turned around and looked at me like I was crazy. "In the dark?"

"I'm meeting a friend."

"Are you that TV woman?"

"Just go. Please."

He waved off a uniformed door attendant and drove on, passing a row of hotel tourist vans, turning left at the exit, and stopping again beneath a long row of palm trees. I reached for the wallet in my purse and the small canister of pepper spray. It was pink, the color of Pepto Bismol, but I didn't care so long as it worked.

"Already paid for," said the driver. "Be careful. Managua isn't safe."

Yeah, I thought, someone should have told me that last night. I thanked him, climbed out into the warm night air with the canister of pepper spray, and looked for Kodak. The hotel parking lot was filled with Mercedes, Beamers, a Porsche, and expensive SUVs, mostly black and shiny. The side street was an endless line of older, smaller, and less expensive cars.

Dammit, what happened to Kodak? He wouldn't have gone inside without me. Aside from the autos, I saw only a parking attendant with a flashlight, two or three men in the shadows smoking cigarettes, and the hotel door attendant.

"Hey, Miami, over here."

There was movement, and then he emerged from the shadows looking like the cameraman he was—shoulder-length hair, faded blue jeans, ball cap, a jacket with a thousand pockets, a minicam in his hand, and a bulge beneath his jacket that could have been a spare battery but was likely a Glock Nine. He took the burning cigarette out of his mouth, dropped it on the pavement, and crushed it with his sneakers.

"What's going on?" he asked. "Gringo said you'd explain."

"Mystery man in the dining room. I'm going to interview him."

"Who?"

"Gringo didn't say, but we'll soon find out."

"Great. I love intrigue. Did you tell the boss?"

"There wasn't time."

"He's going to be pissed."

"He'll be upset no matter what."

"So, what's my role here? What do I do?"

"Same as always. Hang back and keep the camera rolling. Pan left and right. If this character is as important as the gringo says, he'll have a backup. Try to spot them. I'll hesitate a moment at the entrance. Then you trot on down and follow me inside."

"That's a fancy tourist hotel. They may not let me in."

"Of course, they'll let you in. You're with me."

He patted the bulge in his jacket. "What if they frisk me?"

"For God's sake, Kodak. This is Nicaragua. Everybody carries a gun."

"You don't."

I held up the pepper spray canister.

"Really Miami? Pink? It looks like a reward you'd get at Victoria's Secret for buying hot pink panties. What you need is a purse pistol."

"Just shut up and follow me. And stop calling me Miami. Okay?"

"That's what they call you at the station."

"No, Kodak, it's only the manager and he doesn't know any better. My name is Adriana."

"Okay, Adriana, got it. Don't you want to mic up?"

"Too obvious. It'll frighten them away. Do I look okay?"

"You look fantastic. Who does your hair? I like it."

"Just shut up and follow me?"

"You already said that. I'm ready when you're ready."

"Be careful. If anything happens, you know what to do."

"Not to worry. I know the drill." He brushed back his long greasy hair and lifted the camera. "Go! You're hot in five seconds."

CHAPTER 3

I took a deep breath and trod toward the entrance the way the Sandinistas taught me—look, listen, sniff the air. Always be aware of your surroundings. Kodak followed, sticking to the shadows and the row of hotel vans like a stalking spy. I couldn't see him and didn't look, but I sensed the comfort of his presence.

My heels clacked on the tiles. Dammit, why hadn't I worn sneakers?

A car door slammed off to the right. A man got out. It was too shadowy to get a good look. I kept going but had covered only half the distance when a sensation I'd never felt before came over me. My head swirled. My legs weakened. The parking lot became foggy, and the distinctive odor of exhaust fumes became damp, swampy smells.

What was going on? What was wrong with me? Was I having a stroke?

I staggered toward a hotel van, thinking to hold it for support—and that was when a bell dinged. A bell? I looked left and right, and as if the bell weren't weird enough, a woman appeared. Not just any woman, but an indigenous-looking woman with wild hair who looked like she'd just stepped out of the jungle. It happened too fast to describe her skimpy clothes, but not too fast to notice the blue color of her skin.

Or the spear in her hand. She glared at me, her dark eyes blazing into mine. The bell dinged again and she was gone, vanished, as if she'd ducked behind the hotel van. Or had existed only in my mind, and I found myself back in the middle of the parking lot, nowhere near a hotel van. I needed to see a shrink. I shook my head and went on.

The glow of a cigarette. The same two men I'd seen before. A woman too, standing next to a car and staring at me, not a jungle woman, but a woman in normal clothes. The engine of their car was running, exhaust fumes polluting the night air.

The hotel loomed up like a modern version of a massive Mayan pyramid, all lit up in a city that was usually cloaked in power-failure darkness. Until fifteen years ago, when I'd marched inside with a mob of gun-toting Sandinistas, I'd never imagined a waif like me in the elegant dining room. Now, I had a small army of paid informants in the hotel.

A night bird warbled in a tree near the entrance. Would Kodak notice? Of course. His biggest fault, other than endlessly whining about the girl who got away during the war, was to waste his shots on every little detail—anything that moved or made a noise.

Had he seen the blue jungle woman? Or was it all in my head?

A taxi drove up and stopped, blocking my progress. I waited. Someone else came up behind me—the same woman and two men I'd noticed before, so close I smelled their cigarettes.

The taxi door opened. A young man in a blue guayabera stepped out. Behind him came an attractive younger woman in a short skirt. Wife? Paid escort? Mistress?

The door attendant greeted them the way he'd greeted me last night when I'd gone inside with Matt, all smiles and welcome as if to say, "I know who you are, and I know why you're here. Enjoy your evening."

Damn it. I should have worn a wig last night. Tonight too.

The couple stopped at the door. The woman turned around and looked in my direction. She nodded as if she recognized me, and they went inside. Was she nodding at me or the people behind me?

I hesitated, thinking the people behind me would go around and get out of my space. They didn't. Instead, one man stepped forward and stood beside me as if we were a couple. Jerk!

I sighed and headed for the entrance. So did the other three, right on my heels. What was wrong with them?

The entrance door opened, letting out the sounds of a piano and conversation. The doorman stepped aside. Out came the same young woman who'd just gone in, walking fast, heels clacking on the tile, nodding as if to say, "Mission accomplished." As she swept past me, I found myself enveloped in the scent of Chanel Number 5.

Behind me, a man said, "*Ya listo,*" which in Spanish means "Ready."

Ready for what?

As if that wasn't bizarre enough, the double doors burst open again. Three men rushed out, one in dark glasses, looking this way and that. Was he the mystery man? Was I too late? No, I could still question him.

I stepped to his front. He stopped.

A who-the-hell-are-you look crossed his face.

"Murdering son of a bitch!" shrieked the woman behind me.

Someone or something slammed into my back.

The force drove me into the man in dark glasses. Gunfire detonated—bang, bang, bang. There were flashes of light. A spray of blood. Down went the mystery man, clutching his chest.

Down I went too. Hard. Too hard. My face hit the cobbles.

Don't move. I told myself. Play dead.

For a horrible moment, I was back in a sweltering jungle with the Sandinistas, hugging the ground in the chaos of ambush, praying, too scared to scramble away, a comrade's body touching mine, blood pooling around me. There were shouts and screams back then too, as well as curses and footfalls of running people.

The sound of slamming doors brought me back to the present. A car drove away, maybe two cars, tires squealing on the cobbles. I pushed away from the body, trying to absorb what happened. Had I been shot? No. The victim lay beneath me on his back, eyes open, blood draining from his mouth. A crude wooden spear protruded from his chest. Even in my panic, I noticed the beads and feathers. A spear? Why would the killers spear a dead man?

"Adriana, are you okay? Are you hurt?"

It was Matt, his arm on my back, kneeling beside me. I struggled to my knees, unable to speak. My ears rang. Blood covered my hands and the cobbles beneath me. People were gathering around, gasping, staring, asking questions. "Is he dead?"

"Is that a spear?"

"Come on," Matt said and pulled me to my feet. "We need to get out of here. Now."

I didn't ask why. I knew why. People would recognize me. I'd just witnessed a bizarre assassination. I'd been part of it, and witnesses to murder in Nicaragua don't always live to tell their story.

CHAPTER 4

Matt half-pushed and half-pulled me across the cobbles toward the darkness. I desperately looked around for Kodak but saw only the chaos of panicked flight—car doors slamming, engines starting, cars driving away. No one was running toward the scene.

"Where's Kodak?" I asked.

"Haven't seen him. He must have left."

"No, Matt. He wouldn't abandon me."

A SUV stopped beside us. It was one of those black things with dome lights and bumper protectors, the kind used by smugglers for crashing through jungles and roadblocks. At least two men were inside. The killers? I jumped back. A wiry little man sprang out and opened the back door.

"My driver," Matt said. "Get in."

"Wait, I have to find Kodak."

"Dammit, Adriana, you've got blood all over you. We need to get you away from here. Kodak can take care of himself. Come on."

I jerked loose and turned away, looking for Kodak. More cars raced by, horns blowing, illuminating us in their headlamps. And then Kodak was at my side. "Oh, my God. Are you all right?"

I led him away from Matt. "I'm fine. Did you get it?"

"Got it. Also caught the men racing away. Faces and all."

"What about the spear? Did you see it?"

"Saw it. Crazy bastard just rushed up and plunged it into the body. Weird."

"Did you see his face?"

"Couldn't. He wore a mask."

"What about getaway cars?"

"Kept the camera rolling. Not sure license plates will show up."

"Did anyone see you?"

"Not likely. They were too caught up in the excitement."

"Great. Good job. Burn an extra copy. No, make it three copies. One for me, another for the station. Keep the original in a safe place. Don't tell a soul. And Kodak…"

"What?"

"Disappear for three or four days. Get out of Managua."

"You too, Miami. Do you know who they shot?"

"I have no idea. The gringo knows."

He stepped closer. "There's blood on your face."

"It's not mine."

"Christ, Adriana. You need to get home. You need a ride?"

"Gringo will take me."

"You trust the gringo?"

"No, but I need answers. I'll let you know. Go. Stay safe."

"You too, Miami, and be careful with the gringo."

He trotted away. I climbed into the back seat with Matt, and then we were racing away from the hotel with other cars, the driver blowing the horn and weaving in and out of traffic like a madman. Matt handed me a box of tissues and introduced the driver by the code name of Lead Foot, which seemed appropriate from the way he was driving. He also introduced the man in the front passenger seat, but I was in too much turmoil to catch the name or even look at him. "Where are we going?"

"Your place. You need to clean up and change."

"And go where?"

"To Masatepe. We have reservations at a restaurant."

"Are you out of your mind? How can you be hungry after what just happened?"

"We don't have to eat. We can sit and talk."

"I need to call my station manager. He'll be furious that I left the scene of an assassination."

"You sure you want to tell him?"

"How can I not tell him? I'm sure someone recognized me."

"It'll be worse when he learns who got shot."

"Who was he?"

"You didn't recognize him?"

"Everything was too sudden. Bang, bang, bang, and I was on the ground. Who was he?"

He motioned toward the men in front as if to say we shouldn't be discussing the matter in their presence. Then he leaned into me and whispered two words I did not want to hear.

"Contra Uno."

He might as well have said, "You're screwed. Run for your life."

CHAPTER 5

I sat back in stunned silence, shivering, trying to get my thoughts together. Contra Uno was the elusive political and military head of the contras, a man despised by one side and loved by the other. I'd interviewed him once before, clandestinely. It had not gone well. Hate mail and death threats had flooded into the office.

And now I had his blood on my hands. Literally.

"I'm sorry I got you into this mess," Matt said. "I had no idea."

I didn't answer. I couldn't. Did he realize how dangerous this was for me? There'd be an interrogation, Nicaraguan style. They'd fingerprint me and learn all my dirty secrets and what I'd done with the Sandinistas. It would be on TV and in the newspapers. I could lose my US passport and, worse, the killers would come after me.

"This your place?" the driver asked.

I glanced up, not even realizing we had stopped. The lights at my apartment building were out. Residents had gathered on the patio and parking lot with their lanterns and flashlights the way they always did during power failures—which meant every night—listening to battery-powered radios, eating and gossiping, and polluting the air with laughter, music, cigarette smoke, and cooking smells. Children were also laughing and playing as if all were normal in the world.

Matt stepped outside with me. "Can you be ready in thirty minutes?"

"Are you going to tell me or not?"

"Tell you what?"

"How you knew Contra Uno was at the hotel."

"I'll tell you at the restaurant." He squeezed my arm and turned to go.

"Wait. Are you just going to leave me here by myself?"

"Are you afraid?"

"Why would you ask that question? I'm shaking. I just witnessed a—"

"Is your place safe?"

"It's safe. We've got good security."

"Okay, listen. I've also got blood on my clothes. I need to change. I'll hurry. Just go inside and lock your door. I'll be right back."

"You promise?"

He took my blood-stained hand in his. "Oh, Baby, never think like that. We're in this together." He kissed my cheek, whispered, "I'll hurry," and climbed back into the SUV.

They drove into the night, and for a scary moment, all my insecurities came down on me. Was all that affection a farce? Had he been using me last night and tonight? Why hadn't he at least walked me to the front door? Would he come back for me?

"Señorita?"

I turned toward the complex and came face to face with a white-haired old man with a Yankees baseball cap on his head and an AK-47 slung over his shoulder. It took me a moment to realize he was the night security guard. He shined his light in my face. "Who are you?" he asked in a wheezy voice.

I held up my hand. "Turn off that light. I live here."

"Sorry, señorita, but I need to see identification."

"Don't you recognize me?"

He came closer and stared into my face. "Ahh, you're that TV woman. I'm sorry to bother you, but we got orders to check all the comings and goings. I need to log you in. Something bad must have happened."

"What happened? Did they tell you?"

"Nicaragua," he said as if that explained everything. "I heard the sirens, but they never tell us anything. We're just another gear in the machine."

He led me across the parking lot, through the crowd of residents, up the steps where people were sitting, and into a shadowy lobby lit by candles and lanterns. The desk attendant, a young man named Marco with shoulder-length hair, looked up at me and smiled in recognition.

I forced myself to smile back. *Please don't let him see the blood.*

"She's okay," Marco said to the guard. "She lives on the second floor."

"I still need to get the number on her identity."

"No problem. We've got copies of all our residents here."

He reached for his files and nodded at me to go ahead. The guard protested, but I dashed up the stairs anyway, careful not to stumble in the darkness. But when I came to the door, I couldn't find the keys. Did I lose them at the hotel when I'd gone down? Please, dear God, no.

I kept digging, getting frantic. Yes, there they were, buried beneath my makeup pouch and pink pepper spray canister. I clicked on the little penlight on the chain, got the key in the lock, let myself into the privacy of my apartment, and bolted the door behind me.

CHAPTER 6

God, what a night! I'd come to Nicaragua to escape a stalker in Florida. Now I was in a bigger mess. My mom would have said I jumped out of the frying pan into the fire. And she'd be right, staring down from heaven in her green apron. Maybe I should forget Matt and head for the airport. No, that wouldn't work. The alert had gone out. I'd be Suspect Uno. Witnesses would report that I'd been the attacker. They'd arrest me at the airport. They'd say my attempt to flee proved my guilt. Then they'd throw me into a dungeon for the next hundred years.

"Shit! Shit! Shit!" I should have gone to Canada instead of Nicaragua.

I lit the hurricane lanterns and hurried into the bathroom. What I needed was a long, hot shower. Scrub off the blood. Scrub away the sound of gunfire that was still in my head. Scrub away the memory of that man with his open, dead eyes. And that spear. What was that about? Why would they plunge a primitive spear into a dead man's chest?

And Matt. Was he who he said he was? Suppose he just disappeared?

I reached for the faucet. No water. Shit. Of course, there was no water. This was Nicaragua. When power goes out so does the water. This was why everyone in Nicaragua had an emergency water supply—milk containers, wine bottles, buckets, cooking pots, bathtubs, and anything that could hold water. I had three containers and even a cooler of water.

I wiped the blood off my leather jacket and stripped off the rest of my clothes, tossed them into the tub, climbed on top like a barefoot grape smasher, and poured cold water over my head, ruining my hairdo and the makeup I'd so carefully applied for a romantic evening with Matt. How could romance go so wrong so quickly?

Idiot! What was wrong with me? I should have known better than to get involved with an embassy gringo. Was I that needy, that weak? My face burned. I wanted to scream in frustration. Or throw something across the room. Or kick the bathtub. Instead, I lathered my body with soap and kept scrubbing and rinsing. How much time did I have? Matt said thirty minutes. I needed an hour. I needed a blow dryer for my hair, needed a mirror light, needed new makeup.

Needed to hurry.

A knock sounded at the door.

"Señorita?"

I froze. Were the killers coming for me already? Would they bust down the door and put a spear in my chest? I eased out of the tub and grabbed a towel. The glow of flashlights bled through cracks in the door.

More knocks, louder. "Señorita? Are you there?"

"Who is it?"

"Marco from downstairs. The night guard needs your passport."

"Why does he need my passport?"

"Because you're not a Nicaraguan citizen. ID card is not good enough. It's just routine. He'll write the number and give it right back."

If it hadn't been for the assassination, I'd have thought nothing of them checking my passport. I'd shown it at military checkpoints more times than I could count. And always, the guards wanted a small fee. Was that the issue now? Was the old night guard trying to shake me down?

I took the passport from my purse, stuffed a few Nicaraguan Córdoba notes inside—about five US dollars for each of them—and handed it through the mail slot in the door.

Then I waited. What was taking so long?

There was a discussion outside the door. Marco's strong voice and then the wheezy old-man voice of the guard. I couldn't make out their words, but it sounded like a disagreement. Marco tapped the door. "Be right back," he said, and their footfalls faded down the stairs.

This wasn't routine. I needed my passport.

I towel-dried my hair, brushed it, and pulled it back in a damp ponytail. My makeup routine was more difficult in the poor light. Jitters didn't help either, yet I managed to moisten my lips with gloss, touch up my lashes with mascara, throw on a dark knee-length skirt and a Wrangler denim jacket, and go to the mail slot again, hoping to find my passport.

It wasn't there.

Oh, God, had they made the connection? Was the guard on the phone with his superiors at the dreaded security police headquarters, telling them he'd located the black leather jacket woman?

No, that couldn't be. The power was out, and when the power was out, so were telephones. Maybe it was nothing. Maybe I was just paranoid. The passport was probably on Marco's desk.

I finished dressing, took my purse, and eased down the stairs, hoping, praying Matt would be waiting for me. The lobby smelled of lamp oil and cigarettes and was still shadowy and dimly lit. Marco looked up from his desk, his face illuminated by a single burning candle.

"Where is my passport?" I asked him. "I'm going out."

"Old man didn't give it back?"

"No, Marco. You're the one who promised to give it back."

"*Demonios!* He's out there somewhere. Ask him."

I pushed through the exit and passed through a small crowd that had gathered around a couple of teenagers who were belting out a Julio Iglesias number on their guitars. The night guard was there too, standing in a little pool of light next to a stocky man in a military uniform.

Military man? Shit! A pistol was on his hip, and he wore the boots, cap, and insignia of a Sandinista Colonel of State Security.

Had they reported me already? I turned away, hoping he wouldn't see me in the poor light, hoping to find Matt in the parking lot.

Hoping to escape.

Matt wasn't there, and it was too late to run.

The old geezer recognized me.

"Señorita!"

CHAPTER 7

Vega was the name of the officer in uniform. It said so on the little green and white patch above his shirt pocket. His thick mustache reminded me of Saddam Hussein, and in his hand was my passport. This wasn't good. Worse, a military Jeep was parked a short distance away, and two or three other soldiers in boots and combat fatigues stood around it.

Colonel Vega looked into my face. "Señorita Alvarez?"

"Alvarado, not Alvarez."

"You're the TV lady. Correct?"

"What's this about, Colonel?"

"I need to ask where you're going. You were out before, and now you're leaving again?"

"I'm meeting a friend. The guard took my passport."

"I asked where you're going, not who you're meeting."

"I'm going to a restaurant. I don't know where yet."

"Where were you before? The guard says you returned about a half hour ago. Correct?"

"Correct. I was with a friend."

"Señorita, do you have a hearing problem? I asked where you were, not who you were with."

"It's a private matter, Colonel. It's work-related."

"The guard tells me the vehicle that dropped you off bore an MI designation—*Mision Internacional.* That's an embassy vehicle. So, your…ah…friend works for a foreign embassy?"

"Please, Colonel, I told you already. It's a private matter. Confidential. I can't discuss it."

"Why did you refuse to show the guard your identity?"

"I didn't refuse. They have my identity papers at the front desk. The desk clerk showed him, but they took my passport, anyway. I'd like it back, please. I need it for my work."

"Just calm yourself, señorita. We'll discuss your passport later. I'm told you had blood on your clothes when you arrived. What happened? Were you injured?"

I blurted out the first thought that came to my head. "No, no, *Coronel.* It was wine. *Vino Tinto.* Spilled it all over myself."

No sooner had I said it than I regretted my lie. Nicaraguan agents weren't stupid. He'd go upstairs and check my apartment. He'd find my clothes in the tub. Bloody clothes, not wine-stained clothes. Then he'd quote me an obscure legal article that it was a crime to lie to a state agent.

Oh, God, I might as well drop to my knees and beg for mercy.

The Colonel took my arm, guided me away from the security guard, and got right in my face. Even in the poor light, I could see his eyes were shrewd and dark and penetrating, and I got the feeling he could see right through my denim jacket to my lying heart. I expected him to yell at me and threaten me with crude language. He didn't. Instead, he wiped his mustache and spoke in a soft voice. "Listen, señorita, please understand I'm just doing my job."

"I understand, but you should also understand I need my passport."

"*Bueno*, let's talk about your passport. If you've done nothing wrong, if you're being open and truthful, then you can have your passport back with my blessings. No problem. It's also okay if you're trying to…um…hide a little romance thing with your gentleman friend."

The hint of a smile crossed his face. "I'm a man. I understand these things. But I still need to know where you were. An address, a location. It's important. I also need to know the identity of your gentleman friend." He held up a hand to cut me off. "We have a way of checking these things. So be very careful what you tell me. Please be honest."

He stood there looking at me in the dim light, waiting for an answer. There was no point lying. He'd check my room. But if I told him the truth, he'd put me in that Jeep and drive me to the dreaded security headquarters. There'd be questions I couldn't answer. Accusations too. They'd fingerprint me and discover a name that differed from the name on my passport. The friends of Contra Uno would learn about me. So would the killers, and my life would be in jeopardy whether or not they released me.

"I'm waiting," said the Colonel. "If you prefer, we can go down to State Security to talk."

I was fumbling for an answer when Matt's black SUV drove up and stopped beside us, engine running, bumper guards glistening from flashlights and lanterns. Relief swept over me. The old night guard, who'd been standing a short distance away and coughing his cigarette cough, unslung his AK as if to protect Nicaragua from an invasion of foreigners.

Matt stepped out of the passenger side and opened the back door for me, all six feet of him, now dressed in a dark jacket, dark slacks, and a dark pullover, looking like the handsome hero of every woman's dream, coming to save me from the villains.

I rushed into his arms like a scared child.

I thought the Colonel would drag me away. He didn't. I thought there'd at least be a big fuss in front of all the residents who were watching. It didn't happen. Colonel Vega just stood there with a look of disappointment on his face, as if I'd let him down.

"We're going," I said to the Colonel. "May I please have my passport?"

"*Mañana*," he said. "State Security office. Oh-nine-hundred hours. I'll be waiting." He touched his cap in a half salute. "Have a nice evening."

CHAPTER 8

I jumped into the back seat with Matt, buckled up, and began blurting out my problems, happy to escape without cuffs on my wrists, happy that Matt had kept his promise. He laid a hand on my arm and nodded toward the front. "Radio. They're talking about the assassination."

Lead Foot turned up the volume, and out came live, on-the-scene coverage by a male announcer who sounded like he was dodging bullets in a war zone. There were shouts and curses, blaring horns, slamming car doors, and the stir of animated conversation.

"According to eyewitnesses, there were four assailants, two women and two men. The unidentified woman leading the attack was dressed in a black leather jacket..."

"No!" I yelled at the radio. "It wasn't me!"

Lead Foot cranked up the volume as if irritated by my outburst.

"Witnesses say she flew into the victim like a crazy woman, screaming obscenities. She knocked him to the ground. She pummeled him with her fist—"

"That's not how it happened," I said to Matt. "No! They got it wrong. I was pushed. I didn't shoot him. It was someone behind me."

"I know, Baby. We'll talk about it when we get to the restaurant."

"Another assailant, a man in a mask, plunged a spear into the body..."

I took a deep breath and tried to keep my mouth shut. By then, the announcer was going witness to witness, asking questions, but he seemed unable to corroborate what he'd just reported. The hotel door attendant said he'd heard shots but hadn't seen a thing. Another witness, a woman, said, *"All I saw was blood and a dead man with a spear in his chest. A woman in a black leather jacket was on top. Maybe she was the killer..."*

Someone else said, "black leather jacket," or I may have imagined it. None of the witnesses wanted to identify themselves or speculate on why he had been killed—and yet here I was, sitting in the back seat of a speeding SUV next to a gringo who had all the answers.

Was he involved in the assassination? Was I an accessory? What I needed was for him to put an arm around me and tell me it would be all right, tell me the embassy would get my passport back and get me out of the country, tell me the two of us would take an around-the-world cruise or a long vacation to an exotic location like the Gobi Desert or Mars or Jupiter until the truth came out and the world would be sane.

But all he did was sit there and listen to warped accounts from witnesses of the way it didn't happen, which made me even more suspicious.

We passed around a traffic circle, took Highway 1 out of Managua, and drove up a long incline that put the lights of the city far below us. The voice on the radio turned into garbles and static, but even in the garble I heard the words, "black leather jacket."

Lead Foot cursed the radio, cursed the potholes, and was twisting the dials when we rounded a curve and came to a series of flashing lights—and there before us, looming out of the mist, stood a group of soldiers at a checkpoint that was little more than an army truck with flashing lights, a Jeep with a machine gun, and a barrier in the road.

CHAPTER 9

We rolled to a stop. This is it, I thought. They were waiting for us. Colonel Vega had gone upstairs, seen my bloody clothes, seen my black leather jacket, and radioed ahead to nab me. I fought back an urge to jump out the door on the opposite side and dash into the darkness.

Matt powered down the window. A soldier with a clipboard walked to the rear to check the plate. He came back and flashed his light inside, focusing his attention on Lead Foot, whose window was also down. He looked at Matt in the back seat, then held the beam on me much longer—on my face and clothes as if looking for a woman in a black leather jacket.

I held my breath. Any second now he'd make the connection and whip out his pistol. He'd call the others and they'd drag me out and throw a bag over my head. Then they'd toss me into their truck and throw me over a cliff. And Matt's seedy little driver would probably help them.

"Go ahead," said the soldier, and waved us on.

How long it took my heartbeat to return to normal I don't know. All I know is that when I found my voice, I said to Matt, "What was that about? They never let me off that easily."

"They know better than to mess with people in a car like this."

"What's so special about this car? Is it like the Batmobile?"

"No, Baby, we've got MI plates, diplomatic.."

"Does that mean we can pass through any checkpoint in Nicaragua?"

"Sure, as long as you don't shoot one of the soldiers."

"So, what's to stop us from driving to the Costa Rican border?"

"Nothing, but I wouldn't advise it if you're thinking of running."

"Why?"

"Because diplomatic plates don't allow us to cross the border. We'd have to show our passports, fill out forms, and pay a fee. They'll have extra security because of the assassination. If they identify you, which they would, they'll haul you back to Managua. It'll be much worse if they catch you running."

"Isn't there another way? Don't they have back trails for smugglers?"

"Would you listen to yourself? There'll be guard dogs and barbed wire fences. Bounty hunters too. We could get shot or captured. Imagine how that would look in the newspapers, both of us bandaged up, beat up, and stuck in a prison hospital in striped prison garb."

I mumbled a silent curse and we sped on, Lead Foot driving like a maniac, honking the horn, slamming on the brakes, and cursing anyone or anything in our way. I'd never been on this road before, and now I saw the real Nicaragua in the headlights—little adobe houses with wash on the line; people on the road on foot, bicycles or horseback; banana trees and coffee groves on both sides; bromeliads clinging to power lines.

We detoured around a washed-out bridge, dodged a herd of cattle, drove through a sulfur-smelling volcanic fallout zone that looked like a moonscape, and were stopped at another checkpoint with the same outcome as before.

Matt gave me a running commentary of the little villages we passed—Masaya, Catarina, Niquinohomo—and he was pointing out "love" motels with names like Venus, Aphrodite, and Palacio de Amor when Lead Foot turned off the road onto a graveled drive.

Up a hill, a swing to the left, a drive alongside a forest of tall trees, and we pulled into a parking lot beneath a flashing neon sign that read CINE LUMINOSO—Shining Cinema.

"You're taking me to a movie?"

"A restaurant. It just has an interesting name."

I'd heard rumors about the Cine Luminoso—a place where guys took girlfriends to plot seduction and where adulterous couples came for wine, good food, and a few hours in one of those little love motels. Was that what Matt had in mind? Food, wine, and a tumble at the Palacio de Amor. If so, he was in for a big disappointment. No way was I in the mood, not after the madness of the last couple of hours.

Besides, the warmth I'd felt for him the night before was fast fading.

Lead Foot stepped out and shut the front door. I thought he'd open the back door for us. Instead, he lit a cigarette and strode into the darkness. I reached for the door handle.

"No, no, no," Matt said and laid a hand on my arm. "Not yet."

"What's wrong?"

He lowered the window, letting in fresh night air and the sound of music from the restaurant. "There," he said and pointed back toward the road that had brought us here.

In the distance, partially obscured by a row of trees, came the lights of two vehicles. "I think they're following us. They've been behind us since the first checkpoint."

CHAPTER 10

The vehicles slowed and stopped as they approached the turnoff. They were too far away to see if they were military or civilian, but I saw a large truck—possibly army—and a Jeep. A man got out of the smaller vehicle and walked back to the truck. The sight didn't help my stomach, which was doing nervous flips even before the assassination.

"They look military," I said. "What if they come up here?"

"We're okay as long as we're in the car. We can always drive back to Managua."

"I'd rather go to the Costa Rican border."

"Didn't we already have that discussion? I will not be a party to you getting mauled by dogs or tangled in barbed wire or shot or worse."

I sighed in frustration. Damn gringo. He wasn't in trouble. No one had confiscated his passport. He didn't have to face interrogators at the dreaded State Security office and reveal his darkest secrets. For him, there were no consequences. He could at least help me out of the mess he had created. But he would not do a damn thing. Nothing. Which meant all that sweet talk and passion last night had been a farce.

The conference at the truck ended. A door slammed, and the two vehicles roared away. We watched until their taillights faded over a hill. Then I stepped out into the parking lot beneath the brilliance of the Milky

Way. Unlike Managua, where volcanic dust and city lights obscured the night sky, the starry sky at the restaurant looked like it had been created for the canvas of Vincent Van Gogh.

"What happened to Lead Foot?" I asked.

"Don't worry about Lead Foot. He can take care of himself."

"I'm not worried about him. I'm just wondering if he's going inside or staying out here to warn us if soldiers come."

"That's why he works for me. He watches my back."

He reached for my hand. I yanked it away. "Look, let's get one thing straight. All I want from you is an explanation. After that, I want you to drive me back to my apartment. Okay?"

He stood there as if shocked by my reaction. "Damn, Adriana, where did that come from?"

"Do you even have to ask?"

He shook his head and led me up a winding path in silence, beneath low-hanging lanterns and arbors of sweet-smelling honeysuckle. Couples sat at outdoor tables back in the shadows, cigarettes burning, wine on the tables, faces dimly lit by lamplight. A bearded man was reading poetry to his girlfriend. They ignored us as we walked by, and the way they sat there looking at each other made me think they'd soon be heading for one of those little love motels. Hadn't they heard about the assassination?

Did they care?

The dining room had a woodsy smell mixed with cigarette smoke and the pleasant aroma of cooking. It was also poorly lit, for which I was grateful. I didn't want to be recognized as the TV woman and didn't want guests to look up and say, "There's that crazy woman who killed Contra Uno." All I wanted was a long overdue explanation from Matt and a drink to settle my nerves. I could even use a cigarette, but I would not fall into that habit again.

A tuxedoed maître d' welcomed us at the door. "Ah, yes," he said with a big smile. "You have a reservation for the Casablanca table."

I didn't know what that meant until he led us to a table beneath a window that opened to a patio. Beside it hung a framed poster of Bogie and Bergman in that famous scene with the getaway airplane. Posters of other popular movies lined the walls, but without my distance glasses, the only one I could make out was a shark that could be from *Jaws*.

The maître d' lit candles and placed cloth napkins on our laps with all the dignity of a funeral director. Other couples sat around us. No kids, no white-haired seniors like in Florida, and no family gatherings, as if night dining at the Cine Luminoso was for lovers only, all slim, young, and well dressed. Matt, whose humor had kept me giggling the night before, did a Bogey imitation about all the gin joints in all the cities in all the world.

It fell flat, but I smiled anyway and concentrated on the podium where a young woman in a black minidress was singing about a poor country girl named Maria who goes to Managua in search of a better life, only to end up washing clothes by day and selling her body at night:

Poor little Maria/ and her fantasia...

Yes, I thought, change a few words in that song could be about me.

Poor little Adriana, and her fantasia,

That the gringo was the man of her dreams.

I put on the nerd glasses I used for distance and glanced around, hoping no one noticed. The only couple that seemed interested was sitting at the *Gone with the Wind table*, but they may have been looking at Matt, whose gringo face and six-foot frame always attracted attention. Everyone else was too much into each other, drinking and eating, chatting and laughing. "How come there are no married couples here?" I asked Matt.

"How do you know there are no married couples?"

"Just look at them. They're devouring each other. Married couples don't do that. They just sit and rarely talk to each other."

A skinny server named Antonio wanted to know if Matt spoke Spanish. When I said yes, he rattled off the specials and took our order for wine.

I needed something stiff—like a martini—but thought better of it and settled for a Cabernet Sauvignon. "You're not hungry?" Matt asked.

"Later."

He reached for my hand. "Are you okay?"

"No, Matt. I'm not okay. I'm still shaking."

"I'm sorry, Baby. Is there anything I can do to put you at ease?"

"Yes, you can answer my questions." The server may or may not have understood because we were speaking English. I waited for him to leave and said to Matt, "Okay, Mister Embassy Man. It's time. What I want is an explanation of how you knew Contra Uno was in the hotel dining room and why you were even there."

"Are you sure you're not hungry? We can order warm bread, tapas, whatever you want."

"Didn't I say I'm not hungry? Just tell me the damn story."

CHAPTER 11

His expression was like that of a little boy wronged, and for a moment I felt a tinge of guilt for being harsh. He looked over his shoulder and slid his chair closer. "It's a long and complicated story."

"I'm a journalist, Matt. I want details."

"Okay, fine, I'll give you the long version." He sighed as if this would not be easy, and when he spoke it was in a low voice. "This morning when I went to my office, I was still in a happy mood. All I could think about was you. You, Adriana, and last night and your smile that melted my heart and how we met and how we planned to get together again tonight."

I squirmed in my chair. I didn't want to be reminded about last night and how foolish I'd been for drinking too much, falling for his sweet talk, and going to his room like a paid escort.

"I thought about calling you. I wanted to hear your voice again, your accent, the way you say my name. I had the phone in my hand, ready to call, and that's when I was summoned into Easton's office and—"

Our wine came to the table in the hands of a barrel-chested sommelier. He had a towel over his arm and did his thing of uncorking the bottle and pouring it for a taste test, and when he finally left us alone, I clinked my glass against Matt's and took a long sip.

"Okay," I said, "you were telling me about Eastman."

"Easton. Holbrook Easton, he's our legal attaché."

"Code name or real name?"

"Real name. He's a snooty Harvard type. Also, an anglophile. Speaks with a British accent. Thinks we'd all be better off if the Brits had won the war."

"Which war?"

"Revolutionary. Are you recording this?"

"I'm not interviewing you for my show, Matt. And I'm not asking about George Washington fighting the Brits. I just want to know what happened tonight at the hotel."

"You said you wanted the long version."

"Yes, but I don't need a history lesson."

"Fine, just don't use the names I tell you, not even code names. Now, where was I?"

"You were talking about Easton with a British accent."

"Easton. Right, so he summons me to his office and tells me the ambassador's office had been getting strange phone calls from a woman who claimed to be communications director for Contra Uno. She said to tell the ambassador that Contra Uno needed to see him, that it was urgent. And please meet him in the hotel dining room. Which is crazy."

"Why is it crazy?"

"Because the ambassador would never—and I mean never—agree to a clandestine meeting in a public place. No way. He's a public figure like you. Only way he'd meet the top contra in the country would be in a private place under tight security. You know—Marines, embassy spooks, locked doors. So, we figured the phone calls were a prank. A hoax. We get those all the time, but we still needed to check it out. That's why I was at the hotel."

"Why was it your job? Why not someone else?"

He had his mouth open to answer when our server came to the table again. "I'm so sorry to disturb you, but that couple over there,"—he pointed to the *Gone with the Wind* table where an attractive young woman sat with a man old enough to be her father—"they wanted me to ask if you're that TV woman from the show, 'Nicaragua Exposed.'"

I wanted to run out of the place. My nerd glasses weren't good enough. Neither was the mood lighting. Matt shrugged as if to say, "It's up to you to answer." I'd already told one lie that night and figured another wouldn't hurt my chances with St. Peter, so I feigned a laugh. "Funny they should ask. I get that all the time. Tell them I'm not the woman they think I am."

The man thanked me and went back to their table. I hoped that was the end, but the woman waved. She stood. The man grabbed her hand, but she pulled loose, "No!" she said in a voice loud enough to turn heads. "You're not my boss. I don't take orders from you."

Then, with everyone watching, she marched straight to our table.

Her face was as flushed as Scarlett's after she'd shot the Yankee. She wore heels, a tight skirt, a blouse with open-top buttons, and a pair of dangling earrings. "Excuse me," she said, slurring her words, "but my boyfriend over there says you're that TV woman. I say you're not."

She held the back of an extra chair for support and gestured toward Matt. "Does he speak Spanish? He looks gringo. Does he understand?"

"He understands."

"Good, like I was saying, I watch that show all the time. I bet Carlos a hundred Cordobas, but now that I see you up close, I see the resemblance. Would you mind if we took a picture? Carlos has a camera in his car."

I sensed stares from other tables and imagined the whole place was debating my identity and taking bets, and I was trying to think of a nice way to get rid of her when Carlos stepped over and took her arm. "Please accept my apologies," he said and led Scarlett back to their table. But even there, the turmoil continued. The music drowned them out. I took another sip of wine, and then Matt placed his hand over mine.

"We can leave and go somewhere else."

"No, we're here now. Our cover is blown. Finish your story."

"Are you okay? You look flustered."

"Can you answer the question please?"

"What was the question?"

"I asked why you got the assignment to look for Contra Uno. Don't they have 007 types at the embassy for clandestine stuff?"

"Maybe because I'm the single guy at the embassy. No wife, no children. They give me all the dirty work. Next week is equally crazy. I'm supposed to keep an eye on this troublemaking botanist from the States. She claims she discovered magic mushrooms in Nicaragua."

"Magic mushrooms?"

"That's what she claims, says she discovered them in a cave out on Lake Nicaragua. She's an *exiliada* like you. Hates the Sandinistas. There might be a story in it for you."

"Wait a minute, Matt, just hold on. I don't give a damn about mushrooms and Sandinista haters. What I want to know is why you were at the hotel. You were telling me about this Easton guy. He asked you to check out the hotel dining room. Right? Then what happened?"

He refilled my glass and touched my arm. "Well, I get all dressed up like a tourist. Right? Then I go to the bar in the dining room, hoping it's a hoax. But wouldn't you know it? There he sits with his bodyguards. Dark glasses and hairpiece, looking over his shoulder. He was so obvious he should have had a sign on his back. That's when I called you."

"And?"

"Aren't you getting hungry?"

"No, Matt. Are you going to finish this story or not?"

"Well, I'm watching him and waiting for you, and then…then a man I hadn't noticed hurries over to his table. He leans down and speaks to Contra Uno. I don't know what he said, but Contra Uno shoots out of his chair like he'd just been told a bomb was under—"

Something crashed behind me, like a plate falling to the floor.

CHAPTER 12

I swiveled around in time to see Scarlett in a fight with her boyfriend. "It's the same puta story again and again. How many times have you promised to leave her? How many times, Carlos? You say that all the time, but it never happens. NEVER!"

Carlos looked like he wanted to crawl under the table. He tried to wave her back into a chair. They were close enough for me to hear him saying, "Calm down, Dulce. Not so loud. Sit down and we'll talk about it."

"DON'T YOU FUCKING TELL ME CALM DOWN!"

She sloshed her drink in his face, grabbed her purse, and marched over to our table. "Lying bitch. I hate your puta show."

She staggered out of the room. Carlos followed. Everyone stared at me as if I'd caused the fuss. There was silence and then laughter, and when the normal stir picked up again, Matt said, "What was that about?"

"She doesn't like my show. A lot of people don't. I get hate mail."

"I hope you never get that angry with me. I just never imagined..."

"I'm not angry, Matt, but I'm going to slosh wine in your face too if you don't finish your story. You were saying this man went to Contra Uno's table. So, what happened?"

"Well, Contra Uno rushes out of the dining room, and you saw what happened next."

"No, no, no, you're leaving out the woman?"

"What woman?"

"A woman got out of a cab in front of me at the hotel entrance. Young. Very pretty. Early twenties. Maybe late teens. She made eye contact with me. Then she went inside and dashed right back out. She looked at me and nodded her head. Brushed by so close I caught a whiff of her perfume. Chanel Number Five."

"Venus Twenty-five."

"No, Matt, I said Chanel Number Five."

"I'm talking about the woman. Her code name is Venus Twenty-five."

"She's twenty-five years old?"

"Younger. We call her Twenty-five because she packs a .25 Beretta."

"Why not just Venus?"

"Because there's another informer called Venus. Women like the name. We've also got an Isis, a Luna, a Cleopatra, a Dreadlocks, and others I can't remember. Go figure."

"Dreadlocks is a woman?"

"A man. Big dude. Scary looking."

I shook my head as if trying to absorb all the code names. "Okay, so this Venus comes hurrying out of the hotel only seconds before the shooting. What was that about?"

"Venus Twenty-five."

"Right. So why did she go in and come right back out?"

"Because I asked her to keep an eye on you. She was my backup."

"Your backup? I'm getting confused, Matt. Last night you told me you worked with US/AID. That's foreign aid, not intrigue, not dangerous stuff where you need a gorgeous backup named Venus Twenty-five and a cover story and a pistol-packing driver. What's going on?"

He took my hand and looked into my eyes. "I'm so sorry for getting you into this mess. I never imagined things would go so wrong."

"You're not answering the question. Do you have a backup here as well, in this restaurant?"

He didn't answer, which itself was an answer. "Who?" I asked. "Where?"

"Sancho. He was in the car with us after the assassination."

"Sancho? Like Don Quixote's sidekick?"

"Well, yeah, except now he's my assistant."

"Is Sancho his real name?"

"No, his real name is…um, never mind. He's sitting back there with Venus Twenty-five."

I turned to look and, sure enough, there sat Sancho at the *Bonnie and Clyde* table, smoking a cigarette and dressed in the same blue guayabera he'd been wearing when I first met him in the car. Venus faced away from us, so I couldn't see her face. Sancho caught us looking and waved. Then he came over, limping slightly with the aid of a homemade walking stick.

He nodded at me. "You okay now?"

"No, I'm not okay. I'm still trying to get a grip on what happened. I'd like to talk to your lady friend. I want to know what she saw."

"Venus isn't feeling well. I'm going to drive her home."

Matt nodded his approval as if he were the boss. Sancho limped away without me getting a good look at the woman.

"Is Venus his squeeze?" I asked Matt.

"You'd have to ask them."

"Why is he limping?"

"Old war wound. He was conscripted into the army like other kids. Wounded in some no-name battle in the mountains and taken to a field hospital. Can you imagine that—kids getting conscripted at age fifteen?"

Yes, I could imagine very well. They also conscripted me against my will at age 15. Never mind that I was an American, and I had vivid memories of a field hospital in the mountains, a team of medics bandaging my leg while I lay there in agony, wondering if I was going to lose my leg or even survive. But I couldn't tell Matt. He worked for the US Embassy, and I wasn't about to tell him I'd fought with the Sandinistas.

Damn war. Damn contras. Damn gringos.

Matt waved a hand in my face. "You okay? You look lost?"

"You didn't answer my question. Why do you need backups?"

"Would you believe me if I said I was just helping friends?"

"Helping friends? Really, Matt? Do you always help your friends by bringing in armed backups like Venus and a war veteran like Sancho?"

I waited for his answer, but all he did was smile and take another sip of wine. It was obvious he had secrets he wasn't willing to share. Just like I had secrets. No point pushing the issue. Not yet. Besides, the wine on an empty stomach was affecting my head. My judgment too because I didn't pull away when he traced a finger down my cheek.

"Why did you bring me to this place?"

"Do I have to tell you?"

"I'd still like to hear it."

CHAPTER 13

He looked away as if embarrassed, and when he spoke, he came so close I felt the warmth of his breath. "Look," he said, "I don't know what you did to me at that reception last night. It was as if you slipped a magic potion in my wine and cast a spell over me. All I know is I fell in love the moment you smiled at me—your dark eyes, your moist lips, the way your hair fell to your shoulders, the way you walked…"

"I think this wine is affecting your judgment."

"In that case, I need more wine."

He bought a rose from a flower girl and pinned it in my hair. "I'm so happy I met you. I never want to lose you."

"Really, Matt? You don't want to lose me, but you don't seem the least concerned that they confiscated my passport, or that I'm the suspect in the black leather jacket, or that I have to report to State Security tomorrow morning for questioning—Nicaraguan style. Do you know what Nica style means? I'll be lucky to get out of there with my fingernails. And even if I do, my name will become public, and I'll be on the killers' hit list."

"Wait, wait, wait. Just hold on. You don't think I'm going to let you go to that interrogation alone, do you?"

"What's that supposed to mean?"

"It means I'm going with you."

"Are you going to protect me from the assassins?"

"They'll have to get to me first."

His positives suddenly loomed. The indefinable little glow I'd felt for him last night ignited, and I leaned into him as if drawn. God, why did I feel this way? Was I that needy? That trusting? Why couldn't I control my emotions? It had to be the wine.

We ordered warm bread and tapas and stuffed food into each other's mouths like lovers. We finished our wine and ordered another, and soon we were sharing bios like a first-date couple. I told him about the confusion of growing up in both Florida and Nicaragua, and he told me about growing up in South Carolina near Charleston and getting drafted into the army and sent to Vietnam at age eighteen.

He clicked his goblet against mine. "To the gods for bringing you into my world."

"To the gods."

He turned around and lifted his goblet to the *Casablanca* poster. "To Bogie and Bergman. May their characters always have Paris."

"I've never been to Paris."

"Neither have I, but if you and I are together, I will show you the world—Paris, London Rome. Hell, even Casablanca.."

"That's what my first husband promised."

Matt almost choked on his wine. "Your first husband?"

"Second one too. Now I've got four kids by two men and two mothers-in-law, and never been anywhere except Florida and Nicaragua."

"What happened to number one?"

"Starkey. That's a state prison in Florida. They got him for holding up a 7-Eleven."

"And number two?"

"They say I offed him with a sawed-off twelve gauge."

"Why?"

"Because he never spoke to me in restaurants. That's why. All he did was sit back and read the financial pages of *The Wall Street Journal*. Turning the pages. Ignoring me. That's why I'm in Nicaragua. You should see the wanted posters with my mug shots. They're all over Florida. They call me Adriana Twelve-Gauge."

"I think we better order coffee for you."

"I'm having too much fun. Let's drink another toast."

"To what?"

"How 'bout to that couple back there in the shadows? They're kissing."

The more we drank, the sillier we became, and by the time midnight rolled around and the pretty woman on the podium was doing a sultry version of Tammy Wynette's, "Stand by Your Man," I was leaning into him and thinking this evening might turn out well after all.

And it might have except for the soldiers. They roared up the drive in a convoy of army trucks and stopped near the entrance, bringing with them exhaust fumes, panic, and a cloud of dust.

"The hell?" said Matt and took my hand. "Let's retreat out the back."

I didn't move. I couldn't without falling on my face. All I could think about was that famous line from the movie, *Jaws*— "Just when you think it's safe to go back in the water..."

CHAPTER 14

Soldiers bounded out of the trucks—dark-faced teenagers in combat fatigues and black berets, pants tucked into boots, assault rifles at the ready. Female soldiers were also in the mix—wiry-haired, rumpled, and bleary-eyed—looking like they'd rather be home with family than harassing citizens out for an evening of pleasure.

I knew the feeling. I'd been on their side of the gun more times than I could count. Now I was on the wrong side.

"Damn it," Matt said, "we should have left sooner."

"I thought Lead Foot was going to warn us."

"They must have taken him by surprise."

The music came to a ragged halt. A couple on the dance floor bolted toward the kitchen, overturning chairs in their haste. Soldiers in hot pursuit raced after them, a blur of clopping boots and clattering equipment. They caught the man and shoved him against a movie poster of Harrison Ford wielding a whip in *Raiders of the Lost Ark.*

"Do you know who I am?" the man raged at a lieutenant who confronted him. "I'll have you court-martialed. Kicked out of the army. The comandante will hear about this."

"Idiot," Matt said. "He must be a lawyer."

"He's bluffing. He'll soon be offering money and begging them not to tell his wife."

Soldiers led the couple away. Other soldiers began rounding up drivers and guards. And still others corralled couples on the dance floor, penning them in like cattle for slaughter. We remained at our table next to the large poster of Bogie and Bergman. "I'm screwed," I said. "I should have confessed to that colonel at my apartment."

"No, Baby, you don't know that for certain. It's always like this after a bombing or assassination. Round up the usual suspects."

"Usual suspects? Did you say usual suspects?" I burst into giggles. Wine always did that to me. "I'm the usual suspect. I'm the reason they came here. I'm the killer in the black leather jacket. I might as well throw up my arms and surrender now. Raise the white flag, drop to my knees, and beg for mercy." I saluted. "Yes, sir, Lieutenant whatever your name is. No gambling here. Just take me out and shoot me."

Matt lowered my arm and shook his head.

I jerked loose. "Why'd you do that? I'm just showing my respect."

"You sure you're, okay?"

"Of course, I'm okay. All they're going to do is shoot me. No big deal."

"Stop it, Baby. Nobody's going to shoot you."

"They might shoot you too. They don't like gringos."

The lieutenant caught us talking and slammed his fist on a table. It became so quiet I could hear the swish of a wobbly ceiling fan above us, and each swish seemed to tell me to shut up. I popped a hand over my mouth. Stop it, I told myself. Don't make a fool of yourself in front of Matt. No more nervous giggles. No more wine. I'd already had too much.

"Listen up," said the lieutenant. "Take out your identification papers—your driver's license, passport, *cédula*, student I.D., voter I.D., work permit, anything with photo I.D. If you're armed, show your permit, and do not under any circumstances reach for a gun. Repeat: under no circumstances reach for a gun. You don't want to make my soldiers nervous. And we don't want you or anyone else to get hurt. Understand?"

"Yes, sir," I responded and saluted.

Matt lowered my arm again. The lieutenant stopped what he was doing and glared at me a second time. I slid closer to Matt. "Don't worry. I won't do anything stupid. I'm in enough trouble already."

"It's okay, Baby. You're with me. I'll take care of you."

"How are you going to take care of me?"

"That officer doesn't look that tough to me. Neither do those two soldiers with him. One's a female. I'll take out the LT."

"LT?"

"Lieutenant. I'll take him out. You take care of the woman. Then we make a run for the car. Get the hell out of Dodge."

I slapped him on the shoulder. "Are you out of your cotton-picking mind? Soldiers are all over the place. They're outside as well. We'll never even make it to the exit."

"It always works in the movies."

"You're teasing, right?"

"Well, yeah, but if we put our heads together, we might come up with a plan that works."

"What's Plan B?"

"We could shoot our way out."

"Good idea, Clyde. We can rob a bank on the way to the hideout. Shoot the sheriff too."

"You don't like it?"

"I don't like gunfire."

"Okay, let me think." He emptied his glass of wine, poured another, and looked into my face with the expression of a man who was as wasted as I was. "Okay, here's Plan C. I march over to the LT and start an argument."

"How are you going to start an argument."

"I don't know. Maybe I'll just call him a prick. That'll get everybody focused on me. You climb out the window, get to the car, and lock the door. If I'm not out in ten minutes, you drive away. Got it?"

"What about those female guards at the window?"

"Dammit, Miami, stop making it so difficult. Just tell them you need to pee. Then you go to the ladies' room and climb out the window."

"My name's not Miami."

"That's what they call you at the station."

"How do you know what they call me at the station?"

"Okay, from now on I'll call you Baby. Did you hear my Plan C?"

"I heard it. Climb out the window and get to the car. What you're forgetting is windows have burglar bars. This is Nicaragua."

"Okay, so in that case, go to alternate Plan C."

"What's alternate Plan C?"

"Overpower your guards and run away. You can do it. And don't forget to take their guns. You don't want to get shot in the back."

"Sure, Matt, no problem. Give me the car keys?"

"Oh, shit. Lead Foot has the keys."

"That's okay. I'll steal one of their big trucks. I'll hot wire it."

"Oh, my God, you are a genius. That's what Yaritza did."

"You mean the Yaritza? The legend? You're comparing me to Yaritza?"

"Why not? She's got special powers. You've got special powers. She's been arrested again and again. Always escapes. Last time she knocked off an abusive army officer and escaped in a truck. Big army truck. Just like those trucks outside. Now she's on the most-wanted list. If you can hot-wire one of those trucks and get us away, I'll marry you."

"You'll marry me? Oh, my God. I'm so happy, Matt. I need to call my mom and tell her to make a guest list. When's the wedding?"

"I'm talking about a truck."

"But you said marriage. You're already changing your mind."

"No, Baby. I already bought the ring. Oh, shit! Here comes the Gestapo."

"What's Plan D?"

"Hide under the table. They'll never see us."

CHAPTER 15

The lieutenant and the soldiers stopped at a nearby table. A man and woman sitting there looked like they wanted to run out of the place. The lieutenant asked for ID. Out came a wallet and a wad of cash. The lieutenant stuffed the money into his pocket, then he dismissed the couple with a wave of his hand and looked in our direction.

I didn't crawl under the table, couldn't in my condition, but the thought burned in my mind. They marched over. I tried to stand up and salute like a good soldier, but Matt pulled me back.

"Well, well, well," said the lieutenant, "look what we found here, señorita Black Leather Jacket herself. Why did you leave the scene?"

"What scene?"

"You know very well what scene."

Matt said, "What is this about, Lieutenant? This señorita is with me."

"And who are you, *caballero*?"

Matt took out his wallet and a black diplomatic passport.

"No, no, no. Keep your money. Keep your passport. I want to see the señorita's passport."

"I don't have it with me," I said.

"Oh, really, and why is that?"

I didn't answer. I couldn't without lying. Besides, he already knew the answer. "We've wasted enough time," said the lieutenant. "They're waiting for you at State Security. Say goodbye to your boyfriend. *Vamanos!"*

He reached for my hand to pull me up. I didn't move.

"Did you not hear me, señorita? Stand up. Move your pretty little bottom out of that chair."

It grew so quiet I could hear the swish, swish of the ceiling fan again. The lieutenant turned to Matt. "You speak Spanish, caballero. Would you please ask your lady friend to cooperate?"

"I've got a better idea," Matt said. "Why don't I drive her to Managua? She wants to report voluntarily to State Security. I promised to go with her. We can follow you."

"Bad idea, caballero. We do the driving." He turned back to me. "I asked you to stand, señorita. I nicely asked you. Either you walk out with me, or we drag you out." He bent over me and glared into my face. "What'll it be—cooperation or force?"

Everything about the lieutenant filled me with contempt. The nastiness in his voice, his corruption, his attitude, the smell of his cigarette breath on my face, and the way he reminded me of an officer we used to call Little Napoleon. I'd taken abuse when I was a skinny kid wearing an oversized Sandinista uniform. I'd let them slap me around. I'd let them force me to do every dirty job in the camp—and other things I couldn't talk about—and I'd been too afraid to resist. But that was then, and this was now, and I'd be damned if I was going to take it from this jerk.

He grabbed my arm and tried to pull me up. I clung to the chair. He pulled harder. Another soldier joined in the effort, and they began dragging me out, chair and all. Matt rushed to my aid. I jumped up and latched onto his arm like a protective lover.

The soldiers tried to pull us apart. I held tight. More soldiers joined the melee, clutching, pulling, pushing, cursing, and yelling. An arm came around me from the back, lifting me off my feet. I kicked, I flailed, and I screamed every dirty Spanish word I knew.

The momentum carried us against the table. Chairs crashed to the floor. So did our empty bottle of wine, the dishes, the goblets, candles, the tablecloth, the rose in my hair, and even the framed print of Bogey and Bergman—and then we were all on the floor.

"What the hell is going on? Stop it!"

The soldiers sprang up and snapped to attention. I glanced up, and there stood a stocky man in the military uniform of a Sandinista Colonel of State Security. In my wine-blurred vision, it took a moment to recognize him as Colonel Vega, the same polite Colonel who had confronted me at the apartment parking lot.

Matt struggled up and pulled me to my feet, and there we stood, breathing hard, red-faced, and straightening our clothes. By then, everyone else in the place had gathered around—customers, servers, musicians, cooks in their white hats, and soldiers—all staring with a What-the-hell-were-you-thinking look on their faces.

The lieutenant saluted the Colonel, wiped a trickle of blood off his lower lip, and pointed at me, saying he'd picked up my trail at the checkpoints, followed us to the restaurant, rounded up other suspects, and was in the process of doing his duty when I'd turned hostile.

"You're the one that's hostile," I said. "I'm a kind and gentle lady."

Colonel Vega pulled the lieutenant to the side, out of earshot. They talked. The Colonel listened, sometimes shaking his head and glancing at me as if disappointed by my unruly behavior. When the conversation ended, the Colonel stepped over and stared into my face the way a father might do when learning his child came home with a bad report card.

"How did it come to this?" he asked, still shaking his head. "You could have saved yourself a ton of trouble if you'd simply told me the truth back at your apartment. I believed you. You shouldn't have lied. Now it's going to be worse. *Mucho, mucho peor.*"

The way he said it made me feel as if I'd betrayed his trust. I even thought about apologizing. But only for a moment. No, I told myself, don't apologize. Don't say a word. They were playing good cop and bad cop and I'd almost fallen for it.

He turned and marched away. "Finish your job," he barked at the lieutenant as if to say take them out and shoot them.

The lieutenant watched him leave and got in my face again, leaning forward and baring his stained teeth, assaulting my senses with his cigarette breath. He even drew back his fist and might have punched me if it hadn't been for Matt and all the witnesses.

"Who do you think you are, woman? Show some respect! Don't you ever lie to a State Security officer again, and don't you dare defy me either. Same goes for your gringo boyfriend. You hear me, girl? Are you listening? You understand what I'm saying?"

I suppressed an urge to punch him in his ugly face, kick him in the balls, and set him on fire. Or at least tell him where to stuff his fist. But I was in enough trouble already—and it was equally bad for Matt, who was struggling to come to my defense.

The soldiers shoved him against a brick column on which hung Clint Eastwood in *The Good, the Bad, and the Ugly*. They pulled up his jacket, and when I saw the pistol strapped to his belt in the small of his back, James Bond style, I knew his diplomatic passport would not save either of us.

The lieutenant yanked the pistol from Matt's holster and ejected the clip. "Nice pistol. I've always wanted a Sig Sauer. Do you have a *permiso*?"

"Of course, I have a permit. It's in my car."

"Good. I want to see it." He turned back to me and began rattling off the charges. "Lying to an officer of the law, assault, resisting arrest, murder suspect, disorderly conduct, abusive language, public intoxication—"

"I didn't murder anyone, and I'm not drunk."

"Oh, really, señorita, you are so inebriated you can barely stand, which is good. You can use it as a rationale for your belligerence. Now you can enjoy a ride to Managua in the back of one of our hospitality trucks."

He turned to the soldiers and made a "Get-them-out-of-here" gesture with his thumb.

CHAPTER 16

They patted me down and checked my purse for weapons. The lieutenant pulled out the pepper spray canister and held it up for all to see. “What is this? Do you have a pink roach problem?”

I reached for it, but he stuffed the canister into his pocket and pushed us out the door, next to a poster of *Doctor Zhivago*. Then we were under the arbors again, heading back down the path toward the parking lot. Soldiers on each side. The lieutenant behind us. The sweetness of honeysuckle in the air.

I clung to Matt’s arm to keep from stumbling. He leaned into me. “Ever considered joining AA? They’ve got a big chapter in Managua.”

“Shut up, Matt. I don’t have a drinking problem.”

“That’s not what the lieutenant says. Just turn around and ask him.”

“That lieutenant needs a class in anger management.”

“You should tell him how you feel. Just don’t use any f-words.”

“I don’t friggin’ use f-words. I’m a nice woman.”

The lieutenant poked Matt in the back. “No talking.”

The outside was as dimly lit as everything else at the restaurant, but there was enough light from hanging lanterns and the flashing neon sign to see that entire families with their children and dogs had come up from the road to see what the fuss was about. One man galloped around on a smelly horse. Others wore war medals on their jackets and carried pistols or assault rifles like Second Amendment crazies in the US. They parted on our approach, and I heard snickers and unkind comments like "slut" and *"puta gringo."*

The lieutenant stopped us as if enjoying the opportunity to show off his prisoners. This allowed the road people to break into small clumps around us, each with its gray-haired, poorly-shaven authority holding forth on the assassination attempt:

"It must have been the gringos."

"Not the gringos. They're friends with the contras."

"The problem in this country is a woman president."

"Never would have happened if Daniel was still president."

An army truck like the one Yaritza had stolen backed toward us with a roar, scattering the road people and polluting the night with noise and blue smoke. An army photographer and another soldier with a notepad took pictures. Then a skinny female soldier in baggy trousers climbed out of the truck and lowered the tailgate.

The lieutenant whipped back the canvas and ordered us in—and that was when another commotion broke out down in the parking lot, a woman screaming, "DON'T TOUCH ME, YOU BASTARD."

"*Mierda*," groaned the lieutenant. "Not another drunk."

He trotted away, leaving us at the back of the truck with other soldiers. A sergeant ordered us to get in, and we climbed into the back like hostages from a Second World War movie, struggling and groaning until we settled onto a wooden bench with other detainees.

Matt put his arm around me. "It could be worse."

"How could it possibly be worse?"

"Remember the magic mushrooms?"

"What do magic mushrooms have to do with this?"

"Well, instead of sitting here on a hard bench with all these nice soldiers protecting us with guns, we could be lost on an island in the middle of Lake Nicaragua, looking for magic mushrooms and getting chased by Yaritza and hostile natives."

The skinny female soldier burst into laughter. Did she understand English? One or two others also laughed, and then everyone was laughing. Every woman in Nicaragua knew about Yaritza. She was their hero. It was said she hunted down abusive men and murdered them in their sleep.

Those in the truck who didn't understand English, meaning everyone else, asked for a translation, and then all the women were chattering about Yaritza, even saying she could walk through locked doors and windows, and this went on until another noisy commotion outside interrupted us.

"DON'T YOU TOUCH ME, YOU DIRTY BASTARD."

CHAPTER 17

The canvas swept open, and there came Scarlett, the same obnoxious woman who'd come to our table, still mumbling and cursing. The skinny female guard who'd been laughing with us directed her onto a bench on the opposite side, directly across from us. I lowered my head, hoping she wouldn't recognize me in the poor light.

Please don't, I prayed.

"You," she said.

I glanced up. "Yes, you, TV woman. This is your fault."

"Why is it my fault?"

"Because you lied to me."

"What kind of stupid logic is that?"

She jumped up. "ARE YOU CALLING ME STUPID?"

Matt squeezed my arm as if to say, "Let it go." The guard shoved Scarlett back onto the bench, but still, she mumbled and complained like a homeless person with mental illness.

"Waterboard us."

"Shock us with electric cables."

"Take us out back and shoot us."

Everyone in the truck yelled at her to shut up. The skinny female guard said, "Nobody is going to shoot you. Nobody is going to torture you. We don't do that."

Right, I thought. Not anymore. I'd had the same duty as her years ago, sitting in the back of trucks with military captives and civilian collaborators, witnessing their agony and fears, dropping them off at interrogation centers. And I'd heard the screams and the gunfire.

Did they still do that? No, that was fifteen years ago. But still...

A helicopter swept low overhead, stirring up dust and illuminating the grounds in a bright glare, shaking the truck and almost blowing off the tarp. Why was a helicopter here? Was I that important? The only thing missing was a Sherman tank.

Dogs barked. The road people cursed the helicopter, cursed the soldiers, and took turns peeking into the truck. The army photographer climbed in and took more pictures. An old woman whose head barely reached the top of the tailgate shrieked, "Gringo murderer! You bombed my village. Killed my brother."

Soldiers led her away. And then Antonio, the server who'd served us in the restaurant, pushed back the canvas and demanded to know why we were leaving without settling our account. "Please pay, caballero. Otherwise, they'll make me pay."

This created a debate in the truck, with one group saying the soldiers should pay, and another agreeing with the server. Even the skinny female guard had an opinion. "Those servers are poor," she said to Matt. "They're only kids. They put up with a lot of abuse."

Matt took out his wallet and handed Antonio a Visa card.

"Sorry, caballero, we accept only cash or American Express."

"I don't have American Express."

I fumbled in my purse. "I've got American Express."

"No," Matt said and handed over a wad of cash. "Keep the change."

Antonio counted the money and smiled, and as he was leaving, Matt yelled to his back, "How about a couple of *cafés con leche* to go?"

Everyone laughed. "Yeah, right," said Scarlett, "like he's really going to bring you coffee."

How long we sat in the back of that smelly truck, breathing second-hand smoke and listening to the whining, I don't know. What I do know is I'd consumed an entire bottle of wine and a glass of water and needed to pee. "Sir," I said to the sergeant in charge, trying not to slur my words. "I really, really, need to go to the ladies' room. Can I go, please?"

"Of course, señorita, we don't want accidents in this truck."

I thought he'd cuff me and assign two or three of his toughest female soldiers to take me, like the chunky one who looked more male than female. Instead, he assigned the task to the skinny little girl who'd laughed at Matt's mushroom comment.

Weird. She couldn't have been over five feet tall and a hundred pounds. Wasn't I a dangerous assassin? Hadn't they warned the sergeant about me? I could easily overpower her, grab her AK, and dash into the darkness, even in my half-inebriated state.

Matt must have thought so too, because as I was standing, he handed me a card with the number for the US Embassy. "Ask for Easton," he whispered. "Tell him what happened."

"It's after midnight, Matt. They're closed."

"No, Baby. Marine guards are there. They always answer."

"You sure?"

"Plan C," he whispered. "Be careful."

I pushed aside the canvas flap that hung over the back of the truck, took a deep breath of moist night air, and stepped to the ground with the help of my scrawny guard. My head swirled. I leaned against the truck, trying to regain my balance. The guard said, "No hurry, señorita. Take your time."

Lightning flashed in the distance. There were no stars as before, and the cool wind that had blown down from the mountains when we first arrived was blowing from a different direction. "Rain's coming," she said. "I can smell it."

I tried to focus on the name patch on her olive-drab shirt, but it was as blurry as everything else around me. "What's your name?" I asked.

"They call me *La Piña*—Pineapple."

"Why do they call you Pineapple?"

"Because I get outbreaks of pimples." She leaned toward me. "See. Happens each month at certain times. It's my code name."

"You don't find it offensive?"

"Why should I be offended? It's like that in the army. We poke fun at each other. See that sergeant over there? We call him *Calvo*—Baldy—because he's losing his hair. Gringos are too sensitive about stuff like that." She slung her AK over her shoulder as if she were going on a trek with friends, and we set off into the night.

CHAPTER 18

There were too many soldiers to run so I resigned myself to listening to her chatter, and by the time we reached the entrance to the dining area, which was a long hike from the truck, I'd learned she was 21 years old, had been in the army for three years, was from a mountainous village in northern Nicaragua, didn't have TV because her house didn't have electricity, and she had also been arrested for drunkenness and disorderly conduct.

"What did they do to you?"

"Not much. Just a small fee and a night in a cell with other drunks."

"Are you saying that's all they'll do to those people in the truck?"

"Sí, *señorita*, just ask a few questions and send you home."

"That's it?"

"Well, there are exceptions."

"What exceptions?"

She stopped to light a cigarette. "They always check your identity. Always. Then, they run a check to be sure your name doesn't pop up on a wanted list. Stuff like that."

"Fingerprints?"

"Depends on why they take you in."

I didn't like that answer. If they fingerprinted me, they'd match the prints to my service record. I'd never seen the record, but I knew it was buried in a filing cabinet at State Security, breathing like a nasty little demon and waiting to expose me as a deserter under a different name.

"They're also looking for assassins."

"Assassins?"

"Didn't you hear? Somebody smoked this honcho in Managua. They say it was awful. Machine-gunned him gangster-style, like they used to do in Chicago." She aimed her AK at a tree and mock-killed it. "Pow-pow-pow-pow. But that's not the worst of it. The killer or killers lopped off his head with a machete. Can you imagine?"

"Wow. Is that what this raid is about, all these soldiers and trucks?"

"*Sí, señorita*. That's what I hear. But they never tell us anything. Only rumors. We're just little worker ants hauling food to the queen. Damn army. I'll be so glad when I get out."

"When do you get out?"

"Five days. I'm hoping to get a job with the gringos. They pay better."

She took a long puff, said she could use a stiff drink, and led me back into the dining room where movie posters lined the walls, customers were paying their bills, and musicians were packing their instruments. She pointed to a poster of Steve McQueen in *The Great Escape*. "Puta Nazis! Our life is no better than those prisoners. Never get a break, food is lousy, and officers think they're God. People hate us just for doing our job."

She stopped her gripes long enough to ask Antonio, our server, for directions to the ladies' room. By then I'd sobered up enough to realize she did not know who I was or my involvement in the killing. Neither did the sergeant who'd assigned her.

Typical army blunder.

But suppose she was pretending? Suppose the sergeant had chosen her because she possessed some kind of special kung-fu skill that would prevent me from carrying out my escape. Maybe she knew English and was trying to loosen my tongue to get a confession.

Or worse. She could be setting me up for a hit. Her assignment was to get rid of me, shut me up. Yes, that had to be it. The assassins had sent a woman I'd never suspect. The sergeant was in on it too. So was that damn lieutenant.

And what better place for a hit job than the ladies' room?

It was located where it always is in Latin American restaurants—*al fondo y a la derecha*—to the back and the right. The old panic surfaced again. What to do? Only one thing came to mind: assault her now, while the gun was over her shoulder.

I turned. Damn it, she'd already unslung her AK.

"Go," she said and guided me into a darkened corridor around a corner from the dining room, beneath a framed poster of Marlon Brando from *The Godfather* movie. My breath caught. I was going to die right there in that shadowy hallway. Bang! Bang! Bullet in the head, just like Vito Corleone. Blood and brains on the floor and the walls next to a door marked SEÑORITAS. No time to pray or ask forgiveness for my sins.

I closed my eyes and waited.

"Are you okay?" Pineapple asked.

"Huh?"

"Are you sick? You look like you need to throw up." She nodded toward the door with her AK. "Go. Don't you need to pee?"

"God give me courage," I said to myself and pushed open the door.

CHAPTER 19

Pineapple walked behind me as silent as a cat creeping up on a mouse. I braced myself. Would she shoot me in the back? Knife me?

Again, I swiveled around to face her, expecting to see a silencer pointed at me, or a hypodermic needle, or a dagger. Made no difference. I'd struggle until the last breath.

But there she stood at the washbasin, partially turned away, her cap and the AK on the counter, and she was prettying herself up in the mirror, wiping the smeared mascara from under her eyes. "Oh, this puta hair," she said, trying to fluff it with her hands. "It's so unruly. I wish it were long and straight like yours. Got it from my mother."

I stood there, motionless, silent, and I might have collapsed if I hadn't grabbed the wash basin for support. "Easy," she said. "Careful. You must have had a lot to drink."

She motioned toward the stall. "Go ahead. Take your time. Maybe that puta truck will leave without us. Wouldn't that be hilarious?" She laughed. I feigned a smile. I still had doubts. Maybe a killer companion was lurking in the stall, waiting to pounce. Maybe Little Napoleon himself.

I opened the stall door slowly. Nothing. No one. Only a clean lavender smell. There was even a window high above the toilet, small, but not so small I couldn't climb out.

My spirits soared. How stupid of me to suspect Pineapple. Now I could climb out the window without an altercation. Run off with the road people. Find a telephone and call Easton at the embassy. He could get me a new passport. He might even help get me out of the country. No interrogation at the State Security office. No fingerprints. No discovery of my service record.

Do it, said the voice in my head. Take charge of your destiny.

I hopped onto the toilet seat for a look.

Shit! Burglar bars.

My world crashed again. No escape through the window. Back to alternate Plan C. Dammit, if I just grabbed Pineapple's gun and ran, she'd scream, and they'd catch me even before I got out of the restaurant. If I didn't grab the gun, she could shoot me in the back. The only other way was a violent confrontation, a surprise blow to the head.

But could I attack a little country girl like her? She trusted me. She could have killed me, bossed me around, pushed me with her AK, threatened me, and made my life hell.

She didn't, and I felt guilty just thinking about hurting her.

She was leaning against the washbasin when I came out of the stall, looking relaxed and smoking a cigarette. Her AK was still on the counter. "You should know better than that," I said like a mother, pointing to the gun. "For all you know, I could be a dangerous criminal. I could grab that gun and shoot you."

She lit up with a big grin that showed her crooked teeth. "Oh, I'm not worried. You're not a troublemaker. Sergeant said all you did was defy the lieutenant. Scratched his face. Busted his lip. Good for you. He's such a *pendejo*. Always yelling at us, threatening us."

"Didn't the lieutenant tell you anything about me?"

"No, comrade. If he did, I didn't hear it. Last I saw him, he was busy with another drunk in the parking lot. He forgot about you by now."

"Are you saying you could go back alone and he wouldn't notice?"

"He's too busy hitting on innocent women, thinking he'll get lucky."

"He does that?"

"All the time. He even hits on me."

"So, I could just slip away and disappear into the night?"

"I've seen prisoners jump out of trucks."

"You wouldn't, like, scream for help or shoot me?"

"Are you crazy, girl? Why would I shoot a nice woman like you?"

"You wouldn't get into trouble?"

"Ha, that truck is so packed with drunks, the only person who'd miss you would be your boyfriend. Speaking of which, he's cute—*guapisimo*. Is he, um, married?"

"No, Pineapple. Not married. Neither am I. We just met."

"Wish I could meet a man like that. Get me out of this crazy country."

She took a final puff on the cigarette, ground it out on the floor with her boot, shook another cigarette out of a pack, and offered me one.

"I don't smoke, and you shouldn't either. Cigarettes are addictive. They cause cancer. Breathing problems. Halitosis. Not good for you."

"Oh, my goodness, now you're sounding like my mom. But what you don't understand is army life is hard. We smoke to calm our nerves."

Yes, I thought. Hadn't I smoked a pack a day when I was a soldier?

Fifteen years ago.

She picked up her AK and motioned me back into the hallway where I'd died and gone to hell with Vito Corleone. The dining room was almost empty, with workers cleaning the floor and stacking chairs, the smell of ammonia in the air, and we were heading toward the exit, passing movie posters of *Lawrence of Arabia, Cleopatra,* and *Spartacus,* , and I was trying to work up the courage to walk away and fall in with the road people when Antonio came rushing over with two paper cups in his hands.

"Café con leche," he said and hurried away.

I stared at the cups in my hands. This was the kind of bizarre stuff that happened only to drunks and in dreams. "Oh, my God," Pineapple said. "How much did your boyfriend tip him? I need a boyfriend like that. Does he have a brother? Would you introduce me?"

She kept on talking, telling me about a boyfriend who dumped her, a sergeant who'd been making romantic advances, and how lucky I was for having a *guapo* hunk like Matt. This went on for so long that by the time we exited the building and were back in the sweet night air beneath the arbors, I was ready to dash into the darkness just to escape her chatter.

I handed her one of the coffees. "I don't want to go to that truck."

"What do you want to do?"

"If it's okay with you, I'm going down to the road."

She took a long sip of coffee. "I'll watch your back. Go."

"Are you sure?"

"Didn't I tell you already? Go. Be careful."

"You won't get in trouble?"

"*Por el amor de Dios, mujer*—For the love of God. How many chances do I have to give you? If you don't go now, I'm going to shoot you. Go! Get your puta butt in motion."

We hugged like old friends, Latin fashion. I thanked her for understanding, told her it was nice meeting her, took a long sip of coffee, and trod into the shadows.

Soldiers moved about in the darkness, shining lights into faces and questioning customers who were leaving. Other soldiers had built a blazing fire. They stood around it, faces and arms all aglow, the glint of fire on tree leaves, rifles, and brass buttons.

On I went, sticking to the shadows, hoping no one would notice. Thunder rumbled. Was it going to rain? The night had been starry before. Now there were no stars, and the air had a heavy feeling of moisture. Keep walking, I told myself. Don't run, and I had just come within sight of the road people when a pop sounded down by the parking lot.

I stopped. Was that a gunshot? A light streaked up like a Fourth of July rocket, higher and still higher, arcing above the trees until it burst into a floating flare, illuminating the trucks and trees, the parking lot, and even the road people in eerie colors.

The lieutenant dashed out from behind a truck. "Who fired that flare?"

A second flare went off, and another, giving the illusion of a troubled daylight. Shadows moved. The surrounding trees went from white to blue and back to white. I knew this was a bad sign. I'd seen it before, and I had scars to show for it, but before I could react, there were gunshots down by the main road, pow, pow, pow, and then a blast of automatic gunfire.

CHAPTER 20

The road people rushed in all directions. The horse reared in panic and galloped away, leaving its rider on the ground. Dogs barked. Soldiers cursed. Glass shattered, and then Pineapple rushed up behind me and pushed me to the ground.

The coffee I'd been nursing took flight. Pineapple said, "Stay flat. Keep your head down."

A soldier hurried over to where we lay and opened fire, spraying the clouds with bullets as if shooting at airplanes. I put my hands over my ears. Spent cartridges fell into my hair and on my back, a shower of hot metal, flashing lights, smoke, and sharp acrid smells.

"What are you shooting at?" Pineapple asked him.

"Cover fire." He slapped in another clip.

"Cover fire for what?"

"Ask the sergeant."

"Get away from us. You're too close."

He fired another blast, and then Matt appeared on the ground beside us. "You, okay?"

"How'd you get away?"

"Simple. Just jumped out of the truck with everyone else."

"What's going on? Why are they shooting?"

"Who knows? This is Nicaragua. Everyone is armed. It's the nature of the times. Why didn't you run when you had the chance?"

"That's what I'm doing—running—then this fiasco happened."

Pineapple rolled over and looked at me like I was hopeless, her face lit by the dying flare. "You could have run off with the road people. You'd never make it in the army."

Right, I thought, which was why I'd deserted.

The helicopter was now sweeping back and forth above us, soldiers running this way and that, firing their weapons, tracers blazing into the night. And just when I thought it couldn't get any crazier, the commotion triggered car alarms, setting off flashing lights, blaring horns, and even sirens. Into this fray came the lieutenant, waving his arms.

"What is wrong with you idiots? It's the assassins. Get after them."

Soldiers piled into trucks and roared away, leaving a cloud of choking fumes. The lieutenant and two or three others followed in a jeep. Then the remaining customers and even the workers began evacuating the place as if a missile had targeted it, wheels throwing out gravel.

How could this be happening? It was as if chaos was following me—gunfire and panic at the hotel, gunfire and panic at the restaurant. Cars racing away and me on the ground. Twice in one night. Was God punishing me for sins I'd committed in a previous life?

Pineapple touched my arm. "Stay safe," she said and ran into the night.

I moved to get up. Matt pressed me back down. "Not yet. Wait until the shooting stops." He turned to face me. "Pineapple treat you well?"

"How do you know her name?"

"Didn't you notice? I slipped her a hundred-dollar note in the truck."

"I didn't see you talking with her."

"Couldn't in front of the other soldiers. They started laughing about her after the two of you climbed out, even taking bets on whether she'd return with you. The sergeant said she was such an airhead he doubted she could even find her way back to the truck."

"She's not an airhead. We had a friendly conversation."

"You should have escaped when you had the chance."

"You should shut up."

In time, the noise and fury died down, and the only signs of the drama that had taken place were residual smells of smoke from the shooting and the dying campfires. "This is so damn crazy," Matt said. "Nobody was shooting at us. The only shooting was outgoing."

"So, who fired those flares? What was that about?"

"Probably some idiot did it as a prank."

Lights flickered at the restaurant. Then the lanterns and the flashing neon sign went out. It was as if God had flipped a switch and turned off all the lights in the world. "Dammit to hell," Matt said. "Power just went out. Rolling blackout for six hours. No telephone service either and it's going to rain. We need a phone."

"I thought you guys at the embassy have mobile phones."

"We do, but that lieutenant confiscated mine. Passport too. Doesn't matter. No service out here anyway. Next week we're getting sat phones, but that's next week."

"What about Lead Foot? Maybe he's hiding in your SUV."

"It's so damn dark, I don't even know where the parking lot is."

CHAPTER 21

We waited until our eyes adjusted. The only light came from distant flashes of lightning. Then we shuffled down to the parking lot in silence, listening for suspicious sounds but hearing only the coo of nightbirds, the sound of a passing vehicle, and the rumble of an approaching storm.

The car was locked, and Lead Foot was not in it.

"No problem," Matt said. "You can hot-wire it."

"Are you kidding? I barely know how to put gasoline in a car."

"But you said you could hot-wire a truck."

"I was lying."

"You're a bad girl, Miami. I believed every word."

"Oh, really, Gringo? How many lies did you tell tonight? Didn't you say you'd take out that lieutenant and get us away? So, why are we stuck in this stupid parking lot?"

"Fate. It was meant to be. The universe helped us escape."

"It's about to rain. Is the universe going to find us a place to shelter?"

"It's telling me the perfect place. Come on."

"Come on where?"

"Palacio de Amor. It's just down the road. They charge by the hour."

"Are you friggin' crazy? They'll be searching every love motel between here and Managua. Imagine how it'll look if they catch us in a love motel. It'll be in all the tabloids."

"The guys would pat me on the back and ask how it was."

"Can't you be serious for a minute?"

"Okay, I'm just trying to think of a solution. Do you have a better idea?"

"We could bust out a window in your car."

"Bad idea. Eventually, that lieutenant will come back and check the parking lot."

"Your car has MI plates. Diplomatic. They can't touch us. Right?"

"Wrong. Diplomatic plates won't protect us if we committed a crime."

"I didn't commit a damn crime, but you did."

"What crime did I commit?"

"Getting me into this mess. You belong in jail."

"Me in jail? Funny. How is that going to solve our problem?"

"So, what's your suggestion?"

"We could start walking toward Masatepe. It's four klicks that way."

"We'd just get picked up by soldiers."

A flash of lightning lit up the parking lot, and in that flash, I saw movement, someone coming from the direction of the restaurant. Matt saw it too. "Christ," he said. "It could be soldiers. Get behind the ca."

We huddled behind Matt's SUV like kids playing hide-and-seek. Whoever it was came closer, and closer still, footfalls on pavement. No flashlights, which was a good sign since soldiers would have flashlights. Matt put an arm around me, and then they were close enough to hear their voices: a man and a woman, and they were having the same conversation we'd been having.

"Best place is Palacio de Amor," said a man. "It's just a short hike."

"No, Carlos, that's where we went last time. It's got bedbugs. Let's go to the Aphrodite."

Carlos? Wasn't Carlos the boyfriend of obnoxious Scarlett? Had she jumped out of the truck?

"Did you bring the stuff?" she asked Carlos.

"*Sí, mi amorcita.* Also got you something new. You'll love it."

She giggled, and they passed by so close I could have reached out and touched them. Their voices faded, and then they got into a car and drove away. "Wow!" Matt said. "Wonder what he got her."

"I don't know, and I'm not going to guess."

"Maybe it was like…you know."

"Would you shut up? Is that all men think about?"

"Hey, I was going to say he got her a big diamond. Champagne too. What better place to pop the question than a place called Aphrodite?"

"You're impossible."

Another flash of lightning lit the night, followed by the sharp clap of thunder. The wind gusted, bringing in debris and damp earthy smells. Then it started. Not as a sprinkle, but like a torrential downpour, with wind, flashes of lightning, and cracks of thunder.

"Do it," I yelled at Matt. "Find a rock and bust out the damn window."

"We don't have to bust the window. It's a Ford Explorer. Got combination lock on the door."

"You gotta be kidding."

He punched in the code, opened the door, and we jumped inside.

CHAPTER 22

What happened in the back of Matt's Explorer as we snuggled beneath a blanket while rain beat against the windows and thunder crashed around us, I shall never tell. What's important is the universe didn't bring soldiers back that night. I was so beaten I fell into a drunken slumber and didn't wake until the rain turned to mist and the early morning light hinted of sunrise. Then it all came back—the assassination, the wine, my fight with the lieutenant, the appointment I was going to miss at State Security, and my bad behavior with Matt for a second night in a row.

I also had a massive hangover and couldn't even find my panties.

God, what a slut! What I needed was a river to jump in and drown.

Matt handed me a bottle of spring water. I chugged it like a thirsty horse, brushed back my hair, opened the door, and stumbled out into the fresh morning air.

Unlike in Managua, where daybreak begins with the hellish sounds of roaring traffic, construction, low-flying airplanes, sirens, church bells, the chatter of people, and even street vendors hawking freshly killed chicken, the morning greeted me with the happy chirps of canaries, a swarm of green, yellow, and blue. There were other bright-colored birds as well, fluttering and singing like all was well in the world.

How could they be so happy when I wanted to throw up? My mouth tasted as if the army had camped out on my tongue. My head pounded. There was a kink in my neck. I could smell myself and could only imagine how awful I looked to Matt.

Not that he looked better—his clothes all rumpled and stained, his hair a mess, face unshaven, and his eyes with that droopy, feel-like-hell look.

He yawned and stretched his arms. "What a nightmare. I dreamed we were having a nice romantic evening up there in that restaurant and then the whole damn Nicaraguan army showed up in Jeeps and trucks. Roughed us up and pushed us into the back of a truck."

"My nightmare was worse. I dreamed I was stuck with a gringo who got me into a heap of trouble. And I'm still stuck with him."

"That's not polite, Adriana. That nice gringo apologized to you a thousand times. Can't you think of at least one sweet thing about him?"

"It might take a while."

The sound of an approaching vehicle interrupted us. We retreated to the opposite side of the Explorer. Matt nodded to a thicket of woods behind us, back where trees grew tall, thick underbrush flourished, and things moved in the brush and made noises unfamiliar to my ears.

"We can hide back there," he said. "It has trails."

"No, Matt, I'm not going into that damn jungle. It has snakes and spiders and wild animals. Jaguars and wolves too. Maybe contras. I've even heard rumors about chupacabras."

"Okay, you wait here. I'll take my chances with the chupacabras."

The vehicle came closer. Birds protested with noisy squawks. Then a large, open-bed farm truck appeared on the road, workers standing in the back with their hoes, forks, and other farm implements. Were those the road people from last night, going to work on a banana or coffee finca? The truck passed. Bird squawks turned to happy chirps. We breathed again. Matt fished a piece of fuzz from my hair. "I'm still waiting," he said.

"Waiting for what?"

"That one sweet thing about a certain gringo from your…um, dream."

"The only thing I remember is Pineapple. She helped me escape."

"You didn't escape. You're still here. Can't you think of something?"

I thought of those sweet moments when we were stuffing tapas into each other's mouths, and I wondered what would have happened if soldiers hadn't shown up. Would we have gone to his place instead of spending a miserable night in his Explorer? Would I be wearing one of his T-shirts and the two of us sipping coffee in his kitchen instead of standing in a parking lot in smelly, wrinkled clothes, hiding behind his SUV like escaped convicts?

"Can't you think of at least one thing?" Matt said. "'You can get one hell of a story about this for your show. Maybe two episodes, one about the assassination, another about what happened last night."

"Would you shut up before I kill you? My head hurts. I need a shower. Need an Aspirin, need a big steaming mug of café con leche."

"We can get coffee up there at the restaurant. Power should be on in about an hour."

"They're closed, Matt."

"Doesn't matter. They'll have night guards."

"Night guards are war veterans. They don't like gringos."

"Are you always this grumpy in the morning? We need to stop at a pharmacy on the way back to Managua. Get you a box of happy pills."

"I'm worried, Matt. That Colonel expects me in his office at nine this morning. If I don't show up, they'll put me on a wanted list. I'll never be able to work or even go back to my apartment. I don't know what to do."

"Do nothing until we talk to Easton."

"Can Easton get my passport back? Can he get me out of the country?"

"We'll know when we talk to him. Now come on. Let's find a phone?"

The warmth of his hand on mine comforted me despite my misery, and I followed him up the same meandering walkway we'd taken the night before, beneath the arbors with their sweet-smelling honeysuckles that were now glistening with dampness, past the table where a man had been reading poetry to his love, and alongside manicured beds of impatiens, brilliantly white and red in the early morning sun.

Amazing the soldiers hadn't trampled them. The only signs of their presence were truck tracks, a pile of wet ashes from their campfire, spent cartridge casings on the walkway, and the paper cup that had held my café con leche. Was this where scrawny little pimple-faced Pineapple had knocked me to the ground to protect me?

I scooped up the paper cup and dropped it into a trash container—and that was when the birds started protesting the approach of another vehicle. "Christ," Matt said. "Now what?"

It was too late to dash into the woods, so we hid on the opposite side of a flowering trellis. The noise came closer. A battered pickup turned into the drive that led to the restaurant and stopped.

Out of the truck stepped Sancho and Lead Foot.

CHAPTER 23

They were as relieved to see us—or at least see Matt—as we were to see them. Sancho hugged me. Then he took Matt's arm and led him away. They talked, now and then looking at me. Matt's face went from curiosity to alarm. He said, "Dammit to hell," loud enough for me to hear, and when he came back, he spoke to me in English.

"Witnesses saw Kodak at the scene. He's in danger. Your picture is also on the front pages of *La Prensa* and *La Republica*. They know you're the woman in the black leather jacket. They're calling it a hit and run."

My headache grew worse. It was bad enough that State Security knew. Now the entire world knew. "We need to talk with Easton," Matt said. "Sancho talked to him this morning. Told him we were missing. He's sending out someone to look for us. They should be here soon."

"Why can't we go in your car?"

"Because they know that car. They'd stop us no matter what?"

We stared down at the road like passengers waiting at a bus stop, checking our watches and listening for the sound of a vehicle. Canaries flitted around in their rainbow colors, chirping as if asking for a handout. Sancho asked what happened to us the night before. Matt said it was a horror show and began relating our adventures. He talked about the soldiers, the scuffle with the lieutenant, and how we ended up in the back of a truck.

When he came to the part about the flares, Lead Foot waved his arms.

"No, no, no, *Jefe*. That's not the way it happened."

He pulled Matt to the side. I was so irritated at being left out of conversations that I followed anyway. Lead Foot turned his back on me and said to Matt. "Listen, *Jefe*, I don't want that woman to hear. She'll put it on her show. She makes everybody look like a terrorist."

"That woman has a name," I shot back. "It's Adriana, and I was also here last night. I know what happened. I saw everything."

"No, señorita, you did not see everything. You could get me into trouble."

"Look, Lead Foot, if you don't want your version on the show, I'll pretend this conversation never happened. What happens at the Broken Cinema stays at the Broken Cinema."

"It's called the Shining Cinema," Matt said.

"I like Broken Cinema better."

Matt told Lead Foot that it was okay for me to hear what he had to say. Lead Foot showed his disapproval by turning his back on me and lighting a cigarette. He took a long puff, blew it out, and said to Matt, "Listen, *Jefe*, the reason I couldn't warn you about the soldiers was they sent an advance patrol. Sneaked up on us like night owls. Me, I hid in the woods. I saw everything, Jefe, saw them bringing out the drunks. Saw how they pushed them into trucks. I saw the road people coming up to watch. I saw the locals with their guns and war medals. That gave me an idea. Good idea. You won't believe what I did next."

"What did you do?"

Lead Foot shot me another drop-dead glance. "Well, I mixed with them. I wasn't dressed like them and that worried me, so I came down here to the parking lot. Opened the door to your SUV and took the AK."

"You took my AK?"

"The idea came to me in a flash, like God speaking to me. I took the AK and went back up to where they parked their trucks. Saw the two of you being led out by the soldiers."

"You were up there with that bunch?"

"God knows I was there, so close to you and that woman you could have touched me."

"That woman's name is Adriana," I said again.

Lead Foot took a long drag on his cigarette and rolled his eyes as if wishing I'd go away. Matt said, "Okay, you were saying you were up there with my AK?"

"Yes, *Jefe*, but that's not the best part."

"What's the best part?"

"Well, after they pushed you and that…señorita into a truck, I went scouting around. Guess what I found in their Jeep? Found a flare gun and flares, and I know how to use them."

We all looked at one another. Lead Foot kept talking. "So, I sneaked back down here with the flare gun and went over there, near that stand of trees, away from the soldiers. Nobody was around, so I started lighting up the night, uno, *dos, trés*. Boom, boom, boom."

"You shot those flares?"

"*Sí, Jefe*, it was me. *Yo mismo*."

"Good job," Matt said. "Those flares got us out of a lot of trouble."

Lead Foot grinned as if Matt had pinned a medal on his chest. "But I figured flares weren't good enough. Right? So, I went flying down the drive fast as I could run, yelling and shooting the AK.. Pow, pow, pow. Put it on automatic and keep shooting until it was out of bullets. That's when the earth opened and all the demons from hell rushed out."

"Demons from hell?"

"*Sí, Jefe*, horns blowing, lights flashing, everybody shooting and running like crazy."

Matt and Sancho burst into laughter, and we were still talking about Lead Foot's adventure when a Toyota Land Cruiser with MI plates drove up and stopped. Out stepped two thick-necked, crew-cut men in dark jackets and sunglasses who looked like they settled scores for the Corleone family. They nodded without speaking and opened the back door.

"Where are they taking us?" I asked Matt.

"My house. Not a good idea to stop by your place."

He was right. Soldiers would be at my apartment—Jeeps in the parking lot, soldiers on the steps and in the lobby, and a scary guy named Igor or José the Knife waiting on my sofa.

"What about checkpoints?" I asked.

"We'll know when we get there, won't we?"

"What kind of answer is that? They'll recognize me. They'll stop us even if we have diplomatic plates."

The crewcut in the driver's seat turned around and narrowed his eyes at me as if to say he'd had enough of my whining, and I should shut up.

CHAPTER 24

The soldiers at the checkpoints waved us through. I didn't know the reason, and I wasn't about to ask the crewcuts. They didn't speak during the hour-long drive to Managua. Didn't turn around to look at us either. They just sat in the front seats like robots, unmoving, until we drove through the wrought-iron gate at Matt's house in an upscale neighborhood, on a no-name street lined with bougainvillea.

They let us out without a word, turned around, and drove away, leaving us standing in the drive in our wrinkled clothes, beneath the spreading branches of a flowering Poinciana. "Who are those guys?" I asked Matt.

"All I know is they work for Easton. There's a running joke at the embassy that he keeps them caged in the basement."

"Can they speak?"

"I've never heard them."

The door opened and a husky housekeeper in a polka-dot apron let us in. Her name was Teresita, and she looked like she spent more time lifting weights in a gym than taking care of Matt's house. The inside was as orderly as the outside, with marbled floors, wood-paneled walls, clean smells, and ceiling beams.

I needed coffee. Needed hangover medicine. Needed a hot shower and sleep. I also needed to do something about that damn security Colonel who'd be waiting for me in his office.

"Stop worrying," Matt said from the kitchen counter where he was brewing coffee in a drip maker. "That Colonel had a rough night too. He's sleeping it off with his mistress."

"Doesn't matter. When they tell you to be there at a certain time, you better be there. I should call him and explain."

"No, Baby, don't do a damn thing until we talk to Easton."

"Can we call him now?"

He glanced at his watch. "Thirty more minutes and he'll be in his office. Let's get cleaned up. There's a robe and fresh towels in the guest room. Toothpaste and toothbrush too."

"A toothbrush, Matt? You keep a supply for all your girlfriends?"

"I work for the embassy, Baby. Associates come over. Sometimes we work late. Christ, I'm too tired to explain. Anyhow, just give your clothes to Teresita. She'll take care of them."

He took a couple of large mugs from the cupboard, rinsed them, and filled them with coffee. The pleasant aroma spread over the room. I added cream to mine and was enjoying the heavenly taste when the phone rang.

"Gotta take this," Matt said and went into another room.

The kitchen table had folders, notepads, books, and articles on mushrooms, bats, and tropical flowers scattered all over it. I glanced around for a newspaper, wanting to read what they were reporting about the assassination. There was nothing, so I picked up a Xerox copy of an article titled, *"Maria Sabina: Saint Mother of Sacred Mushrooms,"* and was reading about the mushroom rituals of a Mexican *curandera* when Matt came back with the phone in his hand.

"Easton," he said, holding his phone. "He wants to talk to you."

Easton skipped the usual niceties. "I'm told you're in a great deal of trouble," he said in a nasal accent that sounded faux British. "I know what you're asking for—passport and exit—and I understand your concerns, but please understand that before we can take any action, anything at all, we need to put together all the information in your possession."

"All I know is what I saw and heard."

"Which is what we want, Ms. Alvarado. Every tiny detail. Everyone and everything you saw at the shooting. Even the smells. We've heard from other witnesses. Their accounts are murky at best, but they point a finger at you."

"I had nothing to do with that damn assassination. Matt knows it and you know it. I was an innocent bystander, wrong place, wrong time."

"Yes, Ms. Alvarado, I understand, but I'm not the one you need to convince. You're in the newspapers. You're on television and radio. You're also a US citizen and that creates problems for the embassy."

"The embassy created this mess."

"Yes, Ms. Alvarado, I understand."

"You keep saying that. My question is what are you going to do?"

"We're working on it. We're walking a thin line with the Sandinistas. We have to work together to put out the fires."

I rolled my eyes. "What am I supposed to do in the meantime—just wait until the killers put a spear in my chest too? Is that what you want?"

"You have a lovely way of expressing your frustration, Ms. Alvarado. No one at the embassy wants to silence you. No one wants you to come to a bad ending. What we want are two things. No, make it three. First, we need a statement from you, everything you remember about the…um, unfortunate incident. I'll send someone over later today. They'll take your statement. Second, I understand that your camera operator, Mister…?"

"Kodak, but that's not his real name."

"Ah, yes, Kodak. Anyhow, I understand he captured it all on camera. We need a copy. We're also going to need a statement from him."

"That video belongs to the station. We never allow outsiders to—"

"Please, Ms. Alvarado. That video could exonerate you. It could reveal the killers. Imagine what the perpetrators would do if they knew about that video. It could disappear. Witnesses could disappear."

"Do you think I don't already know that? That's why I need my passport. That's why I need to get out of this country. I can answer your questions just as well from Florida as I can answer them here."

"Perhaps you didn't understand what I said earlier. We need to see that video. Only then can we discuss an escape plan."

I blew out a breath of exasperation. "You said there are three things. What's the third?"

"The third? Oh, yes, the third. I'm told you missed an appointment today at State Security."

"There was a good reason."

"The reason isn't important. What I'd like you to do is call their office. Call them now. Speak to Colonel Vega."

"How do you know Colonel Vega?"

"We're the US Embassy, Ms. Alvarado. You need to schedule another appointment with him. Arrange it for tomorrow morning. By then, we'll have a better handle on what you can and cannot tell them."

"Wait. You're going to dictate to me how to answer their questions?"

"No, Ms. Alvarado. We're going to listen to your statement and make suggestions. Nothing more. Nothing less. We have experience in these matters. We're trying to help you."

"Help me? Seriously? If you gave a damn about helping me, you'd get me another passport and get me out of the country."

"I'm sorry, Ms. Alvarado, we don't fabricate passports and even if we did, we couldn't hustle you out of the country. They'd stop you at the border or airport or wherever."

"Don't you folks have airplanes?"

"Please, Ms. Alvarado. Just cooperate with us."

I closed my eyes and muffled another curse.

"Oh, and there's one more thing," Easton said.

"What?"

"Keep a low profile. Take a week off from your work. Don't show your face in public. It could be dangerous. But you already know that, don't you?"

He hung up without saying goodbye. I felt like throwing my coffee mug against the wall. Instead, I gritted my teeth and called Colonel Vega at State Security. It wasn't a pleasant conversation. I called my station manager and got another tongue-lashing. I called Kodak and tried to convince him that gringos were more trustworthy than State Security. Then I uttered dirty words that rarely came out of my mouth and headed for the shower.

CHAPTER 25

The rumble of a passing truck brought me out of a merciful sleep. The bedside clock told me I'd slept four hours. I rolled out of bed, stretched and yawned, and felt almost human again. No headache. No nausea, only the dread of being stuck in a terrible situation. I dressed in the same clothes I'd worn the evening before—Teresita had cleaned them—and went to the kitchen to look for Matt.

He wasn't there, but he'd left a note saying he'd gone to the embassy and to make myself at home. Good idea, I thought, and would have gone snooping like a spy, opening drawers and closets, if it hadn't been for Teresita who seemed to watch my every step. Odd that she had a real name like Teresita instead of a code name like Eagle Eye.

She didn't ask if I was hungry or offer to fix a snack, so I made myself a ham and cheese sandwich, squeezed lemons for lemonade, and sat down to eat at a small kitchen table where Matt had left his folders and books about magic mushrooms.

A folder labeled Yaritza caught my attention. Yaritza? Wasn't she the serial killer we had joked about at the restaurant? The legend? The one who climbed through locked windows at night and murdered abusive men? The one who'd killed her jailer and escaped in an army truck? Was she even human? And what did she have to do with magic mushrooms?

I opened the folder, and found a mugshot of an attractive young woman with Hispanic features. Could this be the infamous Yaritza? On it, someone had penciled, "Rumored to project special powers."

Special powers? What did that mean? That was what I needed: special powers to become invisible and fly back to Florida.

There was also a folder labeled Catia, which was the name of a bitchy girl I'd known in high school. I was about to open it when Kodak showed up in an embassy vehicle driven by the same two crewcut and sunglass robots who'd driven us from the Cine Luminoso to Managua.

They dropped him off and left.

He was as rumpled and grumpy as I had been. "Who the hell are those guys?" he said, watching the crewcuts drive away. "Bastards never even spoke to me. *Ni una palabra*. Not a word. I was worried they'd beat me to death, steal the video, and drop my body at the garbage dump." He glanced around the place—at the spreading Poinciana tree, at the tall brick walls that surrounded the house, and at the paved outdoor patio that was bordered with blossoming flowers. "Nice. You live with the gringo now?"

"My place is too dangerous."

"Are you sure we can trust the gringo?"

"No, but I'd rather put my life in his hands than State Security."

"I don't trust either side. Hell, no. Not the damn gringos and not State Security. One of them—I don't know which—engineered that killing. They don't want our video to see the light of day. It might expose them."

"Did you review it?"

"Affirmative. Light's poor, but it shows everything—faces, automobiles, the gunfire, you on the ground, even that crazy bastard with the spear. It's bizarre. But you know what's shitty about this whole puta disaster?"

"What?"

"You and I were just doing our job. Didn't do a damn thing wrong. *Nada*. Now we're screwed. But do you know what? Anything happens to either of us, the whole puta world will see that video." His face went from deep tan to crimson. His voice got louder. "I will SHOUT THAT PUTA MESSAGE FROM THE ROOFTOPS. I will tell that to the puta gringos. Tell that to the pendejos at State Security. Fuck all those *hijos de puta*!"

"Okay, I get it. Let's go inside so we don't disturb the neighbors."

"The neighbors should know it too. We should shout it together, Adriana. That video is our life insurance. We've got to work together."

"Okay, okay. Not to worry. We're in this together."

I waited for Kodak to calm down and then we went inside, sat at the table, drank lemonade, ate sandwiches, and talked in hush tones. Kodak wanted to talk about an old girlfriend he'd lost in the war. Flower Girl, he called her, the love of his life. I'd heard the story many times and didn't want to hear it again, so I changed the subject back to the video and guided him to the back garden where we conspired some more.

Daylight turned to dusk. The wind blew. Dark clouds were building up for another storm. Teresita came out the door with an umbrella, said, "*Buenas noches*," and left for the night. I waited for the gate to close behind her and was telling Kodak about my adventures with Matt the evening before when the gate opened again and the crewcut twins arrived in an embassy vehicle with Matt and three other gringos.

CHAPTER 26

Dr. Tinted Glasses directed me to sit on one side of the table and the two women on the other. The women still hadn't spoken to me or even made eye contact. Like I was toxic and this whole disaster was my fault. Matt sat off to the side like an observer. The women opened folders, took out sheets of paper, and began reading in silence.

They took their time and, as they read, I noticed they had not been blessed in the looks department. Their brown hair was swept back in ducktail fashion, and they could have been sisters for all I knew—or lovers. The only difference was that one wore a Cross pendant and the other a Star of David.

"When are we going to watch the video?" I asked Matt.

Ms. Star of David put away her notes and looked at me for the first time. "Video comes later," she said in a snarky voice that sounded like she'd grown up in a bad neighborhood in New York. "First, we need your account of the assassination—everything you saw. Everything you heard."

"It would help if I could first see the video."

"No, Ms. Alvarado, we want to hear your version first. Then we'll compare it with the video. There may be discrepancies."

Ms. Cross Pendant adjusted her bifocals and spoke for the first time. "Your interrogation at State Security will not be pleasant. They'll put you at a table in a secluded room. Two men will question you, maybe three.

Others will watch through a one-way window. They will yell at you. They will threaten you. They will cajole you, accuse you, offer money, or escape if you cooperate. They'll dig up dirt from your past. Maybe even fabricate dirt. There may be other…um, intimidating elements in the room."

"What kind of intimidating elements?"

"You already know the answer. You're a respected journalist. It's not likely you'll be treated like a hardened criminal. However…"

"However, what?"

"Your crime is that you're a witness—a witness with a journalist's eye for observation. You saw the killers. You could pick them out of a lineup. You might even know them. That's a big problem. The killers may have friends at State Security. That could be dangerous for you. Extremely dangerous."

"You're not telling me anything I don't know."

"That's why we're having this meeting, Ms. Alvarado—to help you forget what you saw. Your best defense is you saw nothing. It happened too suddenly. So, what we're going to do tonight is listen to your story. You tell us exactly what happened and who you saw. Then we'll review the video. After that, we can tell you what to forget. Any questions?"

"Yes, why can't Holbrook Easton just get me a passport and get me out of the country."

"That will not happen. Do you need a glass of water?"

"Yes."

Matt went to the refrigerator and took out a bottle of spring water.

"No, no, no," said Dr. Tinted Glasses, wagging a finger. "Not yet."

I thought Matt would give me the water anyway. Instead, he put the water on the table. Ms. Cross Pendant picked up the bottle and unscrewed the cap. She lifted the bottle to her mouth in slow motion, took a sip, licked her lips as if to torture me, and screwed the lid back on.

"I'd also like a bottle," I said.

"You'll get water about midway through the interview."

"Why can't I have water now?"

"Didn't we explain already?"

"I'm not deaf, but you asked if I needed water."

"They'll do the same tomorrow," said Ms. Cross Pendant, adjusting her bifocals, "but they won't be nearly as accommodating as us."

"Can someone go with me tomorrow, like a lawyer?"

"All we can do is inform them that you're a US citizen and we expect them to treat you professionally and courteously."

"And one more thing," said Ms. Star of David, leaning across the table. "Tomorrow, you fudge the details. But tonight, you tell the truth, the whole unadulterated truth."

"Unadulterated?"

"Unadulterated means you don't stick your opinion into the conversation or add extra details. Isn't English your native language?"

"I'm bilingual. The word in Spanish is *sin mezcla* or sometimes *sin adulterar* depending on context. Do you speak Spanish?"

Her face went from pasty white to crimson. "We're asking the questions, Ms. Alvarado, not you. As I was saying, we want the truth from you but with only two or three exceptions."

"What exceptions?"

"First, no one from the embassy called you from the hotel. So, when they ask why you were at the hotel with your camera operator, you answer that it was an anonymous tip."

"Isn't that adulterated?"

"No, it's a bald-faced lie. Better to lie than create more problems."

"I got it, anonymous."

"Anonymous will satisfy us, but it won't satisfy State Security. They'll want details. Was it a man or woman that tipped you off? What language? Did he or she have an accent? What were the exact words? Did you hear background noises? We expect you to be creative."

"I can be creative. Can I have water now, please? My mouth is dry."

"Water comes later. The second exception relates to Venus 25. You never saw her either. She was not there. You do not mention her."

"Don't mention who?"

"Venus 25. Didn't I just tell you?"

"Yes, but you told me to forget I saw her."

"Good, glad you have a faulty memory. And number three, they'll want to know why you left the scene in an embassy vehicle. You'll have to embellish. You're a journalist. You can do that, can't you?"

"Do you think I haven't already thought of that?"

"Fine, just remember if it gets ugly it isn't personal."

They dimmed the lights and spoke to one another in whispers. Lightning flashed through the windows like a horror movie. Thunder rumbled, and then the rain started, beating against the windows and drumming on the roof, making the scene even more ominous. By then I felt like I was already in an interrogation room with three sadistic agents who'd come with pliers for pulling out nails and a bucket of water for dunking my head.

Dammit, why hadn't I expected this and tanked up on water?

Dr. Tinted Glasses arranged a desk lamp to shine in my face. He switched on the recorder and stated the date, location, and the names of those present. Then he asked me to identify myself by name, birth date, occupation, and citizenship.

"Could you get me a bottle of water?"

"I asked you to state your name, birth date, occupation, and citizenship."

"My name is Maria Adriana Alvarado. I'm a TV journalist working in Nicaragua, and before I finish my answer, I want to make one thing clear. My cameraman burned multiple copies of the video. He did so at my request. These were placed in secure locations. In the event anything evil falls on either of us, there will be consequences. Is that understood?"

Matt squirmed in his chair. Ms. Star of David let out a breath of frustration. Ms. Cross Pendant said, "You're a US citizen, Ms. Alvarado. Why didn't you entrust your video to us?"

"Because I don't trust you any more than I trust Nicaraguans. May I have water?"

"Later, can you please answer the question that was asked?"

"I'm not answering a damn thing until I get a bottle of water."

CHAPTER 27

Kodak's "statement" wasn't as long or as contentious as mine. No heated words. No dispute over water. They even let me remain in the room. Part of it, I suspected, was that he was just the cameraman who'd been summoned to do his job. Another part was that none of the embassy people except Matt spoke passable Spanish. But the greater part was the clock. It was almost seven p.m., and we were facing a power shutoff that always occurred at eight.

"Let's view the video," Matt said, tapping his watch. "We've got less than an hour."

Someone dimmed the lights. The screen was adjusted. Note pads came out. I finished the bottle of water I'd been nursing and took a deep breath. The rain slacked as if the rain gods also wanted to see the video, and it was so quiet I could hear the movement of the night guard on the outside porch. A shiver came over me. What would the video show? Would it show the faces of the killers? Would it show the jungle woman?

Would it exonerate me?

Matt squeezed my arm. The PowerPoint came on with a hum. I braced myself, and there I was on the living room screen—back at the scene of my nightmare.

"Go!" said Kodak's voice in the video. "You're hot in five seconds."

Again, I relived every moment of my slow walk to the hotel—the slamming car door, the hotel vans, the people off to the side, the glow of cigarettes, the looming hotel in the shape of a Mayan pyramid. Kodak's camera caught every detail and sound, even the clack of my heels on the pavement. But no jungle woman. No movement or shadow. The only hint of that creepy moment was a momentary pause in my gait.

Christ, I didn't just need water. I needed a shrink.

A night bird warbled in a tree near the entrance. Kodak followed my glance into the tree and even focused on a small bird. Weird? His camera captures a little bird but not a crazy-ass jungle woman with blue skin and red facial markings.

The woman and the two men I'd seen before came up close behind me. Annoyingly close. Did they know Contra Uno was coming outside?

Yes, and they were using me as a shield.

"Pause the video," said Ms. Star of David.

She twisted around to look at me. "Do you know those people?"

"No."

"Did you hear them talking?"

"Only one word—*Listo*, which means 'ready,' like they knew he was coming out."

She scribbled on her pad. The video resumed.

Out of the hotel came Venus 25 who'd just gone in, her heels clacking on the tiles. She glanced at me as if to say, "Here he comes," and brushed by so close that even now, sitting on the sofa between Matt and Kodak, I caught a whiff of Chanel Number 5.

The hotel doors closed and burst right back open. Three men rushed out, Contra Uno in dark glasses, looking this way and that. All shown on

Kodak's video, faces and all. The people behind me closed in for the kill. "Murdering son of a bitch!" shrieked the woman.

She shoved me into Contra Uno. Gunshots and flashes of light. A spray of blood. Down went Contra Uno, clutching his chest. Down I went too, directly on top.

Kodak's camera didn't show who fired the shots.

My heart sank. The video would not prove my innocence.

There were shouts and screams and curses. Contra Uno's bodyguards dashed into the darkness. And that was when the weirdo with the spear—who was now wearing a mask—dashed up and plunged a spear into the dead man's chest.

Ms. Star of David gasped at the sight. Matt tightened his grip on my arm. Kodak didn't move. Dr. Tinted Glasses paused the video. "I don't get it," said Ms. Cross Pendant. "The victim was already dead. Why would they stick a spear in him?"

"A message," Matt said. "It's like a warning."

"Warning to who?"

"Maybe his friends. Like saying this could happen to you."

There were more scribbles on notepads. The video started again. The panic intensified—car doors slamming, driving away, horns blaring, tires squealing, women screaming, people running to and from the scene, Matt kneeling beside me.

Kodak panned the area with his camera like the professional he was, focusing on car plates and faces, zooming in and out. He captured the small group that had gathered around us—the faces, the looks of horror, the pooled blood, the spear with its feathers and beads.

Matt stiffened beside me. "Pause," he said. "Rewind."

Tinted Glasses backed it up. Matt said, "See that man in the dark shirt? He was in the dining room. He's the one that went to Contra Uno's table."

Dr. Tinted Glasses enlarged the frame and centered it on two men, one with a badly pocked face. I stared at them, at their silvery hair. At their ugly faces. Could it be them—the sons of bitches who'd ruined my life a long time ago? Were they still alive? Were they involved in the assassination? Did they recognize me?

The memories flooded back. The uneasiness I already felt ratcheted up a notch. It spread to my stomach. Nausea swept over me.

"Bastards!" I said without thinking.

I dashed away and barely made it into the bathroom before everything came out—the water, the sandwiches, and the outrage at how I wanted to find those two *hijos de puta* and drive a stake into their evil hearts.

CHAPTER 28

Matt found me sitting on the bathroom floor with my back against the wall. He pulled me up, guided me into the bedroom, handed me a damp towel, and sat on the bed beside me.

The rain started again, loud, with lightning and thunder. Matt took my hand. My soul told me I needed to tell him, needed to confess. I didn't have anyone else, not a living soul, not a mother or father or siblings, not cousins or close female friends. Not even a shrink. I only had Matt, and maybe that was why I'd fallen so hard. "That man in the video," I said, "the one that you said went to Contra Uno's table."

"You know him?"

"Ramos—Leopoldo Ramos-Garcia. He should be in jail. He was a lieutenant in Somoza's National Guard. The other man, the pock-faced one, his name is Facundo Morales. You have files on them in the embassy. *Americas Watch* named them as war criminals."

"How do you know Ramos?"

"It could ruin our relationship."

"Nothing you say will change the way I feel about you."

"Not even if I tell you I was a Sandinista soldier?"

He didn't blink. No change in facial expression. It was as if he already knew. And maybe he did because he worked for the US Embassy, and they had secret files on everyone in Nicaragua who was anyone.

"Doesn't matter," he said. "There were conflicting emotions back then. I'd rather hear you were a Sandinista than a Somoza supporter."

I showed him the scar above my ear where Ramos had struck me with a brass candleholder, and I was about to tell him the entire story when the room lit up in a flash of lightning followed by a sharp crack of thunder.

The lights went out. There were curses and grumbles from down the hall. Matt lit a lantern, went out to say goodnight to his embassy friends, and came back with two icy cold Coronas.

"Where's Kodak?" I asked.

"Down the hall, past the kitchen, other side of the house. He's staying here tonight, in the other guest room. He can't hear us."

I took a long sip of beer and set down the bottle. "It's a long story."

"We've got all night."

"It's a sad story. I'll cry."

"It's okay, Baby. Cry all you want."

The gods became as outraged as I was, bringing back the storm in a fury. Rain beat against the bedroom windows. The roar of wind became Somoza's airplanes. Lightning and thunder became his bombs. Something was burning. I could smell it. The present slipped away, and through the tears, I told Matt how I was alone with my mom in my childhood home when Ramos and his sergeant burst into our house during a battle.

"I was only fifteen, dressed in my Sacred Heart uniform. I won't tell you what they did to us, but you can guess. I buried my mom in the back garden beneath an avocado tree."

I broke down in long bitter sobs. Matt held me against him, and for the first time since I'd been in Nicaragua, I felt secure with this man who cared for me. "Where was your dad?" he asked.

"Don't know. We didn't have a good relationship. He was a heavy drinker, always angry. I'm pretty sure he had a younger woman in another part of Managua. I thought he'd come looking for us. He didn't. Never saw him again and don't want to see him."

I went to the bathroom to straighten up, and when I returned, I finished the bottle of Corona and told Matt how I'd wandered around the streets in a daze. "It was terrible, Matt. Dead bodies, destroyed houses, burned-out trucks and tanks. Vultures. Dogs. I didn't know what to do. I kept walking until I found myself at the cathedral. It was packed with survivors. They were praying, crying, looking for relatives."

I paused to wipe away tears. Matt put his arm around me, and I continued my story. "I lit a candle for my mom. Many of my high school friends were there, dressed in Sandinista uniforms. They told me that my best friend Angelina was killed in the fighting. I was so exhausted and beaten I couldn't even cry. All I could do was light another candle."

"Is that when you joined the army?"

"More like coercion. Fighting was still going on. You could hear the shooting. An officer asked if I wanted to fight the dictator. Yes, I told him, but what I wanted was to hunt down Ramos and his pock-face sergeant. Kill them. Make them pay. I lied about my name and told the officer my name was Angelina. I don't know why. My friends said nothing. They were fifteen-year-old kids like me, too scared to talk. That's how confusing it was."

"Did you look for Ramos?"

"Couldn't. I was just a flunky, a water girl. A gofer. A cook. A pack mule. The army sent me to places in the mountains and jungles I could never find again. We ate nasty Bulgarian spaghetti with monkey meat. I was wounded in some no-name battle. After that, I just took off my uniform and walked away. Deserted. Changed my name back to Adriana. Left Nicaragua and went to the US."

A rumble of thunder shook the room. When it settled down, Matt said, "It's been fifteen years. How did you recognize them after all that time?"

"How could you ever forget that ugly pocked face? He's the one that killed my mom. The other reason is I studied journalism in college. Did my research. Pored over publications about the war, things like *Americas Watch* until I saw their names. Found their pictures too. I've got an entire file on those bastards in my office."

"Is that why you left Florida and came back to Nicaragua?"

"That's one of the reasons, but there's something else."

"I'm listening."

"They fingerprinted me when I was a soldier. I'm sure they still have the files. Tomorrow, they'll fingerprint me again. They'll find me in their service records under Angelina's name. They'll know I'm a deserter, and desertion is a serious crime. They shot deserters back then. I saw it happen. They may not shoot deserters now, but they could put me away for a long, long time. That's why I need my passport. That's why I need to get out of this country."

CHAPTER 29

The hellish crows of a rooster woke us at daybreak. I used to love the cock-a-doodle-dos of the morning. Bacon and eggs and coffee and the sunrise of a new day. Now they sounded like, "Run, Adriana. You're doomed. You're screwed."

My mood darkened even more when Kodak dragged himself into the kitchen looking like today was the day for his execution. And then Holbrooke Easton called to say in his stuffy voice that State Security had changed my appointment from morning to afternoon to give them time to review the video—and to be on time and not to fight them, and to remember my instructions from last night and that it was in my best interest to cooperate.

"You're also free to return to your apartment," he said.

"Are you saying my apartment is now safe?"

"No, Ms. Alvarado, what I said was Colonel Vega informs me you can return to the apartment if you wish without fear of arrest. It's as safe as any other place in Nicaragua. Just remember what I told you. Keep a low profile and don't go out in public. Your picture is in every publication in Managua. You should see the headlines—Murder by Spear, Hit and Run, Lady in the Black Leather Jacket. The entire country is in an uproar."

"I'm also in an uproar. You people got me into this mess. Why can't you get me out of it?"

"Oh, please, Ms. Alvarado. Haven't we had that discussion?"

He hung up without saying goodbye or good luck. I yelled, "Prick!" into the dead mouthpiece and wanted to throw it against the wall. Matt and Kodak looked up from their coffee, but they said nothing, which was good because I was in a fighting mood.

Matt took the day off and drove me to the complex where I lived. Our arrival created wide-eyed stares in the lobby and at the check-in desk. Marco asked if I was okay. I said, yes, and then we dashed up the stairs to my apartment expecting to find a ransacked mess. But the entire place was as tidy and orderly as if the cleaning fairies had spent the night there. State Security—or whoever—had even replenished my water emergency water supply. The only thing missing was my black leather jacket and the wet clothes I'd left in the tub.

The arrow in my chest sank a little deeper. I imagined a team of forensic workers in white lab coats examining my clothing at that very moment, photographing the leather jacket, going through the pockets, and analyzing the blood stains.

It grew worse when I checked the message machine. It was full. The first half dozen or so were from my station manager asking what was going on. His voice grew angrier with each message. There were other recorded calls with only silence, and then came the nasty ones from voices I didn't recognize, and the final one: "Prepare to die!"

The rooster was right. I was doomed.

CHAPTER 30

I chose jeans and a flowery crimson blouse to wear to the interrogation, and at precisely 1400 hours, I stood with Matt in front of an ugly brownstone building that served as headquarters for the General Directorate of State Security.

Soldiers stood in front with assault rifles. The sharp smell of sulfur from a nearby volcano hung in the air like an evil omen. A tank with a menacing cannon pointed toward the street as if to say, "Don't mess with State Security." There were also Jeeps off to the side and a green army truck that looked like the one they'd put me in at the restaurant.

A terrible dread came over me. I'd heard rumors about this place—the Cuban advisors, the wiretaps, the interrogation centers, and clandestine prisons. The torture. Now it was my turn to go inside, and it's fair to say at that moment I'd have been a perfect fit for the leading role in Pedro Almodóvar's movie, *Women on the Verge of a Nervous Breakdown.*

Matt took my hand and led me to the entrance. "It'll be okay," he said. "Holbrooke Easton had a long conversation with Colonel Vega."

The door swung open. A chunky female soldier with cropped hair and a surly look stepped out. "Only the señorita," she said, and before either of us could protest, she grabbed my arm like I was a dangerous criminal, took me into the lobby, and shut the door in Matt's face.

The place reeked of fear and cigarette smoke and had the grimy appearance I expected. Four or five other soldiers stood around smoking cigarettes or staring at me from wooden benches. An older soldier with sergeant's stripes looked up from behind a caged counter.

"Empty your pockets," he said.

"Pockets are already empty. No purse or jewelry either."

"What kind of woman doesn't carry a purse?"

"They told me not to bring anything."

"Must have been a man," grumbled the female soldier behind me. She patted me down anyway, feeling my breasts and between my legs. "Clean," she announced to the sergeant.

The sergeant nodded and asked me to sign a form to the effect they had not taken any personal possessions. I signed the form and had no sooner handed back the pen than two of the other soldiers, both male, gripped my arms from either side and marched me across the lobby, through double doors, and down a long corridor.

A side door opened and closed as if someone wanted a peek. Other doors slammed behind us. There were clattering and buzzing sounds. I turned to look. No one. Nothing. Was I hearing things? A few more steps and the soldiers ushered me into a room that smelled of chemicals.

By then, my mouth felt as dry as the sands of Morocco. Sweat trickled from my armpits down my ribcage, and it wouldn't have surprised me at all if that blue-skinned jungle woman with wild hair and feathers materialized with her spear.

"Fingerprints and mugshots," said one soldier, and directed me to a desk where sat an attractive middle-aged woman in a Sandinista uniform.

The woman stood. "Oh, my goodness. Aren't you…?"

“Yes, I’m the woman in the black leather jacket.”

“No, no, I’m talking about your show, ‘Nicaragua Exposed.’ I love that show. Love the way you interview guests. Love the way you blend it with action shots.” She turned around, rustled through a pile of newspapers, picked up a gossip tabloid called *La Estrella de la Mañana* (The Morning Star), and slapped it into my hand. “What a great picture. You look like a Hollywood star. Would you mind signing it for me?”

At that moment, I’d have signed over my life savings. She handed me a pen and motioned me into a wood chair that looked like it had been bought in a fire sale. Three or four others gathered around to watch me sign, including the mugshot guy, all staring down at me like mourners around the coffin. “What is your name?” I asked the fingerprint lady.

“They call me Apocalipsis.”

“Why do they call you Apocalypse?”

“My ex says I’m a walking disaster. I destroy everything I touch.”

Everyone burst into laughter. I forced a smile and signed her tabloid, and then others wanted my autograph. I signed their tabloids and newspapers too, and then asked Apocalipsis, “How long does it take to analyze fingerprints?”

“It takes a while. We’re not Interpol or the FBI.”

“How long?”

“Depends on urgency. High priority gets back in two or three days. No priority takes two or three weeks. No urgency just means we file it and forget it. Why are you asking?”

“I’m a journalist. It’s my job to ask questions.”

“Ask any question you want.”

“Am I high priority, low priority, or no urgency?”

"Depends on Colonel Vega. He'll let us know. But since you participated in that crazy assassination, I'm guessing…"

"Guessing what?"

"I don't know, señorita. We're not supposed to discuss this subject."

I didn't like that answer and sat still for the fingerprints. Then, I stood for my mug shot, and when they finished, everyone in the room, including the two soldiers who had hurried me into the room, wanted to take a picture with me on the mug platform.

They patted me on the back, shook my hand, and wished me luck. And just like that, I was among friends, Comrade Adriana in State Security.

Apocalipsis walked me to the exit, said goodbye, hugged me like we were old friends, and then I was back in the corridor's dimness with the two guards, doing a perp walk past doors marked with letters of the alphabet. The concrete walls and floors smelled of mold and mildew. The courage I'd mustered only moments before diminished with every footfall. Had the kindness in the fingerprint room been genuine?

Did they do this for everyone, knowing what was about to happen?

Yes, that had to be it. Wasn't that the way it was in the Old West—the sheriff and witnesses posing with the outlaw before they put the noose around his neck? As a final blow to my courage, there came a loud crash from one of the side rooms, followed by the screams of a woman. "No! No, please don't. Noooo!"

I almost broke into a run. The guards didn't flinch, as if screams were normal, and suddenly an image of that nasty lieutenant flashed through my mind, burning some poor woman's face with a cigarette. Would they do that to me? Damn Matt for getting me into this mess. Damn

Holbrooke Easton for not getting me a passport. Damn those embassy people from last night for not hiding me in a safe house.

And damn me for falling in love with Matt like a silly teenager.

The screams faded behind me. We passed through double doors on which was posted a sign that read, RESTRICTED. My legs weakened, and if it hadn't been for the guards holding my arms, I might have collapsed.

At last, we stopped in front of an ugly door with peeling black paint. It was marked with the letters, DID, which I'm pretty sure meant Directorate of Defense Intelligence.

"This is the back door," said one of the guards.

He knocked.

The door swung open.

"God give me courage," I murmured and stepped inside.

CHAPTER 31

What I expected was a medieval-looking torture chamber with chains, dunking tubs, and other instruments of pain. What I saw was a plush office with a leather sofa and large desk behind which sat Colonel Vega in his uniform—the same Colonel Vega with the bushy mustache who'd confronted me in the parking lot and later at the restaurant.

A large portrait of ex-President Daniel Ortega hung on the wall behind the desk. Another door with a frosted glass window was off to one side. Beyond it came muffled voices and the clatter of typewriters. I was so scared of what would come next that it took a moment to notice a woman in uniform against the wall. She was standing and looking at me, her eyes wide and red as if she'd been crying. Her kinky hair was a mess, and she had the terrified look of a woman who wanted to run out of the place.

Pineapple?

What was she doing here? Had they tortured her for letting me escape?

Colonel Vega stood, pressed a red button on his desk, and motioned both of us onto the sofa. He took his time lighting a cigarette and then came from behind his desk and pulled up a chair to my front. I stared at the cigarette, at the glowing tip, and dreaded what would come next. Would he yell at me, slap me around, burn me with his cigarette?

He took a long puff, blew out the smoke, and stared into my face with the same penetrating look as when I'd first met him. "So, here you are at last," he said without a trace of a smile. "You can thank your embassy for the pleasure of meeting here, in my office, instead of down the hall."

He paused as if giving me time to absorb the meaning of "down the hall" and then gestured at Pineapple. "You two know one another. Eh?"

Pineapple squirmed but didn't speak. I said, "*Sí, Coronel*, we met at the Cine Luminoso."

"Under what circumstances did you meet?"

"Your lieutenant had me thrown into a truck. I needed to go to the ladies' room and she's the one who escorted me at gunpoint."

"And she was under strict orders to escort you back to the truck. Eh?"

"I don't know what her orders were. All I know is she marched me to the ladies' room."

"Did she then escort you back to the truck?"

"Not exactly?"

"I asked you a yes or no question. Did she return you to the truck?"

"It's complicated. Didn't she tell you about the flares?"

"Please, señorita, do you have a hearing problem? I'm the one asking the questions. She told me her version. Now I want to hear yours." He held up a hand to stop me from answering. "Be careful what you tell me. I want the truth, *la verdad*—and it better coincide with her explanation. Otherwise, it's not too late for a little stroll down the hall. Eh?"

I sensed the uneasiness of Pineapple beside me and didn't know how to answer. Had she told him the truth? No, no way. She'd have lied. And I should lie too—for her benefit and mine.

"Well," said the Colonel. "I'm waiting."

"Look, it was confusing. I'd been drinking.."

He slammed his palm on the coffee table. "I didn't ask how you felt. I asked what happened. Get on with it, señorita. Answer the question. We don't have all day."

"I'm getting confused, Colonel. What was the question?"

"The question was...*Mierda*, just tell me what happened."

"Well, what I remember is she was courteous. She liked to talk. She told me her call sign was Pineapple. She's not big, so I thought she'd be a pushover. I begged her to let me go."

"Did she?"

"No, *Coronel.* On the contrary. She refused and even apologized."

"Apologized? She apologized to you?" He glared at Pineapple as if she'd committed a terrible offense. Pineapple looked like she wanted to crawl under the sofa.

"*Sí, Coronel.* She was very professional. She said she was sorry to disappoint me, but she had to perform her duties. I even offered money."

"How much money?"

"Not sure. I was drunk. I can't remember everything. I can't even remember her answer, but I think she said, 'What good is money if I'm in a military stockade?'"

"And?"

"She poked me with her gun. Told me to shut up. Said she was following orders. And that was when the flares and the shooting started. People running like crazy. Some idiot was riding a horse. He fell off. The horse galloped between us...or it may have been the road people. It was so confusing. I just took off running."

"*Ya, basta*," said the Colonel, which means enough. "I don't believe a puta word from either of you. It's total horse manure. You're lying to protect her, aren't you?"

"All I'm telling you is what I remember."

He stared at me with those dark penetrating eyes, and this went on for so long that I imagined he could see through my blouse to my pounding heart. Finally, he stabbed out his cigarette in the ashtray and turned back to Pineapple. "Get out of my office, girl. Go! *Vete*! And I better not see your face again. Do you hear what I'm saying, girl? Do you understand?"

Pineapple sprang to her feet and snapped to attention. *"Sí, mi coronel. Gracias* for your kindness." She scooped up her backpack, saluted, said, "*Viva Nicaragua libre*!" and dashed out of the room as if she'd been pardoned from death by a firing squad.

The Colonel watched her go and shook his head like she was hopeless, "Stupid girl. She can't even find her way to the outside."

CHAPTER 32

I hoped he'd throw me out as well. Instead, he lit another cigarette, took a long puff, and leaned forward. "Did you see the video?"

"*Sí, Coronel.* I saw it, but before we discuss it, I should inform you that I made multiple copies of the video, and in the event anything bad happens to either me or my cameraman—"

He slammed a palm on the coffee table so hard that I jumped. "Spare me the speech! Do you think we're incompetent fools? Do you think we wouldn't know you made insurance copies?"

"I just wanted to be sure."

"You made your point, señorita." He reached into his desk, took out a folder, opened it as slowly as if contained a bomb, and handed me a picture of Matt. "Tell me about this man."

"All I know is what he told me—that he works at the gringo embassy."

He shook his head and showed me a picture of Sancho. "How about this man?"

"I'm told he's the gringo's assistant."

The next picture was Venus 25 in her short skirt and dangling earrings. "Do you know her?"

"No, *Coronel.*"

"Are you sure?"

"I saw her at the assassination, but I don't know her."

The pictures and questions kept coming. Yes, I told him, I recognized the door attendant and Ignacio, but I didn't know any of the killers or the person with a spear or any of the other faces in his pictures—until he showed me a picture of Pock Face and Ramos.

I hesitated.

"Well?" said the Colonel. "Do you know them or not?"

"No, *Coronel.*"

"You look a bit pale. Would you like a bottle of water?"

"Huh?"

"Bottle of water. Don't you understand Spanish?"

"*Sí, Coronel.* I'd be grateful for a bottle of water."

He stood, walked to the back of his desk, and came back with a bottle of spring water. I thought he'd pull the same dirty trick as Matt's embassy friends, but he handed me the bottle and waited for me to screw off the cap and drink. "Are you sure you don't recognize either of those men?"

"Positive. I watched the video very carefully."

"I also examined it carefully. It doesn't show who fired the shots. It doesn't exonerate you. And it doesn't answer questions you'd lie about."

"I'm telling the truth."

"Oh, really? Suppose I asked why you were at the hotel with your cameraman at the time of the murder? Eh?"

"It was an anonymous tip."

"Oh, please. I should lock you up for implying that we're that incompetent. We know it was your gringo friend. We know he called you. He didn't just happen to be at the hotel. He's the one with the answers. So, there's no point in wasting your time or mine."

I took a gulp of water. "Does that mean I can get my passport back?"

"No, señorita. You're not getting your passport back. Not yet. You can go back to work if you want. You can leave the gringo's house and move back to your place if you want, but from this moment forward there are restrictions on your movements."

I almost fainted with relief. "What restrictions?"

"Number one, you are not to leave this country. Not even Managua. Understand?"

"But Colonel, with all due respect, do you realize how dangerous it is for me to remain in Nicaragua and go back to work? The killers saw me. They know who I am."

"We live in a dangerous country, señorita. You knew you were playing with fire when you went to the gringo's room at the hotel, didn't you? And you knew it was dangerous when you and your cameraman went back to the hotel on the night of the assassination."

He took a long puff on his cigarette, blew out the smoke, and went on. "You also knew it was dangerous when you lied to me. Lied to me with a straight face. Then you and your gringo friend went off to that, that, restaurant with all the movie posters."

"*Cine Luminoso*."

"Correct. Did you behave at the restaurant? No, on the contrary, you made yourself as *borracha* as a sailor and picked a fight with the lieutenant. Then you seduced that stupid Pineapple girl into letting you escape. What is wrong with you, woman? What were you thinking? That's why I can't believe a puta word you tell me."

He held up a hand to stop me. "And one more thing. My job is also dangerous. Do you know how many people want to put a bullet in my head? Do you know how many death threats I get? So don't you dare lecture me about danger. Do you hear me, woman?"

"*Sí, Coronel*, I hear you."

He marched to his desk and pressed the red button again. Within a minute, a female soldier in uniform came in with a red folder. I stared at the folder. Was that my service record? Had they already matched my fingerprints to Angelina's name? *Please, dear God, no.*

Colonel Vega took the folder, smiled as if to say, "Now we've got you," and slapped it into my hand. "This is your pledge."

"Pledge to do what?"

"Pledge to abide by two conditions."

"What conditions?"

"Number one, you promise to cooperate in our investigation. That means you share any information that would help us. *De acuerdo*?"

I breathed again. "Yes, Colonel. I agree. No problem."

"Condition two, you promise to abide by the travel restrictions. Not to leave this country and not to travel outside Managua. *De acuerdo*?"

I held up my hand like a schoolchild. "May I ask a question?"

"Ask anything. Just don't expect a favorable response."

"What about witness protection? You're requiring me to remain in Nicaragua. Shouldn't you also provide a guard or lookouts or something?"

His face darkened. He closed his eyes and shook his head as if I'd just asked the most outrageous question he'd ever heard. "Excuse me for pointing this out, señorita, but wasn't it the gringo embassy that got you into this nasty situation? Wasn't it your…um…your gringo friend who lies about his job? The embassy has more resources than we do. They should be the ones looking out for you. Don't you agree?"

He was right, but I said nothing. I was so grateful the red folder wasn't my service record that I could have kissed it. "Read it and sign it," said the Colonel. "Otherwise, you're going to spend a lot of nights in this building as our special guest."

I read the document. "It says nothing about returning my passport."

He snatched the document from my hand, mumbled something that didn't sound polite, and penned the words, *Once the investigation is complete, and if it fully exonerates Señorita Alvarado, the General Directorate of State Security will return her passport and she will be free to remain in Nicaragua without restrictions.*

He read it aloud to me. "Is that good enough?"

"*Sí, Coronel.*"

"Do you understand the consequences if you violate this pledge?"

"*Sí, Coronel.* I understand. Thank you for your kindness."

He initialed his handwritten words and signed the document. I signed it, too, knowing full well I'd violate the agreement at the first opportunity. The woman in uniform also signed as a witness and stamped it with an official seal. They gave me a copy, and then Colonel Vega reached into his desk and pulled out my pepper spray canister.

"Pink?" he said. "What kind of person uses pink pepper spray? The woman covered her mouth to hide her smile. Colonel Vega handed the canister to me. "Thank you for your cooperation, señorita. This lady will show you out."

CHAPTER 33

Early the next morning, after another deluge that cleaned the air of volcano dust and smells, I went to the station where I worked, expecting them to fire me for leaving the scene of the assassination. Or at least yell at me. Instead, Marcelo, the editing manager, turned his wrath on State Security for not letting the station air the video.

"Edit it anyway," he barked at me in his loud voice. "Do the voiceover. Enhance the sounds. I want it available for airing the moment we get permission."

"I'll need to interview witnesses."

"Do it. Just don't get yourself killed."

There was only one witness I wanted to see, and that was Ignacio, the maître d' in the hotel dining room. He was my best informant, my go-to for anything. Need information about a hotel guest? Ask Ignacio. Need fake papers? Ask Ignacio.

I called Kodak into my office. "Can you do me a favor?"

At noontime, while everyone was at lunch, Ignacio showed up at the studio in jeans, guayabera, and boots, looking nothing like the tuxedoed maître d' in the hotel dining room.

I guided him out the back door, onto the patio, and to a table far away from others who were eating lunch. He lit a cigarette, reached under the table as if feeling for listening devices, and lowered his voice, "Kodak says you need to talk with me."

"I assume you've heard about my problems."

"Ha! Everyone in Nicaragua has heard about your problems. They're even airing it on CNN in the States. It's the biggest thing since Oliver North. How can I help? Tell me what you've got in mind?"

We plotted in hushed tones. We explored every avenue for getting me to neighboring Costa Rica. The biggest hurdle was checkpoints. There would be two, maybe three, and I'd need to change my appearance and get fake papers. And even if I got past the checkpoints, there'd be questions at the Costa Rican border and forms to complete.

"Why not wait a few days?" he said. "They might catch the killers. Then you'll be okay."

My heart sank. His solution was no better than Holbrooke Easton's.

Or Matt's.

Another day went by, and then two. There was no word from Ignacio and no one else was willing to help. I jumped at every ring of the phone. I glanced over my shoulder in parking lots and considered every stranger an assassin or agent of State Security. Any day now they'd match my fingerprints to my service record.

Or the assassins would find me.

And the worst part was Matt. When I'd first met him and foolishly gone to his room at the hotel, he'd been the hunk of every romance novel that had ever been written. He was the knight in shining armor, the fearless warrior who'd risk his life to save the damsel in distress. Now he'd morphed into a paper tiger, a yes man for the embassy, more concerned about following the orders of Holbrooke Easton than helping me.

"Just be patient," he kept telling me. "We're working on it. Trust me. It'll be okay."

Yeah, right. If I trusted him and Easton and the other gringos at the embassy, I'd end up in a dungeon or a jaguar's belly. Damn him and damn myself for continuing to share his bed like a co-dependent housewife. Like a prostitute. Not that I had a choice. The embassy didn't offer witness protection, and I didn't dare return to my apartment.

On the third day, during a torrential downpour, Matt told me he needed to spend a night or two at the hotel where the assassination had taken place. Crucial for his work, he told me.

"You're leaving me alone in this house?"

"No, Baby, the housekeeper is here during the day. She'll take care of you. And there's a guard at night with an AK. His call sign is Ox. Nobody messes with Ox."

He kissed me on the cheek and left. I shouldn't have cared. There was no future with a man who put his work ahead of my safety, but, oh God, did it hurt to watch him walk out the door with his overnight bag. I'd given my heart and body to him. I'd endangered my life. I'd dreamed of a future with him. But now, even he was abandoning me.

I read about myself in newspapers that were either controlled or strongly influenced by the Sandinistas. I listened to TV reports about the assassination. I looked around the house for evidence of Matt's work but the only thing I found was the folder of Yaritza. No background information or address. No last name. Only a photo of a beautiful Hispanic woman with the notation that she possessed "special powers."

What did that mean? Black belt? Witchcraft? Divination?

Note to myself: Ask Matt.

The daily rain became a metaphor for misery. The empty bed radiated loneliness. Where was he? What was he doing at the hotel? I asked Ignacio, but he wouldn't give me a straight answer either—which meant he was hiding the truth as well.

I lost my appetite. I cried myself to sleep. I couldn't concentrate on my editing work at the studio. I became the loser in every tear-jerking country song that had ever been written. Despair became the monster under the bed, and I became so depressed that I considered moving back to my apartment and waiting for the inevitable.

On the fourth night or the fifth—I'd lost track of time—I was alone, lonely, and getting ready for bed in the dimness of lamplight, wallowing in my misery, when someone knocked at the kitchen door. A loud knock, loud enough for me to hear from the bedroom.

My heart seemed to jump right out of me.

"Senorita? Are you in there?"

I pulled on a house robe, grabbed a hurricane lamp and the canister of pepper spray, and tiptoed down the hall to the kitchen, careful not to make a sound.

The knock grew louder. "Senorita? It's me, Ox, the night guard. There's a message for you."

"What's the message."

"Pineapple. She needs to talk with you."

Pineapple again? What did she want? I opened the door and stepped into the shadowy darkness of the front patio, my hand on the canister, still wary of a trick. The night was cool and damp with flashes of lightning and the earthy smell of rain. "Where is Pineapple?"

"Not here yet." He backed away as if not to appear threatening and told me in his *campesino* accent that his "woman"—meaning his wife or girlfriend—usually came at ten or eleven to keep him company until his shift ended at midnight, but tonight the woman would be Pineapple. "Must be careful," he said. "Soldiers are down the street."

I glanced toward the front gate as if expecting them to bust it down in a T-34 tank. "Not to worry," said Ox. "They're used to seeing my woman. They'll think it's her."

"But why are soldiers here? Are they watching this house?"

"No, señorita. It's the neighborhood. It's where gringos and diplomats from foreign embassies live. The government wants to keep them safe." He consulted his watch. "Any minute now. You should talk with her in the garage. I'll bring chairs and a lantern."

"Why the garage?"

"I don't trust the house. It could be bugged."

I changed into jeans, grabbed an open bottle of Cabernet Sauvignon, and was back on the front porch with my hurricane lamp when Ox opened the gate for Pineapple. She wore a dark hoodie over her head and carried a large tote bag. She also smelled like cigarettes.

We hugged. "I'm so sorry to bother you this late," she said in her little girl's voice, folding her umbrella, "but we need to talk. It's important."

CHAPTER 34

I wanted to hear the bad news at once, but the rain started with a fury, blowing spray onto the front porch. Ox took shelter in the kitchen. I guided Pineapple into the garage. Our lamps cast spooky shadows on the walls. The place had a musty smell and was cluttered with boxes and the usual storage junk. "What's going on?" I asked. "What's so urgent?"

"Hold on. Wait a second." She settled into one of the wicker chairs Ox had put out for us, took off the jacket with the hoodie, shook off the rain, and fluffed her kinky hair with her fingers. "Puta hair. It's always a mess. Why didn't God give me nice, straight hair like yours?"

I poured her a glass of wine. She took the glass, looked at it, and set it on the floor. "No, no, I better not. It'll aggravate my pimples." She held the lantern close to her face. "See, they're almost gone. That's clean living for you. I'm also trying to cut down on cigarettes."

By then I was ready to kill her. "Would you please tell me what is so urgent?"

"Right. You remember Apocalipsis, don't you?"

"The fingerprint woman? What about her?"

"She called me today. Your fingerprint analysis came back."

The panic in my chest bubbled to the surface. "And what?"

"It's strange. It matches a conscript named Angelina Quintero. Is that your real name?"

I didn't answer. I was busted. Angelina had been my neighbor. My closest friend in high school. My confidante. She and her entire family had been killed during the fighting that brought Ramos and Pock Face to our house, and I'd shamelessly signed up to fight bastards like Ramos under her name, too cowardly to use my real name.

Pineapple stuck a cigarette in her mouth and clicked her lighter. It didn't work. "Puta lighter. What is wrong with this stupid thing?" She kept clicking and complaining until it flared to life. She lit up, took a puff, blew it out, and fixed her gaze on me. "You should have told me you were in the war. I had no idea. Wounded too. Awarded a medal. But there's no record of your discharge. All it says is you'd been admitted to a hospital and gone missing."

She paused for another deep puff. "But that's not the bad part."

She reached into her tote bag and pulled out a yellow folder. On the cover, in large block letters, were the words, SERVICE RECORD, Angelina Liliana Quintero-Perez. The sight of it couldn't have created more turmoil in my overburdened system if it had been a rattlesnake.

"Look at the last page," Pineapple said.

I didn't want to see the last page or any other part of it. What I wanted was to use her lighter to set the damn thing on fire. Burn it to cinders. But the snake was already out of the bag, ready to strike, and Pineapple was holding up a lantern for me to see. I took a deep breath, opened the folder, took out my service record, and flipped through pages of bad memories.

The first page featured a conscription picture of me that I'd never seen before. It had been taken two days after Ramos assaulted me and I looked like the victim of a traffic accident.

"Oh, my God," said Pineapple. "What happened to your face?"

The second page showed the date of birth, race, address, and service number, and was stamped with the kind of seals and initials that Latin bureaucrats love to put on documents. Other pages listed locations and units, dates, company commanders, roll calls for battles and skirmishes, a medal I didn't deserve, and the name of the hospital in Chinandega where they'd treated my wounds. But the smoking gun was on the last page:

Missing. Failed to report to her command after discharge from hospital.

And stamped in big block letters—DESERTER.

"Is that what happened?" Pineapple asked, putting down the lantern and staring into my face. "Did you just walk away and change your name?"

I wanted to tell her all the dirty details—how Little Napoleon had gunned down a close friend for disobeying an absurd order, how one of his bullets had struck me, and how the little bastard had penned a medal on me as if that would compensate for his cruelty and poor aim. Instead, I told her, "I was an orphaned kid. They made me enlist. I didn't have a choice. I was like Omar Sharif in *Dr. Zhivago*, taken at gunpoint."

"Dr. who?"

"Zhivago. Didn't you see the movie?"

"It's not me you've got to convince. It's Colonel Vega. Otherwise, he's going to...well..."

"What did he say?"

"He hasn't seen it yet. Today is Sunday. It's on his desk. He'll read it in the morning."

I took a swig of wine directly from the bottle. If Matt had shown up at that moment I'd have bludgeoned him to death with a tire iron. Holbrooke Easton too, and all those other gringos who'd denied me their help. Bastards!

Pineapple must have sensed my distress because she put her hand over mine, and at that moment Ox stuck his head into the garage. "Kitchen phone. It's ringing."

My headache grew worse. Who would call at this hour? It couldn't be good news. And why did the phone work during a power failure? Mine didn't. Damn gringos. They had everything.

"Better answer," Pineapple said. "It could be them."

"Them who?"

"Just answer, and then we'll talk."

CHAPTER 35

I dashed into the kitchen and scooped up the phone, not knowing what to expect. Was it Colonel Vega? Had he already gone to his office and seen the record? Or was it Matt? Or another death threat?

It was Marcelo, my station manager.

"Pack your gear," he yelled on the other end. "This is urgent."

"What, Marcelo? What's so urgent?"

"I need you to get to the landing by daybreak."

"Huh? What landing? Where?"

"Asese Landing. Lake Nicaragua. Take Kodak with you."

"What's at the landing?"

"Your contact."

"Who's the contact?"

"They didn't say, but I'm guessing you'll be on the lake for two or three days. It's beautiful out there. All those islands, the jumping fish. I love the smell of water."

"Are you serious? Have you forgotten I'm a murder suspect? State Security ordered me not to leave Managua. They'll throw me into a dungeon."

"Oh, please, Miami, you're a TV journalist. You work for us, not the puta government. Show some spark. Be tough. Wear your tight jeans.

Wear your Miami T-shirt. If you run into those pricks at State Security, just smile and say you're following orders."

"I don't have a Miami T-shirt. I never lived in frigging Miami. I'm from Tampa. Do you even know where Tampa is? And why are you sending me an assignment without providing details? It's not only State Security I'm worried about. It's—"

"Just do it," he yelled into the phone and hung up, leaving me standing in a dark kitchen with a dead phone in my hand.

"What?" Pineapple asked, holding up the lantern.

I led her back into the garage and told her about the conversation.

"What a relief," she said. "They finally came through."

"Who came through? What are you talking about?"

"I'm talking about Lake Nicaragua. It's huge. Dozens of rental boats. Get on a boat out there and you're lost to the civilized world. The best bet is Ometepe Island. It's the biggest island on the lake. You can take one of those excursion boats that goes down the Rio San Juan."

"And do what?"

"Escape. Isn't that what you want?"

She took a map of Lake Nicaragua from her tote bag, unfolded it, spread it on the concrete floor, and showed me Ometepe Island and the San Juan River. "Here's the river. See how it borders Costa Rica. All you have to do is jump off the puta boat on the starboard side and there you are—Costa Rica. Freedom. Celebration."

"Are you crazy? I can't swim. I'm terrified of water. It's also the rainy season. And put out that damn cigarette. I can't breathe."

"What is wrong with you, girl? Opportunity is knocking. It's already been arranged."

"Arranged? What are you talking about? Who arranged it?"

"You'll find out when you get to the landing."

"But what about checkpoints? I'll never make it to the landing."

"Oh, señorita, what is wrong with your head? Don't you want to escape? Everything's been arranged. We already thought about checkpoints." She dug in her tote bag again and pulled out a green Sandinista uniform with sergeant's stripes. "Congratulations, soldier. You're back in the army. This is for the checkpoints. You can change back into civvies at the landing."

"Are you out of your mind? Do you know what the penalty is for posing as a soldier?"

"Can't be any worse than the penalty for desertion. There's also a fake military ID card and driver's license. No passport yet, but we'll get you a new one when you get to Costa Rica."

I didn't know what to say. I'd always thought of Pineapple as a lowly soldier like I had been—and not very smart at that. Now it was obvious she had connections in high places. "How did you arrange this?" I asked. "Is Ignacio helping you?"

"If I told you, I'd have to shoot you. Just go, pack your things, and change into your uniform. Bring cash. You'll need to leave with Ox at midnight."

CHAPTER 36

I suspected Ignacio was the brain behind the plan, but no one would tell me, not Pineapple who insisted I take her hoodie for the rain, not Ox who walked me out the gate and down to the Masaya Highway, and not the soldier who picked me up in an army Jeep and drove me past two checkpoints while I cowered in fear in the front seat.

There were flashlights in my face and questions from the guards, and it seemed like a miracle from heaven when they waved us on. The noxious fumes from Volcán Masaya didn't help my mood. Neither did the army trucks we passed, nor the hilltop fortress of Coyotepe that was as ugly in moonlight as the barbed wire fence that surrounded it. And it wasn't until we drove into the parking lot of the landing and stopped beneath a giant Ceiba tree that I began to relax.

Fireflies flickered around like little angels. Hoots and chirrs blessed the darkness, and over at the landing, a long line of boats for rent bobbed in the surf. Was I supposed to hire one of those rickety boats to take me to Ometepe Island? Was it safe? Why hadn't Pineapple been more specific? And where was Kodak? Wasn't he supposed to meet me here?

No sooner had I thought about it than he drove into the parking lot in a company van. The soldier—whose name I never knew—wished me good luck and refused the hundred dollars I offered, saying he'd already been paid. I thanked him, watched him drive away, and then climbed into the back seat of the van and changed out of the uniform.

Kodak wanted all the details. Why was I wearing a Sandinista uniform? How did I get past the checkpoints? Who was the soldier?

I didn't answer. Pineapple had sworn me to secrecy and instructed me to act like I was on a legitimate mission. Besides, it was going on three in the morning, and I was so stressed and exhausted that I fell asleep in the back seat amid cameras and gear.

Kodak shook me awake at five and handed me a thermos of coffee. It was still dark, and the air was filled with the swampy dampness of the surrounding area.

"Contact should be here any minute," he said. "We need to be alert."

I rubbed sleep out of my eyes. "Who is our contact?"

"No idea."

"How are we supposed to recognize him or them?"

"He'll recognize our van. It's got TV Channel 4 on the side."

"Do you have any idea what this assignment is about?"

"We'll find out when our contact arrives."

"I've heard bad things about that lake."

"Like what?"

"Like disappearances. People go out and never come back. That lake is like the Bates Motel."

"The Bates what?"

"Motel. Didn't you see the movie? Check in but don't check out."

"It's a big lake, Adriana. Storms come up. People are stupid. They go out in shabby little boats. Lake Nicaragua is no more dangerous than anywhere else in this country."

"Oh, really? What about sharks? What about chupacabras?"

He turned to face me. "Chupacabras?"

"Jaguars too, and giant snakes. It's also rainy season. There's a hurricane in the Caribbean. We could get caught in a storm."

"Would you just relax and—"

Something shrieked. Loud. I jumped. Kodak yanked out his pistol and slapped in a clip. "Nicaragua," he said and placed the pistol on the dash. "You never know."

I shuddered and checked the door lock.

"What's going on with you and the gringo?" Kodak asked.

"Stop calling him gringo."

"So what? No one uses real names anymore. It's too dangerous. Do you use your real name? Of course not. They call you Miami at the station. And look what they call me: Kodak."

I didn't answer, in part because he kept talking. "Hell, they even took down street signs. Imagine how that affects the postal service. What a mess!" He pulled out a pack of cigarettes, lit one, and rolled down the window, letting in damp fresh air and the insect noises from a nearby swamp. "So, what's going on with you and the gringo?"

"His name's Matt."

"Okay, what's going on with you and Matt?"

"Nothing. It's over."

"That's what you said last time."

"Oh, stop it, Kodak! I don't want to talk about it."

"He dump you or you dump him?"

"Just shut up, Kodak, and put out that damn cigarette!"

"Heyyy, don't be so sensitive. I've been dumped too. I know how it hurts." He took a deep drag on his cigarette. "Did I ever tell you about my little flower girl?"

Please, no, I wanted to shout. I wanted to talk about the lake and its dangers. I wanted to wait for our contact and learn how to get to Ometepe, but I had nothing else to do so I sat back, closed my eyes, and listened again to his sad tale of a cute little señorita with big eyes and kinky black hair. Oh, how he loved her. Oh, the things they'd done in the jungles and in the clear waters that flowed down from the mountains. "She loved flowers," he said. "You cannot imagine how it hurt when I lost her."

"What happened?"

"Busted up our unit. Ordered me to one place and her to another."

"Why didn't you go after her?"

"I did. I searched everywhere. Couldn't find her."

As he spoke it occurred to me that maybe she didn't want to be found. Maybe she had a new love. Or she'd gone into exile like many other Nicaraguans.

"It was like she never existed. Where did she go? We made vows beneath the stars." He leaned into the steering wheel and pointed. "See, look at those stars. I know she's out there somewhere, thinking of me this very moment."

He choked up. I choked up too, remembering my struggles in the jungle—the endless treks, the hiding, the hunger, the fear, the abuse, the love triangles, and my heartbreak—and he was still trying to get out his words, saying she'd given him the nickname Kodak because of an old camera he always carried when the darkness of night eased into a pale imitation of dawn.

"Are you crying?" he asked.

I wiped my eyes. "It's pollen."

"Pollen, my ass. It's the gringo. He put a lot of hurt on you."

A yellow bus that had once been an American school bus roared into the lot, trailing smoke and drowning out his words. Passengers crawled off with bags and boxes. More vehicles arrived. Beggars and peddlers mysteriously appeared and began working the crowd, selling soft drinks, water, coffee, and snacks. Then an army truck drove in and stopped near us. A stab of fear shot through me. Were they coming for me?

Soldiers with assault rifles jumped out, but instead of coming toward us, they headed down toward the dock, lugging chairs and a folding table.

"What's that about?" I asked Kodak.

"Checkpoint. We'll need to show IDs before going onto the lake."

"We already cleared two checkpoints."

"It's just their way to extort money. Give them a few *Córdobas* and they won't give a damn if you have horns, and your name is Satan."

The words were scarcely out of his mouth when a battered pickup drove into the parking lot and slid to a stop beside us. A man got out. Kodak leaned forward. "*Demonios*! Is that Sancho?"

CHAPTER 37

I bounded out. Sancho was the last person I wanted to see. He was Matt's assistant, his sidekick, his Tonto to the Lone Ranger, a reminder of my shattered heart, and there he came in a faded red T-shirt, ball cap, jeans, and big grin, limping from his war wound.

"There you are," he said and hugged me. "Ready?"

"Ready for what? What's going on? Why are you here?"

"Come on. Get your stuff. I'll tell you in the boat."

"No, Sancho, I'm not going to move until I know what this is about."

By then, Kodak was out of the van, stuffing his pistol into his waistband. Both he and Sancho had been conscripted by Sandinistas as teenagers and acted like brothers. They even looked like brothers except Sancho was taller and better looking with dark indigenous features. They hugged, bumped fists, and began asking about old so-and-so.

I stepped between them. "You two can chat later. I want to know what this is about."

Sancho turned to face me. "You've heard about the magic mushroom cave, haven't you?"

"Everyone in Nicaragua has heard about the magic mushroom cave. It's fantasy. Fairytale stuff for kids"

"No, Adriana. They discovered it on one of the islands."

"Is that another one of your unfunny jokes?"

"No, Adriana. That's why we're here—to do a story on the discovery."

"Who says we're doing a story on magic mushrooms?"

"You'll have to ask the gringo. Now come on, I'll explain later."

I didn't move. I had no interest in magic mushrooms. It was all nonsense anyway. There'd been rumors for centuries of a mysterious bat cave filled with mushrooms that when mixed with other ingredients and ground into powder could heal the sick, restore youth, cure impotency, prolong carnal pleasure, and even grow hair on the bald. It was called Blue Magic, presumably because it had a bluish tint. Matt had told me about it and joked about it, but for me, it was as absurd as the Fountain of Youth.

"What's the gringo's role in this?" I asked Sancho.

He tapped his watch. "We've got to go. I'll explain on the boat."

"No, Sancho. You tell me here."

He turned to Kodak as if pleading for help. Kodak said, "Tell her, for Christ's sake. I also want to know. Gringo got her in trouble and got me in trouble. We don't need more trouble."

Sancho rolled his eyes and was fumbling for an answer when an enormous black man with dreadlocks and gold teeth stepped from behind the Ceiba tree. His greasy short-sleeved shirt was open. A jade amulet dangled from his neck, and the single earring on his left earlobe gave him the looks of a pirate.

I backed away. What made him scary—other than his size—was the machete in his hand and the way he was blocking our path. You don't do that in Nicaragua.

Kodak whipped out his pistol. Dreadlocks dropped the machete and lifted both hands. "Not to shoot," he said in melodious Caribbean-accented Spanish. "The gringo, he send me."

"Sent you to do what?" Kodak asked.

"Take your van. Hide it. No problem, Mon. Put gun down."

Kodak backed away as if to say no way in hell. Sancho said, "Put that gun away. That's Nelson. He works for us. Your van's got Channel 4 lettering on the side. They'll see it and know we're on the lake."

"Who will see it?" I asked. "What are you talking about?"

"I'm talking about bad-asses you don't want to meet."

I glanced around the parking lot as if they were already there. "Who?"

"You'll have to ask the gringo."

"No, Sancho, I'm asking you."

Sancho said to Kodak. "Just give him the damn keys."

"That's a Channel 4 van. It's got company equipment in it."

"Not to worry. Dreadlocks will take it to the fortress."

"What fortress?"

"Gringo embassy. It's got barbed wire and watchdogs. Guarded by Marines. You don't mess with Marines. You don't mess with Dreadlocks either. He'll put a curse on you. His wife communicates with the dead."

Kodak, looking like he'd been mugged, pulled out his keys and tossed them to Dreadlocks. "I better not see a scratch on it when I get back. Understand? No joy rides either."

Dreadlocks muttered words I didn't catch and hopped into the van, slamming the door harder than necessary. Before he could drive away, a couple of soldiers who looked like they should be in high school stepped in front of the van.

"What's going on?" asked the taller of the two.

"Nothing," Kodak answered. "He took our van."

"He's stealing your van?"

"No."

"Why did you point a gun at him?"

"Mistake. I didn't recognize him."

"Are you serious? Look at him. He's got dreadlocks and gold teeth. And you don't recognize him? Do you think we're stupid peasants?"

Dreadlocks rolled down the window. The soldiers backed away as if a curse had struck them. Kodak looked like he wanted to run away.

"Do you have a *permiso* for the gun?" the soldier asked Kodak.

"Of course, I have a permit." He took out his wallet and handed each soldier the equivalent of five dollars in Nicaraguan currency, which was twice the going rate for petty extortion. The soldiers took the money, nodded, and turned their attention to me. I turned away. Damn it, I should have worn a wig. Dark glasses too. Now they were going to recognize me and figure I was worth over five dollars.

"You that television woman?" asked the soldier in charge.

"She's with me," Sancho said.

"I'm not asking you, Comrade. I'm asking the señorita." He turned back to me. "I asked you a question. Are you the TV woman or not?"

"What difference does it make?"

"Either you answer me, or you answer the lieutenant. Let's see your identification."

This was getting worse by the second. The only ID I had was fake, and fake ID would get me cuffed and hauled back to Managua in their truck.

Dreadlocks must have seen my distress because he started the engine, gunned it, and blew the horn.

The soldiers jumped aside. Dreadlocks drove the van forward, spun it around, fishtailed, and tore out of the parking lot like a NASCAR driver, showering us with gravel.

"*Pendejo*!" Kodak yelled after him. "Be careful with that van."

We watched our van disappear into the grayness of morning, leaving behind a cloud of dust. The soldiers watched and then turned back to me. "Okay, señorita, time's up. Show us I.D. or you explain to the lieutenant."

"It's inside my pack."

Sancho touched my arm. "Don't show him a damn thing."

The soldier turned on Sancho. "Step away, Comrade, or I'll call the lieutenant."

"Call him. Call him now. Get him over here. Tell him what's going on. When he recognizes me, he'll have you digging trenches."

Sancho pulled out his wallet and showed the soldiers a badge. The soldiers looked at one another as if he'd shown them the stars of a general. The expression on their faces went from hostility to apologetic.

"Sorry," said the soldier. "All we wanted was to pose for a picture with the señorita."

They trod away, leaving me to wonder what Sancho had shown them.

"We need to get moving," Sancho said. "Let's get to the boat."

CHAPTER 38

Kodak picked up his gear and followed Sancho toward the wharf. I didn't move. They kept going until Sancho turned around and hurried back to me. "Come on Miami. We need to leave."

"No, Sancho, I'm not moving until you answer my question."

"What question?"

"About the gringo. About the bad-asses you mentioned."

"I told you to ask the gringo."

"So, you're admitting Matt is involved in this little adventure. Right?"

"You already know the answer."

Kodak put a hand on my arm. "Listen, Miami, we don't have to go."

"Dammit, my name is not Miami."

"Okay, Adriana. Isaid we can take that bus back to Managua."

I looked at the bus. It was as broken as everything else in Nicaragua—muddy with shattered windows and slick tires. The motor was already running, stinking up the parking lot with black smoke. But I didn't want a bus back to Managua. I wanted a boat to Ometepe.

Sancho touched my arm. "Listen, I'll explain everything on the boat."

"You promise?"

"As God is my witness."

I put on my backpack. "What about the checkpoint?"

"Don't worry about the checkpoint. Everybody in Nicaragua's got something to hide. I'll handle it." He reached again for his wallet.

"Hold on," Kodak said. "We need to get shots of us boarding the boat." He put down his pack, brushed back his long hair, and got the camera rolling.

Oh, great, I thought. This was supposed to be my opportunity to escape, to put danger behind me. Now Matt was getting me involved in another fiasco and Kodak wanted to get it on film.

With Kodak filming, Sancho marched to the checkpoint table and shook hands with the soldiers sitting there. The soldiers stood and saluted as if Sancho was their commanding officer."

The soldiers sat back down. Sancho motioned for us, and a moment later we were following him along a wharf that smelled of creosote, ducking beneath ropes and cables and passing along posts on which were perched seagulls and pelicans, Kodak filming from behind.

"Where's the boat?" I asked Sancho.

"Over there, end of the dock." He pointed toward a tall flagpole on which a yellow banner snapped and billowed in the breeze.

"Why are they flying a yellow cholera flag?"

"That's not a cholera flag?"

"Didn't you read *Love in the Time of Cholera?* Yellow is for cholera."

"I saw the movie, Adriana, but that doesn't make it a cholera flag. Out here it's a caution flag for swimmers and boaters. It means be careful. If there were danger, they'd be flying red."

He pointed out the little plywood-roofed boats that were already heading out on the lake, many of them painted in rainbow colors. Locals who'd already passed the checkpoint were also at the landing, waiting with suitcases and boxes to board a ferry. "See there," Sancho said, "if there was danger, do you think those people would get on a boat?"

Passengers moved aside. A few stared as if they recognized me, and I distinctly heard the words, "Contra assassination." Kodak must have heard it too because he pushed me ahead. A group of girls in school uniforms, their black hair plaited with red ribbons, followed us down the wharf, giggling and asking for autographs.

One girl pulled a small yellow camera from her backpack and asked if I would pose with them for a picture.

By then I felt like jumping into the water and swimming to Ometepe—except I couldn't swim. So, I posed for pictures and signed their notebooks. They grinned and thanked me, brushed back their hair, and gathered around to stay in front of Kodak's camera.

"Where are you going?" asked a young girl with crooked teeth.

"The islands. Watch the next episode of my TV program. It's called 'Nicaragua Exposed.' Fridays at eight PM."

They giggled and said they'd watch. Sancho herded them away and guided us to the end of the wharf, stopping at a small outboard that looked like it had fallen off a moving trailer. It had scuffs and dents, flaking paint, holes that looked like bullet impacts, and a small pool of water at the bottom. The boat's name—crudely painted on the side in blue letters—was *Princesa Layla*—as if you could dignify such an ugly boat with royalty.

Kodak aimed his camera. "Who is Layla?" he asked Sancho.

"Hot *chica* I told you about. Now, come on. Climb aboard."

Kodak climbed aboard and plunked into the front passenger seat. I didn't move. "Are you saying we're going into a dangerous lake in that?"

"What'd you expect, the *Queen Elizabeth*?"

I turned to look at the other boats: yachts and sailboats of all descriptions. Brightly painted fishing boats and a ferry too, bobbing in the swells. And there was Sancho with his sorry little outboard that smelled of motor oil and fish. "But what if a storm comes up? What if—?"

"Oh, stop worrying. It's not far. We'll be fine." He pointed to my cap. "Caps on backward. You too, Kodak. Otherwise, they'll blow away."

I still didn't move. Didn't adjust my cap either. It wasn't too late to rush over to one of the other boat owners and bargain to take me to Ometepe.

"Come on," Sancho said. "We need to go."

I pulled in a deep breath, climbed aboard, kicked a beer can out of my way, and wiped down the rear seat. Kodak handed me a life vest. Sancho hung an image of the Virgin on the rearview mirror. "Our just in case," he said and hit the starter.

The engine sputtered but didn't start.

He tried again. Still nothing.

"Did you tank up?" Kodak asked.

"Full tank. We'll be okay."

I twisted my cap around and was strapping on my vest when Kodak, who was panning the place with his camera, said, "Uh oh."

I followed his gaze to a black SUV that had driven right down to the landing. Out of it sprang four or five beefy men who looked like tough ex-military types. "Shit!" Sancho said. "We better get out of here."

CHAPTER 39

He hit the starter and kept hitting it, calling it names I won't repeat. The men were trotting down the wharf toward us. They blasted right through the schoolgirls. The young girl with the camera fell backward into the water. She screamed. The other girls screamed and pointed and cried for help. So did bystanders, and into this madness came the same two soldiers who'd harassed me back at the van.

They plunged into the water to save her, and at that moment our engine sputtered to life. An oily smoke drifted over us.

"Stay low," Sancho yelled, and we roared into the lake like bandits fleeing a bank robbery, scaring up a flock of sea birds and passing the wreckage of a half-sunken ship.

The boat bounced. Spray washed over us. I clung to my seat like a tourist on a Disney rollercoaster, praying for survival. Island after island went by, some no larger than a house, others a little forest of jungle and mango trees.

Here and there children waved at us, and on one of the islands a group of girls in bikinis held out their thumbs like they were hitching a ride. Kodak and Sancho waved and blew kisses, and I'd have waved too if I hadn't been all curled up with my legs to my chest.

Relax, I told myself. Think of escape. Think of magic mushrooms and Blue Magic. Yes, I could get a story out of this and develop it once I got back to Florida. Maybe I could dose up on it myself and keep my thirty-year-old body looking as young as those girls in bikinis.

But I couldn't shake the peril of this damn lake. The water at my feet was sloshing around like a devil's brew. The boat could sink. I couldn't swim, and even if I could, the sharks would get us. Or those men at the landing would catch up and shoot our boat to pieces.

I was also getting nauseated.. Damn Sancho anyway. Surely they paid him enough to afford a better boat than this piece of bouncing junk. I leaned forward and touched his shoulder. "Slow down. I'm getting sick."

He tapped his ear. "CAN'T HEAR YOU."

"I SAID SLOW DOWN! I'M SICK!"

"WE'RE ALMOST THERE!"

"HOW MUCH LONGER?"

"THERE," he said and pointed to an island. "ISLA CALABAZOS."

He throttled down and wheeled the boat away from the island, letting us drift on the swells. The only sounds were the squawk of birds and water slapping against the boat. Kodak kissed the love note he'd penned to Flower Girl and tossed it into the water as if she could read it.

"Why did we stop here?" I asked Sancho. "Is the boat okay?"

"Boat's fine. I need to brief you on basic rules."

"Brief us on what, Sancho? I want to get off this boat. It's leaking."

"It's not leaking. That water is from spray."

"I don't care what it is. I want to get off."

"Just hold on. You know how it is in the military. You served. Officers always came out to brief us before we set off on a mission. Right?"

"Why can't you brief us on the island? I'm sick."

"Only take a minute."

"But what about those men at the landing? They'll see us."

"No way they can find us out here. Not with all these little islands."

"Come on," Kodak said to Sancho. "Hurry it up."

"Okay, first rule. If for any reason we're around other people, we use only code names. I'm Sancho. Don't ask why. You'll understand later. Kodak, you're Kodak. No need for an explanation. And you, Adriana, like it or not, you're Miami. Okay?"

At that moment I didn't care if they called me Crazy Bitch. Didn't have the desire to ask about Matt either. Or those men at the landing. All I wanted was to be free of this bouncing, leaking, stinking nightmare called a princess. "Fine," I said. "Can we go?"

Sancho lit a cigarette. "There's one more thing."

"What, Sancho? Just say it."

"You know I work for the gringos, don't you?"

"Everybody knows you work for the gringos. So what?"

"Yeah, but here's the problem. People in this country hate gringos for what they did to us during the war. Right?" He pulled up his pants leg and showed us an ugly scar that ran from his ankle to his knee. "Look at this. We were good guys. Right?"

Kodak waved his arms to stop him. "You making a political speech or asking a question?"

"I'm making a point. Gringos called us Communists."

"Why the hell wouldn't they? Our leaders were commies."

"I'm not a damn Communist. My point is the gringos supported the wrong side."

"So why are you working for them?"

"Where else in this country can you get a decent-paying job?"

"What the hell kind of principle is that?"

"More than the money. They're not all bad. Gringo treats me well."

I sat forward. "Would you two shut up? Let's talk on the island?"

Sancho shook his head. "I need your answers first."

"Answers to what?"

"About how you feel, Miami. You wore a Sandinista uniform."

"That was fifteen years ago, for God's sake. A lot of us got caught up in the hysteria. I was a kid. I did laundry. I did the dirty work."

"You still swore an oath, Miami. You lived in the jungle. You drank river water like the rest of us. You ate that puta Bulgarian spaghetti with whatever kind of meat we could scrounge up. Remember?"

"Monkeys too," Kodak said. "We ate monkeys."

By then my stomach felt like it was coming out of me. I retched and leaned over the side. Kodak said, "Come on, Sancho. Get to the point."

"Point is we all hated gringos back then."

"So?"

"So, how do you feel about collaborating with them now?"

"I'm a cameraman," Kodak said. "I've filmed plenty of bad shit. Long as they're not killing Nicas, I don't give a damn."

Sancho fixed me in his gaze. "What about you, Miami? You in or out?"

I didn't answer. The nastiness in my stomach was bubbling up inside me. Kodak said, "What kind of stupid-ass question is that? Miami was born in the US. Went to a big university in Florida. Speaks perfect English. Carries a US passport. She's even got a gringo boyfriend."

"Well?" Sancho asked me again. "You in or out?"

"Just go," I said.

Sancho turned to Kodak. "How come girls never answer?"

Kodak rolled his eyes like he'd been asked the dumbest question in the entire history of asking questions. "They don't answer because they're girls, you idiot. You gonna go or do I have to throw your skinny ass overboard?"

Sancho tossed his cigarette into the water and fired up the boat, but instead of taking us straight to the island he turned starboard and took us to the opposite side, throttling down and drifting us beneath a tangle of limbs and vines that trailed into the water. Into this silence came splashes of water and the songs of birds whose plumage I could only imagine.

Kodak began filming the beauty around us—the sandy white beach, the tropical undergrowth, the mango and banana trees with their dangling fruits, the butterflies, the brightly colored orchids and bromeliads, and another boat that was anchored nearby. I twisted out of my life jacket and was so intent on getting my feet ashore that I paid no attention to the other boat until we bounced lightly against it, making a watery thunk.

"*The Ana Maria*," Sancho announced as if he'd discovered hidden treasure. "It's a Sea Ray 260 Sundancer. Got berths, cabin, and galley. Twenty-six feet of the luxury you deserve."

"Are you saying we're going somewhere else—in that?"

"You didn't think the mushrooms were on this tiny island, did you?"

CHAPTER 40

The prospect of going back into the lake twisted the knot in my stomach tighter. I leaned over the side and threw up the morning coffee, and I was trying to regain my dignity when a mean-looking little fellow with dark mestizo features stepped out of a palmetto thicket and lashed our boat to a coconut tree.

It was Lead Foot, Matt's cranky driver, the man who'd set off the flares at the restaurant. He lit a cigarette and glared at me the way he always did—like he wanted to bury a pickaxe in my head. His tattered cap and the pistol holstered to his hip made him even more menacing.

"Don't take his picture," Sancho said. "He doesn't like cameras."

Sancho helped me out of the boat, and I was stumbling around, trying to find my balance when I glanced up and saw Matt in sunglasses, a ball cap, boots, cargo khakis, and one of those travel vests with little pockets, talking into his new mobile phone.

I'm not going to say my heart skipped a beat. Not going to say my breath caught either. Or that I suddenly became aware I hadn't put on makeup or that my hair and pullover were wet and messy, and my stomach was in turmoil. It was just one of those awkward moments of swirling emotions where sadness, anger, and sickness clash with pain. Dizziness swept over me. I grabbed the trunk of a coconut tree for support and slid to the ground.

Matt rushed over and looked down as if to be sure the waif who'd just arrived was really me. Kodak lifted his camera. "No, no, no," Sancho said, waving his hand. "No pictures of the gringo."

Matt squatted down and put his hand on my cheek, his grey-blue eyes boring into mine. He hadn't shaved, and he was more tanned than the last time I'd seen him. "Oh, my poor baby," he said in English. "You okay?"

"I'm okay."

"You don't look okay."

"It's the boat. I'm seasick."

He turned and spoke to Sancho. "Dramamine."

"What?"

"Motion sickness meds. It's in the aid kit. Also, get her a towel. Clean."

Sancho lumbered aboard the *Ana Maria* and came back with a small container of tablets, a can of Diet Coca-Cola, and a red beach towel. The Coke can was icy cold and covered in condensation. Damn gringos! They had everything. I took a tablet and washed it down with Coke. Lead Foot, who'd been watching, nodded to Matt and climbed into the little boat that had brought us here. He fired it up and raced into the lake.

As it faded, I said to Matt. "Okay, you took our van. You took our boat. Now it's just the four of us on this little island. Now what?"

He stared a moment longer, prolonging my discomfort.

"Let's take a hike," he said.

"Do I look like I'm up to a hike? Tell me here. What is going on? Why are you here? Are you the brains behind this little excursion?"

I said this in Spanish so Kodak and Sancho would understand. They shuffled around a bit and strolled a short distance away.

Matt lowered his voice. "Okay, just sit there a while."

"Who were those men at the landing?"

"What men?"

"Ask Sancho. He saw them."

Matt straightened up and strode over to Sancho. They had a hushed conversation, glancing now and then at me. Kodak joined them, and the conversation continued until Matt came back. He knelt beside me, took my hands, and gently pulled me from the ground. "Feeling better?"

"Are you going to answer my questions or not?"

"I'll tell you, but you should walk around a bit. Take deep breaths."

"I might throw up."

"I've seen you throw up before." He reached for my hand.

"Where are we going?"

"Other side of the island. It's not far."

"Why can't you tell me here?"

"Because what I have to say is between us."

Damn him. Why couldn't I just say no? What scary, mysterious power did he have over me? Every meeting I had with him led to disaster, and yet I gave in like I always did, conceding a bit of my soul.

He yelled to Sancho to keep a sharp lookout—he didn't say for what—and then he led me toward a jungle that loomed up like a mountain of green, pulsing with noise and life.

CHAPTER 41

Giant butterflies flitted around us. Things moved in the trees. I caught pleasant scents of orange blossoms. Songbirds serenaded us from above, and it seemed as if every tree was festooned with bromeliads, creepers, and dangling flowers of many colors.

"I could live in a place like this," Matt said.

I didn't answer. I had no interest in living like Tarzan in a jungle. I'd already done that with the Sandinistas and even now, fifteen years later, my mind filled with images of sweaty men and women in single file, glancing into trees and shadows, everyone weighted down with packs, assault rifles, and ammunition. The scenery was beautiful back then too, but I couldn't enjoy it for fear of snipers or ambush or snakes and other hidden dangers.

The dizziness came back. I grabbed a dangling vine for support. Matt rushed to my side and held my arm, and for a fleeting moment, it seemed as if all was well between us. "Poor baby? Do you need to sit down?"

"Give me a minute."

The spell passed and on we went. Do not stumble and fall, I told myself. Don't give in to his charms either. I'd fallen for his sweet talk too many times, fallen for his line that nothing we did in the name of love was wrong, no matter where we did it—like in the back of his Explorer—and he could never make love unless his heart was in it. Yeah, right.

"How much farther?"

He turned and mopped his forehead. The smile that had melted my heart was on his face. He held out his arms. "Come here."

"No, Matt! I didn't follow you into this jungle for that."

"Christ, Adriana, I just wanted to give you a hug."

"Well, all I want is an explanation. Last I heard, you were at the hotel—or supposed to be. Now you're out here in your jungle gear, tanned and unshaven. You either tell me what's going on or I'm going back."

"Back to where? We're on an island."

I turned around. He grabbed my arm. "Fine, let's talk on the beach."

A few more stumbles and we came to a beach that was as pretty as everything else on the island, with white sand, coconut trees, noisy lake birds, gentle waves that slapped against boulders, and a spectacular view of Volcán Mombacho in the distance, brilliant in the early sunlight. Matt put a hand on my back. "This is the place I wanted to show you."

"You brought me back here to show me the scenery?"

"No, Baby, I brought you back here to talk."

"I need to sit down."

He led me past a coconut tree that had grown horizontal and was motioning me toward an outcrop of lava boulders when the ground seemed to move beneath my feet. I stumbled. He grabbed my arm and eased me down on a boulder. "Just sit there a moment. Relax. It takes a while for the meds to kick in." He took a bottle of water from his jacket and handed it to me. "Here, drink this."

I took a sip, laid back, and closed my eyes, but closing my eyes caused the earth to spin faster. I sat up and drank more water. Matt ran his hand through my hair. It felt good, soothing, comforting. Damn it, why couldn't I get over him? Why was I so weak-willed?

He leaned over and kissed me on the cheek.

"Don't," I said and pushed him away.

"Hey, don't be so hostile."

"You said you were going to explain. I'm here. Let's talk."

He drew in a sharp breath. "First, I have to tell you about Catia."

"Who is Catia?"

"A botanist. Didn't you see her file at the house?"

The more he explained, the more I realized Catia was the same entitled little slut I'd known when we were teenagers. The sound of her name felt like a punch to my stomach. Catia, who'd gone after a boy I liked in high school and bragged how they'd "done it" all night. I could still see the little bitch, sneaking into the dorm at dawn, her hair a mess, clothes wrinkled, a big grin on her face, saying she needed a long hot shower to wash off the lovemaking.

And now Matt was bringing back the memories.

"I don't want to hear about Catia. I want to know what is going on. How did you engineer this mushroom mission?"

"For God's sake, Adriana. Would you just zip it up and listen?"

"Is this about Catia or escape?"

"It's about everything. Would you please let me tell you the story?"

CHAPTER 42

I already knew more about Catia than I was willing to let on, a lot more. But I wanted to hear what he had to say, so I crossed my arms like a pouty teenager and listened. Her family had been supporters of the Somoza dictatorship. The Sandinistas retaliated by confiscating their mansion, and it was now occupied by a general. Catia had fled to Miami with her family and then moved to France. I'd never been to Europe. A struggle for survival had delayed my exile to Florida.

And now we were both back in Nicaragua.

"Where is this story going?" I asked. "She's a botanist. What does botany have to do with those men at the landing?"

"Everything. She claims to know the location of the mushroom cave."

It took a moment to make the connection. "You brought me out here to do a story on Catia? Build her up. Give her the glory for a major discovery. For God's sake, Matt, I didn't come out here to do a story on Catia. I came out here to escape. I thought you'd help me. You didn't. You were spending your time at the hotel with Catia."

I struggled up. The sudden movement brought on more dizziness. I grabbed the boulder and sat back down. The only thing Matt knew about the toxic little bitch was how well she performed in bed. He didn't know that even at age fifteen she was destroying relationships and turning friends against friends. Worse, back then she was prettier than me. She had bigger boobs. She could afford beauty spas, stylish hairdos, flashy jewelry, and designer clothing. I couldn't afford any of those things. We were poor.

"You didn't let me finish," Matt said.

"If it doesn't involve escape, I don't want to hear it." I forced myself to take another sip of water.

"Look, we'll talk about escape in a minute. First, I need to explain about Catia. Please?"

I didn't answer. He said, "Look, here's the problem. Catia can't keep her mouth shut. She's been blabbing to everyone, saying she found a magic mushroom cave. That's like an invitation to tomb robbers—*depredadores*. They're notorious for robbing pre-Columbian sites."

"Were those men at the landing tomb looters?"

"That would be my guess."

"Why would tomb looters be interested in mushrooms?"

"Isn't it obvious? If those mushrooms exist—and if they could be made into Blue Magic—they'd be worth billions to the pharmaceutical industry. The tomb robbers would kill to find the location. Kill Catia too."

"Why is that your problem?"

"I'm coming to that. She's also been bad-mouthing Sandinistas."

"What's wrong with bad-mouthing Sandinistas?"

"Nothing if you do it discreetly. But you don't call them low-life ignorant scum in public, not in Nicaragua. They control security. They run the army. That's why no one in Nicaragua is going to protect her. She even went to her old family home and confronted a Sandinista comandante. Imagine that? Uppity women get killed in this country."

"Are you saying I'm uppity?"

"I'm talking about Catia, not you. An assertive woman can't come to this country and be bitchy and bossy to men. That might work in the US, but not here. *El hombre manda*—men rule. You know it and I know it."

"What does all that have to do with you?"

"It's simple. Her family was big in the sugar and rum industry in Nicaragua. Now they're big in the Florida sugar business. They've got connections. The ambassador asked me to keep an eye on her and keep her out of trouble. That's what I've been doing the last few days."

His cell phone buzzed. "Christ. I gotta take this."

He walked a short distance away, nodded a few times, and said into the phone, "Primary rendezvous, waiting. Just give us a holler."

He folded the phone and came back. "My spotter. He thinks they're about to shove off."

"Who is about to shove off?"

"Catia and her crew."

"Where are they going?"

"I'm hoping to Ometepe. It'll solve most of our problems."

"Why can't we just forget Catia and go straight to Costa Rica?"

"Can't. We'd need to refuel in Ometepe."

"Okay, let's go to Ometepe and tank up."

"No, Adriana. We're in the ambassador's boat. It's monitored by satellite. If we deviate from the plan, all hell's gonna break loose. They'll think someone has hijacked us. Next thing you know they'll send out search planes and gunboats. It's best to play along. Film the surroundings, take notes, all the usual journal stuff. It'll make one hell of a story."

"That's what you said last time—hell of a story—and look what happened. Maybe you didn't hear they took my fingerprints and matched them to my service record. I'm busted, Matt."

"We're on a huge lake, Baby. They wouldn't know you're out here, and even if they did, they wouldn't know where to find you."

I struggled to my feet, waited for the dizziness to pass, walked around the boulder, and kicked a dead piece of brush out of the way. "Dammit, Matt, every time I listen to you and your smooth talk, I get deeper into trouble. All I want is a plane back to Florida."

My face grew hot, and I'd have thrown more accusations at him if it hadn't been for a flock of yellow, blue, and green canaries that appeared in the trees above us, tweeting as if to tell me to calm down. Matt stepped closer. "Listen, Baby. I'm sorry for getting you into this mess. It's been hard on me too." He reached for me. I twisted away. He shrugged as if his feelings were hurt. "Damn it, Adriana, I've got a job to do. Sometimes they make me do things I don't want to do."

"Did you sleep with her?"

"Sleep with who?"

"Catia?"

He let out an exasperated sigh and glanced at his watch. "Shit. We need to get moving. We'll talk later."

"You're avoiding the question."

"You'll get your answer. Now, come on."

He tried to take my hand. "No," I said and stalked away.

CHAPTER 43

The canaries followed, tweeting as if they were taking his side. Damn him anyway for keeping me in the dark about his plans.

"Hey, don't get so far ahead. Didn't you hear about chupacabras?"

I stopped and stared into the shadows like a scared child, into the tangle of overhead vines where exotic flowers blossomed, and things moved and croaked. Did chupacabras even exist? I could almost believe it in this creepy place. Matt caught up and put his hands around me from the back. "Not to worry. This island is too tiny for monsters."

I shoved him away and pushed on so fast that I didn't see the protruding root. Down I went into a tangle of creepers and underbrush..

Matt dropped down beside me. "Don't move. You've got spider webs in your hair." He brushed them away, pulled me to my feet, and stared into my face. I thought he was going to pull me into his arms. Instead, he reached above me and broke off a large blue and magenta flower that brightened the surrounding foliage.

"These flowers are rare," he said. "They grow only in tropical forests."

"What is it?"

"The Latin name is *Cochliostema odoratissimum.*"

"How do you know so much about tropical flowers?"

"I've been studying them." He put the flower in my hair. Its sweetness was like a romantic potion, and I'd be lying if I said his hands on my cheek didn't cause my heart to beat faster. Damn him, I didn't need Dramamine; I needed a stiff dose of anti-Matt medication.

I shoved him away and trod on, and a minute or so later we emerged from the thicket near the boat. I smelled cigarettes before I saw Sancho and Kodak sitting on the stern with their legs stretched out like tourists on a Carnival cruise ship, drinking Coronas. They stared, taking in the flower in my hair. Sancho nodded as if to say, "We know what you've been up to," but Kodak looked like he was about to burst into tears. His little flower girl, I thought, and took the flower out of my hair.

"Show her the locker," Matt said to Sancho.

Sancho opened a deck locker and pulled out an assault rifle with a distinctive banana-shaped magazine. "You know what this is, don't you?"

I knew very well what it was. I could field strip it, clean it, put it back together with my eyes shut, pop in a magazine, pull the trigger, and shred a tree with a few bursts.

"It's an AK," Sancho said, which was what Nicaraguans called an AK-47. "Best jungle weapon in the world." He propped it against the locker and pulled out grenades, a shotgun, a rifle with a scope, pistols, another AK, and even a grenade launcher.

"Are you serious?" I said to Matt. "What is it you're not telling me?"

"I told you. Tomb robbers. They're already on the way."

By then I was ready to jump into the lake and swim back to the mainland, turn myself in, and beg for mercy. It was scary enough going onto the lake in peacetime with its hazards and tales of monsters. Now we might have to defend ourselves with sniper rifles.

"Once they see our guns," Matt said, "they'll back off."

"I'm a journalist, Matt. I'm not toting a damn gun."

"You don't have to. We'll tote the guns and stand guard while you get your mushroom story."

"Dammit, Matt. Didn't you hear me the first time? Didn't I already tell you I don't give a hoot about mushrooms? I came out here to—"

He put a finger to his lips as if to tell me that Sancho and Kodak were listening. Did they understand English? Maybe. So, I turned away from them and lowered my voice. "What if your girlfriend doesn't cooperate?"

"Damn it to hell, she's not my girlfriend."

"Okay, she's not your girlfriend, but what if she doesn't cooperate?"

"Doesn't matter. She can't stop you. There's no law out here."

An image of an angry screaming woman popped into my mind—Kodak getting it on film—and I almost smiled at the thought of tangling with the deceitful little bitch, rolling on the ground and scratching her surgery-enhanced face.

Matt switched to Spanish for the benefit of Sancho and Kodak. "Only one restriction," he said, holding up a finger. "This is a Nicaraguan story. No foreigners, and that means us. You don't film me. You don't film the boat, and you don't mention me or the embassy in your report."

"That's more than one restriction."

"Whatever." He glanced at his watch again. "We need to get going."

"What if I don't want to go?"

"In that case, I'll leave you here with a gun and a fishing pole."

CHAPTER 44

We piled aboard the *Ana Maria* and sped into the lake, scaring up birds and heading straight toward a formation of dark clouds, Sancho in the captain's chair at the helm, Matt sitting in the back with me, Kodak filming the receding shoreline. I strapped on a life vest, begged God for courage, and took out my binoculars, half expecting to see tomb robbers with a pirate flag and bristling guns.

Or Colonel Vega in a gunboat.

"Who is coming?" I asked Matt.

"Catia." He pointed to a screen on the control panel. "See that dot. See how it lights up and pings. There's a transmitter on her boat."

"She's transmitting to you?"

"She doesn't know about the transmitter."

"You planted a transmitter on her boat?"

He smiled but remained silent.

"Is that even legal?"

"Nicaragua," he said.

I stared at him. He stared back, sitting there in his rumpled khakis and boots with his cap turned backward. Who was he anyway? He'd told me he worked as an economist for US/AID—the US Agency for International Development—and I'd never questioned his story. Never questioned why he always showed up where crap happened either. God was I pathetic. Journalists are supposed to get answers, not settle for sweet talk and exotic flowers. The only economists I knew, back at the university, smoked pipes and looked like Woody Allen. They weren't tall and tan or handsome. Didn't wear dark aviator glasses either or know the Latin names for tropical plants.

And they sure as hell didn't have a luxury boat crammed with grenades and AK-47s. "Where do you think she's going?" I asked. "Which island?"

"That's why we're watching that little screen."

He unfolded a map and rattled off the names of islands we passed—Sanctuary Island, the Isle of Thieves, Zopango—some so close together that traveling between them was like boating down a river. Others lay a mile or more back: little oases of jungle, hills, and white beaches. Lake birds swarmed and cawed. Fish jumped. And when we came to an island where children played in the water, Matt said, "One of these days I'm going to retire and build a cabin out here. Sleep in a hammock and gaze at the stars."

"You're crazy."

"Why am I crazy? Don't we all want to escape the world's madness?"

"That wasn't my point. What good is all this beauty if you have no one to share it with?"

He put down his map. "I wasn't planning to live out here by myself."

I didn't answer. I'd had those same fantasies when I was camped on mountaintops with the Sandinistas, shivering beneath a smelly blanket, scratching insect bites, and staring at the Milky Way, wondering if I'd survive the war and one day be able to share the beauty of God's creation with a man I loved. But things were different now. Now I wasn't about to give up civilization and live on a tropical island for love and starlight. Wasn't going to fall into his web of seduction and empty promises either. Not again.

"Wouldn't you also like it?" he said. "A hammock stretched between the trees. A nice bonfire. The stars out here are incredible. It's like being back at the dawn of creation."

"I'm not a beach girl, Matt. Catia would like it out here but not me."

He came partway out of his chair. "For God's sake, Adriana, would you stop it? I don't give a shit about Catia. I'm talking about us."

Sancho twisted around to see what the fuss was about. Kodak stopped filming and stared. I was pretty sure they didn't understand English, but they understood anger. Matt settled back into his chair, sighed, and folded the map. "You don't have to be so mean about it."

"I'm just being honest. Beach life isn't for me. I don't like glaring sun and hot sand. Don't like sunburn and wrinkled skin either."

"So why are you going back to Florida?"

I didn't answer. I couldn't without bringing Catia into the conversation. Then I'd lose it in front of Sancho and Kodak and make everyone miserable. Better to save it for later. Besides, I had other things to worry me. Like getting to Ometepe. Like those dark clouds and lightning. Like the turbulent water and my fear of sinking and drowning.

"Those clouds are ugly," I said. "Shouldn't we stop on an island and wait out the storm?"

"We already passed the islands. They're behind us."

"Why can't we turn back? I'm getting nauseated."

He glanced at his watch. "Too late to turn back. We can stop on the Island of the Dead."

"You just said we passed the islands."

"All except the Island of the Dead."

I tightened the strap on my vest. This escape-turned-assignment was getting worse every minute. Kids back in school used to joke about the Island of the Dead, saying it was a spooky place where gangsters dumped bodies and spirits ruled the night.

"What's on the Island of the Dead?"

"Coconut trees. It's one of those postage-card pretty islands?"

"Why do they call it Island of the Dead?"

"Who knows?"

"How much longer?"

"It'll be a while. Don't worry about the boat. We'll be fine."

I wasn't so sure we'd be fine and pointed to the mobile that was attached to his belt. "That thing work on the lake?"

"You need to call someone?"

"The station. Can I borrow it?"

"It's an embassy phone. They monitor my calls."

I visualized Ms. Cross Pendant, Dr. Tinted Glasses, Ms. Star of David, and a bunch of other nerdy gringos in the basement of the US Embassy in Managua with earphones, ready with their notepads and pencils. "Good," I said. "I can rail against the embassy for not helping me."

Matt handed me the phone and told Sancho to throttle down. "Be careful what you say."

CHAPTER 45

The connection to my station chief was so clear I could hear computer keys tapping in the background. "Marcelo, what are you getting me into? Why didn't you tell me about this mushroom business?"

"Speak louder. I can barely hear you. Are you in an airplane?"

"I'M ON A BOAT, MIDDLE OF THE LAKE."

"A boat? Didn't you hear about the hurricane?"

"Are you serious? You sent me out on this lake during a hurricane?"

"It's two days out. Projected to pass to the north. All you'll get are outer bands. Nothing to worry about."

"How can you say nothing to worry about? Spaghetti models are notoriously inaccurate."

Matt, who'd been listening, touched my arm. "It's okay, Baby."

I turned to Matt. "Did you know about the hurricane?"

"Just learned it from your conversation."

By then I was so furious my face heated up. I turned back to Marcelo. "WHY DIDN'T YOU TELL ME ABOUT THE DAMN MUSHROOMS?"

"I didn't tell you because I didn't know. And you don't have to shout. I only learned about the mushrooms a short while ago."

"What did you learn?"

There were muffled voices in the background. Marcelo said, "Hold on." The line went silent and when he came back, he said, "Her name is Catia Arguello." He spelled the name. "Her family is—or was—in the sugar and rum business. They've got connections. She's traveling with a French television crew. Can you believe that shit? Puta foreigners!"

I almost laughed. Were the agents at the US Embassy listening? Was Holbrooke Easton listening? I hoped so. I imagined them adjusting knobs on a monitor, plugging wires into an entire wall of switchboards. "Speak up," I said to Marcelo. "Did you say foreigners?"

"I SAID PUTA FOREIGNERS!"

"You're right, Marcelo. Foreigners have no right meddling in our business." I glared at Matt. He rolled his eyes and shook his head.

Marcelo kept talking. "This is Nicaragua, by God. It's a Nica story."

"What about this Catia woman? Isn't she Nicaraguan?"

"That's not the point, Miami."

"Stop calling me Miami."

"You're from Florida, aren't you?"

"Florida's a big state. I'm from Tampa. What about Catia?"

"Point is she's an *exiliada* like you, and she's doing her story for Paris television. How in God's name did Frenchmen get involved?"

"Did she say which island?"

"Magic Mushroom Island."

"There's no island out here named Magic Mushrooms."

"It's a cover name. Are you sure you're up to this job? I can send Rafael. He's available. He knows his way around the islands."

My face grew even hotter. Rafael was a sexist prick who'd stolen my stories more than once. But that was so Nicaragua—a man's world. "TELL RAFAEL TO GO COVER A WEDDING!"

"That's not nice, Adriana."

"Neither is your suggestion I'm not up to the job. I'm already out here, middle of the lake. Heading into a storm. I'm also hearing about tomb robbers. They're on the way."

"Tomb robbers? Oh, great, that makes it more interesting. Hold on."

Again, he spoke to someone else. There were muffled voices, shouts, and four-letter words like *puta and joda*. When he came back, he said, "I just spoke to our boss. He said you damn well better get that story. He wants it presented on the news by Nicas, not by a bunch of puta Frenchman in berets. You know how much Nicaraguans hate foreign meddling."

He was yelling so loud I had to hold the phone away from my ear. Great, I thought. Keep it up. Let Matt hear. Let the spooks in the embassy hear him. Marcelo might even fly into a rage about Oliver North and Iran-Contra, which he often did. Instead, he said, "Can you put the gringo on the phone?"

"How do you know I'm with the gringo?"

"Because he's the only one on the lake with a sat phone."

"Wait. Didn't you just say you don't like foreigners meddling in our business?"

"Just put him on the puta phone."

What a hypocrite! He was on the embassy's payroll as well. Bastard! I frowned and handed the mobile to Matt. They spoke in Spanish. His expression grew serious. "*Mierda*!" he mumbled and turned his back on me. They spoke a while longer, and when they finished, Matt put away his phone and turned around.

I slapped him on the arm. "Why didn't you warn me about a hurricane?"

"I told you already. I didn't know."

"How is it you know Marcelo?"

"We have a business relationship."

"Yeah, right. How much are you paying him? Marcelo doesn't cooperate with gringos unless he gets something in return."

By then the wind was blowing and the boat was getting so knocked about that we were yelling at each other. "WE DON'T PAY HIM ANYTHING," Matt yelled. "NOT A DAMN PESO. We share information. He helps us and we help him."

"What did he tell you?"

"He said to take good care of you."

"HE WHAT?"

"SAID TO TAKE GOOD CARE OF YOU.

"No, Matt, that's not what he told you. WHAT WAS IT?"

"It's best you ask Marcelo."

"NO, MATT, I'M ASKING YOU."

Sancho swiveled around again. Kodak was also staring. I thought one of them would ask us to speak Spanish so they could understand. Instead, Sancho pointed to the dark clouds that were almost on us. "Not looking good," he said, "Five more minutes and we'll be in it."

"He's right," Matt said. "You should get below and relax."

Relax? How could I relax when we were heading into a storm, maybe a hurricane? Even if we didn't sink and get eaten by sharks, we could get shot by grave robbers.

"I don't want to go below," I said, speaking Spanish for the benefit of Sancho and Kodak.

Sancho turned around again. "Are you crazy, girl? You could get swept overboard. You'll need to lash yourself to a rail."

"He's right," Kodak said, strapping on a lifejacket. "I've been out here before. I'm going below myself in a minute."

I stood and grabbed the seat for support, not sure what to do. My head swirled. Damn them. They knew about the storm. They knew I was terrified of water. Why didn't they anchor us in a safe place?

A flash of lightning lit up the boat.

"Come on," Matt said. "Let's get you below."

CHAPTER 46

He led me down a short flight of steps into a wood-paneled cabin that reeked of cigarettes. Even in the dim light, I noticed the built-in refrigerator, microwave, reading lamps, a galley for cooking, a television set, lounge sofa, and even pull-out beds. Had he brought Catia down here? I imagined I could see them, stripping off each other's clothes. I could even hear Catia's voice—He's just like all the other boys.

"Nice boat," Matt said. "When I retire, I'm going to get one just like it, call it the Adriana."

"You're so full of it."

The boat rose and fell. I plunked onto the sofa lounge and gripped the armrest. "Are you okay?" Matt asked.

"No, Matt, I'm not okay. We shouldn't have sailed into a storm."

"I'm sorry, Baby. It's important we keep going."

"What did Marcelo tell you?"

"Are you nauseated? You're getting pale."

"I asked you about Marcelo."

"Hold on." He opened a cabinet and shook another pill out of a container. "Take this. Drink some more water. The head's over there."

"Head?"

"Nautical talk for bathroom. Wall is bulkhead. Floor is deck."

I swallowed the pill with water from a plastic bottle. A hardcover book called *The Magic World of Maria Sabina* lay on the lounge beside me. I picked it up as if that would calm me and was clutching it to my chest when the boat suddenly rose and plunged, taking my stomach with it. Matt opened another cabinet, took out one of those native hammocks with rainbow colors, and began stringing it from one side of the cabin to the other.

"Don't we have beds?" I asked.

"Queen size, but they rock and roll when the going gets rough. Hammocks work with gravity." He took out a blanket and sank onto the lounge beside me. "You're shaking?"

"It's the boat."

"The boat doesn't tremble."

"Look, I'm scared. Okay?"

"Oh, Baby, don't worry about the boat. It will not sink."

"That's what they said about the *Titanic*."

"Dammit, Adriana, we're not the *Titanic*, so stop worrying." He put an arm around me.

"Don't," I said and leaned away. "I don't feel well."

"Look, I'm not interested in Catia. Okay?"

"You already said that. What did Marcelo tell you?"

"I didn't sleep with her either. She's got a boyfriend named Gérard." He gave it the French pronunciation, which annoyed me even more. "He's a jealous jerk. He's with her now."

"You said before you didn't know who was with her."

"I didn't tell you because I wasn't sure you were coming with us."

"What kind of logic is that?"

"Look, you and I haven't exactly been on good terms lately. I wasn't comfortable telling you everything. I had to be careful with the embassy. I'm going to catch hell when they learn you're on the boat with me. It'll be worse when they learn you're in Costa Rica."

"What did Marcelo tell you?"

"You should get in the hammock."

"No. Tell me now."

"Look, there's six of them. Okay? All French except Catia. The others are her boyfriend and a camera crew. Also, a botanist from the French Academy of Natural Sciences."

"What's so secretive about that?"

He put his hand over mine. "There's something else."

"What, Matt? Just tell me."

His grip tightened on my hand. "It's about the tomb looters."

"What about them?"

"Ramos is with them."

A flash of lightning lit the cabin. Something clattered.

"Shit!" Matt said. "I'd better get topside."

I clasped his hand, suddenly alarmed at being alone. "Why didn't you tell me about Ramos?"

"Because I just learned it from Marcelo. Besides, would you have come if you'd known?"

"I would have been even more anxious to come."

"Why?"

"So, I could kill the sonofabitch, that's why."

CHAPTER 47

Back and forth I swung in my hammock. Back and forth and up and down. In a cabin as dark as the plagues of Egypt. The down plunges were the worst, like a sickening drop on a roller coaster. Now and then it felt as if we'd collided with a boulder. The boat protested with creaks and pops. Flashes of lightning lit the cabin, and in those flashes, I saw the evil face of Ramos, coming to get me. How did he get onto the boat?

Was this real?

I tried to struggle up, to get myself out of the hammock. Find an AK and blast him to pieces. But I couldn't. My arms and legs wouldn't cooperate. Was I hallucinating? Was it the pill Matt had given me? I couldn't even scream. Where was Matt? Why didn't he come below to save me? Had he and the others been swept overboard?

Please, dear God, no.

I prayed like I'd never prayed before. I begged forgiveness for all my sins. I promised God that if I survived Ramos I'd go to church, devote my life to helping the poor, and live as saintly as Mother Teresa.

I opened my eyes. Ramos was still there, glaring from the sofa lounge. And somewhere in that hallucinatory state, a theory began to emerge: the pill Matt had given me wasn't for motion sickness; it was a magic mushroom extract—Blue Magic—and it was filling my head with *tonterias.*

The roar of wind became airplanes. Lightning and thunder became bombs. Something was burning. The boat? No, I wasn't on the boat. I was fifteen years old and caught between government forces and Sandinistas at my childhood home, cowering beneath a window in my Sacred Heart uniform. I should be outside with the rebels, black beret and all, fighting against the hated dictatorship that ruled our country.

There were shouts and gunfire, soldiers running past our house, others behind them, footfalls slapping on the pavement, and there was my beautiful mom in her checkered green apron. I saw her as plainly as the day it happened, screaming to get away from the window.

"Are you crazy, *Mija*? They'll shoot you."

She pulled me away and slammed the window shut, and that was when the door swung open.

In rushed five or six armed teenagers from the neighborhood, breathing hard, now all scraggly and smelling unwashed in their ill-fitting Sandinista uniforms. My best friend Angelina was with them, an ammo belt strapped around her skinny waist. Her eyes were wide with terror, and her hair was all wild and kinky, sticking out beneath a black beret.

"Come with us," she said. "Hurry!" One of the others shoved her to the back door. Out they dashed, scattering chickens and grabbing avocados off a tree. They had scarcely disappeared through a back gate when soldiers pounded on the door.

"Open up! Open this puta door or we'll shoot it open!"

"Run," my mom begged me. "Go with Angelina. Hide."

A truck roared past, or a tank. The door burst open. They charged in—soldiers of Somoza's hated Guardia Nacional—waving their guns and looking right and left.

"Where the hell are they?" barked the officer in charge. "Wher?"

My mom pointed out the back. "Gone. I'm so sorry."

Soldiers trotted out the back and through the gate. Four or five chased chickens in the backyard. Others went from room to room, opening drawers, scattering contents, and knocking things over as if we were the enemy instead of fellow Nicas. They picked up a framed photograph of my mom and dad in their wedding clothes and threw it against the wall. They even smashed an image of Jesus. But the worst of it was when they found the black beret and small Sandinista flag that a recruiting officer had given me.

"God help us," my mom muttered and made the sign of the Cross. I shrank against her, holding on as if she could protect me from their rage. The officer in charge, a squat man with the name Ramos on his name patch, backed us against a wall with his pistol.

"Puta traitors! Who is the Sandinista in the house? Is it your husband?"

My mom didn't answer. Neither did I.

He flung the beret and flag at us. "I asked you a question, bitch. Answer me, damn you!"

My mom broke down in whimpering sobs. I sank to the floor beside her, so petrified that all I could do was tremble. Other soldiers came and left, grabbing and stealing, yelling and cursing, until at last there was only Ramos and his pock faced sergeant. "The old lady's yours," Ramos said to the sergeant. "This little sweetie is mine."

"Don't fight them," my mom whispered. "They'll kill you."

Ramos yanked me to my feet and pushed me toward the bed. I screamed. I fought. I called him every dirty teenage word I knew, and I kept screaming, kicking, and cursing until I realized I was flailing at the blanket in my hammock and Matt was standing over me.

"It's okay," he said and pulled me into his arms. "We're out of it now."

It took a long time for my heart to stop pounding and to realize the storm had ended and Kodak was in another hammock beside me. "Where are we?" I asked Matt, my voice hoarse.

"Coming up on the Island of the Dead. Are you okay?"

I stumbled into the tiny bathroom and threw up everything that had gone into my stomach, wishing I could also purge the memory. The image in the mirror made it worse. Face ashen. Hair a tangled mess. Eyes red and swollen. Yet I managed to get myself together and go out to find Matt taking down the hammocks.

Kodak was up too, his long hair as messy as mine had been, and he was sitting on the lounge with a small copy of Neruda's *Twenty Love Poems* in his hand. He looked up from his book, tears in his eyes. No, I wanted to shout. Please don't tell me your troubles.

"This breaks my heart," he said, nodding at the book. "Just listen to Neruda's words:

'Tonight, I could write the saddest lines.
She loved me and I loved her too.
How could I not have loved her huge still eyes?'"

Matt looked from Kodak to me and shook his head like a doctor telling the family there was no hope. "I'm making coffee," he said. "We've also got boiled eggs and ready-made sandwiches—ham and cheese, chicken, pimiento cheese. You should eat something."

I dashed back into the bathroom and threw up again.

When I came out, Kodak was trudging up the stairs like a defeated lover. Matt watched him go and turned to me. "Poor guy. He told me about his little flower girl."

"He's been mourning her forever. I wish I could help him."

"I might be able to help."

"How?"

"Tell me her full name and the unit she served in. I can ask around."

"You'd do that?"

"If she's alive, I'm pretty sure I can track her down."

I wrote down the information. Damn gringos, they had resources to spy on everybody. Probably had a thick dossier at the embassy on me too. "What was in that pill you gave me?"

"Dramamine." He took out the container and showed me. "You've already had two." He felt my forehead. "No fever. Do you want to go topside for some fresh air?"

"How much longer to the Island of the Dead?"

"Thirty minutes at most. Your boss wants us to get preliminary footage while we're there."

Preliminary footage. Good God, I could barely walk, my stomach was in turmoil, and my clothes wrinkled. My head swirled, and I looked like I'd climbed out of a grave.

"We need to talk," Matt said and motioned me onto the lounge.

CHAPTER 48

Any conversation that begins with "We need to talk "is never a good sign. I took a drink of water and drew in a deep breath. He fixed me in his gaze. I braced myself. He smiled and asked, "What do you know about bats? You know, those creepy fluttering creatures of the night."

"Why are you asking about bats?"

"Because we're going to a bat cave."

"On the Island of the Dead?"

"No, Baby, it's on another island. Do you know how many bat species there are? More than fourteen hundred. Without them, there'd be no mangos. No bananas. No avocados either."

I felt like I'd fallen into an episode of *The Twilight Zone*. Matt kept talking. "They hibernate in caves—in the overhead. Down comes their guano. It piles up, deeper and deeper. Guess what grows in guano."

I closed my eyes and tried to picture a dark, smelly cave with bats clinging to the ceiling.

"Mushrooms grow in it, but there's only one important mushroom. Remember that flower I put in your hair this morning?"

I brushed my hair and looked at my hand without thinking, imagining it would be stained with bat guano."Bats eat many things," Matt said, "but it's the flower that gives mushrooms their magic quality. And there's something else I need to tell you."

"Why do you keep saying there's something else? Just say it."

"Maria Sabina. "Mexican medicine woman. A *curandera*. People came from all over the world to get her mushroom cures."

He picked up the Maria Sabina book atop the lounge. "You should read this. Her mushrooms were the real deal. There are testimonials—women claiming their wrinkles disappeared. Bodies lost fat. Energy levels rose, and they looked twenty, or thirty years younger. Men reported the same. Claimed her cures helped them bang like rabbits."

"So, what's the catch?"

"Catch is no one knows the formula for Blue Magic. Maria Sabina knew, but she took her secrets to the grave."

"Wait a minute, Matt. Hold on. Time out." I waved my arms in front of him. "How many times do I have to tell you I went to the landing this morning for one purpose? To get on a boat to Ometepe. Escape. Get away from here. Go back to Florida. Can we talk about that?"

He put the book down. "I can't believe you're not interested in a hot story like Blue Magic."

"Any other time, yes. But not now. My priority is escape. You've known that all along. So why are you dragging me into this mushroom business instead of helping me?"

He was fumbling for an answer when Kodak appeared at the top of the stairs. "Island of the Dead. Almost there."

CHAPTER 49

Unlike other islands we passed, which were covered in thickets of trees and vines, *Isla de los Muertos* looked as if it had been lifted from a glossy travel brochure—a beautiful white beach, an open field of reeds, and a hill topped with swaying coconut trees.

Sancho lumbered over the railing and lashed the boat to a boulder. A sweet smell I couldn't identify filled the air, and flocks of lake birds circled above us, cawing and protesting.

"Know why they call this place Island of the Dead?" Sancho asked in his country accent, looking up from the beach and grinning.

"Do I have to answer that?"

"No, but it's a good story." He pointed toward the reeds. "Happened right there. Indians used to lay their dead out on platforms in the reeds. Wait for birds to eat the flesh. Then the families would come back for the bones. But that's not the best part—"

The boat rose and dropped in a sudden swell. I grabbed the railing. Sancho kept talking. "The Spaniards also burned criminals and witches here. Burned them up there on that hill. Beneath the coconut trees. They say that at night you can hear the screams."

I turned to Matt. "How long are we going to be here?"

"We'll be gone long before dark. Don't pay any attention to Sancho." He grabbed a blanket and beach towel and helped me off the boat, across the sandy beach, and into a formation of black lava boulders.

Even there the ground seemed to bob in the surf.

"I should lie down," I said.

He spread the towel and handed me the blanket. "When you're better we'll hike up that rise."

The summit he pointed to was no more than three hundred yards away, not nearly as formidable as the hills and mountains I'd climbed when I was a teenager in a Sandinista uniform, but in my current condition it might as well have been Mt. Everest. "What's up there?"

"Could be the witch," Sancho mumbled beside me. He made a bad attempt at trying to emulate the theme music of *The Twilight Zone*.

"Sancho, if you don't shut up, I'm going to throw up on you."

Matt shook his head and told Sancho to get us another bottle of water. Sancho limped away with an impish grin on his face.

"Don't be so hard on him," Matt said. "He likes to joke around."

"What's his job at the embassy?"

"Consultant."

"What does that mean? How can he work at the embassy if he doesn't know English?"

"He knows English very well. He may have grown up in humble circumstances. He may speak Spanish like a peasant, but after the war, he went to the states like you and thousands of other Nicaraguans. Got a degree in music at UCLA."

"Music?"

"Music. You should hear him play the sax."

I should have guessed there was more to Sancho from the way he'd hustled us through the checkpoint at the landing. "You still didn't tell me what he does."

"I told you. Consultant."

"How do you know he's not spying for the Sandinistas?"

"All I know is he's a valued employee."

I sat back and shook my head. There was a lot more about Sancho that Matt would not tell me, so I gave up and asked what was so important about the hill he wanted me to climb.

"You'll see when we get there."

"Why are you so elusive?"

"I'm not elusive. It's just more fun when you learn thingsyourself."

"What's that sweet smell? They smell like gardenias."

"The reeds. I don't know the name, but they have these little white flowers that butterflies and birds love. You'll see when we climb the hill."

He sat beside me and began rubbing my back, the way he used to do when we were curled up at his place. It felt good. Damn it, why was I so weak? I shouldn't give in to him. There were too many other things to worry about. Like a hurricane. Like Ramos and Catia and a cave with bat guano. And getting to Ometepe. And that damn hill. I didn't want to go up there. Didn't want to get back on the boat either. Not now. Not ever.

But I didn't stop him from rubbing my back. I couldn't. He was like Spock in *Star Trek*. Touch me in the right place and render me helpless.

"Matt?"

"What, Baby?"

"What if Ramos shows up?"

"Don't you worry about Ramos. I'll take care of him."

I snuggled closer, and if it hadn't been for his buzzing mobile phone, I'd have been crying in his arms and forgiving his lies.

"Damn it to hell," he said, and stood up. "I've got to take this." He gave me a reassuring squeeze and trod down the beach.

The wind gusted. Seabirds cawed, thunder rumbled, and despite the blanket and the heat radiating off the boulders, I began shivering. Worse, the ugly face of Ramos kept popping into my head. Was he coming because of the mushrooms or was he coming for me? Maybe he was here already. Maybe he was on that hill, lurking behind a boulder.

CHAPTER 50

I rolled over and shut my eyes, and when darkness closed around me, I was fifteen again, trekking through the jungle in a Sandinista uniform, all boots, beret, and an AK-47. One of the other girls was pregnant and complaining about her cooking assignment. Thunder rumbled. Monkeys chattered in the trees, and I distinctly heard a conversation between two soldiers who sounded like Sancho and Kodak.

"What's holding you up? Why don't you get off your ass and find her?"

"Because I'm scared of what I might find. She was so gorgeous back then. Slim. Energetic. And oh, those dark eyes. But how does she look now? Maybe she's fat as a cow."

"Oh, come on. Did she have big boobs?"

"What kind of stupid-ass question is that?"

"Not stupid, Kodak. Young girls with big boobs turn matronly with age. Flat-chested girls stay skinny. If I remember correctly, your little flower girl was flat as fried eggs."

"What makes you such an expert?"

"Because I have more experience than you."

"Oh, please. When's the last time you got laid?"

"Doesn't matter. What's important is I always go for small boobs?"

"Because they age better?"

"No, Kodak. Because they're easier to read. Bet you didn't know that."

There was silence long enough for me to realize I was awake, and Sancho and Kodak were sitting atop the boulder near me.

I kept my eyes closed and listened.

"This is foolproof," Sancho said. "If she's ready for action she will always, and I mean always, mention how small her boobs are. That's to prepare you."

Good God, I thought. Had I said anything to Matt about my breasts?

Sancho kept talking. "Best way to answer is, 'Oh, sweetie, that's wonderful. I prefer small-breasted women.' You say those magic words and she's yours. Guaranteed. And there's one other get-laid secret."

"What secret?"

"Music. It has a direct connection to a woman's soul, especially romance music. Always ask what kind of music she likes. Ask who is her favorite artist. When she tells you, you say, 'Oh, my God, that's my favorite too.' Then you go out and buy her an album. I did that with this Mexican chick. She was into Mariachi, and oh, it did pay off big. She's crazy for me."

I felt my face growing warm. Did Matt ask what kind of music I liked?

"Poetry also works," Sancho said. "It's better than flowers."

He burst into laughter. Kodak said, "Not so loud, you pervert. You'll wake Miami."

"Nah, she's sleeping like a baby, poor thing. Should have never taken this assignment."

"Why did she?"

"Blame the gringo. He called your station and asked for her."

I lay there waiting for more details, but they got back into boobs. "Something else I bet you didn't know," said Sancho. "Girls with small knockers are the smartest, but it's harder for them to get a guy. That's why they're easier. The girls with the biggest knockers are the dumbest, but their advantage is they don't have to use brains to get a guy."

"How do you know that?"

"Proven scientific fact. It's called natural selection. Some guy named Darwin invented it."

I sat up. I'd heard enough. Sancho and Kodak scurried away like frightened deer. I rubbed the sleep out of my eyes and looked around. The sky was dark, and it looked like another squall was coming. I felt better, though, and was pulling myself together when Matt hurried over. "Ready to tackle that hill? You slept an hour."

CHAPTER 51

Matt told Sancho to stay with the boat and keep a sharp lookout. I climbed back aboard the *Ana Maria* long enough to straighten up. Then Kodak hitched up the tripod and other equipment and we followed Matt upward through a winding path amid the reeds with their tiny flowers. Petals from the flowers swirled around like snowflakes, and then a swarm of canaries swooped from the sky and flitted around us, chirping and singing as if welcoming us to the island.

"You, okay?" Matt asked. "We can take a break."

"I'm fine. The Dramamine must be kicking in."

A few more minutes and we were at the summit in the shade of coconut trees, near the edge of a cliff that overlooked a jumble of boulders and frothing surf, at the spot where Sancho said they burned the witches. The lake spread out below us, open water on one side, black mountains in the distance. Seabirds lifted into the air, squawking. A breeze off the lake rustled the limbs above us, and in that breeze came smells that brought back memories of a chicken roost in our backyard. Was it seabird poop? I plunked down on a boulder and took a long drink of water. "What do you want to show me?" I asked Matt.

"You're sitting on it."

I stood but saw only a smooth flat surface that had been carved into the rock by some ancient stone mason. "Not there," Matt said. He led me to the opposite side, to a spot that was dangerously close to the cliff's edge and where the breeze brought up even stronger bird guano smells. "There," he said and rubbed his palm over the back of the boulder.

On it was an etching. "Thousand-year-old petroglyph," he said. "Maybe two thousand years. They're all over this island."

"I can barely see it."

He unscrewed the cap on his water bottle and sprinkled the contents over the etching. An image of a woman appeared, life-size. Then a second woman, smaller than the first, stooping to gather mushrooms. "There you have it," Matt said. "Magic mushrooms." He pointed out other things in the glyph, like celestial bodies that could be the sun and moon and even a plume from the taller woman's mouth. "She's talking," Matt said. "If I had to guess, I'd say she's proclaiming the merits of mushrooms. What do you think?"

I envisioned an ancient *curandera* standing on this very spot, preaching to the masses in the field of reeds. The journalist in me came to life. What a wonderful place to begin a story about magic mushrooms, even if I had no plan of doing the story and returning to the station.

"Set up the camera," I said to Kodak.

I made a mental note of what to say, arranged my hair beneath the cap, and was putting on lipstick when Matt said, "Wouldn't it be better to leave off the makeup?"

"Why?"

"To show how rough it is out here?"

"No, Matt, this is Nicaragua. Latin television. They expect the woman behind the camera to be attractive, young, and sexily dressed. I can't do the sexily dressed part. Not now. Don't look that young either, but I can at least put on lipstick. I slathered it on a little thicker to annoy him and wondered if I shouldn't undo the top button of my shirt. Nope, unlike Catia I didn't have that much to show.

A final check of my face in my compact makeup mirror told me it was no worse than when I'd done other shots in a jungle, and I was concentrating on what to say when the drone of a boat interrupted us. It appeared far out in the lake, against a distant mountain range. My heart jumped. Matt watched it through his binoculars. "Nicaraguan flag."

"Ramos?"

"Too soon. Not Catia either."

I felt the blood returning to my face. We watched a while longer, and then I positioned myself with the lake to my back like one of those hurricane reporters in Florida—ball cap, pocket vest, boots, and a troubled look. Matt pinned the mic to my collar. "Your station manager said to be sure and rail about foreigners."

"I might rail against you."

"You already did. Show a little mercy."

Kodak held up a finger. "You're hot in five seconds. Go!"

"It's a little after noon," I said, glancing at my watch, "and we're standing on the summit of the Island of the Dead, on the very spot where witches were burned and a native medicine woman instructed the early inhabitants of Nicaragua on the benefits of magic mushrooms."

Oh yes, I thought, magic and witch in one sentence.

"We don't know that for certain, but what we do know is this. Even as I speak, a group of botanists are on the lake you see behind me. Foreign botanists. They're heading to a cave on one of our beautiful tropical islands. And in this cave—according to them—is proof positive that magic mushrooms exist. Do they? Do they heal the sick? Do they grow hair on the bald? Do they prolong life and rejuvenate your body? Are they the fountain of youth?"

Matt grinned and gave it a thumbs-up.

"It wasn't easy to get here. The authorities didn't give us their blessing to search for magic mushrooms. But they're allowing a foreign TV crew. Yes, you heard that right—foreigners. But guess what? If that cave exists. If the mushrooms exist. And if the foreign crew finds it, they're going to discover something else when they get there: Nicaraguans, a crew from Channel Four News, bringing you the full story…"

I ranted for another two or three minutes. Kodak panned the island and focused his camera on the petroglyphs, and we were wrapping up when, amid the squawks of birds, I distinctly heard a woman's voice, begging for help.

A woman here? Where? Who? I glanced left and right, but the lake and surroundings, so clear before, had grown as foggy as a cloud bank. My legs weakened. My head swirled like I was about to faint—and that was when a bell dinged, a sharp-pitched ding, like a silver spoon against crystal. What was wrong with me? I tried to focus. I reached for the boulder to keep from falling—and there she was again, that indigenous-looking woman with wild hair and blue skin, the same jungle woman I'd seen at the assassination, now tied to the base of a palm tree.

The bell dinged again. My head cleared and she was gone, vanished, as if she'd never been there. Or had existed only in my mind, and I found myself leaning against the boulder and Matt at my side. "Are you okay, Baby? What's wrong?"

"Dizzy. I need to sit down. Give me a minute."

How long I sat on that glyph boulder, trying to get my thoughts together, I don't know. Who was that woman? Why was she blue? Why did she appear to me not once but twice? There had to be an explanation. Was it stress? Should I tell Matt?

No, don't tell anyone other than a shrink.

Matt handed me water and was rubbing my neck when Sancho appeared in the reeds below us, waving his arms. "They're coming!"

We gathered our things and trotted back down the trail through the reeds, the canaries following. I climbed aboard the *Ana Maria* and glanced around as if expecting to be set upon by tomb robbers. Or a blue woman with a spear. Sancho fired up the engines and away we went, scaring up clouds of sea birds, keeping the island between ourselves and whoever was coming.

"This is getting ridiculous," I said to Matt. "Who is coming?

"Catia. We need to get to the island before they do."

"Ometepe Island?"

"It looks like they're heading to Zapateras."

CHAPTER 52

I'd heard about Zapateras before, about the half-human, half-animal creatures that were said to live on the island in ancient times, and whose likeness had been carved into stone and worshipped by the natives—and there were rumors they still roamed the island like carnivorous versions of Sasquatch.

Worse, there were whispers of chupacabras, and stories about animals and humans ripped to pieces. So, when Zapateras loomed up like the lost island of King Kong, all hills and jungle and craggy shoreline, I asked myself again why I hadn't taken one of those other boats back at the landing and gone straight to Ometepe.

And the answer was Matt. Always Matt. Stupid me. Would I ever learn?

"Island of magic mushrooms," Matt said. "Fifty square kilometers."

"Who lives on it?"

"No one; it's a state preserve. You can still see the ruins."

"What ruins?"

"Sonzapote. The old Spanish priests called it the Sodom and Gomorrah of Nicaragua."

"Why?"

"Because a volcanic eruption destroyed it. Fire from the sky. What was left was destroyed by zealots of the Inquisition. They said it was the wicked getting their just desserts."

Sancho throttled down. Buzzards and seagulls circled overhead. "Creepy," Sancho said. "This would be the perfect place for an Indiana Jones movie: snakes that drop from trees. Hostile natives. Vines that wrap around you and squeeze you to death."

"Didn't you hear the gringo?" Kodak said. "No one lives here."

"Yeah," Sancho answered, grinning, "and you know why? Because no one survives." He crossed his eyes and made a gurgling sound as if being choked by a vine.

"You'd never make it in show business," I said to Sancho. "Not with that bad acting."

Matt tapped the image on the screen. "They're moving fast. We better get out of sight."

We idled past a small landing and followed the shoreline around a rocky point, avoiding boulders and passing beneath low-hanging limbs. Kodak got our camera rolling. I gazed into the trees for hidden dangers but saw only fruits and coconuts, orchids, bromeliads, bananas, flowering creepers, and tropical flowers that looked like the ones favored by bats.

"Get a good shot of those flowers," I said to Kodak.

"Got it, boss. No problem."

Matt gestured to a tiny cove that was barely big enough for the boat. "There," he said.

Sancho cut the engine and let the drift carry us in, and we came to a stop beneath a tangle of vines and vegetation from a giant mango tree. Fog rolled in from the lake, heavy here, wispy there. The smell of rancid water and decaying leaves hung in the air like a Florida swamp.

Matt put a finger to his lips. "Hush, let's listen."

I cupped a hand behind my ear. Not a breath of air stirred, and the only sounds came from birds, buzzing insects, and slaps of surf. "Here's the plan," Matt said in a whisper. "We find a high point that overlooks the landing. Wait for them there. Get footage of them coming in."

"Why are you whispering?"

"Because that's the way we'll talk when we get to the landing."

"Where's the landing?"

"Fifteen-minute trek. Twenty, depending on the trail."

"What makes you so sure this is the right island?"

"Logic."

"That's not an answer. What kind of logic?"

"Occam's Razor."

Kodak looked baffled. Matt kept talking. "First you look at all the possible answers. In this case, we're talking about islands. Which island? There are hundreds on Lake Nicaragua."

"Four hundred plus," I said.

"Correct. But if we eliminate the least likely islands, which they've done for us by passing them up, we're left with only two islands. The largest—Ometepe—is so far out that if they were going there, they'd have left from a different port. That leaves only this island—Zapateras. It's got all the ingredients—volcanic soil, jungle, bats, hills, caves, and those flowers you saw back there. So, there's your answer. Thank you, Mr. Occam."

"You could still be wrong."

"Yes, I could. They might have deliberately chosen an illogical departure port to confuse us, but Catia's not that smart. Twenty dollars says I'm right. Anybody want to bet?"

Kodak and Sancho shook their heads. I didn't take the bet either, mainly because I felt that Matt had known all along that this expedition was headed to Zapateras.

Matt looked at his watch. "We should get moving."

"Not yet," I said. "We need to shoot some footage of us landing."

"No, Baby, I'm sorry. This is an embassy boat. No pictures."

"Look, Matt, you told me to play along and that's what I'm doing. I'm a broadcast journalist. I don't do shoddy work. There's an audience to please, as well as an editor. They'll want everything on film. Every stop and every trek. If you don't want shots of you or the boat, fine, no problem, but I'm not going anywhere until I record a short visual."

He looked at his watch again. "Keep it brief." He strapped on a pistol belt and pulled AKs from the deck locker.

"Why do we need guns?"

He popped a clip into his AK. "How are you feeling?"

"Better. The nausea's gone."

"Good thing," Sancho said with that stupid grin on his face. "You'll need to be strong if we come across any of those jungle devils. How fast can you run?" His eyes widened like a madman, and he burst into another of his stupid faux laughs.

"Shut up, Sancho. I'm scared enough as it is."

Matt handed me a machete. "Here, take this. It'll make a good prop for your audience."

He hopped ashore and lashed the *Ana Maria* to the trunks of Ceiba trees. Kodak and Sancho began unloading our camera and equipment. "Are we going to just leave the boat here?" I asked. "Snakes could come aboard. Rats…and whatever else is out there."

"We'll deal with that when we get back. Only other choice is anchor in the open. Not a good idea. It can be seen for miles."

I sighed in resignation, hitched up my pack, put on my shades and cap, and reached for Matt's hand. And that was when a hideous shriek shattered the calm. Not a bird-like shriek. Not the shriek we'd heard back at the landing. But the kind of out-of-this-world terror shriek you'd expect from a woman being attacked by vampires. Kodak reached for his pistol. The jungle became so silent it felt like a power failure.

"What was it?" I asked Matt, my senses on full alert.

"Something just came to a bad ending. Nothing to worry about. Happens all the time."

"Can you be a little more specific?"

"It's a jungle, Adriana. Animals and birds eat each other."

I stared into the trees and underbrush. What was out there? Was Matt being truthful? I'd heard lots of shrieks in my days with the Sandinistas, some from birds, some from wounded, and some from women fighting off unwanted advances. But never a shriek like that. Never. Not once.

Something chirped. Little by little the jungle came alive with croaks, chirrs, and tweets. The only other sound was the lullaby of waves slapping the boulders. Matt offered me his hand. "Come on. Rock and roll."

"God give me courage," I mumbled and stepped ashore.

CHAPTER 53

Despite Matt's worry that the embassy boat would show in our footage, there were only glimpses through draping limbs, creepers, giant vines, and other vegetation. He and Sancho went to work anyway with their machetes, slashing, covering, and tying, and within minutes there was no sign of the boat, only the wilderness and the fog.

"Was that necessary?" I asked.

Sancho snorted and wiped sweat off his face. "You're missing the point, Miami. It's not your cameras we're worried about. It's those damn jungle creatures."

Kodak glanced up from his tripod. "If you don't shut up," he said to Sancho, "I'm going to toss your skinny ass into the lake."

I'd already told him to shut up a hundred times so decided to save my energy for the camera. Matt wanted to position me with my back to the jungle. No way in hell, I told him—or words to that effect. What I wanted was my back to the lake and a clear path of retreat to the boat.

Sancho plucked a banana from a tree, peeled it, took a bite, and pronounced it delicious. I strolled around with my machete, swatting at mosquitoes and hacking at overhanging creepers.

"Are you scared?" Kodak asked.

"I don't know if Sancho is lying or just teasing."

The two of us hacked away at vines and finally settled on a spot with a view of the lake. It had drooping limbs with the "bat flowers," elephant ears and palmettos, and thick hairy vines with tenacles that trailed into the water. Perfect. There were even mangoes above us and brown and white mushrooms growing along the shoreline.

I pointed them out to Matt. "Are those the magic mushrooms?"

"No, Baby. They're plain old toadstools."

"Poisonous?"

"Well, I'm not going to eat them. You shouldn't either."

He traipsed away with his AK, glancing into the underbrush and trees as if searching for hidden dangers. "Are you sure this island is safe?"

He turned to face me. "Safe as anywhere else in Nicaragua."

I didn't believe him. I had an uneasy feeling that things were in the trees, watching and waiting to attack. Kodak stepped closer and spoke to me in a hushed voice. "Do you believe in the rule of three?"

"What's the rule of three?"

"It's the rule that terrible things never happen by themselves. Never. There's always a second and a third. It's like a curse. You and I already had an assassination. Then the storm. Now we've got to deal with tomb robbers and a hurricane and God knows what else." He patted the pistol on his waistband. "That's why I'm carrying this Glock."

I put on a jungle jacket with all the extra pockets and prettied myself up with lipstick and makeup powder. Kodak set up the tripod for the camera and pinned the mic on my lapel.

"Don't get too close to the water," Sancho said. "You could fall in and get eaten by sharks."

I rolled my eyes. Kodak tested the sound through his earphones and made a final adjustment on the tripod, and when he nodded and gave the thumbs up, I smiled into the camera and began my presentation.

"We're finally here, an island in the middle of Lake Nicaragua. Is it the Island of Magic Mushrooms? We don't know, but it has all the ingredients—volcanic soil, bats, tropical flowers, caves, and massive trees with creepers and gnarled limbs that could have come from a fairy tale."

I sniffed the air and smiled again. "You can smell the humidity. There's a lake to our back and swampy low places in front, some of it rancid, some perfumed with beautiful blossoms favored by bats. Perfect for mushrooms. If that's not creepy enough, there are also tales of witches on this island. But what's scary are rumors about half-animal, half-human creatures that guard the caves of magic mushrooms..."

Matt pointed to his watch as if to say, "Hurry up." Sancho limped this way and that with his AK, looking into the trees and underbrush like a soldier in enemy territory. Maybe he wasn't kidding about jungle creatures. Maybe Kodak was right about the rule of three.

Stop it, I told myself. Concentrate on your report, and I was trying so hard to keep concern out of my voice that I lost track of the point I was making. I stammered and hesitated.

Kodak looked up with alarm in his eyes. So, did Matt. Then Sancho.

Matt made a throat-slashing gesture.

Something screeched.

I froze. And then, as if the gate to hell had opened, an enormous bird swooped down from the trees directly toward me.

CHAPTER 54

The tripod toppled. Sancho cried, "*Joda*!" I flung out my arms. The machete went flying. The bird zoomed past my head, so close I felt a blast of air. I hit the ground and scrambled away on all fours, screaming and flailing. Matt dropped next to me and pulled me into his arms. "It's okay, Baby. It's okay. I got you. It wasn't after you."

I glanced back in time to see the bird in a death struggle with a black snake, pulling, shrieking, flapping its wings furiously, disturbing the air around us. The bird won. It flapped away with the snake in its beak, predator and prey, the snake still whipping and fighting to get free.

By then, my heart was thudding so hard I couldn't talk. Matt rubbed my back and said something about the bird coming out of nowhere. Sancho and Kodak just stood next to the toppled tripod with a what-the-hell-happened look on their faces. I thought they'd come over and comfort me the way Matt was doing. Instead, Sancho pulled in a deep breath and said to Kodak, "Mexican fucking flag."

"What?"

"It's on their flag, an eagle eating a snake. Imagine that poor serpent getting eaten for dinner."

"Poor snake, hell. What about Miami? Probably pooped in her pants."

They burst into laughter. One of them said "poop" again—I didn't hear the context—and then they were laughing like kids, pointing to each other, and slapping their thighs.

"What so funny?" I yelled. "That snake could've bitten me."

The laughter stopped. I struggled up and turned my fury on Kodak. "Your job is to look after me. You saw the snake. Why didn't you stop the shoot and wave me away?"

Matt said, "It was a water snake, Baby. Not that big. They're not venomous."

"How do you know they're not venomous?"

"Trust me. If you'd been in danger, I'd have been a lot faster."

"What kind of bird? It looked like a prehistoric beast with wings."

"All I saw was a big, black bird with an appetite for snakes."

Kodak stepped over and said he was sorry. "I thought you saw the snake. You were talking about half-human and half-animal creatures and then you suddenly stopped. I zoomed in on the snake. Never imagined the bird attack. It's all on film. It'll make a nice addition."

"Hell, yes," Sancho said. "We can market it in Mexico. They'll love the image." He made an idiotic attempt to imitate a Mexican accent. "*Sí, señorita, me encanta la bandera.*"

Kodak glared at him and shook his head. Matt gathered us around him and said we needed to get to moving. He sent Sancho back aboard the *Ana Maria* to check on Catia's progress. I gathered my things and was hitching up my pack when Sancho yelled down at us, "They turned back. Storm must have delayed them. Looks like they're going to the Island of the Dead."

A sense of relief spread over me. I still hadn't recovered from the seasickness and was dreading a trek through the jungle and the thought of spending the night with snakes and killer birds.

Matt walked out of sight with the cell phone to his ear. When he came back, he said, "Well, the good news is we can get a good night's rest, get a fresh start in the morning."

"What's the bad news?"

He didn't answer. I said, "What are you not telling me?"

He drew in a deep breath. "Ramos and his thugs. I don't know where they are. No way to check. For all I know they could also tie up at the Island of the Dead."

"Why is that our problem?"

"Didn't we discuss that already?"

I bit my lip and shut up about his obligations to the little slut. "What about the hurricane? What's the latest?"

"Well, that's the other unwelcome news. We'll get a new advisory in two hours. Right now, we need to get the boat away from land and find a safe place to anchor."

"Why do we need to move the boat?"

He looked at me as if I should know why, and that itself was an answer.

CHAPTER 55

That night, anchored near a little sandbar away from the island, swinging in my hammock, I drifted in and out of sleep. One minute I'd be at the US Embassy soiree with Matt, glitter and glamor all around, women in low-cut outfits, Matt in a tuxedo, leading me out the door. The next minute I'd be awake, the breeze rattling something on the deck above, thunder in the distance, Matt breathing softly only inches away.

The next time darkness closed around me, I found myself on the fifth floor of the Managua Hotel Intercontinental, my heart ablaze with passion, Matt easing me down on the king-sized bed. Even in my dream, I accepted the theory that I was hopelessly in love with a man I had just met. I felt those wonderful moist kisses again. I felt his lips on my thighs, on my stomach, on my breasts. It was his body I embraced around the pillow, his body I lay beneath. We were one, and just when I thought my heart would burst with love, a crash of thunder shook the boat.

Damn this weather. Damn this lake. It was six in the morning. The pillow that had been Matt was now a crumpled mess. Surely there was more to love than erotic dreams.

Everyone climbed out of their hammocks, grumbling, sleep in faces, taking turns in the head, and before long we were on the deck for our second day on the lake, munching on mangos and bananas we'd gathered on the island. Dark clouds hung over us. Sea birds squawked and protested our presence, and we were talking about the hurricane when Matt's cell buzzed.

He answered, reported our position, asked about the hurricane, listened for a moment, and rang off. "No change in hurricane projection. It'll hit far north of us tonight."

"What if it shifts and comes this way?"

"We've still got time."

"What else did they tell you?"

"They said to wait here for Catia's boat."

"What if she turns back because of the hurricane?"

"She won't. She's not going to blow this opportunity."

My face grew warm. How did he know so much about the little bitch?

He glanced at his watch. "They should be loading up right about now."

Kodak and Sancho decided to take a dip in the surrounding shallows. While they were splashing around and laughing, I retreated to the cabin. Matt followed me in and began rubbing my arms and shoulders. It felt good, and I'd be lying if I said the erotic dream hadn't pumped me up. But I pushed him away. I wasn't about to take off my clothes for a man who'd slept with Catia, and even if he hadn't, I wasn't going to fall back into that pattern. Not yet. Not until I knew he was sincere.

"Do your friends at the embassy know I'm on this boat?" I asked.

"I hope to God not. Holbrooke Easton would be furious. He'd order us back to Managua."

"So, who put this little scheme together? Was it Ignacio?"

He didn't answer.

"What about Pineapple? How is she involved?"

Still no answer. "Dammit, Matt, why can't you tell me?"

He was struggling for an answer when Kodak and Sancho began yelling like the boat was on fire. I understood only one word—"Sharks!"

We dashed topside for a look. Kodak and Sancho had retreated to the sandbar, and around their little island that wasn't much bigger than an army truck swam three or four bull sharks, their fins slashing through the water. Matt picked up his AK.

"Are you going to shoot them?"

"Shoot who? The sharks or those two idiots?"

"We can flip a coin."

"Good thinking. Sharks have been on this lake for a million years. They're the only freshwater sharks in the world. They should get priority."

He put away the AK and started the engine without pulling up the anchor. The sharks scattered. Sancho and Kodak jumped into the water and swam toward the boat like Tarzan on a mission to save Jane and were soon aboard in their drenched underwear, laughing and joking.

"What's the latest?" Sancho asked. "Any news about Catia?"

"Nothing."

Nine o'clock came and then ten. No pings on our receiver and no sighting of a boat. Nothing but rain showers and thunder. Nothing at eleven either. Or at noon. What happened to them? Had they turned back? Been sunk in the storm? Captured by tomb looters?

Matt got on his cell to the embassy. He listened, said, "No, no, that's not what happened," and when he put away his cell, he shook his head.

"What?" I asked him.

"Colonel Vega is in an uproar. The embassy is in an uproar. Newspapers demanding to know what happened. The only good news is your station chief, Marcelo. He's lying for you. Says you called in sick and didn't come in. He didn't mention the lake assignment."

I sat back in the deck chair and closed my eyes. Why hadn't I taken a boat to Ometepe yesterday? I could have been in Costa Rica by now.

"If we don't hear within an hour," Matt said, "we'll need to check the Island of the Dead."

He glanced at me, shook his head again, and motioned me to follow him down to the cabin. Sancho and Kodak followed, both looking as if their pet dog had just died.

"No, no, no," Matt said. "Just Adriana."

He closed the door behind us and pulled me as far away from the door as possible. "Don't worry. Worst-case scenario, I'll take this boat to Ometepe, tank it up, and get you down the river to Costa Rica."

"But what if Colonel Vega sends out a gunboat?"

"Not going to happen. Marcelo told them he heard you talking about an overland plan to the Honduras border. If Vega goes looking for you, it won't be on the lake."

"What about Sancho and Kodak?"

"They're not going to object. Kodak might even want to go with you."

"You'll get in trouble with the embassy."

"To hell with the embassy. You're more important than they are."

He hugged me and left me alone in the cabin.

I should have felt relief. No confrontation with Ramos and his thugs. No hurricane. No snakes and shrieking killer birds. No more jungle hoots and chirrs and smells of decay. But all I felt was disappointment. The journalist in me wanted that story about magic mushrooms, even if it was under duress. I could do both if Catia showed up—get the story, escape via Ometepe, do the editing in Florida, and send it back to be aired in Nicaragua. I also wanted to confront that little slut on a lawless island in front of Matt and see whose side he was on.

We ate ham and cheese sandwiches in silence, drank coffee and tea, listened for pings that never pinged, and at precisely 1 PM we pulled anchor, started the boat, and set sail under an ugly sky toward the Island of the Dead.

"How long?" I asked Matt.

Before he could answer, the screen lit up with a ping.

"Coming straight at us," Sancho said and made a wide U-turn.

CHAPTER 56

We tied up and camouflaged the boat at the same scary place as the day before, beneath the same dangling limbs and vines that lined the shore. The same smells of decay and the hoots, chirps, and croaks of unseen creatures greeted us. Matt said Catia's boat should arrive within a half hour, and since we had to trek through the jungle to get to their landing place, which was a fifteen or twenty-minute hike, we needed to get moving.

"Single file," he said. "Watch where you step. Stay quiet."

"Will we get back before dark? It's already going on three."

"Depends on what happens when we get there."

I didn't like that answer and had a brief flashback of standing with my comrades in a dripping jungle beneath the black and red flag of revolution. Boots and dirty Sandinista uniforms. AKs hitched over our shoulders. I could even smell the wood fires and the cook pots and hear our officers telling us to watch out for snipers in the trees and snakes on the ground.

Were Sancho and Kodak having the same thoughts?

Of course. You don't forget trekking through the jungle and getting shot at. You don't forget the fear and the camaraderie. And you don't forget that puta Bulgarian spaghetti.

The images faded. The smells dissipated. Matt ended his instructions by telling us to spray on insect repellent and stay hydrated. Then he handed me the machete I'd lost during the bird attack. "Here, better take this."

What I wanted was a grenade launcher to blow up Catia's boat and watch it sink into shark-infested waters, but I was a journalist, and journalists are supposed to be Switzerland, so I took the machete and followed Matt into the shadows beneath the trees and thick canopy that blocked out the sun.

Kodak marched behind me with his minicam, filming our progress through scrubby oaks, patches of palmettos, and giant ferns. These gave way to taller trees, broken ground, and stagnant swamps, the latter covered with green slime that looked like the Florida Everglades.

There were toucans, parrots, and other colorful birds in the trees. Chattering monkeys too, and as I stumbled along with the others, looking left and right and into the trees like a good soldier, I wondered how I'd so easily shifted from escape mode to wanting this story on mushrooms. Was it the journalist in me, wanting to sniff out a good story? Was it my desire to confront Catia? Or was it Matt?

All the above, I figured, but mainly Matt.

The hellish croaks and shrieks and chirrs grew louder. Mosquitoes and other biting things swarmed around us. We stair-cased into a shadowy ravine, jumped a small stream, and were about to ascend the other side when Matt held up a hand—which meant stop and squat.

I ducked and froze. So did everyone behind me. Matt pointed to a slim plant. It was about eight feet tall with a hairy trunk and rank foliage. "Chichicaste," he said as if we didn't know. "It'll eat you alive. Senses body heat and leans into you. Worse than being attacked by fire ants."

I backed away. I'd tangled with chichicaste before, and I wasn't about to get near it. Matt whacked it in half with his machete and we splashed on, stepping around mossy boulders and following the trail upward.

My lungs ached. My boots became covered with mud, and my legs got wet to my knees. What made it worse was the way Matt darted up inclines like a member of some elite fighting force. Slow down, I wanted to tell him. Couldn't he see how I was struggling along in my sweaty clothes and muddy boots, grabbing for limbs and vines for support? Did he care? Worse still, Sancho and Kodak weren't even breathing hard. How could that be? Sancho had a bum leg. They were both heavy smokers. I wasn't, and yet I was the one breathing like I'd come off a treadmill.

"How big is this island?" I asked Matt, hoping to slow him down.

"I told you already. Fifty square kilometers."

"I have no idea what that means."

"About eight miles long by four or five miles wide. You need a break?"

I did but said I was fine, and we were trudging on when something snarled. An angry snarl. Like a cat ready to fight. Matt held up his hand. I stopped. Kodak said, "What the devil?"

Then came that damn shriek again.

The jungle fell so quiet I could hear the caws of seabirds on the water.

"Just another bird," Matt said.

"What about the snarl?"

"Howler monkeys. Let's go."

There was movement on the right. And then a shower of small stones and broken pottery began falling around us like a sudden hail storm.

CHAPTER 57

Kodak whipped out his pistol. Matt and Sancho swung this way and that with their AKs. I hurried to Matt's side with my machete.

We waited and watched, crouched down like soldiers.

Twigs snapped. Limbs shook in nearby trees. I caught a glimpse of something through the thicket. And it was blue. Was it that damn jungle woman with her spear? Was that why I felt so weak and disoriented?

There were splashes of water and more snarls. More stones and potsherds too. Damn it. Why hadn't I brought a gun?

Sancho noisily racked a round into his AK. "Come on, come on," he yelled into the jungle. "We've got AKs. We've got grenades. We'll blow your hairy asses to pieces."

He turned to Matt as if asking for permission. Matt said, "Warning shots only. Keep it high." I dropped to the ground with my hands over my ears, which I'd done many times with the Sandinistas. Sancho straightened up and fired into the trees, hosing the jungle left to right.

Bark splintered off trees. A limb fell. Foliage shredded in front of us.

The shooting ended. A blessed silence came over us. I straightened up. The air around us was filled with the acrid smells of gunfire, blending with the fog. I saw no signs of whatever had been out there. Only the fog, the splintered tree bark, and a few leaves drifting down like autumn. Sancho popped another clip into his AK. Matt laid a hand on his arm.

"*Ya basta*," he said. "They got the message."

"Who got the message?" I asked.

Matt didn't answer. We waited and watched, staring into trees and underbrush, my heart in my throat. I wasn't cut out for this kind of work. Investigative reporters were supposed to be bold, assertive, and kick-ass. But I wasn't an investigative reporter. I was a broadcast journalist. My job was to get all prettied up and face the camera from a desk in a nice, air-conditioned studio and report the news others had gathered, not lie face down in the dirt and mud of a jungle, praying for my life. I'd already done that with the Sandinistas.

God, what a coward I'd become. Only minutes ago, I'd been Ernest Hemingway, all pumped up to get a story on magic mushrooms.

Now all I wanted was a boat to Ometepe.

There were no more snarls. No more stones or shrieks or movement in the trees. The smell of gunfire faded. The jungle came back to life with the usual hoots and chirrs.

"Howler monkeys," Matt said again. "They don't like intruders."

"Oh, come on. Since when do howlers throw stones?"

"They've been known to poop on people."

"That wasn't poop, Matt." I picked up a piece of broken pottery and showed him. "See. Do you think a bunch of monkeys trekked up to the ruins with their baskets and gathered broken pottery just to throw at us? This isn't *Planet of the Apes*."

"Hell no," Kodak said. "Monkeys can't do that. We used to eat howlers for breakfast during the war. Right, Adriana? Mix them with that puta

Bulgarian spaghetti. I know what howlers look like. I know how they taste. I know how they sound…and those things out there are NOT howlers." He looked at Sancho. "Right, Sancho? You ate howler spaghetti too."

Sancho looked away. Matt shrugged. I knew he was lying, and I would have interrogated him right there if I hadn't been so anxious to get out of that damn jungle. "Come on," he said. "We can talk about this later."

The trail grew steeper. There were forks, washed-out gullies, and downed trees, everything green, lush, and dripping. Birds, monkeys, and insects kept up their commotion, lost amid the foliage. The adrenaline that had driven me wore off. Exhaustion came back, and I began to feel like the horse that collapsed beneath Scarlett during her flight from Atlanta. Would this torment never end?

"How much farther?" I asked Matt.

"Almost there."

"You said fifteen minutes."

"That was before I learned about washouts and downed trees."

I stopped. Matt turned to face me. "What's wrong?"

"Everything. Storms, shrieking birds, tomb robbers. And now those things that attacked us. Why can't you just tell us what they were."

"They didn't attack us, Adriana. They were trying to scare us away."

"They? What do you mean by 'they?' What are they? Who are they?"

"It's a long story. It's complicated. I'll tell you when we get to the landing. Now come on."

CHAPTER 58

We emerged into the sunlight on a hill overlooking the lake. Fishy smells rose to greet us. A blessedly cool breeze blew off the water. Sancho and Kodak sank to the ground and stretched out on their backs. They looked as wretched as I did in our sweaty clothes.

I stood there a moment with Matt, scanning the water for sight of Catia's boat. Nothing. Only swarms of seabirds and dark, distant mountains. Matt pointed down to the water's edge, only about a hundred yards distance. "I'm pretty sure that's where they'll dock, between those boulder formations."

"Is that another Occam's Razor conclusion?"

"It's the only place that makes sense."

"Why wouldn't they dock in a secluded place like we did?"

"Their boat's bigger. They can't maneuver around rock formations. Too dangerous. Besides, they've got loads of equipment. Can you imagine them hauling it up here through the jungle? Catia's so self-centered she's got an entire suitcase of makeup."

"How do you know so much about her makeup?"

"Please, Baby, let's don't start that again."

"Okay, they land down there. They unload their equipment. Then what happens? Do we just march down and surprise them?"

"No, Adriana. We do what we came to do."

"Which is what? Remind me again."

"We take pictures and follow them to the cave."

"Seriously, Matt? You think they're going to just invite us to go along?"

"Of course not. We'll have to do it clandestinely. We can hide over there, near the monsters."

"Monsters?" I tried to look into his eyes, through his aviator glasses, for a sign he was joking.

"Come on. I'll show you."

"No, no, no, Matt. You're weaseling out of your promise. You said you'd explain those things in the jungle. I'm waiting."

He reached over and brushed plant debris out of my hair. "It's a long, complicated story."

"You said that already. Just tell me."

"Can't. Not right now. We need to worry about Catia's boat. Let's set up the camera. Then I'll explain. Come on, everybody. Let's go."

He hiked away. Sancho and Kodak struggled up, grumbling like they'd spent the day digging trenches in the hot sun. "Just like the damn military," Kodak said, "hurry up and wait."

Matt ignored the comment, and we followed him along the ridge to the toppled ruins of two ancient stone statues. They were enormous, at least about ten feet in length, half-human, and half-crocodile, partially buried at an angle, and as broken and battered as I felt.

"Sentinels," Matt said. "Placed here to guard the landing."

I walked around the statues for a better look. They were all teeth and snarls, as ugly as creatures in a horror movie. In my mind, I knew such creatures didn't exist and had never existed. But why did the natives who lived here carve their likeness into stone? What about the "eyewitness" accounts of humans and animals ripped to pieces?

"Can't we find somewhere else to wait?"

"This is the best place. It's got bushes and boulders for cover."

"What happened to these statues? Why are they so busted?"

"Spaniards. They killed the natives and destroyed everything—the statues, the temple, the entire city. It's right over there, behind that hill. It has more statues. If necessary, we can spend the night there."

"In the open?"

"No, Adriana, there are places with shelter."

Sancho, who'd been listening, stepped closer. "Not to worry about these monsters. They've passed on, ceased to be, gone to monster heaven. I would call them ex-monsters except for one thing."

"What one thing?"

"Because at midnight they come aliiiiive."

"Really, Sancho? And what do they do at midnight?"

"You'll find out if we spend the night in the ruins." He burst into faux madman laughter.

I rolled my eyes and unhitched my pack, grateful to be out of the jungle. Lake birds cawed and circled above us. Some dove into the water. Waves splashed against boulders, creating little rainbows in the spray, and if I'd had a change of clothing and wasn't scared of sharks or monsters I might have gone down for a bath.

Matt and Sancho began hacking limbs off bushes and piling them around us for camouflage. I offered to help. Matt said, no, that I should rest, so I sank to the ground and watched.

"What if they don't come?" I asked Matt.

He tossed another limb on the pile and wiped his face. "If they're not here by dark, we'll know we're at the wrong place."

"Dark? I'm not going back into that jungle after dark."

"Let's hope it doesn't come to that."

He went back to work. Kodak lit a cigarette and set up the tripod in a patch of palmettos. I could tell from the way he kept glancing behind us that he was as spooked as I was. He stepped over and spoke in a faint voice. I expected to hear his analysis of what happened in the jungle. Instead, he put on that pathetic puppy-dog face of a broken-hearted lover.

"Nora was only fourteen when we met."

"Nora? Who is Nora?"

"*Por Dios,* Miami, haven't you been listening? Don't you pay attention? I'm talking about my little flower girl."

"You never said her name was Nor."

"Eleanora. We called her Flower Girl. You'd have liked her."

"Why would I have liked her?"

"Because everything about her was poetic—her face, her shiny raven-colored hair, her dark Indian eyes, her trim figure, her smile." He took a deep breath. "Oh, God, that smile. Even her name sounds poetic. Just listen to the rhythm. Eleanora Bermudez-Durán. Hear how it flows?"

He choked up. I gave him a moment and asked, "How old were you?"

"Same as you. Sixteen."

"I was fifteen."

"Fifteen? Christ, we were kids back then."

"Where was Nora from?"

"Diriomo. She was so loving. We took our vows right there in the jungle, beside a gurgling stream."

He sighed and shut his eyes, and when he spoke it was as if he had transported himself back to the stream. "I can still hear its trickle. It was in a cool, shady spot beneath the Ceiba trees. We called it the River of Magic. There were orchids in the trees. Songbirds, too. All assorted colors. They sang for us. And then my sweet little flower girl—God, how I miss her—she put her hand over my heart. She promised to love me to the end of time. And then we… well, you know…"

"She didn't get pregnant?"

His eyes opened. His expression grew tortured. "Too much stress. Not enough nutrition. Too much fighting. Too much grief. I tried to comfort her by reading Neruda to her, but my little book of love poems got destroyed by a gringo bomb."

His voice trailed off. He choked up again. I thought his imaginary messages were touching and told him so. "You must have been inspired by all the Ceiba trees on this island."

"I can't even look at Ceibas without thinking of her."

A rumble of thunder broke the spell. And then, as if awakened by thunder, the things in the jungle began howling and yipping like wolves and coyotes.

CHAPTER 59

Matt and Sancho stopped their work. "You hear that?" Kodak said. "You think that's animals? Hell, no, those sounds are as phony as the Rolexes they sell in the Masaya market."

"What do you think they are?"

"Humans. The contras used to do that too."

"You're saying they're contras?"

"All I know is I'd rather be toting grenades than this damn camera." He stepped so close I could smell jungle on his clothes. "What's going on with you and the gringo? Sometimes you look like you want to kill him; other times you look like you're ready to go off into the bushes with him?"

I didn't answer.

"Okay, you don't want to talk about it. Fine. Let's talk about the assassination." He took a long cancerous drag on his cigarette, ground it out with his boot, and looked in Matt's direction again. "You realize he's lying to us, don't you? Sancho is also lying."

"Why do you say that?"

"Look, Adriana, I may not be as educated as you, but I'm not stupid. Gringo knows what was stalking us back there. He also knows about the assassination. He knew something bad was going to happen. He called you in advance. He called me. We both saw the shooting. Now we're in a shit load of trouble just for being there. Ask the gringo. He knows a lot more than he's telling us. Ask him, Adriana."

Kodak was right. It was time to get answers. Matt realized it too and was heading toward us when his mobile buzzed. He muttered something I didn't catch and stepped back toward the jungle. I swung my Canon in his direction, thinking this was a good chance to film him clandestinely.

"Put that damn camera down," Sancho barked at me.

"Don't be such a jerk. I'm not including it in the report."

I stuck out my tongue like a kid and took pictures anyway. Matt noticed and grinned for the camera. When the conversation ended, he settled in beside me, sitting with his back against a stone monster. "I'm sorry for dragging you out here," he said.

"So why did you?"

"Do you even have to ask? Hasn't it dawned on you that I can't get over you? All I can think about is—" His phone buzzed. "Christ, not again." He stood up and trod away.

Kodak got our camera rolling. He panned the landing, the lake, the statues, and the jungle. I pinned on the mic, brushed myself off, and said a few words about the place and why we were waiting. I ended it by rubbing my hand over the crocodile head of the nearest statue. "You're a good monster, aren't you? Please don't come alive at midnight."

By then, Matt had finished his phone call and was having a hushed conversation with Sancho. Afterward, he sat back down beside me.

"Tell me what you saw back there," he said. "Human or animal?"

"I don't know what I saw. It was just a glimpse—and it was blue."

"Kodak needs to hear this too. I'll explain in Spanish."

"What about Sancho?"

"Sancho already knows. He can stand guard while we talk."

We motioned for Kodak and the three of us sank to the ground with our backs against the monsters. Matt pushed back his cap and mopped his brow. "Remember back when they discovered Japanese holdouts from the war? It was mid-seventies. Soldiers from World War Two. They were still hiding on Pacific islands, not realizing the war was over."

"You're saying those things back there are old Japanese soldiers?"

"No, Adriana. There are no Japanese soldiers on this island. What I'm saying is it's a similar situation. When did you guys kick out Somoza?"

"July of '79. I was fifteen. Kodak was sixteen."

"Right, you marched into Managua just like Castro in Havana, flags flying, people cheering. Somoza and his family and mistress fled to the US with all their stolen money. But what about his henchmen? The top dogs and the criminals. What happened to them?"

Sancho, who'd been listening, stepped over. "Got away, the bastards. Should have lined them against a wall and shot them like Castro did. But no, the US opened the gates for them. So did Spain. Shame on the US. Shame on Spain. Gringos backed the wrong side. They always do."

I glared up at him. "Aren't you supposed to be standing guard?"

He made his mouth-zipping motion and backed away.

Matt shook his head and smiled as if to say Sancho was just being Sancho. "The US and Spain didn't welcome them all. Some were so bad—like the murderers and drug dealers—that they'd have been imprisoned or extradited back to Nicaragua."

"So, what happened to them?"

"Some were shot. Some thrown into a dungeon. Others came here."

"Here? This island? This place?"

Kodak glanced back into the jungle. “Shit. I knew they weren’t howler monkeys. They’re probably watching us right now.”

“Hold on,” Matt said. “Let me finish. It gets even more interesting. It wasn’t only Somoza’s thugs. The Sandinistas emptied the prisons. Remember? Most were political prisoners. But in the confusion they released real criminals.”

I slapped my thigh. “And you’re saying they’re also out here?”

“Only a few. Most were recaptured.”

“Why are you grinning? Are you enjoying this?”

“No. Adriana. Back in ’79, before Somoza fell, someone had the bright idea to clean out the local asylum. It was a horrible place. No medical care, people naked, hungry, sick, caged like animals. They herded them onto those shabby little plywood boats. Intention was to sink them in the lake, get rid of them. They did the same to beggars and the homeless.

“Rumors. That’s what the government claimed.”

“Maybe. Maybe not. What we do know is not all the so-called crazies were crazy. There was mutiny and bloodshed. Not all the boats sank. Some made it to this island.”

Sancho, who was loitering close enough to hear the conversation, burst into laughter. If that wasn’t bad enough, the crazies and the criminals in the jungle began howling and yipping again.

CHAPTER 60

Sancho held up his fingers and began counting.

"One…two…three…four."

"What are you doing?" I asked.

"Hush, just listen." He waited for the yipping to stop. "I count four."

"How can you tell it's only four?"

"Because I'm part Indian. Indians have special powers. Look at me. Look at my nose and dark skin. Look at my beautiful dark eyes that drive the señoritas crazy."

"Oh, really, Geronimo. Almost everyone in Nicaragua has Indian blood. Look at me. Look at my dark eyes and black hair. My mom wasn't exactly descended from Vikings. My only special power is to know you two have been lying from the beginning."

"No, no, no. Just listen. Kodak will back me up. Back in my army days, they trained me to interpret enemy signs. It was my specialty. You know, things like footprints. Sounds. Abandoned campsites. Smells. I could count contras in any number of ways. Right, Kodak?"

"Tell her about the latrines."

"Spare me. Just tell me how you count the crazies by their howls?"

"Piece of cake. Didn't you take music appreciation in college?"

"What does music appreciation have to do with the crazies?"

"Everything. Remember how they did it? They'd play different instruments for you. They'd play a flute, a cello, piano, violin, a harp, a piccolo. Sometimes they even do an inspired pizzicato. Do you know what pizzicato means?"

"Just get on with it."

"It's plucking the strings of a violin. Then they'd do clarinets and trumpets, or tubas, cymbals, and on and on. Once you learned the sound of each, they'd test you by playing a beautiful classical piece like, umm, Tchaikovsky's 1912 Overture."

"It's 1812, Sancho. Tchaikovsky wasn't even alive in 1912."

"Whatever. I can hear it now. Just listen." He closed his eyes and moved his head as if in a trance. "Hear it? Listen to Tchaikovsky. His music is in the trees and the lake and the clouds and all around. Hear it? The thunderous arrangement of the piano. The contrasting dynamics. The sudden lingering violin. The modulations and transposition. And then…then the boom of the cannon. Oh, yes, the boom. The horses, the charging men with fixed bayonets. The smoke of the battlefield."

I stared at him. Was he acting or was he a true aficionado of classical music? I touched his arm. "Sancho, are you okay?"

His eyes opened. "Sorry. I got carried away. Anyhow, they'd stop at certain sounds and ask you to identify the instruments."

"What does that have to do with yips and howls?"

"Can't you see it? Even an amateur like you should figure it out."

"Do you have a death wish?"

"Okay, if they start again, just listen. Listen to the pitch, the intonation. A man and a woman makes the yips. Two people, each has a different sound. Same with the howls, two people but with slightly different sounds, both male. There might have been a fifth person."

Sancho's talents should have intrigued me, but the more he explained, the more he annoyed me. I turned to Matt. "Let me see if I have this straight. You knew this place was teeming with crazies and criminals. You knew it was dangerous. Yet you brought us out here anyway. No warning. No explanation. What were you thinking?"

"Now hold on a second. Calm down and I'll explain."

"Don't you tell me to calm down! There's a hurricane in the Caribbean! Then you've got snakes and giant killer birds and chichicaste and tomb looters and crazies in the jungle, and God knows what else."

"You'll get a great story out of it."

"Are you serious? Our lives are more important than a story. An hour ago, you'd almost convinced me to come along for the story. But now, now, I don't give a damn about effing mushrooms. Not any longer. Do magic mushrooms even exist, or were you lying about that too?"

"Did I hear you right? Did you say effing?"

"I'm just being polite." I stood and brushed off the seat of my khakis. "I want to go back. Can we leave? Please. Now."

All three men looked from me to each other. Matt said, "You didn't let me finish. Things aren't as bad as you think."

"Oh, really? How can they get any worse?"

"Just sit back down and I'll tell you."

I sank down again with my back against the statue, arms crossed in front. Matt said, "Keep in mind it's been twelve years since those people came out here. Twelve years."

Sancho stepped closer. "More like fifteen."

Matt shot him a shut-up look. Sancho made his mouth-zipping gesture. Matt turned back to me. "As I was saying they've been out here twelve years. Many were old even back then. Some had disabilities. Some were mentally deficient and in poor health. There were alcoholics, drug addicts, and street thugs. They weren't equipped to survive in a place like this. Most died already or were killed fighting over the women."

"Women?"

"Some were pretty. And you know what happens when women are mix with volatile Latin men. Then there was Yaritza, a real stunner."

"Yaritza? The Yaritza? The one that hijacked a truck?"

"The same. She also stabbed a military officer."

"What did the officer do to her?"

"Same thing Somoza's soldiers did to lots of pretty girls."

I stiffened, remembering what they did to me. "They should have given her a medal."

"A lot of people thought so. But she escaped. Went on a killing rampage. They locked her up again. She escaped and ended up out here."

"Here? Yaritza is on this island?"

"Let me finish. When she first came here, there weren't enough women. Men fought and killed each other. Only the strongest survived."

"How do you know this?"

"The army. They came out here and swept across the island. Captured Yaritza. I read the transcript of her interrogation."

He rattled on and on about Yaritza and what a knockout she was and her bad experiences with men, and as I listened, I thought her story wasn't that different from what I'd witnessed as a soldier—the men slugging it out over pretty girls in uniform, cursing, shouting, rolling on the ground, getting bloody. Other troops egging them on, taking bets on who would win, the girls exchanging glances and saying how stupid men were.

"So, how many survivors are left?"

"Yaritza said no more than a dozen. That was two years ago. They're scared and pathetic."

"Dozen loonies can be dangerous," Kodak said. "People get murdered out here all the time. I've seen pictures. Bodies ripped to pieces."

"Yaritza said it was feral dogs."

Oh, great, I thought. Dogs too.

Matt said, "They've gone native."

"Native dogs? What does that mean?"

"Not the dogs, Baby. I'm talking about Yaritza and her friends. They live in caves. Yaritza's the only healthy one. She's sane."

"Sane? She's a serial killer, Matt."

"She only kills bad guys."

"How would she know we're not bad guys?"

"She knows. That's why they say she has special powers."

"Who is she anyway? Where does she come from?"

"No one knows. There's no record of her background."

By then I was ready to pull out my hair and run screaming into the lake. But before I could ask another question, Sancho shouted, "Boat!"

CHAPTER 61

Matt told us to keep out of sight. He punched a number on his mobile and spoke to someone in English. "Target contact. ETA twenty-thirty minutes. What's the latest on the hurricane?"

He listened, said, "Roger that," and snapped his mobile shut.

"What about the hurricane?" I asked.

"Same as before. Landfall in Honduras, couple hundred miles north."

"When?"

"Tonight?"

"What if it comes this way?"

"Most we'll get are outer bands."

"Dammit, Matt, how can you say that? Hurricanes are unpredictable."

"Worse comes to worse, we'll shelter in the ruins."

I slapped my knee and tried to calm down. Blue crazies. Tomb looters. Hurricane on the way. And a boat carrying the woman I despised.

It drifted in on a swell of water, birds swarming over the boat, black clouds in the distance, flashes of lightning. Matt was right about one thing: Their boat was larger and boxier than ours, like it was made for comfort.

"Get in position," Matt said. "No jerky movements."

Kodak got our camera rolling. I lay on my stomach and watched through Matt's binoculars. The boat landed. A dark-skinned man in green pants and T-shirt jumped off and secured the boat to a boulder. A pistol was strapped to his hip. He helped another man and woman down with their cameras and equipment. Both wore baggy khakis.

Next came a muscular young man in a striped blue and white pullover. He had blonde hair and looked like a fitness trainer. Even before Matt said it, I knew it was Catia's boyfriend. Had she stolen him too?

And there she came, the bitch: khakis, hiking shoes, and a white blouse unbuttoned at the top. She wore dangling earrings and bracelets and was carrying a blue suitcase as delicately as if it contained her makeup kit.

Even from a distance, I could see she had eyes like Morocco and the boobs of a stripper. The boys at school used to say she was beautiful because of her long raven hair and the way she'd smile with her puffy kissable lips. They also said she was easy, and there were stories she'd take on two or three at a time.

Slut!

"Zoom in on her," I said to Kodak.

"Which one?"

"Blue suitcase."

"You want me to film the blue suitcase?"

"No, Kodak, focus on the woman with dark hair and big boobs."

"How do you know that's Catia?"

"Because the other is blonde."

Catia brushed back her hair and used a hand mirror to check her makeup. She puckered her lips and turned her head this way and that. What a vain little bitch. She was probably drenched in enough perfume to keep away the mosquitos. She waited for the others to set up their camera on a tripod and then marched inland like a Spanish conquistador ready to plant the Cross.

My hatred grew at each step.

She stopped next to a large boulder, sniffed the air, and wrinkled her nose like the fishy smells offended her. Her hair blew just enough for her to keep pushing it back. Then she dramatically swiveled toward the camera. Her words drifted on the breeze. I couldn't hear everything, but I heard enough to know she was narrating her report in French.

French, mind you. She was too snooty to speak English or Spanish.

Kodak touched my shoulder. "What do you think she's saying?"

"All about herself: 'I came. I saw. I conquered. I'm hot stuff.'"

"You sound like you know her."

"Maybe I do."

"Oh, my God," Kodak said. "Look at that."

"Look at what?"

"Camera in her boyfriend's hand. It's a Hasselblad. Looks like a Model 500. Expensive. Do you know how much those things cost? I always wanted a Hasselblad."

"Just keep your camera focused."

A rumble of thunder shook the ground. Catia stopped her narration. The wind picked up. The water became choppy. The clouds grew darker. They ended their filming and began unloading bags, boxes, and suitcases. Kodak said, "Look what those idiots did with the Hasselblad. Left it atop the blue suitcase where it could get wet. We're talking five, ten, fifteen, or twenty-thousand dollars for a camera like that. And they expose it to lake and rainwater. What are they thinking?"

I turned to Matt. "Why don't we go to the ruins now?"

"Best to stay here and watch. It'll take them a couple of hours."

"It'll be dark in a couple of hours. We should look for shelter. I don't want to be struck by lightning when that storm hits."

"We'll be okay. I told you we can find shelter in the ruins."

"What is it you're not telling me?"

"Tomb robbers. We can't see them if we're at the ruins."

The words had scarcely left his mouth when Sancho, who was also scanning the lake with binoculars, said, "Second boat."

I heard the boat's drone before I saw it. Catia and her crew also noticed. Matt pulled out his mobile and began reporting to the embassy.

"*Mierda*," Sancho said. "That boat's going to panic them."

The tomb robbers must have realized it too because they turned their boat away as if to pass the island.

Matt put away his mobile. "Come on! This could get ugly."

"Come on where?"

"Our boat? They'll see it. We need to camouflage it."

"We already camouflaged it."

"Not from the lake side."

"Seriously, Matt? It's getting dark. We're going back into that jungle?"

"Sorry, Baby, we've got to do it."

CHAPTER 62

We splashed back down through jungle and slippery ravines, Sancho and Matt in front with their AKs, Kodak in back with our camera. It was downhill and would have been easy except for the darkness beneath the trees and my fear we'd round a bend and come face to face with blue-painted lunatics with spears and monkey teeth.

We didn't. No howls or rock throwing either, and were almost at our boat when Kodak tripped and went face down over a small embankment.

"*Puta madre*," he yelled. "Chichicaste got me."

"Don't rub it. Splash water over it."

Matt and Sancho didn't see what happened. They were already aboard the *Ana Maria*, frantically pulling down limbs and vines to camouflage the boat from the lakeside. Kodak plunged into the water as if possessed by demons, cursing and screaming.

"Are you crazy?" I yelled. "The sharks will get you."

"Better sharks than this shit!"

He continued to splash around like a madman. I couldn't see our boat because of the thick jungle foliage and was thinking to yell for Matt when that damn bird shrieked like it was coming for me again.

I turned around and there stood the blue people, all feathers, monkey teeth necklaces, scraggly hair, clubs, and wooden spears.

The bird was there too, perched on a low-hanging limb.

I couldn't scream. Couldn't breathe. Couldn't run to the boat either. They had me backed against the embankment that dropped down to the water Jump, my mind told me. Get into the lake with Kodak.

But I didn't. I was paralyzed with fear.

One of them babbled like a crazy man. His rotten teeth and a bone dangling from his long greasy hair made him even scarier. He danced around and poked me with his spear, coming so close I smelled his rancid breath. I raised my hands in surrender and would have dropped to my knees except the only female in the group stepped forward and shoved him away.

"Stop," she said. "Leave her alone. She's mine."

The man puffed himself up and spat on the ground. The woman shoved him away and turned back to me. Not until then did it register in my panicked mind that she was the blue jungle woman in my vision—a spear in her hand, long dark hair erupting from her head like lava.

Was this Yaritza? Was this another vision?

The others—all men—were older and scrawny as scarecrows.

The woman pressed her spear against my throat. In desperation, I grabbed it with both hands. The others came running up to help, and I'm sure I'd have ended up like a spear pincushion if it hadn't been for Kodak.

He dragged himself out of the lake looking like *The Creature from the Black Lagoon*, drenched and covered with green algae, cursing and slapping at his arms.

The blues dashed away like spooked deer. The bird followed. Kodak, still mumbling and cursing, recovered his camera and began brushing off the dirt. He hadn't seen the blue crazies. Neither had Matt and Sancho.

"Get to the boat," I yelled to Kodak, trying to find my voice. "Hurry!"

"No," Matt answered from the boat. "Stay up there."

"Blue crazies," I yelled back.

"What?"

"I SAID BLUE PEOPLE. THEY'RE HERE."

Matt came off the boat with his AK. "Where?"

"Gone already. They scared me. Backed me against the embankment."

"How many?"

"I don't know. Five or six. One was a woman."

"Woman? How old?"

"I didn't ask her, Matt. She looked about my age. Maybe younger."

"Christ. You sure?"

"She got right in my face. I could smell her."

"What did she smell like?"

"Like us, Matt. Sweaty. She had flowers in her hair."

"How was she dressed?"

"Cutoffs and T-shirt. No bra."

"Was she fat? Skinny? Ugly?"

"What difference does it make?"

"Please, Baby. It's important. I'll explain later."

"You always say you'll explain later. You never do."

"The boat's coming. There's no time."

"She wasn't fat. Not skinny either. She'd be pretty if she cleaned up?"

From his jerky motions, I could tell he was as concerned as I was.

"Which way did they go?"

"That way." I pointed to the trail that led to the landing.

"You okay now?"

"No, I'm not okay."

He handed me his AK. "You know how to shoot this thing?"

"Did you forget I was in the army?"

"That was fifteen years ago."

"Makes no difference. I can still shoot it."

He pointed at the spot where the bird had attacked the snake. "That's the best place to set up the camera. You've got a clear view of the lake. We need good footage of Ramos when they pass. Can you do that?"

"Are you out of your friggin' mind? What if the crazies come back?"

"They won't, and even if they do, they're harmless. Don't shoot them."

"How can you say that? If they're harmless, why give me an AK?"

"So, you'll feel better. Okay? There could be gunfire."

"Gunfire? Are you serious?"

"They're killers, Adriana. Murderers."

"You just said they're harmless."

"I'm talking about Ramos and his thugs, not the blue people."

By then we could hear the drone of the tomb looters' boat. "Shit," Matt said. "Gotta go. Get that camera rolling. Keep out of sight."

He hurried back into the foliage and jumped aboard the boat.

"What are you going to do?" I yelled to his back.

Sancho answered for him. "They're war criminals, Adriana. Nobody's going to miss them." He picked up a weapon that looked like a sawed-off shotgun with a big barrel. "M-79 grenade launcher."

"You're going to ambush them?"

"It's either them or us. Now stay down and keep quiet!"

CHAPTER 63

I sank next to Kodak, my heart racing, thudding in my head. What to do? Blue crazies in the jungle. Tomb looters with AK-47s. Snakes and killer birds. Now the threat of gunfire. What a nightmare! I'd seen killings before, but aside from the time when I wore a Sandinista uniform, I'd been there as a field reporter, never as a participant. But now…now, I was part of a team that was going to do the killing.

Kodak touched my arm. His face, all red and swollen from chichicaste, looked like he'd been attacked by killer bees. "What's happening?"

"You didn't see them?"

"See who?"

"The blue people?"

"I got water in my ears. Can't hear very well. What's happening?"

"They're going to ambush the tomb robbers."

He moaned and cursed some more. "What a pile of monkey shit. We've got more damn problems than Jason and the Astronauts."

"Argonauts."

"Whatever. We're in enough trouble already. How are we going to explain another shooting?"

"Just get the camera rolling. Are you okay?"

"No, I'm not okay. This shit burns like hell. Itches too."

"Don't scratch. It'll make it worse."

"Can you see them? I can barely see."

"I hear them. Be sure to film the boat."

"Gringo said not to film the boat."

"I'm talking about the tomb looters' boat, not ours."

"A video can be used as evidence against us."

"Just do what I say. We can destroy the video if we don't like it."

"Fine, you're the boss." He took out his pistol and handed it to me.

"What's this for?"

"Damn it, Adriana, don't you understand anything? I'm going to be busy with the camera. I can't see behind me. I don't want those blue crazies sneaking up on us from the rear."

"They were already here."

"What?"

"I SAID BLUE PEOPLE WERE ALREADY HERE."

"What? You're saying those crazy blue bastards were here?"

"Bird too. They're gone now. GONE."

"*Mierda*. We need to get on the boat."

"Gringo wants us to stay here."

"Gringo's fucking crazy. I'm getting on the boat."

"There's going to be gunfire. Gringo says we're safer here."

"How can it be safer here than on the boat?"

"Gringo says the blue people are harmless."

I picked up the AK, popped out the magazine, checked to see that it was loaded, and snapped it back in. Then I rolled over and glanced around the way I used to do with the Sandinistas—left and right and into the trees, listening and watching for movement, my senses on full alert.

"Adriana!" Matt yelled. "You and Kodak okay?"

"I'm scared."

"Just keep your heads down. Stay alert. They're almost here."

The buzz of their boat was louder now, getting closer. Through the thicket, I caught a glimpse of the bow. It rounded the point and came so close I could make out the name on their boat—*El Tiburón*, the Shark. It looked as sleek and powerful as our boat, like it was made for speed.

Sancho aimed his grenade launcher.

I figured I'd already used up my credits with St Peter, but I prayed anyway, silently. Please, dear God. *Please don't involve me in another killing.*

The drone of their engine stopped. I tried to calm myself by breathing deeply, in and out. Oh. God, how did I get into this mess?

Kodak crossed himself. "Gringo gonna shoot?"

"I don't know what the gringo's going to do."

The boat drifted closer. I sank lower. This was like during the war. Danger behind us, danger in front, danger in the trees, panic in my head.

"What's happening?" Kodak asked. "My eyesight's gone to hell."

"Can you keep the camera on them?"

"Camera is on them."

"How do you know if you can't see?"

"I'm not fucking blind, Miami. I asked what's happening."

I lifted my head and peeked around the tree. "Five men in camouflage clothing, all sunglasses, guns, and boots, scanning the shoreline. And don't call me Miami."

"What about the blue people?"

"Gone."

"What's the gringo doing?"

"Don't know. Sancho's the only one I can see."

"Can you check behind me? I'm worried about the loonies."

"I just checked. There's nothing."

"I got a bad feeling they're in the trees."

"Just keep the camera focused."

The seconds ticked by. If Sancho was going to shoot, now was the time. Ramos was ugly as ever, with the kind of face that only a blind person could love. His old pock-faced sergeant was there too, the one who'd beaten my mother to death—and in an instant it all came back: the screams, the terror, the violence, the foulness of Ramos' breath as he hovered over me, tearing at my Sacred Heart uniform.

That son of a bitch! That low-life bastard!

I racked a round into the AK. *Kill the bastards*! I wanted to yell.

"You're blocking the camera," Kodak hissed. "They'll see you."

I hoped they did. I wanted Ramos to recognize me in the seconds before we riddled the bastard with bullets. I aimed. My hand was on the trigger when Matt suddenly appeared, gesturing for me to get down. The motor kicked in again. The boat sliced through the water, its bow up. Then they were out of sight, lost amid the foliage.

What was wrong with me? One minute I was a little wimp, begging the Almighty to spare them; the next I was Rambo.

Matt sprang out of the thicket with his AK and raced up the trail, boots pounding. I trotted behind him. He stopped at the edge of the cliff, grabbed a small tree for support, and leaned out as far as he could. "Still going!" he yelled down to Sancho.

"Did they see us?" I asked Matt.

"Don't know. Why did you stand up?"

"To shoot the bastards. Why did you let them get away?"

"They didn't get away. They're heading to a landing on the north side."

"How do you know that?"

"Logic." He made his way back along the trail and glanced down at Kodak, whose face had grown even more swollen and distorted. "What happened to him?"

"Chichicaste. He needs medication."

Matt squatted down next to him. "Why are your clothes wet?"

"Jumped into the lake to stop the itching."

"How's your breathing?"

"Breathing fine. Eyesight not so good."

"Christ. Did you film them?"

"I think so. Got them the second they rounded the point."

He helped Kodak onto the boat and out of his shirt. Then he poured water over his head and arms. He also gave him eye drops, treated his face and arms with a Cortisone ointment, and sent him into the cabin to change out of his wet clothes.

"How about you?" he asked me. "Are you okay now?"

"Do I look okay?"

"You always look okay. Tell me about that woman you saw."

CHAPTER 64

I pushed an overhanging limb out of my way, wiped debris off a deck chair, and sat down with my AK pointed toward the jungle. "What's so important about the woman?"

"I'll explain after you tell me."

"No, Matt. Tell me now."

"Please, Adriana. I don't have all the answers. We're working on it."

"We? Who is we?"

He held up his cell phone. "Contacts at the embassy."

Again, I conjured up the image of a bunch of gringo nerds with headphones in a dark basement, turning knobs and plugging things into sockets. Matt waved his hand in front of my face. "I'm waiting."

"Look, there were five or six of them. Okay? All armed with spears. All with monkey teeth beads. The men were scrawny, white-haired, and stooped. Toothless too. Bones in their greasy hair. One had crossed eyes. The bird that ate the snake was there too."

"The woman. She's the one I want to know about."

"Why don't you care about the men?"

"Please, Adriana. Can you just cooperate?"

"All I remember is she was young."

"How young?"

"Mid-twenties. Thirty at most."

"What else?"

"Healthy looking. Dark hair, white teeth, firm breasts."

"Attractive?"

"I told you already. Get her out of those rags, give her a good scrubbing, send her to a spa, get her into a nice dress, and men would be tripping all over themselves."

Matt turned to Sancho. "What do you think?"

"Bingo," Sancho said. "If it's got feathers and looks like a duck, quacks like a duck, and walks like a duck then it's a duck."

I turned to him. "What's that supposed to mean?"

"Ask the gringo."

Matt shook his head like Sancho was hopeless. "Remember what I told you about Yaritza?"

"Are you saying that woman was Yaritza?"

"It's a long story."

"Everything with you is a long story."

He drew in a deep breath. "Look, just let me finish. Okay?"

"No, dammit, I want to know why you left us with a serial killer."

"She doesn't kill women, not unless they're after her."

"She could have killed Kodak."

"No reason to kill Kodak."

"How do you know? Maybe she thinks we came out here to bag her?"

"No, Adriana. You came face to face with her. If she was going to harm you, you'd be skewered to a tree. Kodak too. Just listen. Okay?"

"This better be good."

"If it was her, she's been out here for twelve years, living like Tarzan."

"Thirteen years," said Sancho.

"Okay, thirteen years."

"Wait. Hold on. You said the army captured her two years ago."

"Correct. They cleaned her up, got the blue off her, and got her into nice clothes. Looked like a model. Beautiful white teeth, dark hair, nice shape. Amazing she looked so good after living out here so long. But here's the shocker. She's not young."

"How old?"

"Would you believe sixty?"

"The woman I saw wasn't sixty."

"Fingerprints don't lie."

A rumble of thunder shook the boat, followed by a few drops of rain. It was also getting dark. "We should get into the cabin," Matt said.

"Wait. You said they put her in prison. How could she be out here?"

"All I said was they captured her. Never said they put her into prison. That was the plan, but Yaritza's resourceful. She had other ideas."

Even before Matt told me, I had a good idea of where this story was going. A gorgeous "young" woman in a secure facility, a hot-blooded Latin man in charge, a little flirtation, a promise to help her escape in exchange for love, and then…

"Slit his throat right there in his office," Matt said. "Took the jail keys, released other prisoners, and they busted down the gate in a big truck. That was eight months ago. No one's seen her since."

"And you think the woman I saw was Yaritza?"

"A duck's a duck," Sancho said.

I glared at Sancho. He did his zip-lip motion with his fingers. I turned back to Matt. "Your story is more bizarre by the minute. First, you say she's harmless. Now she's this crazy, dangerous, blue-faced serial killer named Yaritza. I saw the folder at your house. It says she has special powers. Yet you just shrugged it off and left us out there. Climbed back on the boat like we had nothing to worry about."

"That's not the way it happened."

"Oh, really? Tell me what happened. What am I missing?"

"Number one, she wouldn't have harmed you. Number two, you had an AK. Number three, Kodak's got a Glock. And number four, I was watching from the boat the whole time."

"No, Matt. You were watching the tomb robbers."

"It wasn't easy."

I drew in a deep breath, and I wondered if I should tell him about my vision or pound him over the head with the AK.

"Okay," I said. "Let's suppose you're right. Suppose the woman was Yaritza. Suppose she escaped yet again. But tell me this: why would she come back to this godforsaken island and live in a cave? She could be hiding in Managua. Or the countryside or anywhere else, living a civilized life. Doesn't she have friends? Couldn't she just leave the country?"

Sancho said, "Oh, come on, Miami. Haven't you figured it out yet? Yaritza came out here for the same reason as Catia and the tomb looters."

"They came for mushrooms?"

"Bingo," Sancho said.

I looked at Matt. "Yaritza figured out the formula," he said. "That's why she looks so young."

CHAPTER 65

I wanted to ask a hundred other things about Yaritza, like what was the formula, what special powers did she possess, and why wasn't her formula working for her scrawny male friends. But there was a flash of lightning and a crash of thunder. The clouds that had been building up turned into a torrential downpour, and we rushed into the cabin.

We took turns cleaning ourselves and changing, and by the time we finished, it was well after dark. Thunder crashed. The *Ana Maria* shuddered and rolled. Up we went, then down, lifted by waves, then dropped into the shallows.

I locked the cabin door and curled up on a berth with my hands to my stomach, hoping the nausea wouldn't return. Matt and Sancho didn't seem troubled at all. Neither did Kodak. Matt put on his reading glasses and pored over a map of the island.

"You didn't finish your story about Yaritza," I said to him. "I want to know about her so-called special powers. What does that mean?"

"Yaritza's not my number one concern right now." He poked the map. "This is where Ramos will anchor. There's a trail that leads to the ruins. We need to get there in the morning before they do. If not they'll…"

"They'll what?"

"Do you even have to ask?"

"I'm asking anyway."

"They're cold-blooded killers, Adriana. No one is safe as long as they're on this island."

"Why didn't you shoot them when you had the opportunity?"

"It's not my war, Baby. I'm not a hitman."

"Maybe not, but you assured me at least twice that we'd scare them away by showing ourselves. Why didn't you fire warning shots?"

He held up his mobile. "Ask Holbrooke Easton."

"What does Easton say?"

"We'll cross that river when we get there."

"Why can't you answer the question? I've also got a job to do."

He shook his head as if I were hopeless. I sank back onto the lounge and stayed there until the rain stopped. Sancho brewed a pot of coffee and made ham and cheese sandwiches. The cabin grew cramped and foul-smelling. I picked up my AK and went out for fresh air, hoping Yaritza and friends hadn't also boarded.

They hadn't, but there were so many limbs and creepers draped over us, dripping water, that it was difficult to move without bringing down a shower. Matt came out of the cabin with his AK and put a hand on my shoulder. "I'm sorry everything turned out so difficult."

"Tell me about Yaritza."

"I told you already."

"You didn't tell me everything. Why aren't they armed with guns?"

"Isn't it obvious? Most of them have serious mental problems. They're not capable of handling guns. They'd shoot one another. Or themselves. Yaritza won't let them carry guns."

"What about the mushroom formula? Why isn't it helping her male friends? They look like survivors from a shipwreck."

"They're just chewing it, getting a psychedelic high."

"How do you know all this? Did you talk to Yaritza?"

"The embassy got a copy of her interrogation."

"Does Catia know any of this?"

"She knows."

"How?"

"Her dad has powerful friends. Didn't I tell you already?"

"What about the tomb looters? Do they know about Yaritza?"

"They know."

"Dammit it, Matt. Everybody knows everything except me. How do the tomb looters know about Yaritza? What is their connection?"

"The embassy's working on it. They're interviewing contacts."

"Snitches?"

"Valuable informants. We don't call them snitches. What we're trying to do is establish the connection between Yaritza and the looters. And did I mention she has special powers?"

"What special powers?"

"It's weird. Some of her victims—the ones that survived—claim they saw her in a trance before she appeared in the flesh. Like she has cosmic projection powers."

"Before she attacks them?"

"That's what they say."

An icy sensation came over me. I swirled about as if she were behind me. Had she appeared to me as a warning? Was I her next victim?

Matt's phone buzzed. "Gotta take this," he said and jumped ashore with his phone to his ear.

I strained my eyes in the darkness but saw only the jungle in intermittent flashes of lightning. Why did he leave the boat to take the call? Suppose Yaritza and the crazies were out there with that bird and their spears, all on a psychedelic high? Was it the mushrooms that gave her paranormal powers? Suppose Matt didn't come back?

"Where are you?" I yelled into the darkness.

No answer. Only the sounds of the jungle, the smells of decay, and the drip-drip of water.

Damn him! Where was he? If he lied about his work, lied about this assignment, lied about Catia and the hurricane and the blue people, what else was he lying about?

The rain started again. Something growled. Loud, like a jaguar. Things moved in the trees. "Matt, are you there? I can't see you."

I pulled the rain gear over my head and called him again. Sancho came up and asked what was wrong. A flash of lightning lit the boat, and then Matt jumped aboard, landing so hard it brought down a shower of water. "Why didn't you answer? Didn't you hear me?"

"Embassy," he said. "Couldn't talk to you and them at the same time."

"You could at least have stayed where I could see you."

"Sorry, Baby."

"What did the embassy say?"

"Wanted us to have a look now, make sure Catia and crew are safe."

There it was again: Catia. "Kodak's in no shape to do anything."

"Kodak can stay here. You too, Sancho."

"What about me?"

"Better if I go alone."

"You're leaving us by ourselves. What if Yaritza shows up?"

"She won't. She's as afraid of us as you are of her. Besides, it's dark and raining. She's back in her cave with her friends."

"What about the hurricane?"

"Shifted a bit south. We'll be okay."

"How can you say we'll be, okay? What if it shifts some more?"

"We'll worry about that if it happens. I need to go."

"What if you don't come back?"

"I'll be back. Stop worrying."

"How can you say that? You could get struck by lightning. Crocodiles could get you. So could tomb looters or the crazies."

"Sancho will know what to do."

"I'll go with you."

"No, Baby, I can get there and back faster by myself. You should rest." He pulled on his rain gear, slung his AK, jumped off the boat, and sprinted into the darkness.

CHAPTER 66

The minutes dragged by. The rain stopped, started, and stopped again. I sat in the deck chair with my AK, listening to the jungle and trying to figure out how long it would take him to get there and back. What if he was wrong about the hurricane? What if he was wrong about Yaritza? And why was he keeping me in the dark?

An hour went by, then two. Water dripped from the limbs and vines that draped over us. The fog was getting thicker. Something splashed in the water. I jumped, and I got the same horrible feeling I used to get while on watch with the Sandinistas. Yaritza could jump aboard and impale me with her spear. A python could drop out of the trees onto my head.

Sancho seemed as unnerved as I was, sometimes flashing his light into the darkness. "Stop that," I said. "Gringo said no lights."

"Makes no difference. In this fog, you can't see a thing."

"Why don't we drift the boat back into the lake?"

"Not until the gringo gets back."

"What's taking so long?"

"You worried about him?"

"Do you think he's okay?"

"Did you hear gunfire?"

"No."

"Then he's okay."

He peed over the side as if I weren't there. It was too dark to see, but I heard the splash and caught the scent. "That's gross," I said.

"Don't be such a weeny. Would you rather I go below and leave you up here by yourself?"

I didn't have an answer for that and liked it even less when he lit a cigarette and asked why I wasn't getting along with Matt. "Well," he said, "you going to answer or not?"

"Just shut up, Sancho. And put out that damn cigarette!"

He chuckled and sat down beside me. "You know the story of Romeo and Juliet, don't you?"

"What kind of question is that?"

"I'm making a point. Romeo and Juliet had real complications. They had family hatred. They had great tragedy, even death. Compare that to you and the gringo. What kind of complications do you have? None. Nothing. Zero. Nada. You're like a Mexican soap opera on TV, crazy in love but kept apart by stupid little misunderstandings."

I almost came out of my chair. Sancho didn't know my suspicions about Matt and Catia. Didn't know about the apparitions and my paranoia. Didn't seem to care that I was being misled again and again either. But before I could protest, he said, "Let me give you an example."

"Example of what?"

"Mexican soap operas."

"What do Mexican soap operas have to do with anything?"

"I'm trying to illustrate how you're making mud puddles out of droplets. You're an educated woman. Do you know the meaning of a metaphor?"

"Oh, please, Sancho."

"Just listen. You'll see what I'm talking about. There's this Mexican TV series—can't remember the name—with a handsome white guy. Mexican soaps always feature leading characters that look like Norwegians. Anyhow, Señor handsome learns the beautiful dark-skinned woman he loves is adopted. Oh, the shock on his face. Like adoption is a disqualifier. Background music kicks in. It's mariachi. They do this to anchor the show in Mexico. Otherwise, the audience might think it's Spain or Argentina."

"I should check on Kodak."

"Hold on, Miami. Let me finish. Not only is his bride-to-be adopted. Her biological mom is the housekeeper. And she's even darker. Got Indian blood. Oh, my God, the bronzed mother of his fiancé scrubs the master's toilet. How could that be? What a disaster. The wedding is called off. Poor girl goes outside and cries to the moon, 'What does it matter I have the blood of Moctezuma? I am *la raza*. I'm proud of my roots. Why do they shame me?'"

"Does this story have a point?"

"Point is you and the gringo. There's a connection."

He droned on: "So what does this poor little girl with Indian blood do? She tosses her wedding dress into the trash. Then she hops on the Indian bus and rumbles away in a fog of black exhaust. The lilywhite mother of the ex-groom says, '*Adios*' with a smile. Everybody else is in tears. Then the mariachis kick in again—the vihuelas and guitarrónes, the harps and trumpets, and the vocalists. Yeah, mariachi. That's what you and the gringo need. An entire mariachi band with big sombreros, boots, and pants with stripes down the legs."

"Sancho, would you please shut up?"

"Then you've got Kodak down there. Poor innocent love-sick Kodak. You should have known him when he was a soldier. Tough as nails. But then he meets his cute little flower girl and what happens? Turns into a wet noodle. Next thing you know he's reading Neruda to her. Neruda, mind you, all twenty-one love poems."

"Twenty poems."

"Aha, that proves my point. You've been reading Neruda. But let's get back to Kodak. So, he's putting these flowers in her hair. Singing to her. He's still like that. Like a butterfly. Now the same thing's happening to the gringo. He's more worried about you than about mushrooms or hurricanes or blue crazies or tomb robbers. Wouldn't surprise me at all if he comes back with a big bouquet of bat flowers."

I stood up. "I should check on Kodak."

"Good idea. Just don't put flowers in your hair."

CHAPTER 67

I hurried down the steps with my AK and found Kodak on the lounge with a copy of the Maria Sabina book, holding it near a dim wall lamp. His face wasn't as swollen as before, but the cabin still reeked of body odor and dampness. He waved the book. "Don't you dare go to that mushroom cave without me."

"We're not going anywhere until daylight. Are you okay?"

"I'm okay." He held up the book again. "You should read this."

"Why does everyone want me to read that book?"

"Because it tells you about magic mushrooms. It explains why Yaritza looks like a teenager."

"Yaritza doesn't look like a teenager."

"Sancho says she's pushing eighty."

"You need to get your hearing checked. She's pushing sixt."

"Same difference. She's ancient."

I took the book and looked at the picture of a wrinkled old *curandera* who must have been a hundred. The blurb called her a Mexican earthwoman who used magic mushrooms to unlock the secrets and meaning of life. Was that what Yaritza did? No, Yaritza ended life.

I handed the book back. "I'm going to the bathroom."

"Head. It's called a head."

"Whatever."

I splashed water on my face and looked in the mirror. God, what a wretch. I was only thirty and already looked like an *abuelita.* There was even a strand of white hair. And another! If I stayed on this island any longer, I would become as wrinkled as Maria Sabina. What I needed was a week in a beauty spa. Or a basket of Yaritza's magic mushrooms. It didn't help that the cabin P.A. system was playing romantic music, and out of it came the honey-smooth voice of Luís Miguel crooning the lyrics of *La Media Vuelta.* It was a beautiful song but with the absurd lyrics that he wanted his love to go out in the world and meet other men.

And kiss other lips so you can compare me...

Yeah, right, lover boy. There wasn't a man alive who wanted his true love to kiss other lips for the sake of comparison. How would Matt feel if I did that? The same way I felt about him sleeping with Catia.

Bastard!

Kodak was still reading his Maria Sabina book when I came out. "Listen to this. Heal the sick. Remove wrinkles, restore energy, help men get it up and keep it up. Stuff even cures cancer. Imagine that?" He flipped from page to page, reading aloud, and this went on for so long that I felt like a character in that movie, *Ship of Fools.*

"Look at my hair," he said, rubbing his head. "It's falling out. I'll be bald in three or four years. Imagine that? I'm a cameraman. I need long thick hair for my image. Do you ever see a bald cameraman? Camera guys like me have that sexy open shirt look with a single earring and their long hair pulled back in a ponytail. Maybe mushrooms will do the trick. Maybe I need a diamond stud for my ear. What do you think?"

"I think your mind was poisoned by chichicaste."

"Oh, come on, Adriana. There are witnesses. Testimonials."

A series of loud thumps sounded on the deck above us.

"Miami," Sancho yelled down. "You better get up here. Hurry!"

I grabbed the AK and rushed up the steps. Kodak followed.

"What's wrong?" I asked.

"Over there." He shined his light into the thicket in front of the boat. Eyes stared back at us. Red eyes. Not one pair but many. The fog seemed to magnify their creepiness.

"Monkeys?" Sancho asked.

"Monkey eyes are yellow," I said, gripping my AK a little tighter.

"What are they?"

"I don't know."

"It could be the blue people."

"Human eyes don't glow in the dark. And they wouldn't be red."

"Crazies have blue skin. What not red eyes?"

"You're such an idiot. They use wild berries to dye their skin."

"I've seen red eyes in Polaroid pictures."

"That's not the same."

"How can you be so sure they're not monkeys?"

"Damn it, Sancho, weren't you a soldier? Didn't you stand watch in the jungle like I did? Rabbits are the only thing I know with red eyes."

Kodak came up behind me. "You saying they're rabbits?"

"Not rabbits either. With rabbits, you see only one red eye."

"What about jaguars? What color are their eyes?"

"How do I know? Let's just back up this boat."

Something hissed. Loud, like an angry cat. There were also grunts and growls. “Shit!” Sancho said and racked a round into his AK. “Bastards come any closer, I’m shooting.”

“We’ve got grenades,” Kodak said. “That’ll scare them away.”

“Just back up the damn boat. Get it away from the shoreline.”

“Can’t,” Sancho said.

“Why not?”

“We’re tethered to the trees..”

“Cut the damn ropes.”

“Good idea. Where’s the machete?”

CHAPTER 68

Kodak grabbed a machete. Sancho kept his light trained on the red eyes, and I had my finger on the trigger when Matt suddenly emerged from the darkness. "Don't shoot. It's me."

"Be careful! Something's out there."

Matt bounded aboard, bringing with him the smells of sweat and jungle. He was drenched, plant debris all over him, and there was mud on his boots and rain gear. He took the flashlight from Sancho and switched it off, leaving us in darkness.

"Something's out there," I said again. "They've got red eyes."

"Crocodiles. Nothing to worry about."

"Are you serious? Crocodiles eat people. Why shouldn't we worry?"

"Crocs are timid. They're not going to chase you."

"They're also in the trees."

"Crocs don't climb trees."

"Something does. Take a look for yourself."

"It could be owls. They have red eyes."

He opened the cabin door, giving us enough light to see one another. I exchanged looks with Sancho and Kodak, feeling embarrassed for being so scared. "What took so long?" I asked. "We were worried."

He pulled off his rain gear. “Found them at the ruins. Three tents. Lanterns burning like they didn’t give a damn who saw them. Even had a campfire and a grill. Idiots. You can smell it a mile away.”

“It’s raining, Matt. How can they have a campfire?”

“You’d know if you’d been to the ruins. It’s a big pile of rubble, but you can find protected places—overhangs, underground rooms.”

“Did you tell them about Yaritza?”

“Told them.”

“What about the tomb looters?”

“That too. Also told them they should put out the fire.”

“And?”

“It got ugly.”

“What do you mean—ugly? What happened?”

“They’d been drinking. Smelled like a brewery. Catia agreed they should be more careful, but big dumb boyfriend said they’ve got guns and can take care of themselves. Boyfriend wanted to know why we were snooping. Then he and Catia got into a yelling match. I gave up and left.”

“That’s it? Nothing more?”

“I might have left out a few F words. They were fighting when I left.”

“So now what?”

“Same as always. We came out here with a job to do.”

The bird shrieked, so close it could have been in the tree above us, and anytime that damn bird shrieked I felt the presence of the blue people. The darkness and the fog made it even scarier. “Can we back up this boat?” I asked. “Get it away from land.”

“We need to wait. Remember that boat we saw back at the Island of the Dead? That was our backup. They’ll be here soon.”

"Who?"

"You'll see." He stripped to his underwear and plunged into the lake.

"Are you crazy? What about crocodiles? What about sharks?"

"Water's warm. You should join me."

He splashed around and climbed back aboard. I handed him a towel and called him an idiot. He went below to change and came back smelling like mouthwash. There were no stars or moon, only the dampness of fog and an occasional flash of lightning. The wind picked up. The boat rose and fell. Water slapped against us.

Matt took my hand. "I've got something else to tell you."

"What?"

He lowered his voice to a whisper. "Flower Girl. Remember."

"You found her?"

"Hush. Lower your voice. I don't want Kodak to hear." He glanced at the cabin door. "Remember Pineapple, that young soldier who took you to the ladies' room?"

"What about her? Is she okay?"

"Better than okay. She's out of the army now and works for us."

"What? She's only a child, and not that smart. What are her qualifications for working at the embassy?"

"She's an informant. And don't let her looks fool you. She worked for Army Intelligence. Speaks perfect English. Lived in Miami. She was doing undercover work when you met her. And she's not from northern Nicaragua either. She lives in Masaya."

It took me a moment to absorb this. Scrawny little Pineapple an agent? An informant? "What does she have to do with Flower Girl?"

"She did some digging."

"And?"

"Flower Girl is alive. I wanted to tell you before I tell Kodak."

"Where?"

"Masaya. She runs a little flower stall in the crafts market. Pineapple went there. Even spoke to her. Says she's slim and pretty. But..."

"Married?"

"Not married, but she has an eight-year-old daughter. Can't be Kodak's."

"Boyfriend? Widowed."

"Pineapple didn't ask. She'll snoop some more and let us know. Should we tell Kodak?"

"It'll drive him crazy. Let's wait until you hear. Another day won't—"

A light flashed from the jungle in front.

"Tequila!" shouted a voice from the darkness. "It's us. Not to shoot."

"Lemon!" Matt shouted back. He switched on a flashlight and there stood Dreadlocks—he of the muscles and gold teeth who'd taken our van back at the landing. A second man appeared from the darkness—Lead Foot—Matt's driver and gun-toting bodyguard, still in his battered cap with a pistol on his hip. Then came a third person, a young, Hispanic-looking woman in ball cap and rain gear. "Who is that?" I asked Matt.

"Embassy Marine."

"A Marine? What's a Marine doing out here?"

"Hold on. I'll introduce you."

CHAPTER 69

They climbed aboard, all drenched and smelling of jungle. Dreadlocks was so heavy the boat sank a few inches. Kodak and Sancho, hearing the commotion, rushed out of the cabin with their AKs. Dreadlocks mumbled something to Matt in his Jamaican-sounding accent. The only word I understood was "Mon." Matt handed each of them a towel and bottle of water. Then he introduced the woman as a Marine security guard at the US Embassy in Managua.

I stared at her. My image of a Marine was a tall muscular gringo in a blue uniform who looked like Matt. Yet here was this young Hispanic woman with dark flashing eyes who looked like she belonged in a first-year college class—except for the tattoos on both arms. One was the eagle, globe, and anchor of the US Marines. The other looked like an image of a Mayan or Aztec god. "Do you have a name?" I asked her.

She looked at Matt as if unsure how to answer.

"Her code name is Venus Twenty-five," Matt said. "But we call her Venus, goddess of love."

Venus lit up in a big grin.

"Are you the same Venus who was at the assassination?"

"Yes, ma'am. Venus Twenty-five."

"The same Venus who was with Sancho at the Cine Luminoso?"

"Yes, ma'am. It was me. I had a bad headache."

Weird, I thought. First, it was Pineapple, and now Venus, both on the same day. "Is Venus your real name?"

"No, ma'am. My name is Layla. Layla Sanchez."

The name sounded familiar, and then it hit me—Sancho's little outboard, *Princesa Layla*. "Where are you from, Layla?"

"Venus, call me Venus."

"Okay, Venus. I asked where you're from?"

"East L.A. but I'm originally from San Luis Potosí. That's in Mexico."

We shook hands. Hers were softer than I imagined, and she also had the lingering scent of Chanel 5. She told me in her Mexican accent that she'd seen my television show and loved every episode, and what an honor to meet me. I thanked her, told her not to call me ma'am, and was about to ask what a Marine was doing out here when Kodak stepped forward and puffed himself up like he was going to complain to Dreadlocks about our van.

Dreadlocks glared down at him. "You worried about van?" he said to Kodak in his atrocious Caribbean Spanish.

"It belongs to the station. I'm responsible for it."

"You tank up with petrol before you leave?"

"It had a full tank."

"No, Mon, was empty. Bone dry. Run out. Finish. *Se cabo*. Leave me stranded on road. I abandon and walk away."

"You what?"

"Bandits come. Bad men. Strip it down. Now no tires. No wipers. Bad men set on fire. Burn to ashes. Sorry, Mon."

Kodak looked like he was about to cry. Dreadlocks burst into laughter. His gold teeth sparkled in the light from flashlights. "Just teasing, Mon. Van okay. No worries."

Kodak didn't seem to think it was funny and moved away. Sancho, who'd been gawking at Venus like a horny teenager, put down his AK and reached for her hand. Venus jerked back and turned away from him. I resisted the urge to laugh. She was probably upset that he'd put her name on the side of his ugly boat. Everyone else just stood there in uncomfortable silence. Finally, I said, "So tell me, Venus. What's a Marine doing out here?"

Again, she looked at Matt.

"Three Marines," Matt said. "Their boat is on the other side, anchored in a safe lagoon. They came with Dreadlocks and Lead Foot."

"I asked why Marines are out here."

"Nothing but a little pow-wow," he said and motioned for Venus, Dreadlocks, and Lead Foot to follow him down to the cabin.

I thought he meant all of us and followed them down the stairs, but when we reached the door, Matt stopped me. "Sorry. We won't be long."

He closed the door in my face. Damn him. What was going on?

CHAPTER 70

I trudged back to the deck. Thunder rumbled. Gusts of wind blew spray over us. Crocs and whatever else was out there grumped and hissed the way I felt. I turned to Sancho. "Why are Marines out here? And what are they plotting that's so secretive?"

"Plans. They're making plans."

"Of course, they're making plans. I'm not stupid. But plans for what?"

"Can't you figure it out?"

"No, Sancho, I can't figure it out. You and the gringo have been lying from the beginning."

"Don't be so mean, Miami. Things happen."

"So, what's the plan? We need to know."

"Gringo will tell you when he comes out."

"Gringo lies more than you do. And stop calling me Miami."

"Look, our goal is different from yours. Our goal is to keep an eye on that Catia woman. Her father has clout. He's a big sugar tycoon in Florida. Got political connections. That puts pressure on the embassy. But she's a walking, talking, loud-mouth disaster. We need to get her out of the country before disaster strikes. That's bad enough. Now we've got four or five tomb looters to worry about. They're war criminals, armed and dangerous. We didn't expect that. Didn't expect a hurricane either. Then you've got Yaritza and the blue crazies."

"Are you saying there's going to be bloodshed?"

"I'm just saying be prepared. That's why we've got Marines. Their motto is Semper Fidelis. It means always prepared."

"Semper Fidelis means always faithful."

"You're missing the point, Miami. Gringo brought Marine backup just in case. Their job at the embassy is to protect the premises. But it's also to protect American lives. That's preparation. So that gives us just a few good men…uh, and women, to make sure everybody gets off this island alive. I call that preparation."

"Do you realize the kind of trouble you'll be in for collaborating with Marines? They've been meddling in Nicaragua since the 1930s. Look at Oliver North. He was a Marine."

"Does Venus look like a badass Marine to you?"

"She's still a Marine."

"Is she wearing a Marine uniform?"

"Makes no difference."

"She speaks Spanish. She could pass as Nicaraguan?"

"She's still a Marine, Sancho. Get that through your thick head. And her Mexican Spanish would never pass as Nica Spanish."

"She also speaks Nahuatl."

"What?"

"Aztec language. She's got the blood of Moctezuma. Didn't you see that tattoo on her right arm? It's an image of Quetzalcoatl, the Aztec god."

The cabin door opened. Matt came out with Dreadlocks, Lead Foot, and Venus. The open door gave enough light to see. "Okay," Matt said, "here's the plan. Lead Foot stays on the boat tonight. We need him to stand watch. Dreadlocks and Venus go back to their boat with the other Marines. They'll link up with us in the morning at the landing."

"Wait," I said. "Stop! Nicaragua is a sovereign country. Venus and the Marines are foreigners. They're not allowed to operate in this country. My boss doesn't like gringo meddling. He'll go crazy when he learns Marines are with us."

Venus again looked at Matt. Sancho said, "Dammit, Miami. Didn't I explain already? You must have misunderstood. There are no Marines on this island, only us and a few tourists. Right, Kodak?"

"I'm just the cameraman," Kodak answered. "Don't get me involved in your intrigue."

I sighed. This mission was getting more complicated every minute. "So what time are we linking up with the *tourists* tomorrow?"

Matt glanced at his watch. "We meet at 0700 hours."

"Then what?"

"Depends on the situation."

"What kind of plan is that?"

"We'll know when we get there."

Venus touched my arm and nodded as if to say she understood. "We'll talk tomorrow," she said and climbed off the boat with Dreadlocks.

Sancho stared after her like a rejected lover, all slump-shouldered and long-faced. Venus lingered a moment to look back at him. Were they lovers? Of course. They both worked at the US Embassy. Sancho had mentioned the Marines before. And mariachi music. And she was Mexican, or used to be, and she had small boobs.

Dreadlocks motioned for Venus to get moving. And that was when the jungle fell silent.

Sancho rushed to the railing. “What the hell?”

“What?” I asked.

“Didn’t you hear it?”

“Hear what?”

“Gunshot.”

“I didn’t hear anything. How do you know it was a gunshot?”

“Hush. Just listen.”

Into the silence came a second gunshot.

Then a third.

“Where’s it coming from?” I asked.

“Impossible to say in this fog. It could be anywhere. Hush.”

Yet another shot sounded, then two or three more, followed by a long silence. In time a single frog croaked as if to say all was well, that the shooting was over. A cricket chirped. Then the infernal racket of the jungle started again. “How many gunshots?” Kodak asked Sancho.

“Six. I counted six.”

“Christ,” Matt said. “There’s six of them.”

“Six what?” I asked.

“Mushroom hunters. We better have a look.”

CHAPTER 71

Venus and Dreadlocks climbed back aboard. Sancho opened the locker and began pulling out weapons. Matt told everyone to take an AK-47 and extra ammunition. Venus grabbed the first one. "Piece of Communist crap," she said to Sancho. "Don't you have M-16s?"

"No, comrade. AKs are better."

"Don't call me comrade." She noisily popped a magazine into her AK and shook her head as if she'd been tainted. Dreadlocks already had an AK. When it was my turn, Matt said, "Are you sure, Adriana? You can bring the camera if you want. Let Kodak carry the AK."

"You've got that backward. Kodak's the camera operator."

"She's right," Kodak said. "I carry the camera."

Matt looked at me. "Didn't you tell me you weren't going to tote a gun? I'm quite sure you said, 'damn gun.' What changed your mind?"

My face grew hot. Was he trying to embarrass me? "Dammit, Matt? Circumstances change. I'm taking an AK."

"You may have to fire it."

"Do you think I've never fired an AK? I traipsed through mountains and jungles with AKs when I was only fifteen. You don't mess with me either." I picked up the AK, popped in the magazine just as noisily as Venus, and stood back like the ragtag Sandinista fighter I used to be.

Matt shook his head and began passing around flashlights. "Single file," he said like a commanding officer. "Lights pointed at the ground. No talking except in whispers. No smoking. Tank up on coffee now. Take food. We don't know how long we'll be. Refill water bottles. Hurry."

"What about the hurricane? What if it hits us?"

"It's not going to hit us."

"My dad's rule was always assume the hurricane will hit you."

Matt drew in a deep breath. "Look, if it hits us—which it won't—we'll shelter in the ruins. You okay with that?" He clapped his hands. "Come on. Hustle. We need to get moving."

Venus raced below and stayed so long that I was about to check on her when she came back with a stronger scent of Chanel 5 than before. She'd also put on lipstick, and her face had a shiny glow as if she'd put on moisturizer. What kind of Marine did that?

I gulped down my coffee, loaded up on energy bars, refilled my water bottle, put on raingear, and slung the AK over my shoulder.

Matt clapped his hands again. "Rock and roll."

"Wait," I said. "What about the boat? Will it be safe?"

"Didn't you hear me before? Lead Foot stays here."

"By himself?"

"He knows what to do."

We jumped ashore. Lead Foot stood at the railing with his AK, watching in surly silence. Matt gathered us around him again. "Listen up. Stay close together. No lagging. If for any reason we get separated, the password is Tequila. The countersign is Lemon. Got it?"

CHAPTER 72

The noise on the boat had been loud. On the trail, it was a high-pitched chirr of creatures unknown, punctuated by croaks, hoots, chirps, and occasional gusts of wind.

Flashes of lightning lit the forest, and in those flashes, I saw gulfs of dark, stagnant pools covered with low-lying fog, the abodes of no-telling what kind of creepy aquatic monsters. The trunks of fallen trees took on the form of crocodiles. Every upright object looked like Ramos or one of those blue crazies with a sharpened stake, and every overhanging vine was a snake waiting to drop on my head.

Kodak, who was following close behind, touched my arm. "You okay with the AK?"

"I'm, okay?"

"Not too heavy?"

"No, dammit. I'm fine. Gringo said not to talk."

"Gringo can't hear in this racket. You scared?"

"I'm worried."

"Me too. This is just like the war. Miserable weather, contras in the jungle, dark trails, scary as hell."

"Yeah," Sancho said from the darkness, "and we were always starving, thinking of food. Nothing to eat but that puta Bulgarian spaghetti."

"Would you shut up about spaghetti," Kodak said. "I don't like to think about it. Besides, I'm trying to concentrate."

We jumped a run-off stream and were struggling up an embankment when Venus asked Sancho, "How did you hear that gunshot?"

"Music appreciation. Didn't you study it in college?"

"I didn't go to college. Maybe next year when I get out."

"Be sure to take a music course. It'll help you understand sounds."

Sancho rambled on and on about music appreciation, using words like "acoustical magic" and "symphony of the jungle," explaining how all the chirps and warbles and croaks and shrieks were somehow analogous to the distinctive sounds of musical instruments.

I rolled my eyes, tuned him out, stumbled ahead, and didn't listen again until he started talking about Arnold Schwarzenegger. "There's this paramilitary group in Guatemala, traipsing through a jungle like us. Loaded down with guns and ammunition, looking for danger."

"*Predator*," Venus said. "Saw it. They run into some bad stuff."

"Yeah, that's it, *Predator*. They should make a movie about us too. We've got all the drama—crazy-ass blue people with spears, tomb looter thugs, ancient ruins, mushroom hunters, snakes, sharks, and even a hurricane. It doesn't get any better than that."

"Good idea," Kodak said. "What would you name it?"

"Magic Mushroom Island. What else?"

"Island is a place, dumbass. Movies are about people. If you're going to include mushrooms, you should call it something like Escape by Magic Mushrooms."

"Who's escaping?" Venus asked Kodak.

"Miami. You don't think she's going back to Managua, do you?"

I slowed and turned around. "Would all of you please shut up? And stop calling me Miami. My name is Adriana."

If Matt heard any of this silliness, he ignored it. So did Dreadlocks, and we were zigzagging down another deep ravine when Sancho said. "Salma Hayek would play the role of Adriana. She's a dead ringer. Got that beautiful olive complexion. As for the gringo, I'm thinking of a tough guy like…oh, Clint Eastwood. He'd be perfect."

"Too old," Kodak said. "Besides, he'd gun down all the blue people."

Matt stopped so abruptly that I bumped into his back. "Lights out. Everyone down."

I crouched down in place. The others crowded in behind me, mere shadows in the darkness—so close that an enemy burst of gunfire would have killed all of us. "What's wrong?" I asked Matt.

"Straight ahead. You'll see in a second."

A flash of lightning lit the jungle, and in that flash, I glimpsed what I didn't want to see—a man propped against a tree. Naked. His eyes and mouth were open, blood dripped from his chin, and a spear protruded from his hairy chest, the same kind of spear that had finished off Contra Uno, all adorned with feathers and monkey teeth beads.

Venus made the sign of the cross. Kodak said, "*Que demonios*?"

"Who is it?" I asked Matt.

"Looks like a tomb looter."

"Ramos?"

"We need to get a closer look."

"Why would he be here?"

"Most likely he saw me talking to the mushroom hunters and tried to follow me. This is where the blue people threw things at us."

"Are they here now?"

"It's possible. Stay alert."

We waited and listened, fingers on triggers, staring into fog that was lit by intermittent flashes, trying to sort out unusual sounds. No one moved or said a word, though I imagined they were having the same thoughts I was having—that the blues would fall upon us any moment.

But there was only the lightning, the fog, and the hellish noise of the jungle. Sancho stirred beside me. "Nothing. All I hear is jungle."

I shrank against Matt, "Didn't you say this weather would drive them into their caves?"

"Yes, but they think they're being invaded."

"By us?"

"By all of us—tomb looters, Catia's mushroom hunters, Marines. They're not logical thinkers. Not all of them can differentiate. We need to be careful."

"They're here now," Kodak mumbled. "I can smell them."

"What do you smell?"

"Sweet, like perfume. Do the blues wear perfume?"

"Imbecile," said Sancho. "That's Venus you're smelling."

Venus squirmed but said nothing.

Matt crept forward to get a better look at the body. Kodak got his camera rolling and followed for a close-up. Matt's light flashed on and off long enough to see it wasn't Ramos. Not Pock Face either. Matt came back and reported what we already knew—that the dead man was a tomb looter and we needed to be alert. "Why is he naked?" I asked.

"The blues need clothes. You saw how ragged they were."

Something fluttered above us. Then that damn bird shrieked again.

"Shit?" Sancho said. "That bird wouldn't be here by itself. Let's fire a warning blast."

"No," Matt said. "We don't harm them; they don't harm us."

I wasn't so sure. Neither was Kodak. "What do we do now?" he asked Matt. "Do we just keep going? Bastards could ambush us."

"I'm going ahead," Matt said. "It's my job. The rest of you can either go back to the boat or stay with me. It's up to you."

"No way," Venus said. "I'm a Marine. I didn't join the corps to bug out and go back to that damn boat."

"I'm not going back either," I said.

"What about the dead man?" Kodak asked.

"Tomb looters don't get a vote. The jungle will take care of him."

CHAPTER 73

The trail took a sharp upward turn. We struggled again through rocky ditches with run-off from the rain, ducking beneath overhanging foliage and passing in and out of patches of fog. Things crunched and snapped beneath our feet. Limbs whipped back in our faces, spraying us with water, and every few heartbeats, a bird fluttered up before us. As if that wasn't scary enough, that demonic bird seemed to be following, rending the air with shrieks.

Sancho, or maybe Kodak, said something about Alfred Hitchcock's bird movie. I pulled the hood over my head as if that would protect me from an attacking bird. Matt said to knock it off, and we trudged ahead in silence, senses on full alert.

At last, we emerged from the jungle atop the same ridge where we'd gathered only hours before, next to the busted statues that overlooked the lake, away from the giant trees and gullies and underbrush where predators could hide. Relief swept over me, and I was so pumped up on coffee, adrenaline, energy bars, fear, and suspicion that I wanted to fire my AK into the sky just to celebrate the feeling of fresh air around me.

"Down," Matt said. "Douse lights."

I sprawled next to him with my AK. "What?"

"Catia's boat. Can you see it?"

"All I see is fog."

He rolled over. "Can't see a damn thing either. Is everyone here?"

Dreadlocks said, "Here, Mon."

Venus answered like a Marine: "Present, sir!"

Kodak and I also answered.

Sancho did not.

"Sancho, where are you?" Matt whispered to the darkness.

No answer. Nothing but the whistle of wind.

"SANCHO, where the hell are you?"

"Weird," Venus said. "He was right behind me."

Dreadlocks couldn't remember the last time he'd seen Sancho either. A chill came over me, and suddenly I pictured it in my mind—Sancho bringing up the rear. A blue crazy dropping atop him from a tree. Skewering him with a spear.

I twisted around and looked back into the jungle.

Movement. Noise. A dark form. Someone or something was coming.

I racked a round into the chamber of the AK.

"Tequila," Sancho said from the darkness. "Don't shoot. It's me."

"Where the hell were you?" Matt asked.

"Taking a leak. I didn't want to offend Miami. She's a girl."

"Idiot," I said. "You could have told us."

He dropped down next to Venus. "Hush. I need to listen."

"For what?"

"Beethoven's Piano Concerto. Stay quiet."

Again, I cupped my hands behind my ears and listened, but there was only the normal noise of insects and frogs and the breeze and the slap of water against boulders.

"Nothing," Sancho said. "If they're here, they're not even breathing."

"I smell?" Dreadlocks said.

"You smell the crazies?"

He switched to English, which was harder to understand than his Spanish. "You not smell it, Mon? I tink dey barbecue big steak."

"What did he say?" Kodak asked.

"He thinks they're barbecuing a big juicy steak."

Kodak sniffed the air. My stomach growled at the thought of steak, but Dreadlocks was the only one who could smell it.

"Come on," Matt said. "Let's check the landing."

He and Dreadlocks crunched into the darkness. Venus poked Sancho. "*Vamanos*," she said, and they took off together, poking each other like playful kids, their silhouettes visible in flashes of lightning. Kodak and I followed, and the six of us were soon at the landing.

The wind howled. Waves crashed against boulders. Spray blew over us, bringing fishy smells of water-meets-land. "Where is the boat?" Kodak asked. "Did they pack up and leave."

"Dere!" Dreadlocks said, which was his way of saying, "There."

I strained my eyes, looking into the murky blackness. Another flash of lightning and there it was, bobbing and twisting in swells no more than a stone's throw away.

"Christ," Matt said. "It's floating free."

The flash came like a bolt of Florida lightning, followed by heat and the boom of an explosion.

The concussion slammed into me with such fury that I fell to the ground. Matt flung himself on top. "Stay down! Cover your heads."

I thought it had been struck by lightning, but lightning didn't explain the fiery objects that dropped around us like the wrath of God, bouncing off boulders and hitting the ground with dull thuds. Venus yelped like she'd been hit. Kodak also yelled and cursed. Dreadlocks began muttering what sounded like a prayer to an ancient god.

Then came the heavy smell of smoke, followed by showers of cinders.

Matt pulled me up. My ears rang. My eyes flashed white. I didn't know what had happened until I saw the burning boat, cinders swirling around it like fiery stars, fanned by the wind. It cast enough light to see the others. I even felt the heat, and everyone except Kodak was up and meandering around like walking dead.

"Is everyone okay?" Matt shouted.

Kodak sat up. "Piece of burning shit landed on my leg. Look, it's still smoldering." Venus rushed over like a concerned mother and slapped it out. He thanked her and struggled to his feet. "What the hell happened?"

"Catia's boat. Somebody blew it up."

"Who blew it up?"

"Puta tomb looters," Sancho said. "It had to be them."

"How do you know it wasn't the blue people?"

"Blue people don't have explosives."

No one mentioned what I was thinking—that there could be bodies or pieces of bodies on the boat or the ground around us. "Look," Venus said. "It's going down."

Kodak got his camera going. The boat pitched as vertically as the sinking *Titanic*. For a moment it stayed stationary. Then it sank into the water with a final flicker and loud gurgle, leaving us amid the smoldering debris. Venus crossed herself like a good Catholic. “May God bless their souls,” she said and added a few words in her native Nahuatl.

Dreadlocks murmured something unintelligible. Sancho said, “Adios.” And all of us just stood there gazing at the lake like mourners at a funeral.

“Hold on,” Matt said. “Be right back.”

“Where are you going?”

“Just wait there.” He hurried this way and that with his flashlight, zigging and zagging like a soldier in combat, stopping now and then as if to check for a body. He did this along the shoreline, in the bushes and the palmettos, in thickets and gullies, and in a cluster of boulders, and when he came back, he switched off his light.

“Nothing,” he said. “Let’s get back to the ridge. No lights.”

I didn’t ask why. I knew why. Ramos and his tomb-looting thugs could still be on the island. And they could be watching us.

CHAPTER 74

We trudged up the hill like zombies in *The Night of the Living Dead*, dropping down next to the broken statues. No one spoke until Matt took out his cell and reported the explosion to the embassy. He traipsed into the darkness, his voice rising and falling in the breeze. His voice grew louder. A lot louder. "GODDAMIT TO HELL, why didn't you warn us?"

I couldn't see the faces of the others, but I felt their tenseness. Venus, sitting next to me, asked, "Why is he so steamed? Who is he talking to?"

"The embassy. Probably Holbrook Easton."

Matt said, "Fuck!" loud enough for us to hear. Several times, along with a few other four-letter words I'd never heard him use before. It wasn't a good sign. And by the time he ended the conversation and came back, we were all on our feet.

"Warn us about what?" I asked him.

"Hurricane. It shifted south."

"How far south?"

"Nicaragua south. It'll be here soon."

"Here?"

"Here. It's coming straight toward us."

I suppressed an urge to yell at him, to use his crude f-words, throw his Occam's Razor contention in his face, or at least say, "I told you so." But what good would it do?

"Why can't we leave the island now? Find shelter in Ometepe."

"Do you really want to get caught on the lake during a hurricane?"

"No, but—"

"Or trek back down through that jungle in the dark?"

"No, but—"

"We can shelter in the ruins. It's up that hill, ten minutes at most."

"We could be walking into an ambush."

"That's why we're trekking military fashion. One at a time, staggered relay, same order as on the trail. Passwords Tequila and then Lemon. I go first. Sancho brings up the rear. Okay?"

There were no questions. We'd all served in the military and understood the concept. I told him to be careful. Then we watched him set off into the darkness, his light fading into the fog.

"*Mierda*," Venus said. "Where did he go? He disappeared."

Dreadlocks stared into the fog the way I imagined his Jamaican ancestors had done when they were fighting the British. He mumbled something in his native language.

"What do you see?" I asked in English.

"Dere. Gringo signal. Now you go."

I couldn't see Matt's light. Couldn't see much of anything except fog and lightning. But I hitched up, slung the AK over my shoulder by its strap, and set off in the direction he had taken. God, how did I get into this mess? What if I couldn't find him? What if I got lost?

A light flashed, barely visible through the fog. I broke into a trot.

"Tequila!"

"Lemon!"

"You, okay?" he asked.

"No, Matt, I'm not okay. You went too far. We couldn't see you."

"Look, I'm sorry for getting you into this mess."

"Go," I said. "And don't go so far this time."

"Something I need to tell you."

"What, Matt? Another disaster?"

"No, Baby, it's about Kodak's flower girl. Pineapple spoke with her."

"And?"

"Not married. No boyfriend either. You should tell Kodak."

He squeezed my arm and set off into the fog and darkness. I flashed my light backward and kept flashing until Kodak caught up. Should I tell him about Flower Girl? No, not yet. He'd grow crazy for details I didn't have. "Where's the gringo?" Kodak asked. "Did you find him?"

"Found him. Told him not to go so far."

"Look, there's his light. Go. Be careful."

Off I went, breathing hard, the pack straps biting into my shoulder. The wind picked up. There were more flashes of lightning and bursts of rainfall, and by the second or third rendezvous, the wetness had found its way into my raingear and was running down my back.

Worse, the trail turned upward, taking me into yet another creepy forest with smells of decay, draping vines, and uneven ground.

Why hadn't I stayed with Matt?

Why hadn't I taken a rickety boat to Ometepe?

Something moved to my left. Something in the brush.

Panic came over me. An animal? Yaritza with her spear? Ramos?

I unslung my AK and broke into a run.

And went face down in the mud.

Up I scrambled, frantic, turning this way and that.

And there he stood, illuminated in flashes of lightning. Not Yaritza but the same blue crazy who'd danced around me and poked me with his spear. Shirtless. Monkey teeth necklace. Dangling bone. Drenched hair. Water running down his ugly face.

He lifted the spear.

I dove sideways. I might have screamed too.

But he was gone. Vanished.

I swiveled this way and that with my AK. Where was he? My mind told me to spray the forest with gunfire. Scream and curse. Shoot into the trees and all around.

No, I might hit Matt. Might waste my ammo. Might shoot myself.

I drew a deep breath and hurried on, finger near the trigger, looking left and right and into the trees, wondering if he was real or another vision like Yaritza, half expecting him to drop down from a tree in front of me.

Dear God, why couldn't this be easy? I'd done this kind of thing years ago when I was young and stupid and trudging through the jungle in a Sandinista uniform. Now I was thirty years old and trudging up a hill on a jungle island, and I was still stupid.

CHAPTER 75

When I reached Matt, I rushed into his arms and told him what happened. "Christ," he said, "it must have been El Baboso."

"Who?"

"They call him Drool or the drooler. He's scary."

"I thought he was going to spear me."

"He's lucky you didn't shoot him."

"Damn it, Matt. What is it you're not telling me? How do you know what they call him?"

"Learned it from Yaritza."

"You never told me you spoke with Yaritza?"

"I read her interrogation transcript. El Baboso's family abandoned him as a child. He got dumped in the asylum with all the other mental cases and ended up out here."

"Why was he following me?"

"Spying. We should warn the others. They might shoot him."

"He could be watching us now."

"It's possible."

We waited for the others in the driving rain, leaning against a giant Ceiba tree whose spreading limbs and dangling vines touched the ground. By then I was so jaded and used to crazy stuff I wouldn't have been shocked if a UFO full of little green people swooped out of the sky and landed beside us.

"You're shivering," Matt said.

"I'm cold and I'm scared."

He pulled me against him. It felt good, warm, loving, and despite the wind and rain and the possibility El Baboso was lurking nearby, and the danger the tree could blow over and crush us, I felt secure in his arms. He always made me feel that way, as if he had some mysterious, magical power over me, which was why I was on this cursed island instead of on a boat to Ometepe, and which was why I couldn't say goodbye until I knew for sure if he was genuine. Call me weak. Call me addictive. Call me a woman in love.

Kodak showed up, then Dreadlocks, cursing the weather. Moments later, Venus and Sancho arrived, clothes drenched, but holding hands like young lovers. None of them had seen El Baboso. Hadn't heard anything unusual, which bolstered my suspicion that it had all been in my head, another inexplicable cosmic projection.

Matt cautioned them not to shoot him or any other blue crazy unless it was self-defense. "From now on," he said, raising his voice, "we go in pairs. One-minute intervals. Just follow this trail. It goes straight to the ruins. Keep a sharp lookout. No need for light signals."

We continued our trek, following a well-worn path that was miserably muddy and slippery. In time the forest gave way to ancient lava flows, scrubby brush, and broken ground, and on that ground, easily visible in the flashes, lay the remains of what must have once been a magnificent pre-Columbian city.

"Sonzapote," Matt said as if I didn't know. "The doomed city of the Chorotegans. It's a state preserve, but that doesn't stop the treasure hunters."

"Where's the shelter?"

"Middle of the ruins. Beneath the temple. Catia's camp is next to it."

We hunkered down behind upturned slabs of ruins to wait for the others. Matt put his arm around me. I wanted him to say he didn't want me to leave Nicaragua without him. He didn't. Or maybe he did, and I couldn't hear because of the howling wind. Palm fronds and other debris blew around us. Now and then I caught a whiff of wood smoke, sweet and pungent.

"How can there be a fire in this rain?" I asked, yelling into his ear.

"Told you already. Overhangs and shelters?"

"Whose fire?"

"We're going to find out."

Dreadlocks and Kodak showed up, cursing the storm.. Then Venus and Sancho, still holding hands. Matt gathered us around him. The noise was so loud he had to yell. "TEMPLE'S ONLY A SHORT DISTANCE AWAY. Shelter's beneath it. Stay alert. No lights. We can see in the lightning flashes."

We pushed on, leaning into the wind, following Matt in single file, crunching over broken pottery and passing around chunks of giant pillars and busted stone idols, some with the most intricate designs, easy to see in the endless flashes. I tried to suppress the misery by picturing the city in its glory days: temples and priests and beautiful princesses in flowing robes; the locals gathering around their idols for prayers and rituals, all feathers and gold. Now it was only a pile of rubble.

Would Tampa look like this someday? Or New York City?

"There," Matt said, pointing to a mound.

"The temple?"

"Sacrificial altar. It's where they chopped off heads and ripped out hearts. I'll show you tomorrow. It's got runoff channels for blood."

My vision of beautiful princesses in flowing robes turned to blood-soaked priests with malevolent features and obsidian knives, holding up a still-beating heart for the mob.

The smell of smoke grew stronger. "Over there," Matt said. "See it?"

"Smoke?"

"No, Baby. Catia's tent."

We stared into the blackness. In the next flash, it appeared no more than thirty paces away, fluttering in gusts of wind. No lights.

"Where are the other tents? You said there were three."

"There used to be three."

We spread out and approached the tent slowly, AKs at the ready. As we came closer, I saw the other tents flat on the ground, now and then puffing up from the wind like blowfish.

Matt stepped up to the standing tent and motioned us to wait. He yanked back the flap and shined his light inside. "Oh, my God."

I hurried inside with my light. Kodak followed. There were no bodies, but it looked like a bomb had gone off: table and chairs overturned, gear and supplies littering the floor, broken wine bottles, a crumpled map, a smashed television camera. It was a bad sign.

"Tomb looters," Matt said.

"How do you know it wasn't the blue people?"

"Blue people would have taken everything—clothing, blankets, food, even the tent fabric."

He paced around, cursing and muttering to himself. The tent shook and fluttered. "I warned them," he said, "but did they listen? Hell, no." He pulled out his mobile and then put it away. "Don't touch a thing. We need to film this place like we found it. Before it collapses."

By then, all the others had crowded inside, dripping water and looking around, probably as grateful as I was to be out of the wind and rain. Kodak got his camera rolling, lights and all.

"No, no, no," Matt said. "Lights out. Ramos could be nearby."

Kodak switched off the camera. "You said to film the place."

"Not until we secure the grounds. Let's find that smoke."

He led us outside and pointed to a pile of rubble. On it rested a pair of broken stone statues at an angle. "There," he said. "That's the temple. Or what's left of it."

"All I see is a mound."

"There's a shelter underneath. It has steps."

"What if the tomb looters are down there?"

"We're going to find out."

CHAPTER 76

Matt and Dreadlocks took the lead, and again I got that nasty feeling I used to get when approaching a village as a Sandinista soldier. Even now, fifteen years later, I imagined I could see Little Napoleon crouched in front and urging us on, pointing to a burned-out structure in the jungle. *Careful, comrades. Slow. Always assume it's occupied by the enemy.*

My training kicked in. Finger near the trigger. Look left and right. Listen. Smell. Stay alert. "Down," Matt said, though I wasn't sure if he said the word or if it was his hand motion.

"What's wrong? I don't see anything."

"Straight ahead. That's where the entrance is."

A broken tree limb blew past us, tumbling end over end. Matt said, "Wait here." Then he zigzagged to the rubble like a soldier. One second, he'd be off to my left; in the next flash, he'd be in a different place. I held my breath. *Please, dear God.* Then he was lying on his back next to a crumbling wall.

I hurried to his side and dropped next to the wall. It was only about a foot high. "Stairways on the other side," Matt said. "It leads to the shelter."

I peeked over the wall, uncertain what to expect. There were no guards, no tomb looters, no blue people, and no mushroom hunters, only a set of narrow stone steps that led down into blackness.

"What's down there?" I asked.

"Subterranean shelter."

"A cave? A room?"

"More like a basement. The archeologists found it. No one knows what it was used for."

"It could be flooded."

"No, Baby, we're on top of a hill. The ancients understood drainage."

"What about bats."

"No, Baby, it was sealed."

Sancho eased over the wall and onto the top steps. Down he went a few steps and still more. He stopped and did his listening thing. We waited in the rain and howling wind. After a while, Sancho shook his head and pointed to his ear as if he heard nothing.

Matt touched my arm. "You and Kodak wait here."

"In this storm? Are you serious?"

"It'll only be a minute."

"Why do we have to wait here?"

"Please, Baby, It's not good to bunch up. Besides, somebody's got to cover the rear."

"How long?"

"Long enough to check."

"What if you don't come back?"

"Just wait for our signal."

He squeezed my arm and climbed over the wall with Dreadlocks and Venus. They followed Sancho down the steps like a SWAT team, their lights disappearing into the darkness. I might have said, "Be careful," or I might have thought it. Hypothermia does that to the mind. So does heart-pounding fear. All I know is the wind howled, lightning flashed, another sheet of rain poured over us, and I became more miserable by the second, half expecting to hear explosions and gunshots. Or worse, nothing at all.

Kodak leaned against me. "We should wait in the tent. Get out of this puta weather."

"Tent's going to collapse any second."

"I'd like to check it anyway."

"Why?"

"Hasselblad?"

"What?"

"Hasselblad. Expensive camera. Didn't I explain already?"

"For God's sake, Kodak. We're stuck in a hurricane. I'm drenched and freezing to death. A boat blew up in our faces. Our team disappeared into a black hole. There are crazies and tomb looters and killer birds all over this island, and you're worried about a stupid camera."

"It's not just any camera. It's a Hasselblad."

I turned away. Kodak was like that. Get him started on any subject and his internal motor kicked in, whether it was Flower Girl, the assassination, the blue crazies, Maria Sabina, or a camera. "Look," he said. "Over there."

"What?"

"Light. See it?"

"I see nothing."

"It was only a second, like someone running with a flashlight."

We watched and waited, miserable and shivering, but there was no sign of a mysterious light. "What's taking so long?" Kodak asked. "We're screwed if they don't come back."

I thought so too and wondered for the hundredth time why I allowed myself—us—to get into this mess. Couldn't go back to the boat. Couldn't shelter in the tent that would blow away any moment. And couldn't stay in the open and catch pneumonia or get struck by debris that was coming down on us like an avalanche. And why was I in this mess?

Matt, always Matt.

"To hell with this," I said. "Let's at least get out of the wind."

We climbed over the wall and hunkered down on the upper steps. The smell of decay was stronger here, like the menacing presence of death. Would we survive the night? Would I ever get out of this country and back to Tampa? Would Kodak link up with his little flower girl?

I touched his shoulder. "The gringo found her."

"WHAT? I can't hear in this damn wind."

"I SAID THE GRINGO FOUND HER."

"FOUND WHO?"

"FLOWER GIRL. SHE WORKS IN THE MASAYA CRAFTS MARKET."

I thought he'd go crazy and bombard me with questions. He didn't. He just sat there in silence, maybe out of shock or maybe because he was as exhausted and beaten as I was.

"Are you okay? Did you hear me?"

His body began to shake. He made a sound that might have been a sob. "Just can't believe it," he said. "So far and so close. I must have gone to that market a hundred times. Walked right past her. Bought belts and wallets. Hammocks too. And paintings for my wall. I can still see that place in my head. Smell it too—the fresh coffee, the leather, the home-made soaps and perfumes and candles. But I never thought to buy flowers."

"Why?"

"Do you even have to ask? Hurts when I see flowers or smell flowers. God, I miss her."

He wiped his eyes and babbled on and on about the Masaya handicrafts market and its sights and smells, and this went on for so long that I imagined I was out of the weather and inside the market with its warmth and chatter. I could even smell the leather from a purse I'd bought, and I lived in that imaginary world until a crash of thunder snapped me back to reality.

"What is keeping them?" I asked. "Did they forget us?"

Kodak stood and shined his light downward. "Look, there's an overhang. Let's go down a few more steps, get out of this puta weather."

"Gringo said we should keep watch here."

"Gringo's fucking loco. Come on."

CHAPTER 77

I was so weak and wobbly that he had to help me down the steps. By then I didn't care who or what was down there: tomb looters, Catia, crazy blue people, crocodiles, or a den of slithering snakes. I just wanted to find warmth and a place to sleep, and I was struggling to keep my balance when a dim glow appeared at the bottom.

"Tequila!" yelled a voice that could only be Venus's. "Miami!!"

Her voice revived me. "Lemon!" I yelled back. "Is anyone there?"

"No, ma'am, it's just us, but they've been here."

"They who?"

"Mushroom hunters. Come on down. I'm sorry to keep you waiting."

The steps were uneven and slippery. Moss grew on the walls. The overhang was so low we had to bend double to get underneath, but it mercifully took us out of the storm. The musty smells of the underground grew stronger with each downward step. So did the pleasant aroma of food and a wood-burning fire.

At the bottom, which must have been fifteen feet below grade, we came to a landing beyond which a stream of water gushed from the ground like an aquifer, exiting through a hole in the wall.

Venus stood on the other side—or someone who looked like Venus—holding up a hurricane lamp and glancing behind her as if waiting for someone. She wore a red blanket with intricate designs that looked like it came from a native crafts market in Mexico, and she'd marked her cheeks, eyes, and mouth with lipstick like a Hollywood version of a decaying cadaver. Her dangling earrings and headband completed the effect, and in the ghostly shadows and poor light, with her bronze skin, black hair, and indigenous features, she could have passed as one of the original inhabitants of this place, holding up a burning torch.

"Venus?" Kodak asked in an uncertain voice. "Is that you?"

"Venus Twenty-five. You don't recognize me?"

"Why are you dressed like that?"

"Don't you know what day it is? It's the Day of the Dead. Don't you celebrate the day in Nicaragua? In Mexico everyone dresses like this."

"Wait a minute," I said. "You left us out in a damn hurricane while you got all dressed up like a dead person? What were you thinking?"

A pained expression crossed her face. "I'm so sorry. Gringo told me to come for you. I thought he was speaking to Dreadlocks. When I realized my mistake, I dashed back. I'm so sorry, ma'am."

"Don't call me ma'am. And don't call me Miami either. My name is Adriana. Understand?"

"Yes, ma'am." Again, she held up the lantern and looked behind her.

"Why do you keep looking back?"

"Because this place is creepy. It's big. Corridors every which way. One of them has a little waterfall where you can clean."

"What's the gringo doing?"

"Same as always, talking to the embassy."

"Can you help us across this stream? I'll pass our stuff over."

She set down her lantern, stripped down to a tee shirt and khaki shorts, and sailed to our side like an Olympic jumper, bringing with her the sweetness of Chanel. By then I'd unhitched my pack and cleaned the mud off my hands in the stream.

She took Kodak's camera and jumped back across. We tossed over our packs, rain gear, and my AK and then backed up, got a running start, and jumped to the other side—it was about three feet wide—where we found ourselves in a narrow passageway that sloped upward.

"Up there," Venus said, pointing into the darkness.

"What's that smell?" Kodak asked. "Is there a fire?"

"Stew. Dreadlocks is making beef stew."

The mention of stew sharpened the hollow in my stomach. "Where did he get beef for stew?"

"Mushroom hunters. They left all their supplies. Suitcases, boxes, food, blankets. You can change out of those wet clothes."

"What about cameras?" Kodak asked. "Did they leave their cameras?"

"I didn't look."

Kodak got his camera rolling, light and all, and we followed Venus up the passage and around a corner, our shoes squishing on the stone floor. The smell of stew grew stronger with each step. My mouth watered. My mind filled with images of beef stew and a warm fire. But when we rounded another corner and I flashed my light ahead, I stopped cold.

There, guarding an entrance, stood two of those ugly half-human half-crocodile statuesVenus yelled," Tequila, we're coming in."

CHAPTER 78

Venus and Kodak hurried around the statues. I took a deep breath, did the same, and entered a circular-shaped room that looked like a setting for an Indiana Jones movie—hewn stone walls, a paved stone floor, niches in which had been placed glowing hurricane lamps, and another grotesque statue supporting the ceiling in the center.

The pungent smell of burning wood gave it the ambiance of a room with a fireplace. Dreadlocks, enormous as always, was standing in a small side room tending his stew over a small grill. It was vented through an opening in the overhead. He wore a chef's hat and a ridiculously small kitchen apron on which was emblazoned the tricolor of France.

He glanced up and spoke in English. "You hungry, girl?"

"Starving."

"Stew be soon ready."

"How can stew be ready soon? Stew takes time."

"Already cooked. Still warm. I add onions, carrots, potatoes."

"Where are the others?"

"I tink gringo talking with fortress."

"Fortress?"

"Gringo embassy. You need dry off, girl. Clean up too." He pointed to suitcases and boxes against the wall. "Towels and clothes over dere."

The boxes and suitcases were the same that Catia's crew had unloaded earlier that day at the landing. There were clothes, towels, toiletries, blankets, sleeping bags, house shoes, cooking utensils, sacks of vegetables, paper bowls and plates, and other items you'd expect to find in camping gear. There was even a neat stack of firewood.

"Why would they leave everything behind?" Venus asked, her hand resting on a metallic suitcase. "It's so weird. There were six of them. Now there are six of us. We eat their food. We're wearing their clothes. It doesn't feel right. Where did they go?"

The obvious answer was they'd been ambushed by the tomb looters. Probably gone down with the boat. But suppose they'd learned something about this creepy, underground room we didn't know?

Venus, as if reading my mind, said, "Evil came to them. Evil could come to us. This place smells like a crypt. Just look at those monsters."

I followed her gaze to the half-man half-crocodile statue that supported the ceiling and to the two equally ugly monstrosities at the entrance. They seemed to be scowling at me. Hadn't Sancho said they'd come alive at midnight? It was midnight already.

Venus shrank against me. "We should light candles," she said in a little girl's voice. "My mother warned me to stay away from places like this. It could be cursed. Maybe that's what happened to them."

"What good would candles do?"

"To bless their spirits. To keep us safe from harm. Today is November first, the scariest day of the year. Spirits roam the earth. The ghosts of the mushroom hunters could come back."

I stared into the poor child's face, into her dark eyes that had grown wide. Back on the trail, she'd been a sassy, tough Marine. Now the little girl in her had come out and she'd reverted to a childhood where demons ruled the night and witches were as real as the stars and the moon. She needed reassurance. I needed reassurance, but I couldn't tell her I shared her fear of spirits. Her warmth and trust in me almost brought me to tears.

"We'll be okay," I said. "This place isn't cursed."

"You sure? You're not just saying that?"

"No, *Mija*. I've been to places like this before. The only curse I'm worried about is catching pneumonia. I need to get out of these clothes."

"Over there," she said. "Lots of clothes in those suitcases."

She had already commandeered the French woman's suitcase, which left me the choice of taking clothes from Catia's luggage. Catia. Just the thought of her was like a punch in the gut. Under other circumstances, I'd never touch her stuff. Never. But I needed dry clothes. Besides, hadn't she stolen my boyfriend when we were in high school? Hadn't she bragged about it? Hadn't she seduced Matt? What difference would it make if I borrowed her clothes until mine dried out?

But was it right to wear a dead woman's clothes? Shit! Maybe a candle or two wasn't a bad idea. I pushed away the thought and rummaged through Catia's luggage anyway, finally selecting a pair of distressed jeans and a soft pullover. They had a clean, sweet smell. Do it, I told myself. Swallow your pride. It's an emergency.

But I couldn't. Her clothes were tainted. She might have worn those same jeans when she was with Matt.

Worse, her spirit could be here now, in this room.

Venus, seeing my hesitation, handed me a cotton nightgown from the other woman's suitcase. "Take this. It looks like your size."

"*Mierda*," Kodak mumbled beside me. "It's not here."

"What's not here?"

"Hasselblad. I looked everywhere."

"Would you stop it with the Hasselblad? It went down with the boat."

"Damn it, Miami, don't you get it? Don't you know the importance of a Hasselblad? It's the gold standard for photographers. It's the Holy Grail. It's like a Stradivarius for a violinist."

"I'm going to change. You should too."

I grabbed a towel, took my flashlight and AK, and headed into a creepy side passage that smelled of mold and mildew. I walked slowly, my hand on the wall, listening. A few more steps and there it was—the trickling waterfall Venus had told us about, beyond which was only darkness.

Was this place safe? Why hadn't I asked Venus to come with me? I stripped off my wet clothes anyway and tested the water. It wasn't arctic cold, but it was cold enough to bring back shivers, so I took the fastest shower of my life, changed into a soft cotton gown and fluffy house shoes, and was back in the main room toweling my hair when Matt and Sancho showed up, still in their rumpled clothes, all wet and smelly.

Venus gave me a pleading look as if begging me not to tell Matt she'd left us waiting in the rain. By then I'd forgiven her, so I told Matt about the light we'd seen.

"I saw it too."

"How could you see it? You were down here?"

"Come on and I'll show you."

CHAPTER 79

He led me to an area behind Dreadlocks and his pot of stew and pointed to an opening high above us. "Chimney for the fire. It's also a lookout. The archeologists made a wooden ladder. I climbed up to get better reception for my mobile."

"How big is the opening?"

"Just big enough to see outside and let out smoke."

"What about the waterfall passage? Where does it lead?"

"Nowhere. There's no other opening, only the place where we entered, so no one's going to bother us tonight, not in this storm."

"Really, Matt? Seriously? The storm didn't stop El Baboso, did it? Didn't stop us from coming here either, did it? You've been saying from the beginning how everything is going to be hunky-dory. Now look at us—stuck in a tomb during a hurricane. And on the Day of the Dead."

He didn't respond. He looked so beaten and defeated, standing in the poor light in his rumpled khakis and muddy boots, that I felt a tinge of guilt for being so hard on him.

"Shouldn't we at least block the entrance?"

"Well, that's my next project. I'm not worried about humans but there could be crocodiles."

"Crocodiles?"

"Snakes too."

"Snakes? Oh, great, Matt, thanks for telling me. What about jaguars?"

"We're surrounded by jungle, Baby. Who knows what's out there?"

I didn't like that answer and liked it even less when Venus started complaining about fleas, saying she'd seen them hopping about. Matt said to put on insect repellent and then to barricade the entrance.

Everyone grabbed boxes and suitcases. I reached for the blue suitcase that had seemed so important to Catia. "Not that one," Matt said.

"Why not?"

He hauled the suitcase to the wall protrusion and popped the lid, which released familiar smells, one sweet and the other like the ammonia odor of a chicken coop. Inside the suitcase, filled to the top, were plastic zip-lock sandwich bags marked with a date. And in each of those bags, in all their white and gray glory, were the reasons we'd come to this island.

"There you have it," Matt said, "Magic mushrooms. Mushroom gold for big pharma and the tomb looters. Is it the real deal? Who knows?"

All I could do was stare. People had been dying for precious metals and money and drugs and land and even love since the beginning of time—and now they were dying for mushrooms.

"Don't let that suitcase out of your sight," Matt said.

"Do the others know what's inside?"

"Only Sancho."

He took clothes from a box and disappeared down the waterfall passage. I sat beside the blue suitcase like a sentinel, slapping at imaginary fleas and wondering about the smells in the suitcase. Catia had come off the boat with that same suitcase in her hand—and she had kept it at her side. Why would she do that with an empty suitcase? She wouldn't, which meant it wasn't empty when she got off the boat. I opened it for another whiff but quickly closed it when Venus, who was marking Sancho's face with lipstick to give him the look of a skull, asked what I thought of her workmanship.

"Big improvement. It'll scare away the dead."

Matt came back in dark jogging togs and a white T-shirt that accentuated his suntan. He glanced at the others, picked up the blue suitcase, and led me across the room, past the center statue that was getting uglier by the minute, past Kodak who was still digging around for that stupid camera, and to a stone protrusion from the lower wall that was large enough for sleeping or sitting.

On the wall above were petroglyphic images of spirals, celestial bodies, a crocodile, and a warrior with a club and shield.

The shadows around us gave the place an added touch of mystery.

"Ten more minutes," Dreadlocks yelled from his pot of stew.

Matt leaned closer and spoke in a muffled voice. "Connection to the embassy got cut."

"You pulled me over here just to tell me that?"

"No, Baby. I brought you over here to tell you I had an interesting conversation with the embassy before the hurricane knocked out the relay. There's good news and bad."

"There's always bad news. Now what?"

"Hurricane. It's a cat three. Maybe a four. It'll pass right over us. Good thing we're down here. We're safe until morning. If Ramos is out there, he's also hunkered down. No one can stand up in that kind of wind."

"What's so bad about that?"

"Bad for the mushroom hunters if they're alive, caught in this storm. My job was to keep an eye on them. But now, now…"

He sat there with his hand on the blue suitcase, saying nothing. There was no point trying to console him with meaningless words. Catia lived on the daring side. She never listened to anyone. Matt knew it. So did the embassy and her powerful daddy and everyone else.

"What about Lead Foot and our boat? What about the other Marines?"

"They know how to take care of themselves."

"So, what's the good news?"

"Good news is they connected the dots."

"Who connected what dots?"

"Spooks at the embassy. It's bizarre. Yaritza's fingerprints are all over the spear that killed Contra Uno."

"I already made that connection. They could have asked me."

"Yeah, me too, but here's something else we didn't know. Remember what I told you about her escape, how she slit the throat of her jailer? We thought she was the mastermind of the escape. But, no, she was conspiring with another prisoner—someone you know very well."

"Who?"

"You haven't figured it out?"

"No, Matt. Just tell me."

"Ramos. He was also a prisoner. They escaped together. He took her to a contra camp. That's where she met Contra Uno. Holbrooke Easton thinks there was a love triangle—Yaritza, Ramos, and Contra Uno—but that's pure speculation."

"I've got a better theory."

"What's your theory?"

"Yaritza's a good-looking woman. They abused her at the camp, so she did what she always does to abusers—offs them one by one. I put that in the good news category."

"I figured you would. But I didn't finish with the bad news."

"What, Matt?"

"State Security knows about this island. They know it's Yaritza's sanctuary. They'll send out a search party as soon as the weather clears. We don't have much time."

I came to my feet, walked to the stone statue in the center of the room, glared into its ugly crocodilian face, and went back to Matt who was sitting with his blue suitcase beneath the celestial petroglyphs. "When do you think they'll come?"

Dreadlocks clanged his spoon against a metal pot. "Stew be ready!"

CHAPTER 80

Dreadlocks refused to ladle out the stew until we blessed the food—or, as he put it, "Give tanks to Almighty." There was no table, so we gathered in a circle and held hands while he delivered a lengthy prayer in his Creole language. Not a word sounded like Jesus or the Father or the Holy Spirit, but I understood "Amen "and made the sign of the cross.

"Now we eat," Dreadlocks said. "I add mushrooms for flavor."

It grew so quiet we could hear the rumble of thunder through the overhead shaft. Everyone stared at the stew that was still simmering and bubbling in the pot like a witch's brew.

"Where did you find mushrooms?"

"On trail while walking tonight. Grow on dead trees."

He ladled a bowl from the pot and handed it to me. "You try, girl."

I stared at the bowl. The pleasant aromas of onions, beef stew, and other cooking ingredients that had so permeated the room before now smelled like fungus. Did Dreadlocks know the difference between good mushrooms and bad?

"What's wrong?" Dreadlocks said. "You tink I poison you?"

Sancho snickered, and in the ghostly light, his face looked like a grinning skull. Matt poked me gently, then Dreadlocks burst into laughter. "Just teasing, girl. No mushrooms in stew. You eat now."

The stew was too salty, but on my empty stomach, it tasted like a gift from the gods. Bottles of Vouvray from the Loire Valley were uncorked. There was laughter and the kind of camaraderie I hadn't felt since my army days, and the more we ate and drank, the looser became our tongues.

Sancho, waving around his paper cup, said, "Hey, Miami, don't they have hurricane parties in Florida? What's it like? Do you just have fun?"

"I've never been to a hurricane party."

Dreadlocks, who was sitting still in the fading light of the fire, had taken off his apron, and the amulet of his superstition dangled outside his shirt. "Where I from on offshore islands, nobody have hurricane parties. Don't know if live or die. Everybody pray for survival. My wife, she speak with dead. She light candles when hurricane hits, listen to roar of wind, watch lightning flash. We hold hands. Conjure up spirits. Spirits speak to us."

"Where is your wife now?" Venus asked.

Tears welled up in Dreadlock's eyes. "Now she spirit in sky. Tonight, I talk with her. I ax her what happened to mushroom hunters."

"What did he say?" Kodak asked me. "I wish he'd speak Spanish."

Sancho translated Dreadlocks words into Spanish, which sounded even spookier coming from his skull lips. Venus said. "In my culture, when we're in a tough situation like now, not knowing if we'd survive, we'd tell our darkest secrets. We should do that now."

"Good idea," Sancho said. "Everybody has secrets." He strode to the dying fire, picked up the non-burning end of a glowing log, blew on it to enhance the glow, and held it up for all to see. "You know what this is? It's a magic-talking torch. Confess your secrets to the torch and it'll grow brighter. But if you lie, it'll ignite and burn you."

He walked over to me with the torch, trailing a plume of smoke. "You go first, Miami. You're the mystery woman in the room."

I wasn't about to share my darkest secrets. There were too many other things on my mind—like how to get off this island before the soldiers came. Besides, the smoke was burning my eyes. "Get that stupid thing out of my face. A secret's a secret.."

"She's right," Venus said. "We're not State Security." She drained her cup of wine, wiped her mouth, and took the torch. "I used to be ashamed of my story. It isn't easy to tell. But now I'm among friends. I can confess anything. I don't mind. It'll please the spirits."

Sancho kissed her cheek, and she told us in her Mexican accent about a childhood of poverty, an abusive father, a village filled with drugs and violence, a dangerous trek to the US border, a smuggler who wanted more than just money, and the constant fear of being caught and deported.

"That's why I joined the Marines," she said in a voice shaking with emotion. "They gave me pride. They sent me to school. They gave me this nice assignment at the embassy, and they'll pay for my education when I get out." She looked at the torch as if expecting it to respond. It didn't. She stood up anyway and bowed to her audience of five. "Thank you for listening."

We applauded. The conversation became louder. Cigarette and torch smoke fouled the air, then Sancho took the torch and told a similar story of poverty, saying if it hadn't been for the war and his conscription into the army, he'd be raising chickens in a backwoods village.

Venus punched his arm. "What kind of stupid secret is that?"

"I'm not finished," Sancho said and drained his cup. He poured another, took a long sip, and said his mom had earned a living by scrubbing floors and toilets in houses of the rich and selling her body, and what was worse, he, himself, had been abused by the village priest.

"That's my *puta* secret. I should have killed the old bastard."

"Not too late," Venus said. "I'll bring the shovel."

Kodak's secret, which wasn't a secret, was all about his little flower girl and the love they'd shared in the mountains and jungles and rivers and amidst the boulders while bullets zipped over their heads and mortar shells dropped around them. The story became more exaggerated each time he told it, and I'd heard it so many times that I tuned out, closed my eyes, and wished we could stop the confessions and get some rest.

Sancho booed and did a thumbs-down. Then it was Dreadlock's turn. "You wanna know why I move to crazy Nicaragua. Ax me and I tell you. No, no, don't ax me. I tell you anyway. Other man mess my woman. Now other man food for fish."

"Speak Spanish," Kodak said. "I don't understand."

Venus translated for him again, but her words were so slurred, complicated by her Mexican accent, that Kodak asked her to slow down.

"*Pobrecita*," Sancho said. "Indians just can't hold their booze."

Venus punched his arm. "Who you calling Indian, Cochise? Don't you have the blood? Since when did your family stop wearing feathers?"

"Calm down, Dulce, I'm just—"

"Don't you tell me to calm down! I'm proud of my Aztec heritage. My ancestors built great pyramids. They're still standing. They gave us popcorn and chewing gum and vanilla. They gave us the beautiful Floating Gardens of Xochimilco. And do you know what else they gave us, Sancho? They introduced the world to *Xocolatl*."

"What the hell is Xocolatl?"

"Chocolate. Who doesn't love chocolate—dark chocolate, milk chocolate, white chocolate, Swiss chocolate, baking choc—"

"Stop it, Venus! You're missing the point. I wasn't talking about your culture; I was talking about your ability to drink. I'm a man. Men can hold booze better than women. That's why they say *El hombre manda*."

"Oh, really, you think men rule the roost? Well, I've got news for you. I'm a US Marine, and you don't mess with Marines. And I didn't finish with all the chocolates of the world either. You've got chocolate in cereals, in Milky Way, in chocolate milk, in Baileys Irish Cream, in..."

Matt, who'd been in the Army, shook his head as if this conversation was going to hell. Dreadlocks interrupted Venus with words no one understood. Venus, whose eyes had glazed over, began speaking Nahuatl. It morphed into Spanish with the mention of Mexican revolutionary heroes Pancho Villa and Emiliano Zapata.

She held up a balled fist, chanted, "Viva Mexico!" and went back to Nahuatl. Dreadlocks answered in a language that might have been Creole, and this crazy babble went on for so long it sounded like a holy-roller tent revival with everyone speaking in tongues.

It finally ended when Venus, whose cadaver-like face had turned crimson, took the talking torch, held it up like a priestess performing a ritual, shouted, "*Xocolatl*," and was trying to place the torch back where it belonged when several of the boxes at the entrance toppled into the room and spilled their contents on the stone floor.

CHAPTER 81

Matt and Sancho grabbed their AKs and rushed to the entrance. Dreadlocks did the same. Kodak got his camera rolling, and for a scary moment, we stood there expecting the worst. But there was only the roar of hurricane and rumble of outside thunder.

"That box didn't fall by itself," I said. "Something knocked it over."

"Could have been a temblor," Kodak said. "After all this is Nicaragua."

Sancho speculated that it was caused by the vibration of thunder. Dreadlocks shook his head as if he knew better. Matt said he'd go down the passage and check around the corner. "No," I said and held him back, and it wasn't until we cleaned the mess, got the boxes back in place, and were staring as if afraid they would take flight again when from outside the entrance came yips and howls of only God-knows-what.

Matt racked a round into his AK. I did the same.

"Is it the crazies?" Kodak asked.

"No," Sancho said. "Those are animals. We must be in their den."

Matt shined a light down the corridor. Kodak aimed his camera. But there were no animals or blue people, only about twenty feet of stone walls, floor, and ceiling, after which the passage made a turn to the left.

A flash of lightning lit the corridor, and in that flash, silhouetted against the wall like shadow puppets, appeared canine ears and snouts.

"What the hell?" Kodak said again. "Are those wolves?"

"Chupacabras," Sancho said.

If Yaritza and her horde of blue crazies had burst into the place with spears and feathers, they could not have stirred it up more. Everyone grabbed suitcases and boxes to fortify the barrier. Sancho fired a blast down the passage, lighting it up and flaking stone chips off the wall. The creatures yelped like they'd been injured.

"Stop it," Matt yelled. "There's no such thing as chupacabras."

"What are they?"

"Feral dogs. They've got just as much right to seek shelter as we do."

Matt said the barricade was too shaky and ordered us to rearrange the suitcases and boxes lengthwise with the corridor, which we did while keeping our AKs within reach. Matt adjusted the top boxes and suitcases to leave a small gap between each. "For cross ventilation," he said. "This place is at least fifteen feet below grade. It could have radon gas. You can't smell it, but it can be deadly."

We took turns poking the barrier to be sure it was solid. Sancho and Kodak lit cigarettes and fell into an animated debate about whether the creatures were dogs or wolves. I fanned away the smoke and told them it was stuffy enough without their cigarettes. Venus, who looked as if she were about to collapse, mumbled something no one understood and staggered to the wall protrusion to lie down. Sancho covered her with a blanket, and when things settled down, Matt pointed to his watch and said it was long after midnight and we should get some rest.

He offered to take the first watch. Dreadlocks said, "No, Mon, I sleep with back against barrier. No beasts of the night get past me. No tomb robbers or blue crazies either."

He dragged over a large suitcase, plunked atop with his back against the barrier, and wrapped a blanket over his legs. By then, the dogs sounded as if they were on the other side and were fighting over a carcass.

"Everybody go sleep," Dreadlocks said. "Rest. We be safe. I talk with my woman now. Her spirit protect us."

Matt led me to the protrusion where we'd left the blue suitcase and spread out a double sleeping bag that might have belonged to Catia. I crawled inside. God, was I tired. I still had a hundred questions about Yaritza's role in the assassination and how to get away from this island before the soldiers came for her—and for me—but it was late and I'd been drinking, and I'd been up since six and could barely keep my eyes open.

Matt put a comforting arm around me. I leaned into him.

The wind howled. Occasional flashes of lightning penetrated the ventilation shaft high above us. Thunder rattled the dishes we had used for stew, and just when I thought it was safe to fall into the oblivion of blessed sleep, the candle that Venus had placed in a niche flickered and went out. A bell dinged. The radon gas ignited, and the place lit up in a blue glow. The ghosts of the mushroom hunters floated across the room, dogs howled, and then that damn crocodilian monster holding up the ceiling came to life and crashed right through the barrier.

CHAPTER 82

I tried to struggle out of the bag and sound the alarm, but I couldn't move. Couldn't yell for help either. I was paralyzed, and as if that wasn't bizarre enough, Yaritza dropped down from the ventilation shaft like a Ninja warrior, bluer than ever, and pointed her feathered spear at me.

"They will be here sooner than you think," she said.

"Who will be here?"

"The same people who are coming for me. You are in danger."

She wasn't telling me anything I didn't know, and I didn't ask for an explanation. All I know is she took my hand and pulled me to my feet. Matt was not there. Neither were the others. I was alone with Yaritza and a bunch of dead mushroom hunters, all glowing blue in the light from the radon fire. "Where are the others?" I asked. "Where is Matt?"

She ignored the question and led me past the strewn suitcases and boxes and into the corridor that led outside. The dogs morphed into the likeness of Ramos and his sergeant, who also glowed blue. They growled but didn't attack. We hurried down the corridor, turned the corner, and jumped across the little stream that was now filled with crocodiles. I hesitated long enough to check myself in a mirror next to a movie poster of Bogie and Bergman in *Casablanca*, which seemed perfectly normal. The image in the mirror was me, but a younger me, thanks to the magic mushrooms I'd been consuming.

Yaritza appeared in the mirror with her blue face next to mine. "Mushrooms aren't for everyone," she said in a sultry voice. "If you have any side effects like dizziness, weakness, suicidal thoughts, constipation, or turning blue, you should consult your doctor."

"How do I renew my prescription?"

"Come. I will show you the cave."

We climbed the steep steps that had brought us here, ducked beneath an overhang, and emerged from the underground next to the temple ruins.

Catia's tents went flying. Debris and rainfall battered us, but I felt nothing. No danger. No pain. No fear. "I need your help," Yaritza said and pointed down to the lake where monster waves pounded the shoreline and her ugly black bird perched peacefully on a tree limb.

"Why do you need my help?"

"You will see."

She motioned me forward, and in the kind of logic that makes sense only in dreams, I followed her down to the landing and climbed aboard a native canoe. Stars fell from the sky. Colonel Vega's helicopter roared overhead and crashed into the lake. Survivors cried for help. I wanted to pick them up, but Yaritza said to let them drown.

Waves washed over us, warm and soothing. Yariza paddled the canoe, her bird followed, and in that fashion, we crossed the lake to a beautiful island of sandy white beach and a field of reeds, landing the canoe on a hilltop dominated by coconut trees.

Funny how it smelled just like Chanel Number 5.

"The Island of the Dead," Yaritza announced over the canoe's P.A. system. "The landing is slippery. Be careful as you debark."

I slipped and fell anyway. Her bird shrieked—loud, insistent, abrasive. A bell dinged. The island faded. Yaritza faded, and I was suddenly back in my sleeping bag in the real world.

A shaft of light streamed through the opening above our pot of stew. Not the daylight of a sunny morning but the pale light of early dawn. There was silence. No one talking. No thunder or roar of wind or yips and howls. The hurricane was gone. Yaritza was gone.

God, what a crazy dream! I was the one that needed help, not Yaritza.

I reached for Matt. He wasn't there, but the smell of Venus's perfume lingered in the air along with the less pleasant odors of smoke, mold, and mildew. The crocodilian monster had also returned to its perch beneath the ceiling. I sat up and looked around for Matt. Didn't see him. Didn't see Dreadlocks or Kodak or Venus or Sancho either. Their backpacks were gone. So was the blue suitcase, and there remained only boxes and suitcases, empty wine bottles, the low-burning hurricane lanterns in the niches, and the monster with its sharpened teeth and large eyes.

I was alone.

CHAPTER 83

Did the dogs get them? Or the tomb looters? Or someone or something else—like that damn crocodilian monster holding up the ceiling? Get out of this cursed place, I told myself. Find them. But first I needed to pee, needed to change out of this nightgown.

Needed to shoot Matt for abandoning me.

I dashed to the waterfall with my AK and lantern and took another look around. Nothing. No dogs or snakes or blue people or tomb robbers, only the trickle of water and my pounding headache. The cold stone walls worsened the queasiness in my stomach. So did the moldy smells. I splashed water over my face and got myself together as best I could. The clothes I'd worn the day before were smelly and soggy. So were the extra clothes in my pack, so I swallowed my pride and pulled on Catia's jeans and pullover.

Should I take my pack? Yes, I'd learned long ago from the Sandinistas to take everything, so I stuffed my smelly clothes inside the pack and hitched up. The monster holding up the ceiling stared at me in the poor light. Had it come alive and eaten everyone except me?

"Adios," I said and hurried out the entrance.

The passage I'd trod in my dream with Yaritza had the putrid smell of a rotting carcass. I eased to the corner with my AK, ready to shoot. No dogs. No tomb looters or blue crazies either, only an empty corridor and a gushing stream of water. I jumped across, climbed the slippery steps Kodak and I had used to get out of the storm and found myself in the fresh air of early morning gloom, not yet daylight but not dark either.

The ruins—an expanse of rubble and volcanic ejecta that spread out in all directions—looked as if they'd been swept over by a giant broom. Catia's tents were gone, blown away. I looked this way and that for Matt, growing more desperate by the minute, but all I saw was a dark swarm of bats returning to their caves. Did bats go out in a storm? No, the hurricane ended hours ago. They must have gone out while it was still dark.

Damn it, where was Matt? I could hear birds and what sounded like men's voices. Was it them or someone else? I eased around the pile of rubble that had once been a magnificent temple, my senses on full alert.

And came face to face with El Baboso.

My breath caught. The shock seemed to take all the blood from my head. He looked as panicked to see me as I was to see him, and I'm all but certain there would have been bloodshed if he hadn't yelped and darted away, disappearing behind a slab of ruins.

I grabbed a stone pillar for support and was still standing there, trying to regain my composure, when Venus rushed up beside me. She was breathing hard. Smudges of lipstick were still on her cheeks, and she had the hangover looks of a woman who needed Aspirin and two more hours of sleep.

"I'm so sorry," she said, "We thought you were with the gringo. The gringo thought you were with us. He's really upset."

"Where is he?"

"At the pit with the mushroom hunters. Come on. I'll show you."

"The mushroom hunters are alive?"

"Negative. Tomb looters got them. Are you okay?"

"Didn't you see him?"

"See who?"

"Blue crazy. He ran away."

She unslung her AK. "Where?"

"I don't know. But we have to be careful."

I followed her past the sacrificial altar, across the uneven ground of broken pottery, and down toward the landing where Catia's boat had exploded, looking left and right and even behind me for El Baboso. But all I saw were ruins, a gray sky, and a hint of more bad weather. The wind gusted, the sounds of birds grew louder, and at last, we came upon our little party near the edge of the forest where they stood with three or four other young men that Venus said were Marines.

Above them circled a cloud of vultures.

A cold fear gripped my gut. The stench of death permeated the air, and as I came closer, I heard Sancho speaking to Kodak. "Over here. The light is better on this side."

Matt was on his cell, trying to reach the embassy. When he saw me, he snapped his mobile shut and held up a hand to stop me. He needed a shave, and on his face was a look of despair. "You might not want to see this," he said in a weak voice. "It's not pretty."

CHAPTER 84

I walked right past him. He'd just abandoned me in an unholy place. Who was he to tell me what I could and could not see? Dreadlocks and the others had gathered next to a long, trench-like crevice that snaked out of the forest and ran in a broken line along the border of the ruins. It was about six feet deep and at least twice that wide, with rank vegetation on the sides.

"Down there," Venus said, looking like she was about to throw up. "There's six of them. One's a tomb looter." She made the sign of the cross. "May God rest their souls."

A spear protruded from the chest of the tomb looter. I was sorry to see it wasn't Ramos and wasn't Sergeant Pock Face either. The other five bodies had been stripped of clothing and were being fought over by buzzing black flies and an army of vultures.

God, why had I looked? I'd seen worse during the war, but that was years ago. Now I had the kind of stomach that revolted at the sight of a dead roach.

"Disgusting creatures," Venus said and pointed to vultures in the trees.

I dropped my pack and stood there in silence, trying to absorb the meaning. How sad it was. Six people dead and for what? For mushrooms.

For stupid toadstools that may or may not have special qualities. And for stupid Catia, getting all these people killed for her ambition.

"Catia's not down there," Venus said.

A redheaded vulture with a hideous naked neck swooped down from the trees and alighted beside me. I yelled at it and clapped my hands, but all it did was flop along the ground.

I clapped again and pretended to lunge at it.

This time it spread its ugly wings and hissed as if daring me to attack.

What was wrong with that puta bird?

I scooped up a handful of broken pottery and flung it. Bad mistake. A second vulture and then a third dropped down and stood their ground like I was the intruder.

Dammit to hell, I'd had enough. No one or nothing listened to me. Not Matt, not Holbrooke Easton, and not even the fucking vultures. I racked a round into the AK and fired a blast into the trees and the clouds, one short blast after another, and I kept screaming and firing until the magazine was empty, the vultures had flown away, and the Marines were crouched and staring as if I'd gone postal, which in a way I had, except it was buzzard postal.

Silence prevailed. Even the wind stopped blowing, and in that moment it occurred to me that the vultures were only doing what Mother Nature had programmed them to do, and I was the crazy one.

I bent over and burst into sobs.

Matt came over, took the AK, and pulled me into his arms. "It's okay, Baby. We're leaving this cursed island, getting you away from here."

"How many did I kill?"

"Not a single one, but you scared the hell out of the Marines."

"Can't we cover the bodies?"

"We're working on it. Marines are retrieving what's left of Catia's tent. It's over there, caught in a tree. You sure you're okay?"

I didn't answer and wished people would stop asking if I was okay when it was clear I wasn't okay and hadn't been since we'd been on this pinche island. He led me away from the trench. "Another one of Ramos' men is over there," he said, "a live one. The Marines caught him this morning. That's probably the light we saw last night."

I wiped my eyes and walked over for a look. The tomb looter was on his knees, hands shackled behind him, and he was dirty, shivering, and miserable looking, a far cry from the cocky bastards who'd come after me at the Asese landing and knocked the young girl into the water. The Marine guarding him, a young man in cargo khakis and green T-shirt, looked up at me. "He's not talking, but that will change when State Security gets here."

Yaritza's words came back to me in a flood—*They will be here sooner than you think.*

I turned to Matt. "When are they coming?"

"They may already be on the way. We need to get out of here."

"How?"

"The *Ana Maria.*" He pointed down toward the landing. "See it? That's our boat down there."

"I don't see a boat."

"That's the idea. It's camouflaged with vines and branches. From here it looks like a tree."

"How did it survive the hurricane?"

"Lead Foot knows what to do. He brought it in early this morning."

I punched him on the arm. "Why did you leave me alone this morning? I was scared."

"I didn't leave you alone. I went out with Lead Foot before daylight. The others were still there. They should have awakened you."

"Dammit Matt, nobody woke me. I was by myself. I panicked and dashed outside. Almost ran into that crazy old blue babbler."

"Venus told me. They're lurking around here somewhere."

"What happened to the blue suitcase?"

"On the boat. Lead Foot took it." He handed me the AK. "Now go. Grab your gear and get down to the boat. Take Sancho and Kodak with you. And watch out for the blue people."

By then, a couple of embassy Marines were returning with the green fabric from Catia's tent. "Snap it up," Matt said to them. "We need to go. Get it done, secure it, and then get back to your boat. You were never here. None of us were. Rock and roll."

He clapped his hands for emphasis.

Venus said, "What about the prisoner, sir?"

Matt kicked a stone, stomped away, turned around, and came back. "Take him with you, but don't rough him up, and don't interrogate him."

I hiked up my pack and turned to go, expecting to hear the thump of Colonel Vega's helicopter at any moment, but had taken no more than a few steps when the blue people emerged from the forest with their spears, feathers, long greasy hair, and monkey teeth beads.

CHAPTER 85

We dropped to one knee in combat stance—everyone except Kodak who was in his own world of filming the carnage. I didn't count them, but there were at least six or seven—the same scraggly bunch that had confronted me before. And they were all carrying two or three spears as if they'd come to do battle. Others waited back in the forest. Yaritza was not with them.

"Hold your fire," Matt said.

El Baboso, who before had been shirtless, now wore a blood-stained khaki shirt that he'd taken from a dead tomb looter. He danced around as fearless as the vultures, babbled a few words from the corner of his mouth, and stopped no more than five paces away. His rotten teeth and long greasy hair made him just as repulsive as the first time I'd seen him.

He jutted a spear into the ground and pointed a bony finger at me.

Matt rose to his feet. "I think he wants to pow-wow."

El Baboso wagged his finger at Matt as if to say, "Not you," and pointed at me again. I glanced behind me, hoping he was gesturing to someone else, but the looks I got from the Marines told me I was the chosen one.

I stood and pointed to my chest. "Me?"

El Baboso nodded his approval.

"You don't have to do this," Matt said.

I handed my AK to Matt. "I'll see what he wants."

"Make it fast. Vega could be here any moment."

El Baboso danced a complete circle around me, babbling nonsense. When he stopped, I backed away and held out both hands for him to keep his distance, in part because his message—or his attempt at a message—came out in an explosive shower of spittle and foul breath.

He tried again, this time with head jerks.

"I'm sorry, but I don't understand."

Sancho, who still had lipstick marks on his face, came up beside me. "What he said was get the hell off my island or suffer the same fate as everyone in that ravine."

Matt said, "We're leaving. No problem. Can you tell us where they took the mushroom woman? She was in the tent."

El Baboso pointed down at the bodies.

"Not that woman," Matt said. "What about the one with dark hair?"

From back in the tree line came a voice from one of the other blues. "Bad men took her."

El Baboso spun around in a fury, scooped up a handful of broken pottery, and flung it at whoever had spoken. The Marines behind me snickered. I heard the word, "Loonies." Venus told them to shut up. I turned back to El Baboso. "Where did they take the woman?"

He shrugged.

"Did they also take Yaritza?"

He nodded and struggled to say something else. Drool fell from his chin. He tried to speak, but it came out as a painful-to-watch stutter. Matt said, "Let him finish," so I stood there next to a pit of dead bodies, breathing in the evil smells of death and waiting for his answer while my team with their AKs and the Marines with their M-16s kneeled behind me and a cloud of returning buzzards swarmed toward us like kamikazes.

El Baboso finally gave up and gestured for someone back in the forest to speak for him. A cross-eyed man with white hair and a scrawny build stepped forward. The sight of him in the striped pullover that Catia's boyfriend had been wearing turned my stomach even more.

He spoke, and the message was clear:

Tomb looters murdered the mushroom hunters.

They also murdered one of the blues.

Blue people attacked and killed two tomb looters.

The surviving tomb looters captured Catia and Yaritza.

Blue people would attack us too if we didn't leave the island.

"We're leaving," Matt said. "You don't harm us. We don't harm you."

El Baboso didn't budge. Cross-eyes said, "Leave now or you die. *Vete*! Get off our island." His words set off a war dance among the blues, with lots of yipping and howling, waving spears, and chanting, "Go! Go! Go!"

"What is wrong with those idiots?" Kodak said. "Don't they understand we're leaving?"

One of the Marines muttered, "This is what happens when you open the gates to the Funny Farm." Cross-eyes, not to be outdone by El Baboso, scooped up a handful of broken ruins and flung it at us. A piece hit Kodak. Another struck Dreadlocks on his cheek.

"You fucking crazy?" Dreadlocks yelled at him. "Why you attack us?" He marched over to Cross-eyes, yanked the spear from his hand, broke it across his thigh, and tossed it to the ground. "You not hear boss? Boss say we leave. Nobody die. Not us. Not you. Not nobody. You go your skinny ass back to cave and we leave in peace."

If the blues had been rational, they'd have backed off. Instead, seven or eight others stepped from the forest with their spears, grumbling and making threatening motions. And then, while we were focused on them, a terrible scream erupted behind me.

At first, I thought it was that damn bird. But it was another blue, a pregnant woman, and she was rushing at us from behind a broken slab. The Marine guarding the tomb looter must have thought she was coming for him. He rolled to the side with his M-16. "What the fuck?"

The woman kept coming, all wild hair, dangling bones, monkey teeth beads, and a feathered spear, and she didn't stop until she drove her spear right through the captured tomb looter.

With everyone watching, she spit on his dying body, kicked him, did a little victory dance, and lifted both arms as if to thank the gods—and I cannot imagine what would have happened next if it hadn't been for the thump-thump of an approaching helicopter.

"Shit!" Matt said and yelled for everyone to get out of sight.

CHAPTER 86

Everyone scattered. El Baboso dashed away so fast he forgot his spear. Matt pulled me toward the cover of the trees. I grabbed El Baboso's spear—I don't know why—and hurried into the forest with Matt, Sancho, and Kodak.

The helicopter thump grew louder. The four of us crouched beneath the trees. The noise became a roar. The foliage around us vibrated. A dark shadow appeared above us. A blast of wind shook the trees and stirred up debris from the forest floor, and then it was hovering above the site we'd just abandoned next to the ravine.

It descended in slow motion, kicking up a cloud of dust, mist, and debris. When it finally settled, Matt stood up and looked through his binoculars, "Well I'll be damned. That's the embassy chopper."

"What are they doing here?"

"I imagine to check on us. The hurricane knocked out our relay."

He handed me the binoculars. "If I'm not back in fifteen minutes, you get down to the boat. But keep an eye out for the blue people. They're crazier than I thought."

He waved at the copter and set off without looking back, leaving us crouched in the bushes. The helicopter door opened. Out stepped the crewcut twins in pilot headgear. Next came Dr. Tinted Glasses in a jacket and tie. Ms. Cross Pendant was next, and I almost dropped the binoculars when Pineapple jumped down.

Pineapple? What was she doing here? She had sunglasses on and was dressed in stylish dark slacks and a white blouse.

Finally, a tall black man in khakis, a photographer's vest, and aviator sunglasses appeared in the doorway. He looked around and then stepped down and shook hands with Matt.

"*Mierda*," said Sancho. "We're screwed."

"Why do you say that?"

"That's Holbrooke Easton."

"Holbrooke Easton is black?"

"You didn't know?"

"No, it's just that I thought… Never mind."

From our hiding place in the bushes, we watched Matt guide the helicopter crew to the bodies in the trench. Sancho said, "I'm going to see what's going on," and hurried off to join them.

"Get your camera rolling," I said to Kodak.

"Gringo said not to film anything to do with the embassy."

"Forget what the gringo says. We need this on record. Zoom in on Easton and all the others from the embassy. The helicopter, too."

By then the vultures had returned to their feast. Matt drove them away with a burst of gunfire. Ms. Cross Pendant and Dr. Tinted Glasses took a brief look at the bodies and turned away. Pineapple put a hand over her mouth and bent over to throw up. Then Matt and Easton walked back toward the helicopter and got into what looked like a heated discussion.

"What are they arguing about?" Kodak asked.

I didn't answer. I figured they were arguing about me—Easton telling Matt the game was over and that it was time to drag me out of the bushes, shackle me, put me on the copter, and turn me over to Colonel Vega.

Matt looked in our direction. Here it comes, I thought. Why had I trusted him? He gestured for us to come out of hiding. Kodak and I just sat there looking at each other as if we had a choice in the matter, and we didn't move until Matt came within speaking distance.

"Come on out. Easton wants a word with you."

I had never experienced a pleasant conversation with Holbrook Easton and couldn't imagine this would turn out any better, but I found myself cornered like a fugitive in a cave and finally stepped into the open. "What's this about?" I asked Matt. "What does that bastard want?"

"He'll tell you."

"No, Matt, I'm asking you."

"Look, it'll be okay. I've got your back."

"Really, Matthew, you've got my back? Since when?"

"Please, Baby. It'll be okay. You'll see."

I grimaced and followed him to the helicopter. Ms. Cross Pendant fixed me in a gaze as if I were an enemy of the state. Pineapple, the only friendly face in the bunch, rushed over and gave me a sisterly hug. "Thank goodness you're okay," she said. "We were worried."

If ever there was ever a before-and-after for people, Pineapple would have been the perfect fit. When I first met her at the Cine Luminoso, she wore a baggy uniform and had the appearance of a skinny, pimple-faced teenager with wild kinky hair. Now, the pimples were gone, and her hair, nails, and complexion looked as if she'd just come from an exclusive beauty salon.

"We need to talk," she whispered in my ear.

I wanted to talk too, wanted to ask what she was doing with this embassy bunch and what was going on, but Easton stepped between us. No smile. No offer to shake hands, and no other friendly gestures. "Finally, we meet," he said and motioned me toward the helicopter.

"What's this about? I'm not getting on your helicopter."

"Please, Ms. Alvarado. We're not going to nab you."

Matt took the AK from me. "It's okay, Baby. Go ahead."

I still had El Baboso's spear in my hand and drove it into the ground next to Easton's foot. He jumped back and gave me a What-the-hell look. I glared back as if to say, "Don't mess with me," then I unhitched my backpack, let it fall to the ground, and climbed aboard the helicopter.

CHAPTER 87

The cabin had black leather seats and the pleasant smell I associated with expensive purses. I sank back in luxury and looked at the cockpit panel with all its gauges, instruments, knobs, and controls. If I'd been James Bond, I would have kicked Easton off the helicopter, hijacked it, and flown myself to safety. But I wasn't James Bond, and I didn't know how to fly. "Does this thing have coffee?" I asked.

He went into the cockpit and returned with coffee in a foam cup and two small containers of cream. I mixed in the cream, took a long sip, and tried to savor the taste, which wasn't easy considering my head was still buzzing with images of vultures, blue crazies, and dead bodies. Easton sat in a swivel chair to my front—probably the ambassador's chair. For a moment it was quiet enough to hear the clatter of buzzards on the roof.

"You said you wanted to talk," I said. "I'm here, let's talk."

He shook his head as if I'd violated some diplomatic nicety about how to begin conversations. "You just can't stay out of trouble," he said in his stuffy way of speaking.

"Excuse me for pointing this out, Mr. Easton, but wasn't it your embassy that got me into this mess? Wasn't it Matt?"

"No, Ms. Alvarado, that kind of shabby defense would never hold up in court. No one forced you to go to the hotel and film the assassination.

No one forced you to go to the Cine Luminoso and get in a fight with a Sandinista officer. And no one forced you to break your agreement with Colonel Vega. You did those things of your own free will—and as my lovely wife keeps reminding me, no one does anything unless there's something in it for them. So instead of blaming me or the embassy, ask yourself why you made those bad choices. What was in it for you?"

He might as well have slapped me in the face. Jimmy Buffett was right. It was my own damn fault for being so addicted to Matt.

Easten rummaged around in his briefcase, took out a photograph, and handed it to me. "Do you recognize this woman?"

It was the same woman who'd been behind me at the assassination, the same woman who'd shoved me into Contra Uno. "Of course, I know her. You should be interrogating her, not me."

"We already did. Colonel Vega had a long discussion with her yesterday."

"They arrested her?"

"Not exactly. She called Colonel Vega and set up a clandestine meeting. Don't ask for details. What's important is she told him the motive for the assassination. It was vengeance, score-settling if you will. Plain murder. Nothing political about it."

I gulped down the rest of my coffee. "Vengeance for what?"

"For what they did to her and that blue woman—Yaritza."

"What is Yaritza's connection with the woman in this photo?"

"Didn't Matt tell you?"

"All he told me was that Yaritza busted out of prison with one of the tomb looters—Ramos. Then Ramos took her to a contra camp in the countryside. Is that what happened?"

"Yes, and that's where she met the woman in the photo. She was a hostage. Then they made Yaritza a hostage, and the camp commander was none other than Contra Uno. I'm not going to tell what he and Ramos did to those two women in the camp, but you can imagine. What's important is Yaritza killed three men before she engineered an escape. Three, mind you. They say she has these unusual powers—that she can invade dreams."

"Dreams?"

"That's what they say. Drives men crazy with lust. Bottom line: Yaritza is the reason Contra Uno did a stupid thing like going to the hotel. Yaritza lured him there. It was a trap."

He handed me two more photographs. "Mugshots," he said. "These are the men that were behind you at the assassination. They're common criminals. State Security captured them both. I'm sharing this with you because it was your video that made it possible. They confessed. Can you believe they accepted the hit job for only two hundred dollars each? Says something about the value of life in Nicaragua."

Another burst of gunfire startled me. Easton jumped up and glanced out. The Marines had returned and were covering the bodies with what had once been Catia's tent. Venus was there too, driving away the vultures with her AK, probably as angry and frustrated as I was. Ms. Cross Pendant and Pineapple watched with hands over their ears. Vultures scattered, bark flew from the trees, foliage disintegrated, feathers drifted down, and the acrid smell of gunfire came into the cabin. So did a whiff of death.

Easton watched a moment longer and then got me another cup of coffee. He sat back down and said, "Now, where were we?"

"You just admitted that I'm innocent. Right? State Security caught the guys who fired the shots. Yaritza and that other woman were the masterminds. I'm off the hook. Right? So, how about returning my passport and flying me out of the country in this nice helicopter?"

"Oh, please, Ms. Alvarado, you're asking the impossible. You're a wanted fugitive. We can't abuse our diplomatic privilege by flying you to another country in a US Embassy helicopter."

"How would anyone know?"

"Do I have to explain tracking systems and radar?"

"You can at least get back my passport."

"We don't have your passport. State Security does. Colonel Vega is furious that you violated your pledge. He wants your head. And there's also that other little matter."

Easton didn't specify the "other little matter" and I didn't ask, but the word DESERTER might as well have been written on his forehead.

"We're finished here," he said and stood to leave.

"Wait a minute. That's it? What am I supposed to do?"

"What you choose to do is entirely up to you, Ms. Alvarado. You can either go back to Managua and surrender to State Security or you can proceed with your other plans. I don't want to know. I never saw you, and we never had this conversation."

His mobile buzzed. He answered and listened. His expression turned from curiosity to alarm. He clicked off and glanced up at me. "Bad news. Colonel Vega is on the way with a search team. ETA sixteen minutes."

CHAPTER 88

I jumped off the helicopter and grabbed my pack and spear. Easton yelled for his crew to get aboard and for Matt to get his people off the island. Venus kissed Sancho goodbye and said she'd see him in Managua. Then she and Dreadlocks trotted off with the Marines to the other boat. Dr. Tinted Glasses and Ms. Cross Pendant climbed aboard the helicopter without even glancing in my direction, but Pineapple rushed over to me. "I've got something for you," she said and handed me a thick envelope she'd taken from her tote bag.

"What is it?"

"Passport, compliments of Ignacio. It's not your original, but it's got your picture and the same name as the other documents. There's also an entry card that says you arrived a week ago."

I stared at the envelope. A passport? My passage to freedom? Finally? I hadn't expected that. "Does the gringo know about this?"

"Of course, he knows. He provided your picture for the passport."

"Matt did that?"

"*Sí, Señorita.* Didn't you know?"

"What about Easton?"

"He knows too, but he'll never admit it."

By then, Easton was standing in the helicopter doorway yelling at her to hurry. She hugged me, wished me good luck, and climbed aboard.

The helicopter lifted off in a cloud of debris, scaring away the vultures. The four of us—Matt, Sancho, Kodak, and I—hurried across the ruins, down the hill, and through the same creepy forest we'd taken the night before, which wasn't easy for Sancho because of his bum leg. Kodak wasn't that fast either, loaded down with camera equipment. A flock of canaries followed, chirping and singing as if happy to see us go, and we were nearing the edge of the forest when a shower of pebbles, spears, and broken pottery began dropping around us like rain.

The howls and yips started again.

"*Puta locos*," Sancho yelled into the forest. "Can't you see we're leaving?"

The pebbles and pottery kept coming. One bounced off my shoulder. Then a blue crazy dropped from a tree and began beating his hairy chest like a gorilla who just got laid.

Matt flattened him.

We kept going, one foot in front of the other, running as fast as our legs would carry us—which wasn't very fast—and were at the monster statues above the landing when El Baboso sprang from behind the palmettos and crashed into me sideways and struggled to get his spear.

If he had asked for his spear, I might have returned it. But not now. Not after the sneaky way he and his friends attacked us. Hell, no.

Down we went, rolling and tumbling like kids in a wrestling match. I screamed. I fought. I punched, kicked, and scratched. He was stronger than I imagined, and the worst of it was his slobbering drool. Matt pulled him off me, but El Baboso wasn't finished. He dove for the spear. I got there first. "Mine," I said like a child. "Go make yourself a new one."

Sancho fired a burst into the air. El Baboso gave up and dashed into the bushes, spearless, and then we were running again, bounding over downed trees, sliding and slipping down ravines, and jumping streams of runoff until at last, gasping for breath, we splashed into the shallows and climbed aboard the *Ana Maria*.

Which wasn't easy because it was covered with camouflage.

Lead Foot was not there.

"Where is he?" I asked Matt, thinking the worst.

"On the other boat with Dreadlocks and Venus."

Sancho fired up the engine. I thought we'd roar away and put the island with its blue crazies and terrible memories behind us, but Matt said not yet, that we'd create a wake visible from the air. "Hug the shoreline until Colonel Vega lands his helicopters," he said to Sancho.

"But what about the crazies? They'll jump aboard."

"They're not that crazy."

I wasn't so sure. A dozen or more were already in the water, yipping and howling and splashing around in the shallows. They hurled spears and mangos, stones as large as goose eggs, and even coconuts, some of which thudded against the boat.

"Bastards!" I screamed. "What is wrong with you? We're leaving."

They answered with more stones and spears.

I popped a magazine into the AK and fired into the air. I thought gunfire would drive them away. Instead, they sank beneath the surface or vanished behind boulders. Two or three sprang from under the water and swam toward us like Olympian swimmers, arms flailing the water.

“Shoot the bastards!” Sancho yelled from behind the wheel.

“No!” Matt said. “No more shooting.”

I wouldn’t have shot them anyway, and I’d have felt pity for them if they hadn’t been so hostile. Besides, we were out of their range.

Kodak, who’d been watching with a Glock in his hand, retreated to the cabin below. I grabbed a towel to mop drool from my face. Then I squatted in the well that led to the cabin and watched as we maneuvered along the shoreline, passing beneath tree branches and around boulder formations and vines that trailed into the water. Here and there, a blue face popped up, shouting obscenities and flinging stones and mangos, none of which hit us.

“It could be worse,” Matt said.

“How could it possibly be worse?”

“My mom. She lives in The Villages. It’s one of those restricted senior communities in central Florida. Ultra-conservative. She wants me to move in with her. They do things like putter around in golf carts and do group dancing and shuffleboard.”

“Are you crazy? You’re talking about shuffleboard when we’re getting battered by—”

“Copters,” he yelled. “Stay down. Don’t move.”

CHAPTER 89

I heard them before I saw them, not one, but three Soviet-era helicopters. I'd flown on aircraft like that years ago and could still remember the infernal noise, the teeth-rattling vibrations, and the stench of diesel fumes. Two of them headed straight toward the ruins, but the third deviated and swept over us, creating such a blast of air that even the boat shook.

"Recon," Matt said. "Let's give them a few minutes."

We waited, and just as Matt predicted they passed overhead a minute or two later, bringing back noise and vibrations and then fading to silence.

"Gone," Matt said. "They landed at the ruins. They can't see us."

A blessed relief swept over me. No more blue crazies. No more corpses or vultures. No more State Security. No more snakes—but that wasn't true. There were snakes in Florida too, and northerners who tortured locals with lectures on how they do things "back up *noith.*"

But that was a future matter. Today was a day to escape.

I went down to the cabin to straighten up and scrub my face and hands, and when I returned, the camouflage was gone, Kodak was filming the receding shoreline, and Matt was sitting in the front passenger seat with his mobile to his ear. Damn him. He'd been in this escape plan with Pineapple from the beginning and never told me, and I'd thought he was an uncaring prick. He twisted around to face me. "Relay's good. We can communicate with the embassy."

"Where are we going?"

"Ometepe. We tank up and then we're getting you out of here."

"How can we tank up in Ometepe? That hurricane knocked out power, and even if it didn't, people will buy up every drop of fuel."

"Got it covered. No problem, thanks to your friend, Enrique." He stood and motioned toward the stairs. "How about we fix coffee?"

I followed him back down to the cabin and delivered a solid punch to his arm. "Ouch," he said. "What was that about?"

"You were in this all along, weren't you?"

"Into what?"

"Scheming with Pineapple and Enrique to get me a passport."

"You didn't think I was going to abandon you, did you?"

My doubts about his sincerity faded. I wanted to throw myself into his arms, but now wasn't the time. Instead, I kissed his unwashed face, plopped onto the lounge, waited for him to make coffee, and tortured myself about the dream I'd had with Yaritza.

Was it only a dream, or a message? I imagined I could see her lashed to a coconut tree on the Island of the Dead, Ramos standing over her with his AK, demanding to know the location of the mushroom cave. There would be no freedom for her. No life either. Ditto for Catia. I had no love for either of them, but was it right to celebrate my freedom with Matt without at least trying to save them from Ramos?

"I know where they are," I said to Matt.

CHAPTER 90

The Island of the Dead lay to the west. We were heading east. "What makes you so sure they're on that island?" Matt asked.

"Yaritza told me."

"You spoke to Yaritza? When?"

"Last night. She came to me in a dream."

Sancho cut the engine and let the boat drift on the swells. All three men looked at me as if I'd lost it. "That's your evidence?" Matt said.

"Yaritza invades dreams. Didn't Easton tell you? She appeared to me other times too. I can't explain it. Maybe it's from the mushrooms. I'm as baffled as everyone else."

"What about the cave? Why do you say the cave is on that island?"

A gust of wind shook the boat. Sancho pointed to dark clouds as if to say hurry up. "Okay," I said, "first clue was yesterday morning when we were waiting for Catia's boat. Remember? Where was she? I'll tell you where she was. She was on the Island of the Dead. We know that from our snooping equipment. She was gathering mushrooms."

"How do you know they were gathering mushrooms?"

"Simple. When Catia arrived at the landing, she had this blue suitcase with her. Didn't you see it? She never let that suitcase out of her sight. Guarded it like it contained her life savings. Why would she do that? Reason: It was filled with mushrooms. It's down there in the cabin."

Sancho cuffed his hands around his lighter and lit a cigarette. "Maybe she gathered the mushrooms near the ruins."

"Not a chance. The weather was bad. They didn't have time. And here's the third clue. Don't take my word for it. Go down and sniff that blue suitcase. It smells like chicken roost poop. I caught that same smell when we were beneath the coconut trees on the Island of the Dead."

"Poop is poop," Sancho said. "It could have come from anywhere?"

"Yes, it could, but here's the clincher. The contents of that suitcase smell like the reeds we trekked through on the Island of the Dead."

All three men exchanged looks. Sancho said, "There's a flaw in your theory. If Catia already had the mushrooms, then why would she risk going to an island populated with lunatic blue people? Why not just go home with her mushrooms?"

"I can answer that," Matt said. "Mushrooms by themselves are worthless. You can eat'em, smoke'em, drink'em, sniff'em and all you get is a psychedelic high. You need special preparation. And there's only one person on Planet Earth who knows the secret."

"Yaritza," I said. "She's the reason Catia went to the island."

The water became choppy. Dark clouds were building up and we could see streaks of lightning. Matt looked at his watch. "Are you sure you want to risk it? If Colonel Vega captures any of the blues, he'll learn we're on the lake—and he's got helicopters."

"We should at least look. If they're there, we'll see their boat."

Sancho turned us about, and within half an hour the coconut trees of the Island of the Dead loomed up like an oasis in a desert.

I took Matt's binoculars and scanned the island from left to right: its sandy white beach, the jutting boulder formations, the birds dive-bombing the water, and the reeds that were getting whipped up by the wind. Sancho and Kodak also took turns, but it wasn't until we were within a minute or two of landing that I saw it.

"Stop the boat," I said to Sancho. "It's to the right of those boulders."

He throttled down. Matt took the binoculars for another look. "Well, I'll be damned. That's got to be a boat. It's camouflaged with reeds."

Kodak, being Kodak, put a telescopic lens on his camera and took pictures. Sancho surveyed the area with a sniperscope. "No movement. Nothing other than those damn birds."

I suggested we bypass the island and come in from the opposite side. "Can't do that," Matt said. "Other side is nothing but sheer cliffs and breakers. Wind's blowing from that direction. We'd break up."

"So, what should we do?"

"We can either tell Easton or we land and take a quick look. It's unlikely they'll hear us because of wind direction."

"But won't they see us?"

"Only if they have a lookout. They started with five men. Remember? The blues killed three. That leaves two. And even if they see us, they don't know we're after them. They might lay low. There's a lot of hiding places on that island." Again, he glanced at his watch. "Are you sure you want to do this? We're running out of time."

"We have to do this, Matt. Yaritza and Catia could be on that boat."

CHAPTER 91

The closer we came to the beach, the more I remembered my days with the Sandinistas when we approached a building or village that could be in enemy hands. Stay silent. Approach under cover of jungle or darkness. But there was no cover for us, no darkness or jungle, and our boat to my ears sounded like a freight train.

No one shot at us, and we landed on the *Ana Maria* and debarked with our weapons at the same spot we'd landed before, on the beach next to the boulders. "Stay low," Matt said. "Get to the boulders."

We rushed for cover like Marines assaulting a hostile island. Ramos had anchored his boat on the opposite side of the boulders, about fifty yards away. We couldn't see from our side, which meant they couldn't see us either.

Matt took out his cell and reported our situation to the embassy. He listened, frowned like he was hearing unwelcome news, and snapped his mobile shut. "Easton's back in Managua. He's not happy about our detour. Says it's important to get you out of here."

"But we're here already. Let's at least take a look."

"That's what I told him. He said it was up to us. I'll do it. It's my duty. The rest of you can either wait here or go with me. It's up to you."

"We already made that decision. Let's do it."

Matt looked at me and shook his head. "Anybody ever tell you how weird you are? You despise Catia. Right? You're scared to death of Yaritza. Right? Yet you're willing to risk your life and your freedom to save their butts."

"It's a woman thing, Matt. Are we checking out that boat or not?"

We followed him into the boulders that were green with lichen, trekking this way and that, sometimes crawling over boulders.

A shower blew over us. Frogs came to life, the sweetness of reed flowers filled the air, and then canaries appeared in swarms of blue, yellow, and green, flitting about and chirping as if begging for food. "Stupid birds," Sancho said. "They'll give us away."

Matt told us to squat down until they left, and as we waited it struck me that I'd had an encounter with birds everywhere I'd been since the assassination, even in my dreams. Were they trying to tell me something?

They finally gave up and fluttered away. Matt waved us on, and we soon reached the far edge of the boulder field, within a stone's throw of Ramos' boat. Sancho did his listening thing. Kodak got his camera rolling. Matt, looking through his binoculars, said, "Nothing. Don't see a thing."

I thought we'd discuss what to do next, but Matt had a different plan. He stood, said, "Cover me," and dashed to the boat with his AK.

He climbed aboard, signaled as if to say he was going down to the cabin and disappeared. Damn him, did he have a death wish? I'd done things like that back when I was young and stupid but that was because I was following orders and didn't have a vote.

I listened for gunshots, praying for silence, and then Sancho, who I thought had better judgment than Matt, sprang up and hurried to the boat with his AK, limping all the way.

He lumbered aboard, waved as if to say all was well, and stood on deck until Matt emerged from the cabin. He motioned us over. Kodak hung back like the good cameraman he was and followed me aboard.

"Down there," Matt said. "Check it out."

"What is it."

"You'll see. It's not pretty."

I hurried down with Kodak and entered a foul-smelling cabin that might once have been luxurious. Pock Face lay on the deck in a pool of blood, curled up in a fetal position, his pants and underwear down to his knees, his hands curled around the spear that killed him. An army of green flies covered his body and buzzed around the cabin like those damn vultures.

"Bastard," I mumbled, and felt like shooting him anyway.

The smell was so bad, I pulled the top of my shirt over my nose. Kodak motioned me aside so he could catch the scene on camera. Then Sancho came down, swatted at the flies, and checked the body. "Recent," he said. "What do you think happened?"

"Isn't it obvious? He went after Yaritza—or maybe Catia—thinking to get laid. One of them got loose, grabbed a spear, and pounced on him."

"Where'd they get the spear?"

"Same place we go ours. Crazies attacked them as they were leaving the island. I saw more of their spears on the topside deck."

By then Kodak had put down his camera and was rummaging around the cabin, pulling open drawers. "Finally found it," he said like a child who'd discovered a lost toy.

"Found what?"

"Hasselblad. It's a Model 500C, top-of-the-line. Bastards stole it."

I hurried topside and back into the fresh air. Matt was on his mobile but snapped it shut as soon as he saw me. "Just spoke to Easton," he said. "He's in touch with Vega. They captured a couple of crazies. He'll have them talking in no time. We need to get going."

"But what about Yaritza and Catia?"

Matt looked at his watch. "Shit! We've got an hour. No more."

Sancho went into the engine compartment, yanked out the ignition coil, and handed it to me. I stuffed it into my pack. Matt sent Sancho back to our boat to keep watch. Then Matt, Kodak and I got our gear together and set off into the reeds.

CHAPTER 92

Gusts of cool wind blew down from the summit, stirring up butterflies and creating undulating patterns in the reeds. Petals from the flowers swirled around us, their sweetness as powerful as magnolia blossoms in Florida. We eased along in slow motion, listening for suspicious sounds and trying to keep our heads below the reeds. Then the canaries came back.

"Damn birds," Kodak said.

We crept on, ignoring the canaries, and were soon at the summit beneath the coconut trees—at the place where I'd had a vision of Yaritza tied to a tree. The lake spread out below us. Coconut trees swayed in the wind. Flocks of terns squawked and lifted into the air.

But there was no sign of Yaritza.

How could that be? Why did I have that vision? And what about the dream that had landed us at this very spot in a native canoe?

Matt and Kodak looked equally downcast. "They could be in the reeds," I said to Matt.

"Yes, they could, but do you really want to search? Just look at it. Acres and acres. It'll take all day." He curled his hands around his mouth. "Yaritza!" he shouted. "Catia! Hello!"

The birds and the wind answered. The women did not.

He shouted a few more times. Kodak got his camera rolling and was panning the area when I caught a whiff of bat guano. I followed the scent to the edge of the cliff and looked at the foaming surf and pounding waves far below. The scent was stronger there, as if lifted by the wind. I backed away. Heights always gave me that uneasy feeling in the stomach.

And that was when I saw a rope.

It was tied to the same boulder where I'd sat a few days before—the one with petroglyphs on the sides. I eased forward and saw that it swung freely over the cliff, disappearing beyond a jagged outcrop about 12-15 feet below the cliff's edge.

Could Catia and Yariza be down there with Ramos? Inside a cave?

I showed Matt. He pulled the rope up, tested it for strength, and said it could easily support a man. "I'll check it out. You two wait here."

"Ramos could be down there."

"If he is, he can't possibly hear us in this wind and surf."

He tied the end around his waist, slung the AK over his shoulder, and eased over the edge. I told him to be careful. He said he'd be okay and to keep watch on the rear.

I didn't ask what to do if he didn't come back. There was no point. But I remembered the last time he disappeared into a hole and left us waiting in a hurricane. Would he do that to us now?

Kodak lay on his stomach and followed Matt's progress with the camera. I checked behind us, saw nothing out of the ordinary, and lay down beside him. The scariest moment was when Matt disappeared beneath the outcrop.

The rope swung free. "Adriana?" he shouted.

"I'm here. Are you okay?"

"You gotta see this. Come on down. Leave your AK with Kodak."

I pulled up the rope, secured it around my waist, and told Kodak it was more important to keep a watch behind him than to watch me.

The descent was easier than I thought, thanks to the roughness of the cliff face and all the little protrusions that served as footholds. I didn't dare look down, even when sea birds protested my presence with loud caws, and I was soon beneath the outcrop on a narrow ledge.

Matt pulled me to safety. The poop smell was powerful enough to intoxicate an elephant—and would have been worse except for the breeze. The cliff wall was covered with petroglyphic images of bats, celestial objects, spirals, and women with baskets. And amid those images was a dark opening, large enough for a human to enter.

"Bat cave," Matt said and handed me his flashlight.

At first, I saw only bats, hundreds of bats, maybe thousands, or tens of thousands, pulsing with life and clinging to the overhead. The beam of my light glistened off what looked like drops of rain but was a shower of bat poop, and below that, growing from the cave walls and the guano on the floor, were the same things that filled the blue suitcase.

Was this the magic mushroom cave? What a disappointment. A long time ago when I was in the fourth or fifth grade, we'd discussed it in school as if it were a magical place. I'd fantasized about it, dreamed about it, had seen it in my mind as a Fairyland Forest with giant toadstools and pretty girls with magic wands who cured the sick, made old people young again, and turned little girls like me into princesses.

Now I was staring at bat shit in a hole in a cliff in a stinky place that could have been the gateway to hell. No wonder little kids cried when they learned Santa Claus was fake.

"I've seen enough," I said. "Smelled enough too."

"Don't you want to climb inside and collect a few mushrooms?"

"I wouldn't go in that place in a hazmat suit."

"There could be pirate treasure. They say Blue Beard himself was in this area. I'm imagining a treasure chest filled with beautiful jewelry."

"You're a sick puppy. You need help."

I climbed back up, which wasn't as easy as going down, and handed the rope to Kodak. "Don't stay more than a minute."

He climbed down with his camera. I watched until he was beneath the overhang, and then I rolled over with my AK to keep watch on our rear. The wind gusted. The canaries came back, chirping and flitting about as if happy to see me. And again, I stared at the base of a coconut tree where I'd seen Yaritza in my vision. Had she really been tied to that tree? And what about the dream? Hadn't she landed the canoe at this very spot?

If she could communicate with me, why couldn't I communicate with her? "Yaritza," I whispered to the wind. "Where are you?."

I said it over and over in my mind, silently, right there beneath the coconut trees with the canaries looking on, with the stench of bat guano in the air, pouring my soul into that indefinable cosmic connection between us, trying to suck up the energy on the hilltop.

Can you hear me, Yaritza?

A gust of wind was my answer, and the chirps of the canaries, and the swaying coconut trees, and the unmistakable thump of helicopters.

CHAPTER 93

I struggled up and saw them—two helicopters in the distance, flying toward the mainland. They were too far to see the markings, but they were the same shape as the old Soviet copters Vega had landed on the island. Kodak appeared beside me, and then Matt.

"They're flying out the bodies," Matt said. "We need to go."

He cut the rope and tossed it over the cliff, and we were hitching up to leave when his mobile buzzed. He answered it, listened for a minute, and offered the phone to me.

"Easton. He wants to talk to you."

"About what?"

"He'll tell you."

I took the mobile, and before I could utter a word. Easton said, "I just got off the phone with Colonel Vega. He's still on the island. They captured that stuttering character and two other cave dwellers. They interrogated them, Nicaraguan style."

"And?"

"Turns out they were watching your little party the whole time you were on the island. They described each person in detail, especially you, and I don't have to tell you Vega is in an uproar. The ambassador is also having a hissy fit. This will be in the news by nightfall. If it weren't for the hurricane, they'd already be sending out gunboats to search for you."

"How long do we have?"

"It may already be too late. Just get off that island. Now."

Matt took the mobile and listened a moment longer, shaking his head and glancing at me. He snapped it shut. "Change of plans."

"To what?"

"Come on. I'll explain on the boat."

We trotted down the hill and through the reeds until we reached the tomb looters' boat. I thought we'd dash into the boulders and head toward our boat, but Matt said, "Easton wants their boat visible from the air. We need to get rid of the camouflage."

We climbed aboard. Matt used his Swiss Army knife to cut the ropes securing the reeds. Kodak raced down the stairs and retrieved the Hasselblad. I grabbed one of the spears on the deck. We jumped down and hurried into the boulders.

And almost crashed into Ramos.

His AK was pointed directly at us. Mine was slung over my shoulder. Matt's AK was pointing downward, and we couldn't have fired anyway without racking a round into the chamber. Yaritza was on her knees beside Ramos, her skin blue, her hands cuffed behind her back and her mouth covered with a gag.

"Which one of you bastards disabled my boat?" Ramos asked in the same gruff voice I remembered—like he had gravel in his throat. "Who took the ignition coil?"

He poked his AK in Matt's chest. "Answer me, damn you, or I'll blow your puta head off."

There was hatred in his sun-darkened face. I saw it in his furrowed brow and clenched jaw. He'd murdered and raped during the war. He'd murdered the mushroom hunters. He'd watched Pock Face murder my mother. And he'd murder us the moment he got his hands on the ignition coil. Matt knew it. I knew it. So did Kodak and Yaritza.

Yaritza tried to speak. Ramos turned on her. "Shut up, bitch!"

The distraction gave me just enough time to reach for the pepper spray canister in my pocket—the pink one. Ramos saw the movement. "Get your hands up!"

He pointed the AK at me. "You're a sneaky little bitch. You know where the coil is, don't you? Get it for me and I'll let you go."

Yaritza shook her head as if to say *Don't do it.* Ramos poked the barrel into my chest. "You either get me that ignition coil or I'm going to start shooting."

He hadn't seen the pepper spray canister in my hand, but I couldn't click the lever and aim it while his gun was in my chest. I needed a distraction, needed him to look elsewhere. "We buried it in the sand," I said. "It's over there. I'll show you if you let them go."

He glanced toward the boat, and it was clear from his jerky movements that he was as desperate as I was. I tried to click the safety lever with my thumb. Yaritza, who must have been reading my mind, sprang to her feet.

What happened next was so sudden it seemed to happen all at once. Ramos swung in her direction. A shriek rented the air. A dark shadow fell over us, and then that damn bird swooped out of nowhere and raked across Ramos' head.

CHAPTER 94

He stumbled backward. His AK fired into the air. The bird flew away. I pounced with my pepper spray, aiming it at his face. He screamed like a man under attack by vampires, flailing at his eyes and face. Matt kicked away his AK.

Ramos tried to struggle to his feet.

Matt knocked him to the ground, and the fight was over.

"What the hell did you use on him?" Matt asked, wiping his eyes.

My eyes burned too. Kodak was also rubbing his eyes. Ramos was curled up on the ground, groaning and whimpering, blood running over his face from the bird attack.

Matt frisked him and found the keys in his pockets. I unlocked the cuffs on Yaritza's wrist. Not until then did I notice she was dressed in shorts and a tank top sans bra. She rubbed her wrists and thanked us. Matt asked her what happened to Catia.

"Gone," she said in a calm voice.

"Gone where?"

"The water." She didn't explain the details. She didn't have to because I sensed the drama as if she were feeding the vision into my head—Yaritza topside with Ramos in a speeding boat, shackled to a seat. Catia in the cabin with Pock Face. Yaritza invades his mind with erotic thoughts. Catia plays along. Pock Face drops his pants and removes her cuffs, thinking she's a willing partner. Catia grabs a spear and plunges it into his chest. She rushes topside with his pistol, but Ramos is waiting with his AK.

"She dove into the lake," Yaritza said. "Ramos shot at her."

"Did he hit her?" Matt asked, breaking my connection with Yaritza.

"Don't know. She disappeared in the swells. Then we came here."

Matt took out his cell as if to report to Easton but put it away. "We need to leave," he said to Yaritza. "Now. You can come with us."

She gave me a pleading look.

"Don't worry," I said. "We're not going to turn you in."

Kodak pointed to Ramos. "What about him?"

Matt looked at me as if I had a choice in the matter. I didn't know what to say and didn't have to say anything because Yaritza grabbed the spear from my hand.

Ramos didn't see her coming, didn't see the spear until she drove it into his chest, right through his military green T-shirt. He grabbed the spear with both hands. Blood spurted out. A horrifying, animal-like scream escaped his lips. Yaritza pushed the spear deeper.

Ramos twitched a moment and lay still, blood gurgling from the wound. "*Ya echo*," Yaritza said as if she'd done nothing more than smash a cockroach. "It's done."

I looked away. I'd seen enough death. Kodak stood there with a sickly look on his face. Matt said, "Christ, I didn't expect that. Let's go."

Yaritza said she'd be back and raced barefoot toward Ramos' boat.

"Where are you going?" Matt yelled to her back. "We need to leave,"

"Go. I'll catch up with you."

We hurried across the boulders and found Sancho waiting on the boat with his AK. He looked as relieved to see us as we were to see him. "What was the shooting about?" he asked.

"Later," Matt said, twirling his finger. "Rock and roll."

Sancho fired up the boat.

"Wait," I said. "What about Yaritza?"

Matt looked at his watch. Yaritza came racing out of the boulders with a tote bag over her shoulder. She bounded aboard. "Clothes," she said, pointing to the bag.

Sancho gawked at her as if to say, "What the hell?" and then turned the boat about.

"Where to?" he asked Matt.

"How fast can you get us to Rivas?"

"I thought we were going to Ometepe."

"Change of plans. Ometepe's been compromised."

CHAPTER 95

As soon as we were underway, putting the Island of the Dead behind us, Yaritza asked if she could use the bathroom to clean up and change. I led her down to the cabin where she stripped off her shorts and tank top without a trace of modesty. She was blue all over and had the kind of looks and body that would drive women to envy and men to drooling lust. No way could she be pushing sixty. They must have made a mistake.

"I heard your message," she said in a sultry voice that I recognized from the dream.

"You mean when we were shouting for you?"

"No, Adriana, I'm talking about the message you sent from the coconut trees. Next to the cave. Waiting for your friends. You called my name. You said you had come to help. Thank you, Adriana. Thank you." She touched my arm, smiled, took her tote bag into the head, and closed the door.

I stared after her. How could she have heard me? How did she even know my name? How could she have known where I was sitting? Did the bird tell her? Maybe she was a stranded visitor from outer space. Or the future. Maybe blue was her real color. Which explained how she could so calmly drive wooden spears into her victims' hearts. If I'd done that, even to Ramos, I'd be an emotional wreck in need of a shrink.

Matt came down and reported our situation to Easton, which was basically that we'd departed the island and were heading to Rivas. He didn't say a word to Easton about the cave. Didn't mention Ramos or Yaritza either and when he rang off, he said, "Vega will think it's us in that boat. He'll go there in his helicopter. Imagine his surprise. That'll keep him occupied."

Clever, I thought until I remembered the spear in Ramos' body had my fingerprints all over it. I reached into my pocket for the pepper spray canister. It wasn't there. Damn it, I must have lost it in the boulders next to the body. Vega would find it. He'd know it belonged to me.

As if that wasn't troubling enough, Kodak rushed down the stairs. "Gunboats."

Plural, meaning more than one gunboat.

"Shit!" Matt said and dashed up the stairs. I twisted my cap backward and followed. There were two gunboats racing toward us, slicing the water, lights flashing, one directly behind us and another coming at an angle from the starboard rear. I had no idea about nautical distances, but Matt, who was watching through his binoculars, yelled to Sancho that they were about two hundred meters and closing.

"Can we outrun them?" I asked.

He tapped his ear. "CAN'T' HEAR YOU."

"I ASKED CAN WE OUTRUN THEM."

He pulled me partway down the stairs where we could talk. "Gunboats are powerful. They're made for speed…to catch smugglers. It'll be close."

"How much longer to Rivas?"

"Five, maybe ten minutes. We need to get rid of the guns."

"Why?"

"Embassy boat. How would that look in the papers if they find us with a boatload of guns?"

He rushed topside to the locker and began pulling and tossing. Over the side went AKs, grenades, ammunition boxes, a shotgun, pistols, and the M-79 grenade launcher. "Heavy stuff," he yelled above the roar. "That'll get us a bit more speed."

"What about the blue suitcase?"

"No way. Easton wants to analyze those mushrooms."

"Will they shoot at us?"

"They wouldn't dare. This is the ambassador's boat."

Just then, with a roar and a whistle, a shell passed above the boat and blossomed the water to our front. The boat shook.. Splash washed over us. "Are they fucking crazy?" Matt said. "They must think we're narcos."

I uttered a silent curse. Would this drama never end? Kodak had said terrible things happened in threes. It wasn't even noon, and I'd already been battered with so many tragedies I'd lost count. I'd even lost a battle with buzzards. And why?

Matt. Always Matt. He was a Jonah, a jinx. He was that little black-cloud character in the Li'l Abner comic strips that brought disastrous misfortune to everyone.

Stupid me. Stupid, stupid, stupid.

The only good news was that we were fast closing on Rivas. I could already see the destruction caused by the hurricane—broken windows and wrecked cars, downed power lines, boats strewn about, and workers going about the business of cleaning up.

"Hundred meters and closing," Matt yelled to Sancho. He rushed back to the partial shelter of the stairway and reported to Holbrook Easton. "Got it," he said. "Dock C, Berth 37."

"What is Berth C?" I asked.

"Our mooring. Grab your gear. Get everything up here. Yaritza too."

"What happens when we land?"

"Run like hell. Shadow's waiting for us."

"Shadow?"

"Enrique."

I dashed below and found Yaritza calmly brushing her long black hair. The blue was gone. She'd put on lipstick and wore a white knit pullover and faded jeans with fashionable rips at the knees. What a difference from the Jungle Jane look!

"One minute to landing," Matt yelled. "Everybody topside."

Kodak and Matt bounded down in a fury and grabbed their things, including the blue suitcase. Yaritza didn't seem the least concerned, and it wouldn't have shocked me at all if she'd snapped her fingers, turned blue again, and faded away to nothing.

I grabbed El Baboso's spear—I wanted that damn thing. Yaritza put on sunglasses and a ball cap and took her tote bag, and by the time we were topside, the gunboats were almost on us, lights flashing, a voice blaring over a loudspeaker to stand down.

Worse, an army truck was coming down the hill toward us, and if it hadn't been for all the destruction and debris, they'd already be at the dock and waiting for us.

Sancho maneuvered around the flotsam caused by the storm and eased the boat into Berth 37. The gunboats behind us were too large to follow and began landing at a different pier.

We bumped against tires and came to a hard stop.

And there stood my old friend Enrique in a ball cap, jeans, sneakers, and sunglasses. He helped us off the boat with our gear. I didn't look back, but I could hear angry shouts and curses. We raced up the pier to a street where two cars were parked and waiting, engines running.

One was a battered Datsun that had seen more than a few owners. The other was a shiny Toyota SUV with diplomatic plates. Beside it stood the crewcut twins. The robots.

How could they be here this soon?

Were they clones?

I headed toward the SUV. "Not that one," Matt said and guided me toward the Datsun.

Kodak and Sancho jumped into the back seat of the SUV. The door slammed and away they went, taking with them our cameras and the blue suitcase.

Yaritza and I piled into the back seat of the Datsun. Matt climbed into the front passenger seat. Then we were speeding along the back streets of Rivas, dodging around debris, stalled cars, and downed power lines.

CHAPTER 96

I had no idea what was going on, where we were going, or anything else—and didn't ask because I was too busy glancing behind us. Yaritza sat next to me as calmly as if we were going to Sunday mass, cradling her tote bag.

Enrique said, "Almost there" and slowed in front of the cathedral of San Pedro Apostol. He drove into the parking lot and slid to a stop beside a tourist van. On its side in big block letters were the words, NICARAGUA SKY-DIVING.

"Transfer," Enrique said. "Grab your things."

A young man standing beside the van watched until we unloaded. Then he hopped in the Datsun we'd just vacated and drove it away. Enrique climbed into the van and started the engine, and I was hurrying toward the side door when Yaritza pulled me aside.

Her hand on my arm was as warm as her voice. "I've got something for you," she said and reached into her tote bag. She took out a large zip-lock bag that contained what looked like ground coffee. It had a blue tint.

"One teaspoon a week is all you need," she said.

"What is it?"

"Blue Magic. Don't overdose."

I took the bag. "Why is it blue? Is that the magic ingredient?"

"Ask Dreadlocks. He can conjure up Maria Sabina.

"Come on," Matt called from the van. "We need to go."

I headed toward the rear sliding door and was about to climb inside when a flock of canaries appeared from nowhere, a beautiful swarm of yellow, blue, and green. They chirped and flitted for a few seconds, then twirled in formation as if to entertain us, and flew away in a straight line, disappearing beyond the cross atop the cathedral.

I looked back for Yaritza.

She was gone.

Gone? How could she just disappear? It was as if Scotty had beamed her up to the mother ship. I looked this way and that. There were no other cars in the parking lot. No trees or shrubbery. No place to hide.

"Let her go," Matt said. "She obviously doesn't want to come with us."

"But what happened to her? She was standing right there."

"Yaritza," he said as if her name explained all the mysteries.

We drove away, putting the parking lot behind us. I looked out the windows on both sides, hoping to see her hurrying along the tiled sidewalks with her tote bag, but she was nowhere to be seen. Was it the canaries? Was there a connection?

An icy chill shot through me. Could it be?

No, what was I thinking? Canaries were a common sight in Nicaragua.

But still…

CHAPTER 97

We drove up a hill, maneuvered around debris, wrecked cars, workers, downed power lines, fallen trees, and residents surveying the damage to their homes, and finally put the city behind us. I leaned forward and asked Enrique where we were going.

"Private airport."

"Then what?"

He didn't answer.

"What about checkpoints?"

"Don't worry about checkpoints."

Worry? How could I not worry when we were still in Nicaragua? How could I not worry sitting next to Mr. Disaster himself in a getaway van? Any second now we'd round a curve and find the road blocked by trucks, Jeeps, and a hundred soldiers who all looked like Captain Vega.

We didn't, and five or six minutes later we drove across a grassy runway and stopped in front of a small hangar. A red Kawasaki motorcycle was parked in front. Broken tree limbs were scattered about. A portion of the tin roof had been peeled back by the hurricane, and the sign over the door—NICARAGUA SKY-DIVING—dangled sideways.

Sky diving? The knot in my stomach twisted tighter.

A side door opened. Out stepped a wiry little man in a helmet and goggles who made me think of that daredevil who'd attempted to jump the Grand Canyon on a motorcycle.

Good God, was Evel Knievel our pilot?

He nodded as if to say hello and then slid open the bay doors.

A single prop airplane was inside, all white and red and ready to go. "Ever been skydiving?" Matt said. "We'll bail out in the jungle once we cross the Costa Rican border."

I stared into his sunglasses and saw my own reflection. Was he serious? Was this the escape they had in mind? Skydiving? No way in hell was I going to jump out of an airplane, not in Costa Rica and not anywhere else.

"It's only scary the first time," Enrique said. "You'll enjoy it."

All three men burst into laughter.

"Don't worry," Matt said. "We're not bailing out."

Matt, Enrique, and Goggles rolled the airplane out of the hangar. Enrique said he had things to do and climbed onto the Kawasaki. "Suitcases are already loaded," he said.

"Suitcases?"

"You can thank Pineapple. She went to your apartment and retrieved your jewelry. Also, your makeup kit and clothing. She even got your black leather jacket at State Security. There's another suitcase for the gringo."

He saluted, started the bike, and motored away.

By then, Goggles was at the airplane door. "All aboard and buckle up."

I climbed aboard expecting another disaster. Goggles started the engine and taxied to the takeoff end of the runway. We made a U-turn and sat there, engine running.

"What's he doing?" I asked Matt.

"Checking the gauges. It won't take long."

Come on, come on, I wanted to yell. *Get this thing in the air.*

The plane vibrated and shook. No way was this going to work. Not sitting beside the jinxed gringo with the little black cloud hovering over his head. We'd crash during takeoff and die a fiery death. Or Colonel Vega would order up a flight of old Soviet Migs to shoot us down. Or they'd blast us out of the sky with SAM missiles.

I tightened my seat belt and looked around for a parachute. Maybe bailing out wasn't such a bad idea. "*Mierda*," said the pilot.

"What?"

He didn't answer. He didn't have to. I glanced out the window and saw an army Jeep, a truck, and police cars with flashing lights.

CHAPTER 98

Goggles gunned the engine. I sank lower into my seat. Matt took my hand. We bounced along the runway, the pilot mumbling "*Vamos*" again and again, each *Vamos* more desperate than the last, and I was certain we were going to marry the Jeep that had just driven onto the runway when we lifted into the air, banked, and flew low over the lake.

No gunshots. No SAM missiles, and no Migs.

The flight took us past the magnificent twin peaks on Ometepe Island and across a large expanse of lake to the jungles of Eastern Nicaragua. I thought we'd cross into Costa Rica. Instead, we followed the Rio San Juan del Sur to the Caribbean with its spectacular marine blue colors. Blue, mind you, bluer than Yaritza, bluer than the bag of Blue Magic.

I asked Matt why we were flying over the Caribbean. "You'll see," he answered, which was his way of annoying me, and an hour or so later a large island appeared in the distance. I knew from my travels that it was the Colombian island of San Andrés, the birthplace of Dreadlocks and a tourist destination for snorkeling and scuba divers.

Down we went, landing safely on another grassy runway.

In another country that wasn't Nicaragua.

Thank you, God.

We taxied to a shabby hangar. There were no signs of damage from the hurricane. I unbuckled, ready to jump out to freedom, to celebrate, but when I saw a car and driver waiting for us, the paranoia came back. Could he be an agent for Colonel Vega?

He wore a ball cap and brightly colored shirt with patterns of coconuts, pineapples, and tropical birds, and when he spoke, saying, "Welcome to San Andrés," his accent was the same as Dreadlocks. Maybe this would work after all. Maybe we'd get back to Florida safely.

Maybe.

Goggles—or whatever his name was—refused money for the flight, saying he'd already been paid. The other man, whose name was Armstrong, helped us unload our suitcases and kindly waited while we used the hangar's modest facilities to clean up and change.

Reggae was blaring on the car radio when I went back out. Armstrong was grinning and moving his body in rhythm. I wasn't in the mood to dance. Not yet, and even less so when Matt's phone buzzed. He answered and listened, and when he frowned, I knew it was Holbrooke Easton. Was there no escaping that man? Matt offered me the phone

I took it from his hand. "Now what?" I said to Easton.

"Is that the way you always answer the phone? How about 'Good afternoon' or a friendly hello?"

"Good afternoon, Lord Easton. What is going on?"

"I'm calling about the blue suitcase?"

"What about it?"

"Would you be so kind as to explain why it contains only your pack and dirty clothes?"

"What? Are you serious?"

"I'm deadly serious, Ms. Alvarez."

"It's Alvarado, not Alvarez."

"Whatever. Do you have any idea how this happened? We wanted to analyze the contents."

Yaritza, I thought and remembered how she'd cradled her tote bag in her lap as if it contained an infant child. I smiled. I even suppressed a laugh. Yaritza was probably in a dingy witch cave at that very moment, cooking Catia's mushrooms over an open fire, grinding them to powder, and adding a blue ingredient. "I don't have a clue," I said. "Sorry I can't help you."

It was dark by the time we arrived at the Gustavo Rojas Pinilla International Airport. Armstrong "tanked" us for the tip, and we hurried inside to find the place crowded with tourist types in colorful shirts, straw hats, Bermudas, and flip-flops. Reggae was playing as well.

A ticket agent glanced up from behind the counter. So did a man behind a newspaper. Were they looking at El Baboso's spear? Or were they Nicaraguan agents? In my paranoid mind, I imagined they'd soon be on the phone with the head of local security who just happened to be good friends with Captain Vega, and I'd be back in Managua by midnight.

I headed to the nearest tourist stall and bought a floppy hat, pink sunglasses, and a copy of the *Miami Herald* to wrap around the spear.

Enrique had already booked a direct flight to Orlando on American Airlines. We headed toward our gate and fell in line for the security check. My pulse beat faster as the line closed. I'd come this far and couldn't imagine my luck would hold. The agent looked at the spear and shook her head as if I'd been ripped off by a vendor selling cheap tourist junk. She tagged it with the fake name on my passport and directed it to the compartment near the cockpit.

The Blue Magic wasn't an issue either. Matt had packed it in his suitcase. We boarded. I didn't breathe easier or thank God until we lifted into the air over the Caribbean and watched the lights of the beautiful island of San Andrés slip away behind us.

But there was still the matter of getting through US Customs in Orlando with a mysterious bag of Blue Magic and a fake passport.

CHAPTER 99

Our plane touched down on Florida soil at precisely 10:23 p.m. No soldiers were waiting for me. No immigration agents or police officers either. No one was eying me with suspicion. My fake passport was stamped by a nice lady who said, “Welcome to the United States.”

El Baboso’s spear got a good laugh. Matt’s suitcase with its Blue Magic contents passed the dog sniff test, and by midnight we were in a suite on the fifth floor of a luxurious hotel on Buena Vista Drive, a short distance from Disney World.

I felt like falling on my knees to praise God, Jesus, and the Holy Spirit—whatever that was—and to also thank Enrique, Pineapple, Goggles, and maybe even Matt and Holbrooke Easton.

We took long warm showers, separately, and fell into the luxury of a king-sized bed.

Yaritza did not invade my dreams. There was no crocodilian monster holding up the ceiling. No biting fleas either or yapping dogs at the door, and when I woke at nine, the Florida sun was shining through the curtains and Matt was in a white terry cloth robe laying out the breakfast he had ordered from room service.

What a difference from waking up in that damn underground shelter.

Matt said he was expecting a call from Easton, and the words were scarcely out of his mouth when his mobile buzzed. He answered, listened, frowned as he always did when speaking to Easton, and handed the phone to me. “He wants to talk to you, not me.”

Here it comes, I thought, the disaster that was going to ruin my beautiful day. “Good morning, Mr. Easton.”

“Good morning, Ms. Alvarado. “Are you well today? Happy?”

“Happier than I was yesterday. What’s going on?”

“I’m calling about a canister of pink pepper spray.”

“Pink? Did you say pink?”

“Hot pink. It was discovered near the body of that tomb looter. Vega says it belongs to you.”

“Vega is wrong. What kind of person uses pink pepper spray?”

There was silence and then a muffled conversation in the background. I couldn’t make out everything, but I heard the expletives—words like *puta, joda, and mierda*. This went on until Easton came back to the phone. “Colonel Vega asked me to give you a message.”

“What’s the message?”

“I won’t repeat his exact words but what it boils down to is he has a massive headache and says you better not ever show your pretty, um, face again in Nicaragua. Never, ever.”

“He’s such a gentleman. Please tell Colonel Vega that I thank him for his kindness, and not to worry. I don’t plan on returning anytime soon.”

Matt laughed and took the phone. He spoke to Easton for another minute or so and then called Sancho to ask about Kodak. He listened, smiled, and looked up from his cell. “They dropped Kodak off at the

Masaya crafts market. He found his little flower girl. The two of them took off together and now they're catching up at a hotel in Granada."

He laughed at something Sancho said and then rang off and put away the cell. "What was so funny?" I asked.

"Sancho. He says to tell you he's sorry he didn't give you a farewell hug but to let you know that for him your name will always be Miami. Pineapple also sends love. Venus and Dreadlocks too. They all miss you."

My throat tightened. I felt the tears and went to the bathroom to get myself together.

We ate breakfast and wondered aloud about the future for all of them. Matt said he didn't expect things to get any better in Nicaragua and he was sick of his work and the danger and uncertainty. "I'm turning in my resignation. What I want is a tranquil life in a small town."

"And then what?"

"I don't know, and maybe not knowing is a good thing."

"How could not knowing be a good thing?"

"Because if you don't know the outcome, the possibilities are endless." He took a sip of coffee. "I can tell you at least two things I want."

"Tell me."

"First, we're in Orlando. I've never been to Disney World. I'd love to go with you—either to the Epcot Center or the Magic Kingdom."

"Magic Kingdom sounds good. Shouldn't we mix a bit of Blue Magic in our coffee?"

"Let's do it."

We added a dash and then drank a toast to Kodak and Flower Girl. It wasn't fatal so we drank toasts to Sancho and Venus, to Pineapple and Enrique, to Dreadlocks, and even Yaritza.

"You mentioned there were two things you wanted for the future," I said. "One is Disney World. What's the second?"

"Do I have to tell you?"

"I'd like to hear it anyway."

"Second thing is whatever the future brings, I want it to be with you."

He leaned toward me. Our lips met in a wonderful moist fusion of passion. A fire ignited inside me, the same fire I'd felt that first night on the fifth floor of the Hotel Intercontinental, and then we were kissing and fondling like teenagers in the back seat of a car in a drive-in movie.

"I thought we were going to Disney World," I whispered.

"Disney can wait."

EPILOGUE

Colonel Vega's report of the mushroom murders made the evening news. The tabloids called it MURDER BY MAGIC MUSHROOM. The only positive was that my name was not mentioned. Tomb looters were the new villains and I'd become old news.

The soldiers captured eight blues on the island, including El Baboso. Two were identified as escaped criminals, two women were released, and the others were sent to the happy farm. Another eight or ten remained on the island to scare and harass visitors.

Catia's body was never recovered. There was no search, no investigation, and no memorial service. No blowback from her family either, which led me to suspect she had survived by swimming to one of those boulder formations on the lake and was now back in France.

Matt and I spent two fun-filled weeks traveling the state of Florida like tourists, visiting friends and family, getting to know each other better, and looking for a place to settle. We finally chose the charming seaside city of St. Augustine, the oldest city in the US.

Matt secured a position at Flagler University as a professor of international economics. They hired me as a journalism instructor. I also became a weekly columnist with the Miami Herald, writing about the oddities of the state—invasive pythons in the Everglades, UFO sightings, a naked couple making love while driving a speeding car on I-95, and a tourist who perished while trying to hand-feed an alligator with a Double Whopper.

The bag of Blue Magic lasted a year. I'm not ready to pass judgment, but my hair is thicker, my skin is moist and clear, my wrinkles are gone, and my energy remains high. Ditto for Matt, and I have no complaints about his, um, performance in other areas.

On the Day of the Dead, exactly one year after Yaritza invaded my dream, UPS delivered another bag of Blue Magic to my door. No label, no message, and no return address.

Thank you, Yaritza, wherever you are.

We married on Halloween eve two years after my escape, atop the magnificent Castillo de San Marcos, next to an ancient Spanish cannon that pointed out to sea. Matt's mom attended with her gentleman "friend," and they both encouraged us to get a golf cart and move to their retirement community in The Villages.

Maybe in thirty more years. Or a hundred.

Nora, a.k.a. Flower Girl, provided the wedding flowers. She and Kodak had married in Nicaragua, fled to Ft. Lauderdale as *exiliados*, and opened a florist shop and a picture studio.

Kodak took the wedding photos with his Hasselblad 500.

Pineapple and Ignacio also attended. They had moved to Miami and established a successful Nicaraguan restaurant that catered to exiles from Nicaragua, Venezuela, and Cuba. I didn't ask and didn't want to know, but I imagined hidden cameras in their restaurant, audio devices beneath each table, and shady CIA types at the bar in guayabera shirts.

Sancho and Venus 25 showed up as well, Sancho in a dark tuxedo, and Venus, stunning as ever in a white gown that looked as if it had come from Moctezuma's palace. They had not married but were living together in Los Angeles where Venus was proctoring an evening class in Azteca Nahuatl and pursuing a degree in indigenous languages.

Sancho was working on a Ph.D. in music and teaching classes in music appreciation.

Venus caught the bridal bouquet and Sancho got the garter.

Among the wedding gifts was another zip-lock bag of Blue Magic.

Gracias, Yaritza.

Colonel Vega also sent wedding gifts—my original passport that was still valid and a hot pink canister of pepper spray, industrial strength.

Dreadlocks found another woman and started a tourist excursion business on Lake Nicaragua.

Holbrooke Easton lost his credibility with Nicaraguan State Security and was reassigned to the US Embassy in Mexico D.F.

El Baboso's spear hangs over our mantlepiece like a trophy of war.

We submitted a sample of Blue Magic to a lab at the University of Florida. The results: a blend of common magic mushrooms (Psilocybe Cubensis) with Purple Star Apple and three ingredients unknown—which means the mushrooms have no value for anyone other than Yaritza.

The mystery remains.

Yaritza struck again three years after her disappearance. It happened on a busy Miami street inside a Nicaraguan restaurant. Witnesses described the killer as a gorgeous woman in her mid-to-late twenties. She wore no clothes. Not a stitch. And her skin was as blue as the Caribbean. She'd burst into the place with a feathered spear identical to the one hanging over my fireplace. They said she looked around, located her victim—a customer who'd been eating a dish of Gallo Pinto—screamed, "*Hijo de puta*," and drove the spear into the man's chest.

Then she calmly walked out the front door and vanished.

The victim was a former officer in Somoza's Guardia Nacional with a reputation for brutality. Everyone in the restaurant witnessed the incident—cooks, customers, and servers—but not one person on the street or outside tables had seen her enter or leave.

Not one person.

How could people on a busy Miami street not have noticed a naked blue woman?

A gorgeous, naked blue woman.

They did, however, notice the canaries.

ACKNOWLEDGEMENTS

BLUE MAGIC ON MUSHROOM ISLAND would not have been possible without the love, support, encouragement, and critical eye of many friends, associates, fellow writers, editors, government officials, clergy, former students, the Tarpon Springs Public Library, and family members.

In Cajun country, I am deeply indebted to Karen Ritter, Jessy Ferguson, Bea Angelle, Talis Jayme, and Cynthia Thomas. Among my Peace Corps friends who listened, read my chapters, or otherwise shared their thoughts are George Pope, Bill Callahan, and the late George Wildman.

In Florida, I am grateful to my associates in the Tarpon Springs Fiction Writers' Group for energetically critiquing Blue Magic at our weekly meetings. Thank you, Gino Bardi, Shannon O'Leary Beck, Micki Morency, Frank Shima, Donna Lengel, Dorté Zuckerman, Laurie Cotrell, Bill Frederick, Louise Michalos, Raymond David, Bob Dockery, Carl Mitchell, Elizabeth Indianos, Ken Dye, Sandra Sheridan, Deborah Childress, Karen Drobet, and Rosanne Pappas.

My friend, Captain Ken Dye, helped with his police expertise. Attorney Bob Dockery shared his thoughts on the legal issues encountered by my characters, and my son, Dr. Alex Edmonds provided references on the medicinal uses of mushrooms.

Thank you, Vanessa Shen, for your love and patience.

In Mexico, I am grateful to Lourdes Brindis for her thoughts on the ritualistic uses of mushrooms, and to Curandera Rosalinda Konema of the Raramuri community of Ciudad Juarez for her lengthy explanation of mushrooms in healing rituals. Thanks also to her granddaughter, Santi Guadalupe, for translating her Uto-Aztecan words into Spanish.

In Nicaragua, I am indebted to many friends, colleagues, and associates at the US Embassy, the Patrimonio Cultural de Nicaragua, La Prensa, the Estatuaria Zapatera at El Convento San Francisco in Granada, and the Nicaraguan campuses of the University of Mobile, Harvard University, Ave Maria College, and Keiser University.

Among those are Dr. Maria Gallardo de Anzoátegui, Carlos Urroz, Comandante Leonardo Torres, Ambassador John Maisto, Maria Consuelo Maisto, Isabel Alvarado, my driver, Edgardo, my night watchman, Julio Alejandro Suarez ("Ox"), and Dr. Patrick Werner, who introduced me to the mysteries of Isla Zapatera and the Island of the Dead.

DAVID C. EDMONDS is a former Marine, Peace Corps Volunteer, Fulbright Professor of International Economics, and university dean with long experience in Nicaragua and other Latin American countries with the US Government. He currently lives in the Tampa Bay area of Florida and is the author of four other award-winning thrillers.

Other titles by the author:

FLAMENCO IN THE TIME OF MOONSHINE AND MOBSTERS
THE HERETIC OF GRANADA
THE GIRL IN THE GLYPHS
LILY OF PERU
YANKEE AUTUMN IN ACADIANA
THE GUNS OF PORT HUDSON: THE RIVER CAMPAIGN
THE GUNS OF PORT HUDSON: INVESTMENT, SIEGE, AND REDUCTION
THE VIGILANTE COMMITTEES OF THE ATTAKAPAS
THE CONDUCT OF FEDERAL TROOPS IN LOUISIANA

Made in the USA
Coppell, TX
17 April 2024